Copyright © 2013 Janet Waters

All rights reserved.

The right of Janet Waters to be identified as the author of this work has been asserted by the author in accordance with the Copyright, Designs and Patents act 1988. No part of this publication may be reproduced, stored in a retrieval system, or transmitted in any form or by any means electronic, mechanical, photocopying, recording, or otherwise without the prior permission of the copyright owner.

This book is sold subject to the condition that it shall not, by way of trade or otherwise, be lent, resold, hired out, or otherwise circulated without the publisher's prior consent in any form of binding or cover other than that in which it is published and without a similar condition including this condition being imposed on the subsequent purchaser.

This book is a work of fiction. People, places, events, and situations are the product of the author's imagination. Any resemblance to actual persons, living or dead, or historical events, is purely coincidental.

ISBN - 13: 978 1514642252
ISBN – 10: 1514642255

About the author ……………

Janet Waters was born and raised in the countryside near to Cirencester in Gloucestershire. With the lack of other children living nearby to play with, her imagination was fuelled from an early age. Many school holidays were spent playing Cowboys and Indians with her pet terrier Trixie and what adventures they had.

In the millennium year of 2000, Janet and her late husband Michael, decided the timing was right to make changes in their own lives, so they upped sticks and left all things familiar to move to the Costa Blanca in Spain.

Following a successful entry in a short story competition, Janet found that she actually enjoyed writing and decided this was an interest that she would like to explore more. A surprising fact considering she had failed her English Literature GCE. Janet has had two novels published, 'Truth Hurts' and 'The Circle', as well as various short stories. She is currently working on the sequel to Truth Hurts.

I dedicate this book to two very special people, sadly no longer with me. My mother Kitty, whose real life events partly influenced the bones of this story and my husband Michael for his encouragement, his faith in me and predominantly his patience when I hogged his computer for days at a time

Truth Hurts

Table of Contents

Chapter 1 - The Cotswolds - 2006
Chapter 2 - South Wales - 1919
Chapter 3
Chapter 4
Chapter 5
Chapter 6
Chapter 7
Chapter 8 - London – 1938
Chapter 9 - South Wales - 1939
Chapter 10 - The Land Army
Chapter 11
Chapter 12 - The Cotswolds - 2006
Chapter 13 - Tripoli - 1946
Chapter 14
Chapter 15
Chapter 16 - Berkshire, England - 1949
Chapter 17 - The Cotswolds - 2006
Chapter 18
Chapter 19

Chapter 1
The Cotswolds – 2006

"I don't know what I've done to deserve a daughter like you."

With tears in her eyes, Alison's mother looked down into her lap and fiddled with the damp tissue she held in her hand, squeezing it over and over again, as if this would make it dry enough to wipe away the next tear. Alison picked up her handbag from the floor, next to her stool, and inside found a packet of tissues. Opening the packet, she took one out and gave it to Nellie. Her hands looked so frail now, freckled with brown liver spots. The blue veins so prominent, twitching with a will all of their own and looking quite likely to at any moment break free of the paper thin skin that covered them.

"You are so kind, so genuine, I do love you. You know that Alison, don't you? I do love you" her mother gulped, in an effort to compose herself. "I don't know what I've done to deserve a daughter like you."
To bystanders, it may not have appeared strange to hear a mother speaking such endearing words to her daughter, but as Alison well knew, it was totally out of character for her mother and not at all what she had been expecting..........

It had been a week earlier, when Alison's mother had first shown signs that something was not quite right. It was the end of May. Alison and her partner Graham had lived in the small village of Bampton St Mary for the last three years. Alison had spent many an hour glancing through glossy home magazines, dreaming of the type of house that she would like to one day live in. Eventually when she and Graham had decided to move, she had found that house in Acorn Cottage; it fitted the bill exactly. The exterior of the house was just like a picture postcard. Built in Cotswold stone, it had leaded windows and an extra wide wooden door with black iron hinges. An acorn tree stood majestically to the side, hence the cottage's name. Inside it had all the characteristics that Alison sought. The beamed ceiling and inglenook fireplace created such a feeling of cosiness, especially in the winter when the smoky essence from smouldering logs permeated the rooms. The garden was typically English, with an abundance of roses and hollyhocks. To complete the perfect scene, a weeping willow tree gracefully overhung the small brook that ran alongside the far end of the garden. It was all really a dream come true and even now Alison felt like pinching herself to make sure she wasn't dreaming.

Up until now the weather had not been warm enough to breakfast outside on the cobbled terrace, but this morning it was just perfect.
   "I'll just clear these dishes away" said Alison "and then I had better give Mum a ring. She should have had her breakfast by now and be in the day room."
Graham looked up from his newspaper.
   "Yes okay. I'll just finish reading this article and then I had better jump in the shower; otherwise half the day will be gone."

Alison's mother Nellie had been living in Fir Trees Residential Home for the last eighteen months. A spate of falls, combined with her ever increasing memory loss, had eased the difficult decision that Alison had had to face; whether or not it was the right time to put her mother into care? It had not been a decision taken lightly, but at the end of the day, it was for the best and all things considered the only viable solution for everyone concerned.

When Alison and Graham first considered moving house, they had suggested to Nellie that they would look for a larger house and for her to come and live with them. At first, the thought of having her daughter on hand appealed and she was all for it. Nellie though, was not the easiest person at times to get along with and Alison and Graham deduced for them it would not be an easy option; Nellie at times could be high maintenance to say the least. Alison however, had thought it would be a nice way for her mother to spend her remaining years, having her meals cooked and someone on hand to care for her. In the end with intervention from her few friends, Nellie decided not to give up her home and her independence and stayed put.

Nellie depended on Alison very much for just about everything. Although the bus stop was literally outside Nellie's front door, she would never think to hop on a bus and go into town. Invariably Alison would have to drive her to the places she wanted to go. Nellie could also be a bit naughty at times and feign illnesses, or make problems out to be worse than they were, just to attract attention, causing Alison to drop everything and go running. It was a bit like the 'crying wolf' scenario. Therefore, finding a house within a reasonable close distance to Nellie was high on Alison's priority list, as she knew that if she lived further away, she would still have to attend to her mother's needs and a further distance would only add to the disruption. Graham would have preferred to have put a considerable distance between themselves and Nellie. He could see the continuous string of constant demands that she placed on 'his Alison', which occasionally too had an adverse effect on their relationship. Busy working as they both were, they never had as much time together as they would have liked and the little time they did have, often involved something or other to do with Nellie. He loved Alison though and if putting up with Nellie was part of the plan, then that was the way it would have to be.

Graham worked as an Operations Consultant for an I.T. Company and although sometimes he was able to work from home, the majority of his time was either spent commuting into London or attending appointments with clients in locations, not normally close to home. Alison before her recent redundancy had a demanding job as a Liaison Officer for a large Utility Company. Her role involved a fair bit of travelling between Swindon and Oxford, acting as a trouble shooter and link between customers and the company. On the rare occasions that she managed to sneak a lunch break, Alison would pop in if she was close to Nellie and have a quick cup of tea with her. Her mother was always complaining that she spent too much time on her own, so with good intentions Alison thought her visits would alleviate some of her mother's boredom.

Sadly, a year or so after Alison and Graham had moved to Acorn Cottage, it was obvious that Nellie was becoming a danger to herself and no longer capable of living on her own. Her memory was failing significantly and she was getting very confused and stressed. Nellie had from time to time stayed over a few nights at the cottage and the three of them usually had a nice meal, washed down by a few glasses of wine. Sometimes they had a pleasant time, but usually by the end of the evening Nellie could not resist coming out with a vicious comment or two, directed either at Alison or Graham, or sometimes indeed at both of them. There had been so many moments of this kind and it just grated and totally put a damper on everything that Alison and Graham tried to do to please her.

Graham had noticed it first, just how anxious Nellie was becoming. When away from her usual surroundings she would sometimes get herself into such a state; she knew she wasn't in her own home, but more often than not, would have no recollection of where she actually was. The overnight stays at the cottage came to an end, as it was easier for everyone, if Nellie stayed in her own environment, within her comfort zone. Alison and Graham again talked over having Nellie to live with them. They understood that at first she would be upset, as moving to another house would not be 'normal' for her, but Alison hoped that this would not be too much of a problem and that in a short time she would get used to Acorn Cottage and consider it her home.

Acorn Cottage dated back to 1750 and had lots of nooks and crannies, usual for houses of that era. There was a winding staircase with a rope banister to the upper level and stone slab steps down into the kitchen and to the downstairs cloakroom. Nellie, by this time, especially after her last fall, was not very mobile and although she had a walking frame to aid her, was nervous of using it. The cottage as it stood would not be easy for Nellie to move around in and if they decided on building an extension, how on earth would they all manage to live there while it was being constructed?

Sensibly, Alison realised that to care for her mother in her own home, may not be the wisest solution. It would not really be fair on Graham and she knew for herself that life would change completely. She probably wouldn't even have a life to call her own. Alison did not truly believe that it would be the best option for Nellie either. As time progressed, Nellie's condition would worsen and with all the good intentions in the world, nobody could provide twenty-four hour care on their own. Tiredness and irritability would intervene and that is why for everybody's sake, not least of all Nellie's, that Fir Trees Residential Home was considered. In Fir Trees, the staff were so caring and kind. They could afford the gift of such close attention, when the endurance of their responsibility was solely an eight hour shift, not twenty-four like it would be for Alison. Much as Alison felt guilty, she did finally come to a decision and Nellie was moved into Fir Trees.

Wiping her hands on the tea-cloth, Alison moved towards the telephone. Picking up her black, leather filofax, she leafed through the telephone pages, until she came to F and quickly found listed the number for Fir Trees. She sat down on the stool by the telephone table and pressed the number into the telephone. A recorded voice came on the line.

"Oh, not that again" sighed Alison. "I don't know why that happens? I'm not sure if all the lines are busy, or whether it's because I've dialled too fast?"

By this time, Graham was in the shower, so had no hope of hearing Alison, but that didn't deter her, she often talked to herself. She tried again and this time had more success, she could hear the telephone ringing the other end.

"Hello, this is Alison Collier; could I speak to my mother Nellie Collier please?"

"Hello Alison, it's Jane the care attendant. Your mother isn't feeling too well today, she's complaining of a pain in her back."

"Hi Jane, I thought I recognised your voice, but I wasn't sure. Poor old Mum, she does suffer with her back, she has done for a long time. The doctor did warn her that it would get worse in time."

"I'll go and tell her that you're on the phone Alison. I am sure it will cheer her up to speak to you. Just a second."

Alison knew from previous visits to the home that the telephone room was next to the Day Room, where her mother usually sat.

Luckily for Alison, Nellie liked living at the home. She often told Alison that she had no complaints, which coming from her mother she knew to be an unusual statement. Nellie enjoyed living the hotel lifestyle, being waited on hand and foot. Cups of tea and biscuits, three meals a day and the tables in the dining room beautifully set out with napkins and vases of flowers. Considering the fees that were being charged, Nellie rightly deserved to expect five star quality.

"Come on Nellie dear, take your time. That's it, not far now."

It was quite an ordeal for the carers to get Nellie out of her chair and to walk her, with the aid of her frame, to the telephone room. No matter how busy they were, they always somehow found the time. Before now, Alison had apologised for calling, as she was conscious of the extra workload she was imposing on them, but they always insisted that it was not a problem and could never stress enough the importance for the residents' wellbeing to speak to their relatives and friends.

"Hello Sarah", said Jane to the old lady resting on the chair by the telephone. "Can I move you to the chair in the hall, while Nellie takes this call from her daughter?"

'Oh! Sarah's there again', thought Alison. 'I think she must have worked on a telephone switchboard at some earlier part in her life.' Sarah was often to be found sitting on the chair in the telephone room. Sometimes, when she was awake, she would answer the phone, but not being able to remember the names of the people who lived in the home; she would reply "Sorry, I don't know them" and would replace the receiver. The caller would then have to leave it some time and try again; hoping by then that Sarah would be asleep, or had moved to another chair some distance from the telephone.

Alison could hear shuffling accompanied by huffing and puffing, as her mother got closer to the phone.

"What's she doing there?" her mother in her renown manner spat out. "I have a call from my daughter to take and I don't want you listening. It's private."

"It's alright Nellie, Sarah's just moving. Come on Sarah, that's right, put this leg forward."

"I need the toilet," Sarah suddenly remembered.

"Okay Sarah. Let me just get Nellie settled into the chair and I'll take you."

Alison, by now had already weighed up the type of mood her mother was to be found in.

"Hello."

"Hello Mum, it's me Alison."

"Oh! It's you" Nellie disappointedly replied.

'I don't know who else she thinks would be ringing her', thought Alison. 'It's not as if she's got a brood of children, I'm her only one.'

"Jane tells me that you are not feeling too well today?"

"No, I'm not feeling too grand, it's my back." she replied, followed by a long, obvious sigh.

"Why don't you ask one of the carers for a hot water bottle that might help ease the aching a little?" Alison suggested.

"They haven't got time to do that'" Nellie retorted. "They haven't got time to fuss over me."

"Is Jane still there, or one of the carers?" Alison enquired. "Let me speak to them and I will ask them to fetch one for you."

"No, no, there's nobody here. Just leave it" Nellie grumbled.
Endeavouring to lighten her mother's mood Alison continued.

"It looks like it's going to be a nice day today Mum. I thought that I might pot some tubs up with flowers and Graham is going to light the BBQ later. We've got a chicken to go on and we've invited our neighbours to join us."

"What day is it today?"

"It's Sunday, Mum."

"Oh! Sunday. You don't live by me anymore, do you?"

"Yes I do Mum. Not as close as when I lived in Maple Avenue, but I'm only about eight miles away."

"That's right, I remember. You're married now, aren't you? What's his name? David?"

"No it's Graham, Mum," Alison replied thinking it easier all around not to mention that she and Graham were not actually married.

"Ah! Yes, Graham. He's been married before hasn't he?"

"Yes, that's right."

"Ah! Your first love is always your best love, nothing else comes close."

'There she goes again' thought Alison. 'You'd think that she'd be pleased that her daughter was happy and had found someone to take care of her. Why does she always get such pleasure in hurting me?'

"What day is it?"

"It's Sunday, Mum."

"Well, I think I might as well go back to the day room now. I haven't got any news to say, nothing much happens here, you know. Did I tell you that I've got a bad back?"

"Yes, you did Mum. Well I'll let you go and I'll be over tomorrow; maybe we'll go out for a ride in the car if you're feeling better."

"We'll see." mumbled Nellie without any interest.

They said their goodbyes and Alison put the receiver down. It was difficult to hold a conversation with Nellie nowadays, but Alison hoped that at least by ringing, her mother realised that she was in her thoughts.

In a lot of ways Nellie was more fortunate than the other residents at Fir Trees, as she did have a caring daughter. Some of the residents had no family and never saw any visitors at all. Often when Nellie was having a good day, Alison would take her to the garden centre for a slice of coffee cake and a hot chocolate, or otherwise to the local shopping centre, where Nellie never failed to return without a new piece of clothing that she had bought for herself.

Nellie's husband Gerald, before he died, had worked in the control centre of an electricity company, which meant he often had to work nights and week-ends, as part of the shift rota. This in turn caused problems with their social life, as generally when an opportunity came their way to mix with other people, inevitably Gerald was usually working. It had always seemed to be a problem for Nellie to make friends. She loved company and adored going out and partying, but she would never be the person to instigate an invitation to ask someone to go shopping with her or even just to pop in for a cup of tea. She always waited for others to ask her, almost as if it was protocol and not the 'done thing' for her to do the inviting. When the invitations didn't come rushing in, she always used to lean heavily on Alison's conscience saying in a miserable voice, "I haven't seen a living soul all day." Hence, Alison's life in some ways became a drudgery of putting Nellie's social requirements before her own; taking her shopping, accompanying her to the theatre, when really Alison would have far preferred to have gone out with friends of her own age. Nellie did once when she was fifty years old, take up driving lessons, but like most things in Nellie's life, if it wasn't to be grasped immediately, patience and perseverance were not forthcoming.

Gerald died suddenly of a heart attack, leaving Nellie a widow at seventy. Gerald's death was untimely, and with him being six years Nellie's junior, came just six months before he was due for retirement. If Alison had thought her mother was demanding before her father's death, it was nothing to what came afterwards. Alison in retrospect felt sorry for her father, as it wasn't until he was no longer around that she realised the cross that he must have quietly born all of those years, tolerating her mother's whims and demands.

Graham came down the stairs with a towel wrapped around his waist.
    "Have you seen my beige shorts, I'm sure I left them on the floor by the bed?"
    "They're in the washing machine."
A sigh of exasperation emerged.
    "They didn't need washing, I only put them on for an hour or so the other day", Graham grunted.

"Well next time, fold them up and put them in your drawer. How many more times do I have to tell you? You'll have to wear your blue ones; they're in the ironing basket. They haven't been ironed, but they'll do, if it's only for around the house."

Still thinking about her mother, Alison thought she would ring the office at Fir Trees and have a word with either the Matron or one of the Senior Carers, just to check on Nellie's condition; it made her feel the dutiful daughter if nothing else. She picked up the phone and dialled the number. Thankfully, this time she wasn't interrupted by the recorded voice. The telephone was answered on the second ring.

"Oh! Hello. This is Alison Collier. I'm sorry to bother you, but I've just spoken to my mother Nellie Collier and she's not feeling too well this morning. Could I have a quick word with Matron if she is there or one of the Senior Carers?"

"Yes of course you can, Matron is just here. One moment please."
Alison could hear the Matron being advised the reason for her call and the rustle of papers, as presumably she updated herself with the residents' notes.

"Hello Alison, it's Carol the Matron. Yes, I am a bit concerned about Nellie. She did have quite a restless night. I've called for the doctor to come out and see her, so hopefully he'll be here by about one o'clock. Personally, I think she may be suffering with a urine infection; she seems to be in quite a bit of pain. I can't administer anything to her though until the doctor has examined her."

"Do you think she could have a hot water bottle, I thought that might ease her back?"

"Yes, I'll arrange that. She did have one earlier, but she said it hadn't helped. I'll make sure that she gets another one though."

'So she did have a bottle after all' thought Alison.

"Thanks Carol. I was going to come over tomorrow, but do you think I should come today? We've invited our neighbours around for a BBQ, but I'm sure they won't mind if I cancel it."

"Why don't you leave it today Alison; you're always here? Give yourself a bit of time for a change. I think we'll try and get your Mum into bed a bit later anyway; she didn't sleep too well, so a rest would do her good."

Alison walked through into the kitchen and filled the kettle; she felt that she was in need of a cup of coffee. Nellie was nearly eighty-seven years old; it would be her birthday in a few weeks. Alison had already been agonising over what to buy her. Years ago it had been relatively easy; the latest Catherine Cookson book, clothes, perfume, a manicure, but nowadays in some respect it all seemed a bit pointless. Poor Nellie would not even recall it was her birthday and if she did understand for a second or two, the next minute it would be quickly forgotten. Every time in recent months that Nellie caught a slight cold or cough, Alison wondered if this was the beginning of the end. She knew that she could not go on forever, even if Graham did tease that her mother's body should be donated to medical science, as whatever ailment hit her, she always seemed to pull through.

In some ways, Alison was hoping that the end would not be too far away for her mother. Her quality of life was diminishing rapidly and Alison would hate for Nellie to reach the same state as some of the other residents in Fir Trees. Quite a few of them were incontinent, but more distressing in Alison's point of view, was the fact that some of their minds had regressed back to their childhood days. There was one lady in particular, who would get so upset when she was not allowed out of the front door. In her sad, little mind she was late home and was anxious that her mother would worry and tell her off. Often when Alison arrived at Fir Trees, this same little lady would be by the front door asking visitors or anyone passing to let her out. It caused so much anguish for everyone. The doors of course were not normally kept locked, as the majority of the residents enjoyed walking or sitting in the beautiful, parkland gardens, but at such demanding times, it was a necessary precaution.

The kettle boiling sharply brought Alison back to the present time.
 "Do you want a coffee Graham?" Alison shouted, not knowing where he was at the time. There was no reply, so she opened the kitchen window and shouted again; hoping that if Graham was messing around in the garage he would hear her.
 "Yes please! I'd love one. Great minds think alike."
Alison finished stirring the mugs of coffee and wandered out to the garage, taking a sip from hers as she went.

"You look deep in thought" said Graham noticing Alison's sombre mood. "Everything alright? How's 'T.O.B.' today?" Graham's endearing nickname for Alison's mother, which actually stood for 'The Old Bat.'
It was not surprising that Graham referred to Nellie in this way, as more than once he had been on the receiving end of her sharp tongue. Nellie's walking frame on wheels too had its own name and was referred to as 'The Batmobile.'

Graham was always so caring and attentive to Alison and noticed instantly if there was something bothering her.
"She's not too good today; the doctor has been called out to see her."
"She'll be fine; you know she's as tough as old boots."
"Yes, I'm sure you're right", Alison accepted.

Alison was feeling quite uptight, but at the same time relieved that Carol the Matron had suggested she didn't visit today. She had been looking forward to the BBQ and some quality time of her own. The temperature was rising; already twenty-four degrees and it was just 11 o'clock. Alison thought that she would put her swimsuit on under her shorts, hoping that she would get a bit of a tan, in readiness for their holiday in July. Alison wriggled this way and that way to get into her swimsuit. She always bought black, as it was supposed to have a slimming effect, but not a lot of good, when it was impossible to get the majority of you in it to start with.
'Oh God, I really am going to have to go on a diet; this is disgusting.'
Poor Alison had lost 12 kilos the previous year, but with the best of intentions, it had still managed, plus an extra bit, to append itself yet again to her hips and surrounding areas.
'There's no hope is there? I've just gone from puppy fat to middle-age spread, in one fell swoop; no slim interlude in between. My legs and arms aren't too bad; it's just this middle bit. Still, if I took up tap-dancing I'd make a good Roly-Poly' she quipped.
Graham was always telling her that she should do more exercise, but there was always something else that she would rather spend her time doing. Anyway, Alison always considered that doing the weekly shop, loading everything onto the conveyer belt and then packing it all into bags at an ever increasing speed to beat the check-out girl, was exercise enough for her.

Alison kept glancing at her watch wondering if it was too early to call Fir Trees to see if the Doctor had been. Deciding that it was, she heaved the compost from out of the storage cupboard, in readiness to pot the tubs with the colourful plants that she had bought yesterday in the Garden Centre. As Alison arranged the newly planted tubs around the patio, she couldn't help but reminisce over the odd and painful things that her mother had said to her over the years. One that stuck in her mind at that moment was 'I only had a child, so that there would be someone to look after me in my old age.' 'Well it didn't quite work out like that did it Mum?' Alison thought, thinking of Nellie in the residential home. Alison quickly changed her mind, 'On second thoughts I suppose it did really, I'm still at your beck and call.'

Alison recalled another conversation that she had had with her mother, whereby she had called Alison and Graham selfish, because they did not have children. 'You should bring children into the world', Nellie had vehemently stated. 'I want grandchildren.' 'Wasn't that a turn on words' thought Alison 'with Nellie being the selfish one, putting herself before anyone else. Not that it was the case, but never once did she consider that maybe for some reason or another we couldn't have children of our own.' Alison could feel a nauseous, aching pain in her chest. She guessed it was being caused by all the anxiety she was having over her mother. 'Maybe, I shouldn't always take these twinges for granted' worried Alison. 'After all I'm no spring chicken anymore.' She had now passed through the monumental fifty mark. 'In fact I suppose I now must be regarded as middle aged' she assumed, a thought she didn't wish to dwell on for too long.

Later in the day, Alison rang Fir Trees and spoke to Carol the Matron. The doctor had been and confirmed Carol's earlier diagnosis that it was indeed a urine infection that Nellie had.

"The doctor has given Nellie a pain patch, which will control the pain and make her more comfortable and also a course of antibiotics", notified Matron. "I am still a bit concerned though, she is passing very little water and by the swelling around her ankles I would say she is retaining fluid. I've given instructions for her fluid in-take and out-take to be recorded, so we'll carefully monitor her situation."

"Do you think I should come over Carol? I feel so helpless here."

"Well it's up to you really Alison, but to be honest she is being looked after and there's not much you could do if you were here. She's asleep at the moment, so best let her rest I'd say. I don't consider her to be anywhere near critical at this stage, but with older people you just never know how these things will take them; some go down hill rapidly while others, after a course of antibiotics are as right as rain in a few days"

"Okay I'll leave it then. Can you give her my love if she wakes and tell her that I shall be over in the morning?"

"Certainly will" said Carol. "Don't worry, if there is any change in her condition, we have your number, and so we'll let you know. You go and pour yourself a nice, big glass of Rioja and grab a sausage off of the BBQ. Best enjoy the weather while it's here. More than likely it will be raining cats and dogs again tomorow."

The news when Alison rang the home the next morning was not good. She spoke to Linda the senior carer on duty, who told her that the doctor had been called out again the previous evening. Her mother had been running a high temperature and was still unable to pass water, which was causing her a lot of discomfort. Arrangements had been made for the district nurse to attend to catheterise Nellie.

"I don't wish to alarm you' said Linda, 'but I'm wondering if she's had a slight stoke. Her speech is a little slurred and she doesn't seem to have any strength in her legs."

"Is that what the doctor thought?"

"No he didn't. He checked her blood pressure and the results showed nothing to infer a stroke, but she doesn't seem herself to me."

"I'll come over straight away."

"Yes that would be good; I was going to ask you if you could. She does seem quite distressed and keeps asking for you."

Alison found Graham still in the garage; he was having a good sort out. The garage had become a dumping ground for everything that didn't have a proper home. Even though it was three years since they had moved to Acorn Cottage, there were still boxes that hadn't been unpacked.

"I'm going to have to go over to see Mum Graham, things aren't looking so good."

Alison repeated what Linda had told her about Nellie's deteriorating condition.

"Okay" accepted Graham, You do whatever you think best" he said putting his arm around Alison and giving her a squeeze. "Maybe things won't look so bleak when you actually see her for yourself."

"Yes", sniffed Alison, her emotions getting the better of her.

"Do you want me to come with you?" asked Graham as an after thought. "I can if you like; I'm not planning on going into the office today."

"Thanks, but I'll be fine. As you say she'll probably be bright as a button again in a few days. I'll go by myself for now and if I need you I'll give you a call."

Alison felt so fortunate that she had found Graham. She knew that he thought the world of her, as she did of him. They rarely disagreed and the occasional times they did, was usually down to Graham becoming irritable, due to the fact that she was forever putting people before herself, namely Nellie. In retrospect Alison knew it was because he cared and loved her so much that he got upset.

Alison and Graham had a happy relationship. They had first met at a friend's dinner party sixteen years earlier. Neither of them had been looking for romance; Graham had recently divorced and Alison had just bought her own house and was very content being single. That night changed everything and when Graham suggested that they move in together three months later, Alison eagerly agreed. They had never felt the need to get married; they were content as they were and didn't put any importance on a piece of paper to prove differently.

Although it only had two bedrooms, Alison was delighted with the house she had bought and was reluctant to sell it. Graham had no preference and was fine about selling his house, so he moved his belongings in with Alison. They invested part of the money from the sale of Graham's house and with the remainder purchased a holiday home in Spain. They knew that with work it would be difficult at first to be able to spend much time there, but they hoped that in the future it would be a possibility and that maybe one day they would be able to retire there permanently. It was therapeutic to hold a dream. Theirs was a lovely 'Spanish style' villa approximately a five minute drive from the coast. They were so pleased when they had come across it. It was so traditional in its architecture, with white 'stucco' walls, a courtyard garden, a summer kitchen and a beautiful garden with a pool. The garden was enclosed by bougainvillea hedges of deep purple and orange, interlaced with the most fragrant honeysuckle imaginable. Every time Alison took a flight to Spain, she always chose a window seat, but no matter how hard she studied the landscape beneath her, not once had she managed to pin-point her home. It was surrounded by three golf courses, so it should have been easy to spot, but it never was. She couldn't recognise any of the local landmarks, apart from the marina next to the beach that she and Graham frequented and the recently constructed one mile long harbour wall, which protruded into the sea slightly up the coastline.

Within no time at all, Alison was driving her blue fiesta through Cirencester on her way to see Nellie. Graham kept suggesting that they should trade in her nine year old car for a newer model, but she was quite attached to it and didn't want to change. Alison felt at ease with the way 'Doris' groaned a bit on uphill journeys and coughed and spluttered a bit on cold mornings, she felt that they had something in common; both a little bit passed their sell by date. She had bought 'Doris' quite cheaply off of a friend, as when she had been made redundant two years earlier the company car had had to go back. She had only wanted something to run around in and the little fiesta was fine.

Fir Trees Residential Care Home where Nellie lived was in such an idyllic setting. The lane leading up to it was so typical of the English countryside. Beautiful green trees lined the lane with rolling green fields behind, where horses grazed. The idyllic scenery, together with the thatched 'chocolate box' style cottages completed a picture, that even John Constable would have been proud to have called his own.

Alison parked her car in the spaces provided opposite the main entrance of the home. She stretched across to the back seat and grabbed her jumper in case she got a bit chilly; often the case if the sun went behind a cloud. She locked her car and walked across to the main doors.
'I wonder what's in store for me?' considered Alison anxiously. 'What if Mum doesn't know who I am?'
Alison pushed through the heavy wooden front door into the foyer and signed herself into the visitors' book; she knew the routine from previous visits. Turning around to the dispenser which housed the disinfectant solution, she squeezed a little onto her left hand and then rubbed both of

her hands together. Moving further into the hall, the familiar smell engulfed her nostrils. For those who have spent times in similar establishments to Fir Trees, it would be instantly recognisable as a mixture of urine, disinfectant and food being cooked; the unique smell of an institution. It's a smell that hangs around your presence; clings to your clothes and stays with you long after leaving the premises.

As Alison approached the Day Room she could hear her mother's voice.
"Where am I? Will someone please help me? I don't know where I am? Can't anybody hear me? Where am I? Will somebody please tell me where I am? I'm lost. I feel so alone."
Nellie was sat in a wheelchair over by the far window of the Day Room. This in itself was a shock for Alison as she had never seen her mother in a wheelchair before. There were a few residents seated in the surrounding orthopaedic armchairs, but not one of them was taking any notice of Nellie's wailings. No doubt, this type of behaviour was nothing new to them, but it was to Alison. She rushed over to her mother's side and knelt down beside her.
"It's alright Mum, I'm here it's Alison."
"Oh, Alison, I didn't recognise you. How lovely to see you."
Nellie smiled, not her usual smile; her two front teeth were off-centre. She tried aimlessly to straighten them, knowing something wasn't right, but not sure exactly what the problem was and how to rectify it. She had been losing weight over the last few months, but today she looked quite skeletal. Her eyes were sunken and her cheeks drawn into her very pale face. Sensing somebody behind her, Alison looked around and saw Nancy shuffling to the chair next to Nellie.
"Hello Nancy. You are looking so much better than when I saw you the last time. Have you got over that nasty cough now?" enquired Alison.
"Yes thank you, I was glad to see the back of that I can tell you. It's such a shame about poor Nellie; she's not been at all well and she won't eat anything. She needs to eat doesn't she to keep her strength up?"
"That's right Nellie, she does. When I come tomorrow I'll bring her in a little cream trifle, she might enjoy that."
"There's a stool here love, why don't you sit on that. Give your poor knees a rest."

The other residents were always glad to see Alison, not just Alison to be precise, but any visitor who was kind enough to pay them a little attention. The care staff too were also grateful, as Alison never minded easing a distressed situation by picking up magazines or handkerchiefs that residents had inadvertently dropped to the floor, or raising the alarm when one of them had had an accident of a more personal nature. These little actions that came naturally to Alison meant a lot to the residents and carers alike.

The mood of the room changed as Harrison walked in with the tea trolley. Everybody loved Harrison, with his sparkling green eyes and dreadlocks pulled back into a pony tail. At only twenty, working with the elderly wasn't the type of work expected for a young man to be involved in, but then Harrison was no normal young man. He joked with the residents and they gave him just as good back. The morning coffee and afternoon tea breaks were very much looked forward to and a welcome interlude in an otherwise indifferent day. Alison noticed the effect that Harrison had on the majority of the old dears.
'I'm sure a lot of them are wishing they were sixty years younger' she mused. 'They can more than likely picture themselves doing the Jitterbug with him to Glenn Miller; both so light on their toes, not like the harsh, reality of life.'
    "Hello Nellie. How's my favourite lady from the Valleys?" asked Harrison imitating Nellie's welsh accent.
Nellie was very proud of her welsh roots and when she was feeling herself, was forever telling anybody who would listen, that the Welsh were the true Brits. It had been the Welsh who had chased invaders back to the seas, long before any English were around.

However, today Nellie was a long way from feeling herself. Alison took the cup of tea that Harrison offered, along with a chocolate and a garibaldi biscuit. She passed the cup and saucer to Nellie, but soon took it back, as Nellie was not able to keep it steady and Nellie feared it would spill and scold her. Nellie fiddled with the catheter inside her trouser leg; she couldn't make out what it was.
    "What's this?" she asked looking at Alison.
    "It's a catheter Mum. You had a bit of trouble trying to go to the toilet, so that's there to help you."
Alison could tell that her mother did not understand a word of what she had just said. Nellie's face crumpled and her eyes watered with fresh tears.

"I do love you Alison, you do know that don't you?" Her eyes focused with so much need on Alison.

"I'm so unhappy. I know I haven't been a good mother to you."

"Of course you have Mum."

Alison could recall times when Nellie certainly hadn't been the most pleasant of mums, but now wasn't the time to look back.

"Are you in pain Mum?"

Tears rolled uncontrollably down Nellie's cheeks.

"Come on, it's alright, I'm here", Alison soothed as she wiped her mother's tears.

"I don't know what's the matter with me, but I know I'm not right. I don't want to be like this."

Nellie was finding it difficult to speak between the sobs and gulps for air. She was so distressed and it was obvious to Alison that her memory for words had worsened. It was pitiful to witness her struggling to remember the words she wanted to use and then painstakingly trying to form them on her lips.

"I must tell you the truth Alison. I'm so sorry; I know I should have told you a long time ago."

Nellie looked up into her daughter's eyes for forgiveness and the tears flowed remorsefully. She took hold of Alison's hands.

"Please forgive me."

Alison didn't have a clue what her mother was talking about. There had been times when Alison had doubted the content of certain stories Nellie had related over the years of her life. Some of them appeared more like a scene from one of her Catherine Cookson novels than actual true-life, but then Nellie's life had run a similar course, so Alison never really knew if it was make believe or not. Alison was in the opinion that maybe her mother had read so many books, that the fiction was getting confused with the reality. There was the possibility that Nellie's mind could be wandering, but something in her eyes showed real regret and Alison wondered what on earth this secret could be.

Alison and her mother had always had an odd type of relationship, almost as if at times Nellie was intent on upsetting her, or maybe it was a form of jealousy on Nellie's part. Alison had never been able to fathom out the reason for Nellie's outbursts of unkind behaviour. More than once her mother had told her that she had wanted a boy and that Alison should have been her son and not her daughter. "We didn't have a name for you, your father and I when you popped out; you should have been Richard" she used to taunt. None of these statements ever diminished the love that Alison as a little girl had felt for her mother.

Alison studied her mother, so frail and unhappy. A small amount of saliva dribbled from the corner of Nellie's mouth; consciously she wiped it away and started to cry again. Alison could see that Nellie understandably despised the cruel hand she had been dealt.

'Is it really humane to put her through all this?' questioned Alison to herself.

Alison looked fondly at her Mother.

"I love you Mum, I always have" and she spoke the words in earnest.

There had been many good times as well and Alison thought about when she had sat with her mother and listened to the stories of her life, from a little girl through to marrying her father. Some tales had been sad, while others had brought tears of laughter to Alison's and her mother's eyes.

'I wonder what it is that she wants to tell me' thought Alison. 'There can't be much that I don't already know.'

Nellie took hold of Alison's hands and stroked them.

"Please don't think badly of me Alison. I'm an old lady now, time is passing me by. I know I've done wrong and it's important you know everything before I move on to pastures new."

Nellie seemed suddenly composed; as if she was picturing and reliving her life. She lifted her head and looked directly into Alison's questioning eyes.

"It's right you know what they say "The truth does hurt". Do you remember me telling you about my life as a little girl in Wales?

Chapter 2
South Wales – 1919

"Aah! Oh no please not now. Aah!"
Rose heard a loud crash of breaking crockery and a heavy thud to the floor. Jumping up from the table by the window, where she had busily been cleaning the brass, she shouted.

"Mam, Mam are you alright?" as she rushed to the kitchen.
She found Jessie her mother, clutching her stomach and writhing in agony.

"Rose, Rose, the baby's coming. Go and get Peggy." Another cramping pain grabbed her and she screamed out "Hurry!"

As quick as her legs would carry her Rose ran to the front door, leaving it ajar behind her. She raced to number sixty-seven at the far end of the street, where Peggy lived with her seven children and mother. Peggy's husband had died three years previously from blood poisoning, resulting from a scratch on his hand that he had got from his curling box.* Rose hammered on the door and didn't stop until Peggy with flour all over her hands opened it.

"Whatever's the matter? You're making enough noise to wake the dead."

"Quick, quick, it's Mam the baby's coming" Rose informed Peggy.

"What did you say, the baby's coming? Dieu! Dieu! It can't be; she's got another two months to go."
Wiping her hands on her apron, Peggy turned around and shouted deep into the interior of the house.

"Gran, look after the kids, Jessie's gone into labour."
Pushing the piece of hair that had been straggling over her right eye behind her ear, she stepped into a pair of shoes from the row inside the door and chased after Rose, who was already retreating back up the street.

*Curling Box – metal box approx. 60 cm. square with an open end, used when the distance was too far for coal to be thrown on a shovel. The curling box would be pushed into the coal collecting as much as possible and any remaining space would be filled by shovelling the coal by hand. When full it would be dragged or carried to the tram for off-loading

Everyone called on Peggy in their hour of need, as if she didn't have enough troubles of her own to contend with. Peggy's motto was 'If she could help some other poor beggar along the way, maybe St. Peter would look kindly down on her, when it was her turn to enter those pearly gates.' Peggy wholeheartedly believed this and as best as she could, practiced to live by it. From halfway down the street Peggy could hear Jessie's screams.
'Poor girl', she thought. 'You'd think after nine babies and two miscarriages she'd be used to it by now.'

Peggy noticed a few of the curtains twitching and Mrs. Evans who had been mopping down her front step, downed her tools and craned her neck to see if she could see what all the commotion was about. Rushing through the door and rolling up her sleeves as she went, Peggy issued orders to Rose, who was looking helpless by her mother's side.

"Don't just stand there Rose, you know the score. Get some hot water, lots of it and plenty of towels or rags, as many as you can find. Your old man's going to have a shock when he gets home tonight, Jessie" said Peggy trying to make light of what was increasingly looking like a difficult situation. "He's going to have more than his supper waiting for him by the looks of things. Come on Rose, what's keeping you? Is that water ready yet?"

Rose lifted the heavy kettle off of the range, collected the towels she had put on the chair and took them through to Peggy. She went into the scullery and refilled the empty kettle with water from the bucket. There was no running water in the house, so buckets had to be filled from the outside tap in the backyard. They were more fortunate than some of the people they knew, as their house had three bedrooms. Even so, space was still scarce with ten of them living there, soon to be eleven. It should have been twelve, but Freddie had succumbed to tuberculosis and had died when he was just seven.

The house where Rose and her family lived was in Baker St, the last but one in a long row of terraced houses. Most of the men who lived in the street worked in the colliery like her father and the houses were included as part of their wages. The houses all looked the same, slate roofs, a front door with a window to the side and two more windows upstairs. The same tired, grimy look cloaked them all, caused by the residue of the coal dust from the nearby colliery. No matter how many times Mrs. Evans and others like her washed down their steps and the pavement in front, the stubborn shadow of black dust would always remain.

Rose heard a whimper above. With everything going on she had momentarily forgotten about Joyce, her baby sister asleep upstairs. She climbed the stairs and went into the back bedroom. A large iron bed dominated the room and it was here that she slept with her siblings, Idris who was three and five year old Myfanwy. In the corner to the right of the window, stood the wooden cot that Joyce was trying to pull herself out of. She wasn't walking yet, but it didn't look like it would be too long. Rose tenderly remembered the old cot. She could still picture her father making it out of scrap bits of wood, when her mother had been expecting Freddie.
'Where will Joyce sleep when this new baby is here?' questioned Rose.
'I s'pose we'll all have to squash up a bit more in the big bed.'

Being the eldest of all the children, Rose was quite the 'little mother. It was a case of having to really. She could tell when little Joyce needed changing and feeding and without a second thought got on with it. It was just as well that all this was happening on a week-day, as Myfanwy, Owen and Edwin were in school and Idris was across the street playing with his friend. The two elder boys, thirteen year old Arthur and twelve year old Gareth were already working in the colliery with their father. Money was tight in the Edwards' family and every penny counted.

"Rose, Rose", she could hear her name being called from the kitchen. Peggy didn't sound very calm; there was an edge of panic to her voice.
"Go and fetch Dr. Roberts, I can't manage this by myself. Be as quick as you can, don't stop for anyone. Tell him it's an emergency. Don't come back without him, do you understand?"
Rose hurriedly sandwiched baby Joyce between two chairs and the dresser, where hopefully no harm would come to her and for the second time that day flew up the street; this time towards Dr Robert's house.

Dr Roberts had a large three-storey house, the middle one of a block of five at the far end of Richmond Terrace. All the houses had neat little gardens in front, each divided and edged with a pointed, black, wrought iron fence. Richmond Terrace was three streets away, but instead of running up the road and over the bridge, Rose decided on the back way alongside the River Taff. On the rare occasions that she did have some time for herself, she loved to sit and play 'ducks and drakes' with the little pebbles that littered the bank. With so many of them in the family, peace and quiet was not to be found indoors.

By the time Rose reached the doctor's house, the gravity of the situation had set in and tears were running down her cheeks, now flushed from running. Her nose too was streaming, not helped by the cold she had; the reason she had been kept off school that day. Hesitating, as she knew her Mam would tell her off if she saw her, she wiped her nose on her cardigan sleeve. It was Doctor Roberts himself who answered the door. A tall, handsome man who always appeared so smartly dressed. Not many of the men around Llanfaer had a suit and those that did only wore them for funerals or best, certainly not for every day.

"Good Afternoon. It's young Rose Edwards isn't it?"

"Yes sir" Rose shyly answered, sniffing at the same time, wishing that she had brought her hankie. "Me Mam needs you, she's having the baby. Peggy Thomas is with her, but she can't manage. She's bleeding a lot sir."

"Okay Rose, afternoon surgery has finished. Let me just grab my bag and I'll come straight away."

Rose turned on her heel, opened the gate and started to retrace her steps.

"You might as well come in the car with me Rose, no point walking" Dr. Roberts suggested as he locked his front door.

A car was a rare object to be seen in Llanfaer, let alone to own one. The only people that Rose knew that had a car apart from the doctor were the vicar and Mr. Meradith the owner of the colliery. Normally Rose would have been thrilled to be offered a ride in such a vehicle. It would certainly be an experience to make her brothers envious, but today she quietly climbed in with thought only for her Mam, praying inside that everything would be alright.

School was over for the day and Edwin and Owen scuffed their boots on the paving stones, kicking any loose stones that were in their way. Their boots were a bit on the big side for them, as Owen was wearing the ones that Edwin had grown out of and Edwin was wearing the ones that his elder brother Gareth had grown out of. Myfanwy dawdled behind, as usual in a world of her own.

"Last one home's a sissy" taunted Edwin.

"I can beat you any day you old tortoise" Owen jeered back at his brother as he shot off up the road like a rocket.

Owen was indeed first to reach their door and charged through.

"We're home Mam."

As soon as the words left his little mouth, he could sense that all was not as it should be.

"You can't come in here" screamed Peggy. "Your mam's having the ……."

Too late both Owen and Edwin were standing, mouths agape in the kitchen doorway. Their mother lay prostrate on the floor; her legs apart and knees bent. Jessie was not screaming anymore, her pallor was pale and she quietly moaned as she drifted in and out of consciousness. The boys were noticeably frightened by the blood on Peggy's apron and on the towels scattered around.

"This is no place for you three" Peggy said to them. Myfanwy had by now caught up with her brothers and distressed by what she saw, started to cry. "Take Myfanwy over to Mrs Pike; she's already looking after Idris. Tell her your Mam's having the baby. You two boys go and amuse yourself in the street, play football or something. Everything will all be alright here; Doctor Roberts is on his way."

"Daylight at last" said Emrys as he stepped out of the cage at the top of the pit. "At least in the summer months we see a bit more of it than the winter time."

He took a deep breath to inhale the fresher air, but could still smell the coal dust as it was forever in his nostrils. The air in Llanfaer never smelt fresh; always the familiar musty smell of dust hung around, even more noticeable on a rainy or damp day.

"Coming in the Prince of Wales for a well deserved pint man?" asked Huw a fellow haulier.

"Shouldn't really, I promised Jessie I wouldn't be late tonight, but Ah! Go on then, just a swift one. I've got a bit of a thirst on."

Rose constantly boiled water and took it through to the kitchen. Her mother looked so exhausted and she desperately wanted to hold her and comfort her; tell her that she loved her and that everything was going to be alright. Sense told her that it was best for her to stand back and give Dr. Roberts and Peggy the space they needed.

"We're almost there Mrs. Edwards, just one more push will do it" Dr. Roberts instructed, with exhaustion in his voice.

Jessie somehow, she didn't know from where, administered one final burst of strength, pushed one more time and her baby was born.

"Well done" congratulated Dr Roberts and Peggy in unison. "It's a baby girl."

Peggy took the baby from Dr. Roberts and could not help noticing how tiny she was. So intent was she on washing the newborn and wrapping her in a blanket that she failed to notice Dr. Roberts anxiously feeling Jessie's wrist and neck for a sign of a pulse.

"She's beautiful. What you going to call her Jessie?" she asked as she turned around. "No, no, not Jessie" she wailed as she witnessed Dr. Roberts pulling a sheet up over Jessie's pale, so very pale face.

Young Rose hearing the commotion came rushing in and saw for herself her own worse fears.

" Mam! Mam! No, no, not my Mam." She fell to her knees where she stood and sobbed! "What will we do, we can't manage without Mam?"

Neither Dr. Roberts nor Peggy could find the right words to console poor Rose. What could they say at such a time; no amount of comforting words would bring her mother back? Peggy herself was upset and was trying hard to compose herself, so that she could be brave and a pillar of strength for young Rose to lean on. During the 1900's childbirth was very dangerous; one in every ten babies and about the same numbers of mothers died during or soon after childbirth, so Jessie's death was not an unusual event. Dr. Roberts washed his hands in the bucket of water, packed his instruments in his bag and did up the clasp.

"I am so sorry" he said to young Rose and Peggy as he turned to face them.

Peggy took the doctor to one side and whispered her concerns to him about the baby.

"She's so small. What do you think her chances are?"

"It's difficult to say Mrs. Thomas. Apart from keeping her nourished, clean and warm, I'm afraid there's nothing more we can do. She's in the good Lord's hands now. Let's pray he's looking down on her. I dare say the poor little mite will need all the help she can muster."

Putting his hand on Rose's shoulder he quietly spoke to her. "If, there's anything I can do to help, just ask. I will notify Mr Jenkins the undertaker on my way home and he will make all the necessary arrangements for you. Please pass on my sincere condolences to your father Rose; I'll see myself out."

Dr. Roberts sombrely walked down the hall, closing the front door behind him.

"See you in the morning then Emrys."

"Yeah! Make sure your Mrs. kicks you out of bed on time" Emrys joked back to Huw.

They had enjoyed two pints of ale in the Prince of Wales; neither had wanted to owe the other a pint, so they decided to drink an even number. Emrys thought it odd that none of the young ones were sat out on the step watching out for him. Usually, their eyes would be glued to the corner of the street, waiting for him to appear; then whoever spotted him first would be up like a shot running up the road to greet him, closely followed by the rest of the brood.

He opened the door and bent down to take off his boots. 'Jessie will have a right go at me if I traipse all this dust through the house' he thought. Straightening up he saw Rose in the doorway, her eyes all red and puffy from crying.

"Rose dear, what's up. It must be something bad to spoil my girl's pretty face like that."

"Oh Dad, it is. It's the worst thing that's ever happened" she cried and ran to hug him, holding on as if he was the last thing in the world that she had left, which in one sense with her mother gone, he was.

With that Peggy came into view, carrying a small bundle wrapped in a blanket.

"What you got there Peggy? Don't tell me our Jessie's had the baby. Where is she, where's my clever girl?'"

Rose's tears were momentarily forgotten, as he climbed the stairs in search of his wife.

"Emrys, Emrys" Peggy called after him. "She's dead. I'm so sorry, she's dead. There was nothing we could do."

"I don't believe you, she can't be. Not my Jessie, my lovely, smiling Jessie."

"I'm so sorry Emrys. Dr. Roberts has arranged for the undertaker to come, but she's still in the kitchen if you want to see her."

Emrys stormed into the kitchen and fell onto his wife's body, his anguish expelling. His shoulders rose and fell as he couldn't and didn't want to quell the emotion that tore his soul apart. If nothing else he owed his grief to Jessie. His hands grasped the top of the sheet that covered the love of his life's face and gently pulled it down. Unveiling Jessie's face brought his grief home to him. He tenderly bent over her, kissed her forehead, her cheeks, her lips, every part of her face, as he knew, never again would he have the pleasure. His beautiful, caring Jessie, mother of his children was no more. Black smudges of coal dust traced where Emrys' lips had been, equal to his signature on her skin; his final goodbye. Rose had never heard her Dad cry before. If she thought her heart was already broken, it broke some more to hear him sobbing in such agony. Rose went to her father's side.

"Come on Dad, Mam's at peace now, we can do no more. Come and sit down I'll make you a cup of tea."

Mr Jenkins the undertaker arrived; went about his business and left the family to their grieving. Understandably, there was a dark and heavy atmosphere in the house. Arthur and Gareth had returned home from work and both sat with their heads in their hands, trying not to show the tears that they shed. Their father was not ashamed of his tears; they were displayed for the world to see. Edwin and Owen felt uncomfortable, not fully grasping the situation; they had never seen their father cry before and it slightly unnerved them. Unnoticed they slipped out the back door and went and sat on the river bank, sharing their grief silently together. Little Myfanwy, sat on the floor with her arms wrapped around her father's legs; she knew enough to know that he needed her love at this time and she felt comfort from his closeness. Joyce just cried; she was hungry again. She didn't really notice the loss of her mother. Her basic instincts came first and as long as either her mother or Rose attended to them, she didn't have a preference.

Peggy was conscious of the fact that she had to get back to her own brood. They too would need feeding and more than likely George and Tommy her nine year old twins, would need a good clip around the ear for some misdemeanour or other. In her arms Peggy rocked the newborn baby girl. 'She may only be tiny' thought Peggy 'but by God she's got a good pair of lungs on her.' She walked over to Emrys, who as yet hadn't even taken a look at his new daughter. Trying to bring him out of his grief a little, she asked "What you gonna call this one then Emrys, she needs a name?"

Emrys focused on the bundle in Peggy's arms with his red, rimmed eyes.

"I don't know, Trouble? Bad Luck? Grief? That's all she's brought to this family."

"Oh! You can't call her that Emrys; it's not this little mite's fault. It's nobody's fault; it was God's choice. I'll tell you what you should call her."

"What?" enquired Emrys indifferently.

"Well with all this yelling she's doing, how about Ellen? Yelling Ellen. That's what I say."

"Alright Ellen it is then."

It was as if he couldn't bear to look at Peggy, in case he caught a glimpse of the baby. He bent down and picked up Myfanwy, who instantly snuggled into his chest and he kissed the golden curls on the crown of her head. Peggy felt a deep fear that hatred was building up in Emrys and that there was never going to be any love for his new daughter.

Rose loved school. She attended Llanfaer Grammar school, which was quite an achievement, especially for a girl. Rose dreamed of a different kind of life to the one her mother had lived and the other women in Llanfaer. She didn't know exactly her true aim, as her knowledge of the outside world and her vision did not stretch that far, but she did know drudgery. A month had now past since Rose's mother Jessie had cruelly been taken in childbirth and not once in that time had Rose been back to school. Her teacher Mr. Davies had been very understanding of her circumstances and had brought around schoolwork to the house, so that when she did return to her classes she would not be lagging too far behind the other pupils. Rose did her best to study, but with her new-born sister Ellen to care for, as well as Joyce and the rest of the family, spare time was a commodity that she didn't have at her disposal. Rose knew only too well that her dream of escaping the valleys had now completely flown out of her grasp. Money had always been tight, so she knew that her father could not afford to pay for someone to look after them, so unless she took over the role of mother and housekeeper, her brothers and sisters would undoubtedly be split up and put into care. Poor Rose, sadly and slightly peeved, settled down at the wooden table to write a letter to Mr. Davies explaining that she would never ever be returning to school.

Emrys was no nearer to coming to terms with his loss. Life went on, but it was as if it passed by without him being part of it. Rose did her best to take her mother's place and made sure that there was always a bath waiting for him on his return from the pit and a hot meal on the table. She noticed though that his time-keeping wasn't as regular as it had been when her mother was alive and was patently aware that the reason for his lateness was because of his increasing visits to the Prince of Wales public house. More often than Rose liked, her Father would come home a little worse for wear. She hated these times as the drink would never make him cheerful, it usually made him morose or argumentative. Many a time on such occasions he would complain about the meal Rose had painstakingly put together, from the little choice she had in their meagre larder and invariably his raised voice would wake up Ellen and Joyce, who she had only just got off to sleep. Rose loved her father, but during these times she felt so disheartened with him. Each one of their lives had changed since their mother had died, none more so than her own. A small part of her was beginning to despise her father for not pulling himself together and consequently making her life more difficult. Rose had to grow up more quickly than her fourteen years and although she would have wished for her life to have taken a more interesting path, she knew she would do whatever was necessary to keep her family together.

Chapter 3

"Happy Birthday dear Nellie, Happy Birthday to you."
Four years had passed since that fateful day when their mother Jessie had died giving birth to little Nellie as she was now known. Joyce had never been able to say Ellen and the sound always came out back to front in the form of Nellen, which later became Nellie.

Times were hard, but whenever it was somebody's birthday, Rose did her very best to make it just that little bit more special than a normal day. A cake had been baked in Nellie's honour and the look of delight on the younger children's faces made Rose's extra effort all the more worthwhile. Nellie proudly wore the new jumper that the family had given her; it was a mass of stripes in lots of different colours. She was too young to understand that new clothes were unheard of and that they each wore clothes that the others had grown out of, or cast offs from kindly neighbours. In some respects Nellie's jumper was new; she wouldn't know that Rose had knitted it from wool unpicked from her brothers' old jumpers that had become far too holey to mend.

With tea finished, the excitement gathered as they all settled into a circle on the floor to play pass the parcel. Being the birthday girl Nellie won the main prize; a small block of fudge, but so as not to disappoint the smaller children, Rose made sure that they each in turn unwrapped a piece of paper to find a sweet inside.
 "Well you've had a lovely day and I think for you younger two, Joyce and Nellie, it's time for bed" suggested Emrys, as he stretched back in his rocking chair by the hearth.
 "Oh, do we have to Dad, can't we play just one more game of hide and seek?" asked Joyce hopefully.
 "No you can't, but what you can do both of you, is to come and sit on your old Dad's knee and I'll tell you a story."
In preference to any game, the girls loved nothing more than when they were allowed to snuggle up to their Dad and before there was any chance that he might change his mind, they were on his lap with their little heads nestling into his chest.

Rose started to clear the table and carry the plates out to the kitchen. She was so relieved to see how her father had changed, since the early months after her mother had died. There had been a time when she had thought that he was going to reject Nellie and blame her for causing her mother's death, but thankfully as it turned out that had not been the case and he loved his youngest daughter as much as anyone of them. His drinking bouts too had been curtailed and although he did still enjoy a few drinks at the Prince of Wales now and again, Rose was no longer worried, as she knew that he was over the bad times. She understood that he needed to have a break sometimes from the family and have adult time with his male companions.

As time went by, Rose grew accustomed to the chores of looking after her family and surprisingly she didn't miss school, as much as she thought she would. Her days were long and tiring, with little time to get everything done, let alone worry about what might have been. Sometimes, she would bump into school friends while shopping in the corner shop, but nowadays she didn't really have anything in common with them; their lives had taken different paths and Rose accepted that.

Monday was always wash day for Rose; she liked to keep to a routine. It was possible now to buy soap flakes, which indeed made washing a lot easier, but as the corner shop didn't often have any in stock and to make her housekeeping go further, Rose made her own soap flakes using the method she had learnt from her mother. She would reserve left-over animal fat over a period of time and when there was enough, she would boil it with a mixture of lye and limestone. Once set, she would then cut it into bars for their personal washing, or scrape it into flakes for washing clothes. It was a long smelly process and not one that Rose relished, but needs must and she got on with it without complaint.

The weekly wash took her all day to do. Her father's and brothers' working clothes were always exceptionally dirty from working in the pit. Rose repeatedly boiled numerous kettles of water on the range and poured them into the large wooden tub that she had dragged into the kitchen from the back yard. She constantly pounded the clothes with the dolly endeavouring to get the grime out of them. Wash day had been made slightly easier thanks to Peggy, who had given Rose a mangle that somebody she knew had been throwing out. Beforehand, all of the wringing out of clothes had had to be done by hand and sometimes poor Rose just didn't feel she had enough strength left to do it, especially when it came to the large bed sheets. Rose's aim was to keep their little terrace house as clean and tidy as her mother had done. She took a pride in all of the cleaning and household tasks. To Rose it was her way of keeping her mother's memory alive; her own personal tribute. Only yesterday, she had made up some 'black lead' from turps and linseed oil and had rubbed it all over the range until it shone; just like her mother had done before her, to stop it going rusty.

"Edwin, Arthur, c'mon lads it's time to get up."
Edwin sat up in bed and stretched his arms. He had been awake for several minutes, like an in-built alarm he knew that very shortly his Dad would be quietly opening the door and rousing himself and his brother. Arthur turned over and nestled back into the bedclothes, not wanting to embark on the long, hard day that awaited him.

Edwin poured some water from the jug into the basin that Rose had diligently filled up for them the night before. He had a quick swill with the water to wake himself up; it was cold and did the trick. In his mind, he could still hear his mother saying "Hurry along now Edwin, you're gonna be late for school. Go and have a quick cat's lick and get yourself ready." This particular saying had always brought a smirk to his face. They had never had a cat at home, but he had wasted many an idle moment watching the cats in the street. Their little bodies attentively balanced, one leg cocked over their heads enabling them to clean parts that Edwin couldn't conceive washing with his tongue. He loved watching them bring their whole paw over their ears, returning it for another quick lick and then back over again for another scrub. 'Maybe that's where the term 'cat's lick' comes from' he thought to himself. Mrs. Thomas down the street also had a saying recalled Edwin and that was that if a cat put his paw completely over his ear to wash, it was going to be a fine day or was it a wet day? He couldn't remember and thought he must ask her the next time he saw her. A few years before, his father had carefully whittled the form of a cat out of a small piece of wood and had given it to him. He treasured this little cat and carried it with him, wherever he went, considering it his lucky charm. Drying himself with the towel, he walked over to Arthur's side and nudged him. "Time for your wash."

The three of them walked down the street looking near enough the same. They each drudged along in hob-nail boots with caps on their heads. Arthur now had overtaken his father in height, exceeding him by some three inches, whereas Edwin was the opposite and if anything small for his age. Rose had been up before any of them preparing their snap boxes (food containers) and their jacks (drink containers). At the end of the street they could see the red glow of the sun creeping up above the mountain tops.

"Looks like it's going to be a glorious day lads, let's hope there'll be a bit of sunshine left by the time we get out of the pit."

"That would be good Dad and a quick pint in the Prince of Wales, my treat for the end of the week. Shame you're too young Edwin, but if you're good I'll let you drink the froth off the top of mine."

Edwin enjoyed the camaraderie with his elder brother and felt quite like one of the men now that he was working and bringing money into the house. When he had reached the age of twelve he had joined his father and brother working in the colliery learning the same job as his father. His father was now the Master Haulier in charge of all of the pit ponies and when there had been an opening for a haulier, Emrys had managed to secure the position for young Edwin. Edwin found the days long and didn't enjoy working in the darkness for such long periods, but working alongside Daisy the pit pony somehow made it more bearable.

As they approached the pit, they bid their fellow miners Good Morning as they made their way to the lamp station. Before each shift, the miners going underground had to handover a receipt to the lamp man and in return would receive a lamp that was in working order. The same process would happen in reverse on their exit from the pit. This simple procedure acted as a record of who was underground, should there be any accidents whereby people needed to be accounted for.

Rose looked forward to Fridays; it always seemed to be an easier and happier day as the week-end approached. Her father and brothers always came home in good spirits, especially if there was no work on the Saturday, knowing that they had a bit of respite before having to go back down the mine. It was like a celebration day and Rose tried to manage the house-keeping so that there was always enough money leftover to provide a meat stew or cawl as it was known in Wales, as a special homecoming on pay day.

With Nellie tottering behind her, Rose made her way to Mr. Jones' butchers shop at the bottom end of Richmond Terrace where Dr. Roberts lived. By herself the journey would have taken a lot less time, but with Nellie they were constantly stopping so that she could play on the hopscotch marks that the older girls had left behind. She didn't quite yet have the hang of it, although she had figured out that you hopped on some squares and put both feet down on others.

"Hello you two. How are the prettiest girls in Llanfaer this morning?" asked Mr. Jones with a beaming smile.

"We're fine, thank you Mr. Jones" replied Rose, embarrassed and looking down at her feet. Nellie wasn't much better than her big sister, as she too was trying to hide in her sister's skirt.

"I keep saying to young Alfie here, that he should come calling on you and ask you out for a nice walk, or bring you back to our house for tea. You could do with a bit of a break. A fine girl like you should have more fun, not stuck at home all the time."

Poor Rose appreciated his concern, but could feel her cheeks burning up at his suggestion. She would like very much to be on more friendly terms with Alfie, as she did have a soft spot for him, but realised that her chance would never come. What on earth would somebody like Alfie ever see in her? Time only usually allowed her to sweep her long black curls up into a bun and her clothes had seen better days. Rose looked up and in the direction of Alfie, Mr. Jones' son and found him busily sweeping up some imaginary bits of dirt off the floor. His face was also flushed and when he noticed Rose's eyes upon him, he quickly rested the brush against the wall and made his exit into the back room. 'There I knew it' thought Rose, 'He can't stand the sight of me.'

"Right, what will it be then Rose?" enquired Mr Jones.

"Have you got any scrag ends of lamb please? I want to make a cawl for Dad and the   boys' supper tonight."

Mr. Jones packed up the meat and gave it to Rose. She thanked him and turned to go out of the shop.

"Just a minute" called Mr. Jones and he went to the end of the counter and picked up two saveloys. "Here, take these. A little treat for you."

Edwin, Arthur and their Father stepped into the cage that would carry them down into the depths of the pit. The further they descended the square of light above them diminished until it was only a spec. It was dark and gloomy in the pit and the air was dank as they each moved along to find their place of work.

Edwin led Daisy up and down the tunnels pulling the trams of coal, talking to her gently as they went. It was a tough haul for Daisy as a tram of dry coal was a very heavy load. Like Edwin, Daisy also wore protective headwear, which protected her face and eyes in case she bumped into any timber or falling stones. Edwin was feeling thirsty and his stomach was starting to rumble.
 "It must be near break-time Daisy if my stomach's not mistaking me." Daisy let out a little neigh as if she understood exactly what he was saying. As they turned the next corner, Edwin recognised his Father coming towards them.
 "Time to stop for a bite, I reckon" said Emrys.
Daisy started nuzzling up to Emrys, gently pushing his shoulder with her head.
 "What's this ol' Daisy? Cupboard love I call it, I know what you're after."
The miners because of the obvious danger of escaping gases were not allowed to smoke underground and many of them, Emrys included, used to chew on tobacco. The ponies were as partial to tobacco as the men themselves and Daisy used to actually take it from Emrys' mouth.
 "There you go then Daisy, that's your lot for today; otherwise I'll have none left for a ciggie with my pint when I've finished down here."

Back in the house, Rose with Nellie's help, or more like hindrance, was chopping up the meat and vegetables and dropping them into the big pot in readiness to cook on the range over the fire. Rose sharply came to a halt, her whole body stiffened. She listened intently and could hear a faint rumble, almost like thunder in the distance. Rose knew that it was not thunder, she had not heard this sound before, but instantly recognised it from fearful stories she had heard many times before. The crockery on the Welsh dresser started to vibrate and chinkle and with that the sound of an almighty explosion filled the air. The colour drained from Rose's face. Her worse fear had just become a reality; a disaster at the pit and from the enormity of the blast it sounded as if this was a major catastrophe.

Rose literally uplifted Nellie by her arm down from the stool she had been standing, causing it to topple to the floor with a thud and pulled her towards the front door. As she stepped out into the street, she could see the debris from the mine still being discharged into the sky from the mouth of the pit. Dark, heavy, smoke hung all around. Front doors were opening all the way up the street, with people fleeing without a thought of closing their doors or making their houses secure. The state of panic was both intense and overwhelming as family members feared for their loved ones.

Little Nellie was nearly being dragged along the street, as try as she did, her tiny legs would not allow her to keep up with her big sister. Aware of the terror and not fully understanding the situation, she started to cry. Rose bent down and picked her up.
 "Come here Nellie, let me carry you."
Rose's voice didn't sound at all confident. She herself was dreading what the outcome might be and certainly wasn't able to give her sister any words of comfort.

Rose and Nellie approached the pithead, as too did hoards of people from all directions. Most of these were women and children, as their men folk were at work. The time was around half-past one and everyone gathering knew that this was shift change over, therefore the chances were that more men would be underground now than during a normal shift. As the crowds gathered an eerie, almost silent atmosphere blanketed them. Surprisingly there wasn't too much wailing, a state of shock and unknown horror prevailed. The onlookers stood unmoving like stone statues, unable to comprehend the enormity of the situation unfolding before them. Llanfaer Colliery was the largest colliery in the valley and nearly every household in Llanfaer and the surrounding area had at least one family member, if not more working there. An accident of this type would absolutely devastate the close-knit community.

Rose had often listened to her Father and brothers talking about work and she prayed within herself that the explosion had not been in the nine-foot seam, as not only did she know that this was the largest seam where most men would be working, but it was also where her Father, Arthur and Edwin were working today.

'Thank God, Gareth's on late shift today', she thought to herself. For once in her life, she was glad that he'd gone to have a drink with his mate at The Black Lion. It was a sore point with Rose as Gareth was not quite old enough to legally drink, but when she had voiced her concerns to her Father he had dismissed them saying "Ah, he's earning now, he deserves a pint now and again and if he can get away with it then so be it."

Rose was slightly peeved at times that her brothers had time to socialise and enjoy themselves, whilst she was always the 'little wife' at home doing the chores. She often thought that it wouldn't hurt them to help her a bit more, or even to invite her to go with them occasionally, but it was never to be. Today though, she was more than glad that Gareth was safely in the pub, under age or not.

A few ambulances had already arrived and were attending casualties on the surface who had been hit by fallen debris. The sound of clanging bells could be heard in the distance, as more ambulances approached and without doubt they would be needed once the miners were brought up from below ground

In The Black Lion, Gareth leaned against the bar and rolled himself a cigarette, while the landlord pulled him another pint.

"I'll have a box of matches while you're at it John."

At that moment the door swung open and in walked Mel.

"Better make that two pints, I'm sure you won't say no will you mate?"

The bar was sparsely scattered with customers, not too busy, most drinking was done in the evenings. The regular domino players sat in the corner, next to the fireplace. Ray and Jim Miles two bachelor brothers, Archie Webb and Jack Lewis were all retired miners and come what may, each week-day morning they would always be on the doorstep waiting for John the landlord to open up. Many a time Gareth had watched them from his position at the bar and he was amazed at just how long they could keep a pint of bitter going; their concentration being taken up by the game, rather than conversation and sipping. Gareth's gaze followed over again to the corner where the domino players sat.

"You don't make much profit from that little lot, do you John? In the winter those seats by the fire are the best in the house and what they all spend together on beer won't pay your coal bill."

"Ay, you're probably right, but it makes the bar look a bit lively. Some people don't like coming in if there's nobody else around."

Through the bar Mel spied Maggie Clifford an attractive young woman with blonde waves and a neat figure. She was sat with a female companion at a round, wooden table in the centre of the lounge bar, two empty glasses in front of them. It was not customary for women to drink in the public bar, as that was for men only. It was questionable whether this was a gallantry custom, as although the furnishings were more comfortable in the lounge bar, it could have been solely because the men preferred to have somewhere private that they could retreat to, away from their wives and girlfriends and whereby enjoy some masculine rapport.

Maggie eagerly started waving to Mel when she caught him staring at her; her friend looked down at her feet, not so gushing as Maggie.

"Cor! I wouldn't mind waking up to her in the morning" said Mel leeringly.

"Get away man, she's too old for you, she must be all of thirty."

"Nothing wrong with that" smiled Mel. "I like them with a bit of experience. I expect she could teach me a thing or two."

Mel hailed John from the far end of the bar where he was enjoying a cigarette.

"Would you give those two lovely ladies a glass of whatever they're drinking and tell them that we'll join them shortly?"

"Don't tell me that you're after Maggie Clifford, Mel? She's a bit of a goer that one. Had more men than I've had hot dinners you know" John warningly told him.

"And tell me John?" asked Mel "How would you be knowing that?"

John turned and walked through to the lounge with the two drinks for Maggie and her friend without saying a word, but a slight flush of red could be seen creeping up from his collar.

"Right c'mon Gareth, my old mate, grab your pint and let's see if these two beauties are ready for the picking."

"No, No, you're alright. I best finish my pint and go and see if our Rose needs a hand" Gareth sheepishly answered.

"They won't bite your head off you know, it's about time you gained a bit of experience with the opposite sex. C'mon watch the maestro at work."

"Jesus! What the hell was that?" exclaimed John.

The elderly, retired miners playing dominos knew exactly what it was. They had heard that same noise in 1895, when all four of them had escaped with their lives. The vivid memory of the awfulness still etched on their memories, never to fade. Silently they mourned again for their colleagues, those who had not been so fortunate.

Mel and Gareth looked at each other knowingly and instantly rushed outside.

"Oh, my God" exclaimed Gareth, "Dad and my two brothers are on shift."

"My brother as well and my brother-in-law" added Mel.

Further conversation was out of the question, they just ran in the direction of Llanfaer Colliery, dreading what they would find when they got there.

Mrs. Evans who lived in Rose's street approached her and put her arms around her.

"Is your poor old Dad working today luvvie?"

The kindness of Mrs Evans just pushed the anxiety that Rose had been trying to contain over the edge and she bent her head against her neighbour's shoulder and the tears came.

"Yes he is" she sobbed "and so are Arthur and little Edwin. Please God, let them be alright, I'll do anything, just let them be safe."

"There, there now" comforted Mrs. Evans. "We are all going to have to be brave. I've just heard that it's going to be some time before they are going to be able to bring our men folk up from the pit. The explosion has damaged the pit top and the winding gear, so at the moment nobody can get down there to rescue them."

By this time, so many people had gathered at the pit head to hear news of the men trapped underground that the police had to form a cordon around the colliery yard. Gareth and Mel pushed their way to the front of the crowd.

"You can't come through here lads" shouted a burly policeman as they reached the cordon. "We need space for the ambulances to get in and out and for the attendants to do their job."

"You've got to let us through man. You don't understand we work here. We can help, we know the layout of the mine" Mel explained.
The policeman shouted to his colleague slightly further along.
"Fred, move up this way a bit. I'm just going to take these two to the colliery office, they may be of help. Come this way then lads." In a quieter voice he whispered to them both "If you ask me, I think they are going to need all the help they can get and I don't think there are going to be too many survivors."

Eventually news came back to the anxiously waiting assembly. The news was not good. As the crowd had already worked out, because of the shift changeover more people were trapped underground and everything was pointing towards the fact that the nine foot seam had indeed taken most of the blast.

"Thank God I've found you Rose. It's been like looking for a needle in a haystack."
"Oh Peggy, have you heard? It's the nine-foot seam." Peggy understood only too well the significance of this, as that was where her late husband had often worked. Our young Edwin is down there, he will be so scared. It's not only him though Peggy, Dad and Arthur are there as well."
Peggy took little Nellie from Rose's aching arms, trying to relieve her of the weight.
"I know it sounds bad Rose, but let's try and stay positive for the time being love. People have got out of situations like this alive before now. You mustn't think the worst. Your old Dad's been mining for many years now; he knows the ropes and will look after the other two."
"I hope so Peggy, I hope so. I just don't know how on earth we would manage without any of them."
"Well, we'll worry about that if and I say if, the time comes" Peggy comforted.
Rose didn't know if she would have been able to care for the family since her mother's death, if it hadn't been for Peggy. She had been her rock, helping out whenever she could and always offering a sympathetic ear when Rose needed to get things off her chest.
"Now listen, don't worry about the little ones, they're at my house and they can stay there as long as you want."

Rose was so tied up with worrying over her father and brothers that she had forgotten time and had not given a thought that Joyce, Idris, Myfanwy and Owen would be home from school.

"Thanks Peggy, you're so good."

"Ah, it's nothing" replied Peggy. "I'll take this little one back with me as well" she added pinching little Nellie's nose. "You'll come home with your Aunty Peggy won't you precious? I've got some nice bread and some of my home-made jam that I made especially for you."

Nellie smiled at her Aunty Peggy and stretched out her arms to give Rose a hug before she departed.

"Rose, don't stay here too long dear. If there's any news it will find itself back to you, never fear about that. "Granny Bess" as Peggy's mother was called "has got a lovely brown stew cooking on the range and we'll keep a bit back for you. Don't be too long now."

It had been three long hours since the explosion, the damage to the winding gear had been repaired and the first victims of the disaster were now being hauled up to the surface. Rose was relieved to see a couple of men being carried into the waiting ambulances and hoped, as like all the other onlookers that the injured were members of her family. Sadly, the majority of the rescued were being laid out in front of the lamp station, for them the dark hours spent working under ground were well and truly over.

Rose was too far away to recognise any of those coming out of the pit, but she did see her brother Gareth walking out of the lamp station and called his name. Gareth spotted Rose's gesticulating arms beyond the cordon and ran to her side.

"What's happening? Have you found them?" she pleaded.

"It's pretty grim over there Rose; there's more coming up dead than alive."

Rose looked up into his eyes. "But Dad, have you found him or Edwin and Arthur, please tell me that they are alright?"

"I haven't seen them Rose, but quite a few are pretty badly injured, it's going to be difficult to identify them. We're going to move the bodies over to the blacksmith's shop and make a temporary mortuary."

With that he could hear himself being called "Gareth, Gareth, we need you over here, the cage is coming up again."

He turned to his sister. "Gotta go, best you get off home. There's nothing you can do here. I'll let you know as soon as there's any news."
He gave her a kiss on the cheek and encouragingly squeezed her arms before swiftly running back to help in whatever way he could.

The sun was now starting to go down and the temperature was dropping. Rose rubbed her arms and wished that she'd brought her shawl with her. The crowd was thinning out; some poor people had already been told the worse, so for them the waiting was over. No such news had come to Rose, although the odds were stacking up against her, she still hoped that when it did eventually come it would be good. The police cordon broke up, as with fewer onlookers around it was no longer required. One of the policemen approached Rose.

"Why don't you go home love? You've been standing here for hours. There's nothing you can do, so go home that's the best place for you."
She looked up at the policeman's concerned face.

"Will you let me know when you find my Dad and my brothers? Tell them their dinner's waiting for them at home."
The policeman agreed that he would, although privately he surmised that even if they did come up alive, that there would not be much chance that they would want any dinner, but he kept this to himself, not wanting to upset the young girl in front of him further.

Rose called in at Peggy's house to collect the children on her way home.

"Why don't you let them stay here for the night?' suggested Peggy.
Owen had come to the door.

"I'd rather go with Rose if that's alright Mrs. Thomas?"

"Course it is love. I expect your sister would like a bit of company at this time. You're a big boy now, you go and look after her," answered Peggy.

Myfanwy, Idris and Joyce could be heard playing with Peggy's younger children and Rose was quite happy to leave them in Peggy's care.

"I'll take Nellie with me. I don't like to leave her, she's never been away at night before and she might get stressful."

"Okay" replied her neighbour, "but if you change your mind or need anything at all, you just come and knock on my door."

Rose, Owen and Nellie let themselves into the house. It seemed so quiet and depressing without the usual chatter of the children and the banter between her brothers and Father. To keep her occupied and ever hopeful that her brothers and Father would soon return, Rose filled the big kettle and put it on the stove, so that when they did appear she would have hot water for their baths. She picked up the knocked over stool remaining from their sudden exit earlier in the day and carried on making the cawl for supper. Her Father and brother always had a good appetite on a Friday when they came home at the end of the week and Rose prayed that tonight wouldn't be any different, but her heart of hearts told her otherwise.

Chapter 4

Rose and Owen started as a heavy knock was made on the front door. They didn't know why the noise had made them jump, as it was the sound that both of them had been expecting all evening. Owen was first to the door and pulled it open. On the doorstep was a man who Rose recognised, knowing that he lived further up the street, but she did not know his name.

"Rose Edwards?" the man enquired.

"Yes, that's me" Rose answered anxiously.

"Your brother Gareth asked me to call. Arthur's safe."

"Oh! Thank God", cried Rose and Owen simultaneously.

"The ambulance men are checking him over, but apart from a few cuts he seems to be alright. He's a very lucky man. Gareth said to let you know that he'll bring him home shortly."

He took a deep intake of breath before he imparted his next piece of news.

"Unfortunately though, I'm sorry to have to tell you Missy that your Dad's not been so lucky. He must have been hit by falling rock and was already dead when they brought him up. I'm so sorry."

Owen clung to his sister for comfort. He had often thought to himself that now he was approaching twelve that he was nearly a man, but times like this made him realise that he was still a child. Rose gulped and tried to steady her trembling voice.

"And our other brother Edwin, Edwin Edwards, is there news of him?"

"No, I'm sorry I don't know. It's chaos up there; there are still people underground. It's a long, slow job, but they're doing their damnest to get everyone out. Would you like me to fetch someone to be with you Missy, a neighbour or a friend?" he asked feeling that his duty was done and it was time to leave.

"No, no thank you. "We'll just wait for our brothers to come home."

Silently they turned around shutting the door behind them. Words didn't come easy, as there was nothing that either of them could say to each other. The grief that they had endured just over four short years ago for their mother was back again, only this time for their father.

There was hardly a home in Llanfaer and the surrounding area that had not been touched by this most cruel disaster. The whole of the valley was in mourning. Messages of sympathy came from the length and breadth of Britain, even King George V sent his own personal message, which read:

"The King is anxious to express to you personally, to the widows, the orphans and other relations of those who have lost their lives in the recent colliery accident, the profound sympathy he and the Queen entertain for them on the overwhelming calamity which has befallen them. Their Majesties feel most sincerely and deeply for them in their great sorrow."

In total two hundred and thirty-seven men and boys lost their lives on that fateful day, with more than half of the victims being 'lads' under the age of twenty. Sadly Edwin had made up one of those numbers. His little body had been so badly crushed that the only way he could be identified was by the little whittled wooden cat that was found in his trouser pocket, his so called lucky charm. There was little solace to be found when losing one so young, but Rose along with her brothers and sisters were comforted to know that he had not died alone, the body of Daisy the pony, his beloved work companion, had been found alongside him.

The day of the funeral arrived. Rose wanted to make sure that her 'little family' looked their best. Dresses and shirts had been washed and ironed and Owen had been given the job of polishing everybody's shoes. Nobody would say that the 'Edwards' family were not clean and tidy, even if they didn't have parents anymore to teach them values. Rose buttoned up the back of Myfanwy's dress and then picked up the brush to tidy Nellie's hair. Nellie's hair, unlike her sister Joyce, who had beautiful blonde curls, was dark, straight and unwieldy and had a tendency to stick out in all directions.

"Idris, your shirt collar's sticking up and make sure that you have a hankie and that goes for all of you" Rose bossily added. "It's going to be a sad day; we shall all be shedding a few tears without doubt."

Just as they were about to set off, a knock sounded at the door. Opening it, Rose recognised her Uncle Henry, suitably dressed in his mourning clothes.

*Original King's speech sent to the mourners after the Wattstown Colliery disaster of 11th July, 1905.

"Hello Uncle Henry," Rose greeted him respectfully.

Both Rose and Gareth who had gone to answer the door were surprised to see their Uncle there, as he had not darkened their doorstep for some time. Uncle Henry was their late father's brother and over the years there had been a falling out between them. The reason was not completely understood, but Rose had often thought that it may have been jealousy of some kind on her father's part. Uncle Henry had a small holding, which by no stretch of the imagination made him a rich man, but Rose assumed their indifference was in some way down to this.

The farm was hard toil and Uncle could barely afford to employ the one man who helped him.

"I wanted to come and pay my respects. I know that your father and I had our differences over the years, but he was my brother and like they say, blood's thicker than water."

"Yes, of course Uncle Henry. We're glad that you are here, aren't we?" she asked looking around the rest of the family.

The younger ones hadn't set eyes on their Uncle before and probably hadn't even heard his name mentioned in the house either. A muffled "yes" was said in uninterested agreement.

"Right," said Rose, "we'd best be off."

The elder boys Arthur and Gareth, along now with their Uncle would be attending the actual funeral. It was not customary for women and children to be seen at such events, but Rose intended that she would take the children to watch the cortege pass on its journey to the cemetery, so that they could say their final goodbyes.

The funeral of the miners from the Llanfaer Colliery disaster was precedent to anything that had gone before it. The horses were lined up ready to leave the church of St David, looking so regal and proud to be pulling the black, glass carriages that held the coffins. The cemetery was in Powlais, a distance of some three miles and the cortege wound its way through the valley resembling a long, black slithering snake. It was reported that as the head of the procession entered the gates of the cemetery, the tail of it was just leaving Llanfaer; so many were there to be buried.

Unfortunately Arthur's injuries from the explosion had not been as lenient as first thought. On the face of it, it did look like he had escaped with a few cuts and bruises, but in hindsight, this was not the case. One of the cuts on his leg had gone septic and from this he had contracted blood poisoning. It had been touch and go for several weeks if he would survive at all, as he battled with a high fever. One minute his body would be glistening with sweat and the next his teeth chattering from the chill. The illness left him in a very weak condition and if this in itself was not enough, he was then diagnosed with pneumoconiosis, more commonly known as black lung disease. The extensive dust in the mines had caused an irritation to his lungs resulting with Arthur having a chronic cough and being constantly short of breath. There was no cure, but avoidance of further exposure to coal dust was recommended, so even if Arthur had wanted to return to the pit after that tragic day, he was not able to.

If Rose had thought that they were on the bread line before, they certainly were now. With Arthur unable to find a job that his health would let him do, Gareth was the only one bringing in a wage to the house. At just seventeen years old, Rose knew that he shouldn't be expected to carry the burden of financing all of them. At the moment they still had the house in Baker Street, but they were not sure how long for, as this had been incorporated as part of their Father's wages. It was unlikely that Gareth would be able to take over the tenancy, partly because of his age and partly due to the fact that houses usually were only allocated to married men with families.

Twelve years old Owen had left school and taken a job as a delivery boy with 'Daniels' grocery store, in order to help in a small way supplement the family. Although the money was less, Rose had been adamant after losing their father and brother that he would not go down the pit. Nellie was now at school, so Rose too was able to look for employment. Work was in short supply, but she did manage to secure a couple of cleaning jobs, that she was able to juggle with running the house and looking after the family. Being at home, Arthur did help with some small tasks, but the housework was still left firmly on Rose's shoulders. There was men's work and house work was definitely women's work in the eye of any full blooded male in the welsh valleys.

"Rose, Rose, there's a letter for you" Myfanwy excitedly said as she pushed the envelope to her sister's face.

"For me?" Rose looked at the scrawled writing on the envelope and yes it definitely was for her. All eyes were on Rose as she tore open the top of the envelope, took out the single sheet of writing paper and glanced over the words written on it. A flush of colour came to her cheeks.

"Well, who's it from?" asked Arthur.

"It's from Alfie, Mr Jones' the butcher's son. He's asking if I would like to go for a walk with him on Saturday afternoon and then go back to his house for tea."

"What do you say about that then Myfanwy? Our Rose has got herself a fancy man."

"Oh, don't" said Rose. It's nothing like that and well you know it. How can I go and have tea with him, there's too much to do here?"

"You just sit yourself right down at that table Rose and write back to Alfie and tell him that you would love to see him on Saturday. I shall be here to look after the youngsters and I dare say that there's not too much skill to making a sandwich should they get hungry. You get out and have a good time. He seems a nice fellow that Alfie Jones, a bit on the quiet side, but you could do a lot worse for yourself."

"No I can't possibly go. I haven't got anything to wear, certainly not anything smart enough to have tea with Mr and Mrs Jones."

"What about Mum's clothes that we packed away in the box? You're quite a young women now Rose, not the little girl you were when Mum died. I'm sure there must be something in there that would fit you."

"But they're Mum's things, I couldn't possibly wear those" retorted Rose.

"Why ever not?" asked Arthur. Don't you think Mum would rather see you wearing them and looking pretty, than gathering dust in an old box? No more excuses. Myfanwy, fetch your sister a pencil and paper."

So that was how two days later, Rose found herself nervously getting ready to meet Alfie. Her mother had never had many decent clothes, but for Rose who always put the others' needs before her own, it was like looking in Pandora's Box. Arthur had been right, Rose had grown and there was indeed a dress in their mother's box that very nearly fitted her perfectly. She could remember seeing her mother wearing it; she used to call it her 'Sunday Best'. It was a pretty dress in a blue floral print, waisted with buttons up the front and a crocheted collar and edging to the long sleeves. Rose had washed her hair and brushed it until it shone. With it piled up on top it showed off her high cheekbones and emphasised the cream glow of her skin and her long-lashed, dark eyes. Unbeknown to Rose, she had become a very attractive woman.

Rose's stomach churned over and over. Although she had not eaten very much, she knew that it wasn't lack of food that was the cause. Rose had never walked out with a man before. She was used to male company, growing up with her father and brothers had prepared her, but that wasn't the same as being with Alfie. She was fond of Alfie and was flattered and excited that he wanted her company, but what on earth would they talk about? Should she let him hold her hand or kiss her cheek? Listening to her father and elder brothers talk, she understood that there were certain women who were known as being a bit 'flighty' and she certainly did not want to gain a reputation of that type. If only her mother had been here, then they could have had a mother to daughter chat and concerns such as these would have been resolved.

A quiet knock was heard at the door.
"I'll go. I'll go" shouted Idris and ran to the door before Rose could stop him.
Rose quickly followed Idris to the door where she shyly greeted her suitor. Not wishing to embarrass herself or Alfie further by inviting him in to meet the family, she took her coat off of the peg and walked outside. She closed the door behind her, but without looking she knew that there were at least three pairs of eyes if not more, viewing down on them from the upstairs window.

Over the next few months walking out with Alfie became a regular occurrence for Rose and for the first time in a long while, she felt that life wasn't all hard work and that she at last had something to look forward to. Since the death of their father, Uncle Henry too had taken more of an interest in the family and on several occasions had paid them a visit. Uncle Henry and his wife Grace had just one daughter Cynthia, who was twelve years old. Grace had had a difficult confinement and due to problems with the birth was unable to have further children. The younger children especially enjoyed Uncle Henry's visits, as often he would play tricks with them and would make a sweet appear from behind their ears.

It was also good for them to have some involvement with somebody other than their immediate family circle and Uncle Henry became a substitute father figure for them.

Rose should have known that life did not run smoothly for the Edwards family and just as she thought it was making a turn for the better, Gareth came home from the colliery and dropped the bombshell. With Gareth not being of age, it was not permissible for him to take over the tenancy agreement from his late father and the family had been given a month's notice to vacate their home on Baker Street.

"But how can they do this to us?" questioned Rose.

"I know Rose, it does seem harsh. Believe me I did question it, but they just answered rules are rules and that's it. They need the house for somebody else."

Rose just sat down in bewilderment. After everything she had done and given up to keep the family together, it had come to this. Whatever would they do? She felt like her whole world was caving in around her.

"Maybe we could rent a house?" suggested Gareth, but they both knew that to rent a house privately would be far more than they could afford and on top of which they would still have to put food on the table and cover the bills. The only option open to them was the workhouse, there didn't seem to be any other solution.

A few days later Rose was toiling over the weekly wash when there was a knock at the door. "Hello Uncle Henry" Rose greeted him forlornly.

"What's up Rosie, everything getting too much for you?" her Uncle sympathetically enquired.

Rose filled up the kettle and placed it on the range. "Oh! Uncle Henry" she sighed. "Let's have a cup of tea and I'll tell you all about it."

Having listened to Rose's dilemma, Uncle Henry rose out of his chair and stood in front of the range.

"Well there might be something I can help you with" he said, "that's if young Owen is in agreement."

"What did you have in mind?" asked Rose.

"Well, old Joe who has been helping me on the farm has been finding the work a bit too strenuous lately. He's been suffering with his arthritis and with the cold weather coming on; it doesn't look like he's going to make it through another winter. I've been thinking of taking on a younger man on to do the job and under the circumstances I don't see why young Owen couldn't do it. I could give him his board and lodgings with us at the farm and a bit of money for his pocket as well. What do you think?"

"Oh! I don't know. I don't want to see the family split up, but what other choice is there? At least if he came with you, he would be with somebody he knows and not a complete stranger and it would certainly be a lot better than the workhouse."

"Anyway Rose, I'd best be off. You have a word with young Owen and see what he has to say about my offer. I've got another idea up my sleeve, but I'd better have a talk to your Aunt Grace first, so best not mention anything at the moment."

Rose returned to her washing slightly lighter of heart. If Owen was agreeable to go and work for Uncle Henry it would be one less for her to worry about.

Three weeks later, with just four days to go before their eviction, life being what it is, somehow managed to sort itself out. Ideally, it was not as Rose would have wished, but as the old saying goes 'beggars can't be choosers' and in all honesty they were not too far off of that parallel.

Gareth's friend Mel suggested that he should board with him and his widowed mother as they would be more than glad of a little bit of extra money coming into the house to help make ends meet. Arthur too was over the moon to land himself a live-in job as barman in the Prince of Wales and Owen was delighted to accept his Uncle's offer of work on the farm, as he considered this to be real work, much better than delivery boy at 'Daniel's' grocery store. Uncle Henry, true to his word, had returned a few days after his visit and proposed that the younger children, Myfanwy, Idris, Joyce and Nellie join Owen their brother and live on the farm with him and his wife and daughter. Rose could not believe her good fortune; never in her wildest dreams did she think that her Uncle would suggest this. At least now the little ones would all be able to stay together and not be split up. This now only left Rose to sort herself out. Her good friend and neighbour Peggy had offered her a bed. Rose was very grateful for this, but she knew that this could only be for the short-term, as Peggy's house was already crowded with her own seven children and Grannie Bess.

The next day was Sunday and Rose was looking forward to seeing Alfie. His parents Mr. and Mrs. Jones had invited her to join them for Sunday dinner at one o'clock. Alfie had informed her that he would call for her at twelve, as there was something he wanted to show her first. Rose hadn't seen Alfie for just over a week; she knew he was up to something as he was being very secretive, but she didn't have a clue what it was.

As the clock struck twelve, Rose opened the door in answer to Alfie's knock. Rose looked admiringly at him; she had never seen him looking so smart. He was wearing a brown tweed suit, with a matching waistcoat adorned with a pocket watch borrowed from his father and the biggest smile that would fit on his face. In his hand he held a small bunch of flowers, which he presented to Rose.
   "Thank you", she said. "What have I done to deserve you looking so smart and these beautiful flowers?"
   "Nothing but the best for you Rose" grinned Alfie as he offered her his arm.
Alfie and Rose walked up Baker Street arm in arm and then cut through one of the alleyways so that they could walk alongside the River Taff. Conversation between the two of them was stinted. Rose kept talking to Alfie, but his answers were very concise, almost as if he was afraid to say too much in case he let the cat out of the bag.

Alfie's parent's lived in the flat above the shop and access to it was through the door just to the right of the main shop entrance. When they arrived at the shop, Rose was surprised when Alfie led her past the flat entrance and took her around to the old store room at the back. She noticed that the store room had recently been given a new coat of whitewash and as they approached the door she could see that a new lock had also been fitted. Alfie felt around in his pocket and produced a key, and while grinning like a Cheshire cat, fitted it into the lock and turned it. He pushed the door open and turned to Rose.
   "You first."
Rose slowly entered and looked around her. She had only once before been in the store room and then it had been full up with boxes, brooms, buckets and everything else that there wasn't enough room for in the shop. Rose took a deep intake of breath.
   "This is lovely Alfie. Is this what you have been up to, why you have been so busy?"
Inside the store room, again it had all been freshly painted. There was a small kitchen in one corner, complete with a scrubbed wooden table and

two chairs. To the left of the kitchen, on the centre back wall was a shiny, black range that Rose couldn't remember seeing before, but which no doubt at some time had been used by Mr. Jones to cook hams for the shop. In front of the range and placed at an angle, were two wooden armed, threadbare fire chairs. At the far end of the room was a black iron bedstead adorned with a pink and brown feathered eiderdown. Everything was perfect, even the two little windows either side of the door had been cleaned and dressed with curtains.

"What do you think Rose, do you like it?" asked Alfie hopefully.

"It's wonderful Alfie. Are your Mum and Dad going to rent it out?"

"Well not exactly."

Alfie took a step nearer to Rose and gave her a kiss on the cheek.

"I've never done this before" he stammered "but I understand that this is the way it should be done."

Alfie lowered his body, whilst at the same time not taking his eyes off of Rose, and knelt down onto one knee.

"Rose, please don't think this is rushed, it's something that I've been meaning to ask for some time. I suppose if I'm honest, circumstances maybe have pushed me forward a bit, but that's not to say it's not what I really want and hope with all of my heart it's what you want as well. Oh! I knew I would waffle on and mess everything up. Rose, what I am trying to say is please, please, would you do me the great honour of being my wife?"

Chapter 5

Nellie was nearing her seventh birthday and although she missed her elder sister Rose, she enjoyed living on Penbryn Farm with her Uncle Henry and Aunt Grace. The farmhouse was built of cobbled whitewashed walls and had a grey slate roof; a lonesome landmark on the otherwise bleak mountain top that overlooked the small mining community of Ferndale. No longer did Nellie have to share a bed with her siblings. Now she actually had a bed to call her own, one of three in a large bedroom that she shared with her sisters, Joyce and Myfanwy. Owen and Idris shared another room, while Cynthia had a bedroom to herself and Aunt and Uncle shared the remaining one.

Myfanwy, soon noticed that Cynthia was given preferential treatment by their Aunt, not only did she have a bedroom of her own, but if there was a slice of cake left over, it was always offered to Cynthia and should she refuse, was put aside in case she fancied it later. Never was it offered to one of her cousins who looked on in envy. Aunt Grace was forever brushing Cynthia's hair until it shone, or coiling it around rags to make curls. Returning from shopping trips she would take great delight in dressing Cynthia in a new frock or cardigan that she had bought for her, never anything new for the others. On the other hand, Uncle Henry adored having the children around; for him it filled the gap of the family that he and Grace were unable to have. Aunt Grace did not share his feelings and for her, although she was never cruel to them, she was resentful of the extra cost of looking after four children who were not her own flesh and blood, with money that in her opinion, could have been better spent on her cherished Cynthia. Owen of course did not really enter into this equation, as he was earning his keep on the farm.

Uncle did not have a lot of livestock, but there were three cows, which provided milk for the family and a number of chickens that roamed freely around laying eggs. There were also a couple of geese that acted as far better guard dogs than the three dogs that lived on the farm. If anybody approached within a hundred yards of the farm's boundary, everybody was made well aware by their squawking, that rose to a crescendo the closer the unknown wanderers came.

Nellie loved helping her Uncle. She loved being around him and just wanted to please him in any way she could. All the children apart from Cynthia were given chores to do in the house and on the farm. Nellie was nominated the job of going around the farmyard, searching in haystacks and behind buckets for eggs, collecting them and putting them into the baskets, ready for the elder children to take down the mountain to Ferndale where they would go from door to door selling them, along with cabbages and other produce that Uncle had grown.

One morning as Nellie was collecting the eggs, she heard her Uncle calling her. She carefully put down the basket, so as not to break any and ran over to where he was standing next to the hedgerow behind the barn. Patch the Jack Russell was by his side, yapping and wagging his tail, obviously having caught the scent of something enticing.

"Nellie, I think we've got a nest of rats down this hole by'yer, do you see it?"

Obediently Nellie looked in the direction of where her Uncle was pointing. She was nervous to be standing so close to it, in case one of the creatures made a run for it.

"Now I'm going to light this piece of rag and stuff it down the hole to smoke out the little blighters. What I need you to do is pick up Patch and when you see them running out, let go of him so that he can catch them. Have you got that?"

Nellie nodded her head in agreement and moved forward to pick up Patch, who was totally against the idea and wriggled for all his worth. Uncle lit the rag and bent down and pushed it into the hole, while Nellie anxiously watched to see if the plan was successful. All of a sudden out of the hole emerged a large rat, followed by about seven smaller ones. Witnessing the advancing rats, Nellie turned on her heels and sped off towards the safety of the house.

"Drop the dog Nellie! Drop the dog", her Uncle bellowed out behind her.

In her fear not only had she scarpered, but had carried Patch with her, so the little family of rats, much to her Uncle's annoyance, lived to see another day.

By foot, Penbryn Farm was a fair walk from Llanfaer, with the journey each way taking at least an hour and a quarter. Arthur and Gareth had not made the journey very often, but Rose did try to visit on a regular basis.

On one occasion, about a year after they had moved to the farm, Uncle had taken the five of them over to visit Rose and her husband Alfie in their home behind the butcher's shop. Rose had made Welsh cakes and they had all eaten as many as they could manage, before starting off on the long walk back to the farm.

All the children attended Ferndale school. There was a single vehicle road that wound its way passed Penbryn Farm down to Ferndale, but rather than go this way, which added on a further two miles, the children always opted to clamber down the mountain side. It was a bit steep in places and they had to be careful not to trip over craggy boulders sticking up in the grass, but they were well used to this route, as not only did they use it for school, but when selling Uncle's produce as well.

Nellie enjoyed school, as she had an inquisitive mind and was interested in learning new things. As like her brothers and sisters, outside of school hours Nellie never had any friends to play with, due mainly to the location of where they lived; up the top of the mountain and far away from the terraced streets where the other pupils lived. From a very early age, Nellie understood the meaning of 'out of sight, out of mind'. Nellie was undeterred by this and wasn't a child to take it to heart; she found company with the cows, the chickens and the farm dogs and not least of all her day dreaming and vivid imagination.

Walking home from school one afternoon, Nellie was feeling very hot and didn't feel well at all. She was glad when at last she heard the gobbling of the geese to know that she was nearly at the gates of the farm, as she didn't feel that her little legs would be able to carry her much further. As Nellie approached the barn, her hands were feeling very clammy and everything around her started to swirl and she felt as if she was floating above everything on a different plane. The next thing Nellie remembered was coming round with Aunty Grace and Uncle Henry fussing over her. She still felt hot and clammy and knew she wasn't well.

"What happened?" asked Nellie frightened that she couldn't remember.

"It's all right love, you fainted. We've got you now it's alright" comforted Aunt Grace.

"She feels very hot Grace and look at this rash on her neck."

"I'll take her up to bed and give her a hot drink and see what she's like in a bit."

Nellie was carried up to bed and Aunt Grace returned with a cup of hot lemon juice.

"Here, drink this Nellie."

Nellie took a sip, screwed her eyes up and winced.

"My throat hurts Aunty, I don't want anymore."

The next day, Nellie was no better and by now the rash had spread to her chest and back. Her temperature was still high and as well as complaining still of a sore throat, her glands also were up. Owen had been sent down the mountain to Ferndale to ask if the doctor would call on them.

Just before mid-day the doctor duly arrived and confirmed that Nellie was indeed suffering with Scarlet Fever, which was highly contagious. He informed Uncle Henry and Aunt Grace that little Nellie would have to spend some time in hospital and that he would make arrangements for her to be collected. A car with darkened windows arrived soon afterwards, to take Nellie to the Fever Hospital several miles away over the next valley. The car with its darkened windows looked very threatening to Nellie and she didn't like the idea of getting in it by herself. Uncle had explained to her that she had an infectious disease which could be passed on, so because of this Aunty and Uncle were not allowed to travel with her to the hospital and to make matters worse would not be able to visit her for several weeks. Nellie feeling so poorly unhappily accepted the situation and clambered into the awaiting vehicle.

The ward where Nellie was placed had large high vaulted ceilings and iron beds were arranged in a long row against each wall. Large cathedral like windows were strategically set in the opposite wall to where Nellie lay in her bed. A little while had elapsed before she had actually taken much notice of her surroundings, as before she started to get better Nellie's fever had worsened and for several days she had been quite delirious. The windows in the ward were always slightly opened to allow fresh air to creep through. Ritually twice a day they were thrown wide open for the air in the ward to be completely exchanged with new fresh air. At these times the patients were covered over with a sheet until the wards warmed up again, to avoid them breathing in any cold air. The patients were also bathed or sponged down twice a day and rubbed down very quickly afterwards with towels so as not to get cold. Vaseline was then rubbed into their bodies, as within about six days the red rash would disappear, but the skin would start to peel. Strict hospital rules stated that all patients with scarlet fever had to stay in bed until the skin had stopped peeling, which could take up to several weeks. The illness had taken away Nellie's appetite and never having had much flesh on her to begin with, she now looked positively skinny. All she had been given to eat since arriving at the Fever Hospital had been broth and to drink water or week lemonade.

Nellie was quite envious of the other children, who were getting over their illnesses and were allowed out of bed in their clothes and bedroom slippers. Understandably after spending so long in bed, she was over the moon when the nurse told her that her Uncle had been asked to bring some of her clothes in, as she too had improved enough to join them. Imagine Nellie's embarrassment and shame when Uncle brought in a pair of hob-nailed boots for her to run around in, no nice slippers for her.

Six months after her stay in hospital, Nellie was again walking up the mountain on her way home from school. As usual she was daydreaming about something or other and not paying full attention, tripped and grazed her knee on one of the boulders jutting out of the ground. She picked herself up and brushed the remaining dirt off of the grazed area. It stung a bit, but she tried not to let it bother her. As she approached the farm, the usual gaggling of the geese started and she knew that they wouldn't stop until she was well within recognising distance.

Entering the farmyard, Nellie noticed a small black car parked near to the front door of the house. 'Aunt and Uncle must have visitors' she thought, but didn't know who, as nobody normally arrived in a car. A low mumbling of voices could be heard as Nellie walked through the front door and closed it behind her.
   "Ah! Here she is now" exclaimed Aunt Grace. "Come over here Nellie, there's some ladies here that I want you to meet."
Slowly Nellie approached with a sense of foreboding. She had no reason to suspect anything untoward, but realised that Aunt Grace was speaking in her posh voice and that something was different.
   "This is Miss Carter and Miss Jessop" Aunt Grace informed her with a false smile on her face.

Nellie examined the two ladies in front of her and decided they were as different as chalk and cheese. Whereas Miss Carter was of medium height, rotund with a rosy complexion and dark hair tightly pinned up into a bun, Miss Jessop was above average height, thin, with pale skin and fair hair fashionably cut into a bob style. Age wise Nellie assumed that the plump lady would be around her Aunt Grace's age, forty or thereabouts and the slim lady maybe some ten years younger. The only similarity was that they both wore black dresses, the elder one with a high ruffled collar and the younger one with a plain round neck. Politely Nellie said hello to them, as she knew this was expected of her.

Glancing around the room Nellie noticed Cynthia, sat in the armchair by the fire, fingering her crochet, but eagerly listening to all the goings on with a look of the cat who was about to get the cream. On the table, packed in a cardboard box Nellie recognised her clothes and on top, the rag doll that Rose and Alfie had given her for Christmas.

"Nellie" Aunt Grace stated in a loud voice to get her attention. "Miss Carter and Miss Jessop have kindly offered for you to live with them for a while, isn't that nice of them?"

Nellie didn't know what to say or think. 'Had she been naughty?' She couldn't think of any exceptional episodes that would warrant her having to stop living with her Aunt and Uncle. She remembered her Uncle being cross with her over the dog and rats incident, but he had laughed about it at a later time, so surely it wasn't that. By this time, Joyce and Myfanwy had come home from school and were listening to the proceedings. They were upset to think that their sister was being sent away, but too frightened to voice any opinion, as they knew that they would be in trouble if they did and feared they also might be packed off.

"How long's a while?" Nellie meekly enquired.

"Oh! I don't know" replied her Aunt. "Stop asking questions young Nellie and pick up your box and take it to the car."

Nellie obediently did what she was told. She wondered where her Uncle was, surely he wouldn't let her go without saying goodbye, but as she looked around the farmyard he was nowhere to be seen.

"Now you be a good girl for these two ladies, young Nellie and don't get yourself up to any mischief" instructed Aunt Grace, as she opened the door of the car and guided Nellie onto the back seat next to her box of possessions. She closed the door behind Nellie, not even being able to bring herself to give the poor, confused girl a kiss on the cheek.

Miss Carter and Miss Jessop duly settled themselves into the front seats, Miss Carter in the driving seat and Miss Jessop as passenger. The engine started up with a soft purr, followed by a slight jolt and the car moved slowly towards the five barred gate at the far end of the farmyard. Nellie looked over her left shoulder and saw Myvanwy and Joyce hand in hand by the front door of the farmhouse, forlornly waving their other hands after their younger sister. Glancing over her right shoulder, Nellie could faintly make out her Uncle Henry in the shadow of the big barn door. He wasn't waving, but Nellie did notice him wiping his eyes with his big, white handkerchief.

The car trundled down the winding road to Ferndale, passing by Nellie's school and other local familiar landmarks. She could see Bobby Jones and Bryn Morrison playing marbles on the steps of the church hall, but they didn't notice her. For them life went on just the same, not so for poor Nellie who had no idea what was install for her. The journey seemed to take forever. Little Nellie didn't have a clue where she was, the familiar terraced streets of Ferndale had been left long behind.
"Not far to go now" Miss Jessop said as she turned and gave Nellie a friendly smile.
Nellie looked straight back at the stranger in front of her, words would not come to her as she gently squeezed her rag doll for comfort. Eventually they turned right off of the main road and went down a hill stopping outside a large house at the bottom.
   "Well here we are home at last" said the plumper lady, "I certainly shall be glad of a nice cup of tea."

Peering out of the window at her so called new home, Nellie's first impressions were of a daunting nature. The house didn't look very friendly; its blocks of grey granite stone made it look cold and uninviting. There were two large windows either side of a glossy black front door and three equally large windows on the upper floor. The house had a gravelled front, surrounded by a wrought iron spiked fence, which reminded Nellie of Dr. Robert's house in Richmond Terrace. This house though stood alone, not in a block of five like Dr. Robert's, giving it an almost defiant nature as if to say 'Keep away, you are not welcome here.' Nellie wriggled across the seat to get out of the front passenger's door, trying to pull her box with her as she went.

"Leave that!" instructed Miss Jessop. "It will be easier for me to lift it out, once you are out of the car."

Stretching her legs on the pavement outside the house, Nellie looked up and down the road at her surroundings. It was unlike streets that she had seen before; there were no rows of houses on either side. Apart from 'Aberaeron', the name she had gleaned from the brass plaque to the side of the front door, there was just one row of about eight small houses and a few cottages dispersed around.

Miss Carter unlocked the door and they entered into a large, square hallway with a dark passage way leading off at the far end. A highly polished, wooden banister dominated the hallway, reaching nearly to the high ceiling and curving around just before the upper landing. The floor was covered with red and black, diamond shaped tiles that reminded Nellie of days when she had played hopscotch, but she didn't think she would be allowed to do that on this floor. Nellie had never been inside a house such as this, it was all very grandeur to her simple means; the brass light fittings and ornate, gold picture frames appeared so opulent. A far cry from the house she had lived in on Baker Street with Rose and her brothers and sisters, but all the same Nellie knew which one she preferred and it wasn't this one.

"Come along Clara Jane, we'll show you to your room" said Miss Carter already making her way up the staircase.

'Clara Jane' thought Nellie, 'Who's Clara-Jane?' and she turned around expecting to see another person, but there was only Miss Jessop behind her. Feeling the pressure of Miss Jessop's hand on her back, she moved on up the stairs.

Leading off the landing were five doors. Pointing to each door in turn Miss Carter advised, "That's the guest room, that's Miss Jessop's room, this one's the bathroom. Over there is my bedroom and this one here will be your bedroom."

Nellie wasn't sure what amazed her most, having a bathroom and one upstairs at that, or the fact that she was to have her own room.

"We hope you like it" Miss Jessop excitedly commented as Miss Carter opened Nellie's bedroom door and guided her through.

Nellie couldn't believe her eyes when she surveyed the room that was to be her very own bedroom. She had never seen anything so pretty in all of her young life; it was a room fit for a princess. Covering the bed was a silky, powder blue eiderdown and floating down from above the bed was a canopy of white muslin. Sitting on the bed, dressed in a pink dress was the most beautiful china doll that Nellie had ever set eyes on. There was a wicker bath chair in the corner and next to it was a dolls house at least three feet tall, with doors and windows that opened and a complete set of miniature furniture inside. She also took interest in a white, painted bookcase full of children's books.

Anxious to please, Miss Jessop quickly stepped towards the wardrobe and tall boy dresser at the far end of the room.

"Clara-Jane, look in here! Come and see the pretty clothes that we have bought for you!"

Again Nellie looked around thinking that somebody else must have walked into the room, but there was nobody else there apart from the three of them. Thinking that they had forgotten her name or were mixing her up with somebody else, she politely pointed out that her name was Nellie.

"Not anymore." informed Miss Carter sternly. "From now on you will be called Clara-Jane Carter and you will call Miss Jessop here Aunt Tilly and I shall be known as Aunt Beatrice. Understood?"

Totally confused, Nellie didn't understand at all, but thought she had better nod her head in agreement.

After breakfast, a week following Nellie's arrival at 'Aberaeron', she could hear the local children laughing and shouting as they made their way to school. Nellie had watched them playing in the road outside the house and being too shy to join them at that stage, was looking forward to starting school, whereby she hoped soon she would be able to make friends with them. Aunt Beatrice, with a white pinafore over her black dress, bustled back and fore clearing the remains of breakfast from the table.

"When shall I be starting school Aunt Beatrice?" asked Nellie.

"Starting school? You needn't think you will be joining the likes of that riff-raff out there. No, no, my dear girl, we've arranged for Miss Prior to come and teach you here. It will be much better for you, not only will she teach you to read and write, but etiquette as well. Your lessons will start at nine o'clock on Monday morning."

Nellie sat on the hard, wooden window seat and peered out of the window, tracing the raindrops as they trickled down the glass panes. Several months had passed by since Aunt Beatrice and Aunt Tilly had taken her away from Penbryn Farm and not a day went by without her thinking about the family she had left behind. Often she would look out of her bedroom window and see a figure walking down the hill, that she swore was her sister Rose coming to see her, only to be disappointed the closer it came when she realised that she had been mistaken. She knew in her heart of hearts that Rose would not have forgotten her, but remembering the long distance she had travelled from her Uncle's farm to 'Aberaeron', sensibly understood that a journey of such length would not be feasible for Rose to walk and without a car would be impossible.

Nellie could not say that she was not shown attention by Aunt Beatrice and Aunt Tilly. They were forever dressing her up in clothes of such finery, sometimes even changing her two or three times a day. Her hair was washed every day and brushed until it shone and now that it was longer, was either plaited or put in ringlets. It reminded her of the way Aunt Grace had pampered over Cynthia and although at the time, Nellie and her sisters had been a little bit jealous of all the attention bestowed on their cousin, Nellie now wondered if Cynthia had really enjoyed it.

As was customary on Sundays, both in the morning and evening, Nellie and her two Aunts could be seen walking down the road to the Baptist Church at the far end of the village. Dressing Clara-Jane in readiness for church was one of the highlights of the week, especially for Aunt Tilly.
  "Shall we put her in the little white hat with the flower buds Beatrice? She looks so pretty in that and it goes so well with the lacy gloves."
  "Yes if you wish, but I think she had better wear a cardigan on top of that dress, as the weather seems to have taken a bit of a turn today and we don't want her catching a chill, do we?"
  "Yes, yes, you're so right. Come here Clara-Jane; let me put this on you."
Nellie enjoyed going to church. Although she found the long sermons a bit on the dreary side, she loved singing the hymns at the top of her voice. Sometimes Aunt Beatrice would give her a dig in the ribs and put a finger to her mouth, a sign for Nellie to lower the noise level slightly.

One particular Sunday as the three of them made their way to church, a group of boys and girls, slightly older than Nellie and scruffily dressed, could be seen gathering around the lamp post at the top of the road. As they approached, the little gang's sniggering became louder and more frequent. Protectively, both Aunts took hold of Nellie's hand and the three of them continued walking towards and past the offending onlookers. A couple of the boys left the main body of the gang and started following Nellie and her Aunts, whispering and jeering amongst themselves. Several times Nellie turned around, trying to hear what was being said, but not being quite close enough it was difficult for her to hear properly.

"Come on Clara-Jane, don't take any notice of them" Aunt Beatrice told her, as she gave her a sharp tug to pull her around to face the front.
Nellie being self-conscious felt that their taunts were being directed at the way she was dressed. She herself wasn't comfortable with it, as she could well remember the times when she too had worn hand me down clothes that were more than a little on the big side. The two boys who followed started walking hand in hand together and then blew each other a kiss. The rest of the gang found this to be hilarious and fell about laughing.

The wintry nights had drawn in and Christmas was almost here. It would be the third Christmas that Nellie had spent with Aunt Beatrice and Aunt Tilly, away from her own family. Unlike the little terrace house on Baker Street where coal and wood had been rationed to make it last from one week until the next, 'Aberaeron' was a warm house with fires blazing in several rooms.

As Nellie walked through from the kitchen to the front parlour, the front door suddenly burst open and a gust of wind rushed in.

"Hold the door open please Clara-Jane" ordered Aunt Tilly's voice from behind a vision of greenery.

"Aunt Tilly, is that the Christmas tree? Can I help you decorate it?" asked Nellie as she ran to hold open the door.

"Yes of course you can" replied Nellie's Aunt. "We'll just stand it here in the hall while we fetch the bucket from the backyard."
The tree was placed in the front parlour and the whole afternoon was spent decorating the tree and making paper chains and lanterns. Christmas was always a favourite time for Nellie, as for most small

children. Nellie particularly liked Christmas Eve when the expectation and excitement grew inside her and she felt like a balloon ready to pop.

Her Christmases of a few years before had been so different, none of the extravagance of more recent ones, but still they had been a time of great fun and anticipation. Nellie could remember sitting around the range with Rose and her brothers and sisters, singing carols and playing charades. Her brother Gareth was particularly good at mimicking different characters in their street and would have the family in stitches laughing at his antics. There hadn't been a lot of money in the Edwards' family, but that hadn't deterred Father Christmas from paying his annual visits and the children each had a sack with a few little goodies inside, namely an orange, an apple, even sometimes a potato or a carrot. It didn't matter what the contents were, the importance was that whatever was inside belonged to them; it was theirs and theirs alone and they didn't have to share it with anyone.

Nellie woke up Christmas morning, pushed the covers back and sprang towards the foot of the bed. Just as she had hoped, the empty pillow case that she had left at the bottom of her bed the night before, was now full to overflowing with presents wrapped in pretty paper. She opened her bedroom door and could hear Aunt Beatrice and Aunt Tilly busying theirselves in the kitchen.

"He's been. He's been. Father Christmas has been" she yelled over the banister and down the stairs. "Come up and see."

Nellie didn't have too long to muse over her presents of new toys and clothes, as within no time, again she was being dressed ready for church. Usually Nellie quite liked going to church, as it made a welcome change and it gave her the opportunity to mix with more people than just her two Aunts, but today being Christmas she would have preferred to have stayed and played with her newly acquired toys.

"Do we have to go to church today?" resisted Nellie. "It was Sunday yesterday and we went twice then. Can't I stay here and play?" she pleaded.

"No you cannot, young lady" answered Aunt Beatrice. "You well know what day it is today. It's our good Lord's birthday and it is only right that you show some respect and go to his house and ask forgiveness for your sins and to give thanks for all of these presents and the good food on our table. Now come along and hurry up. I shall not hear another word. Understood?"

Winter moved on and spring arrived, bought to life by the yellow daffodils clustered on the grass verge opposite. As Nellie lay on her bed reading a book, she could hear the children who lived nearby playing in the road. Intrigued by their laughter and chatter, she raised herself off of the bed and walked over to the window where she sat down on the window seat, so that she could get a better view. Looking down, she could see three girls, roughly the same age as herself. Two of them held the end of a long rope, while the other one skipped over it.
"Twenty one, Twenty two" they shouted in unison until the girl in the middle missed her step and failed to jump over the rope.
"My turn, my turn" shouted the tallest of the three and swapped places with the girl in the middle to take her turn at skipping.
Nellie would have loved to have gone over to them and asked if she could join in their game, but she knew that it was pointless, as her Aunts would dismiss the idea immediately. Nellie longed to be one of the girls that she looked down on and felt so alone in her little ivory tower.

Nellie knew that in truth she should count her blessings at the good fortune of being taken in by her two Aunts, but she still yearned for her real family, the family that loved her and her days of playing in the school yard. In no stretch of her imagination could she claim that she was not well cared for, well dressed or well fed, but deep in her heart she knew that it was not love in the real sense of the word that her Aunts felt for her. Yes they idolised her and treated her well, but for them she was like a pet or a doll; something to pamper. To Aunt Beatrice and Aunt Tilly she was no more than the china doll that sat on her bed, a sacred object to be savoured.

One night Nellie awoke in the night, not feeling well at all. Her nightdress was damp and she felt very clammy and her stomach churned. She eased herself out of the bed and opened her bedroom door. It was dark on the landing, but she felt her way along to Aunt Tilly's door and gently knocked. Not a sound came from inside, so Nellie turned the handle and gently opened the door. At first she couldn't see anything, but gradually her eyes became accustomed to the darkness and with the aid of the moonlight shining through the thin curtains she could see that Aunt

Tilly was not in her bed, in fact her bedcovers had not been turned down at all. 'Maybe she's already up' thought Nellie, but at the same time thought it must be very early, as there was no sign of dawn breaking. Nellie turned to go back to her room, but was halted outside Aunt Beatrice's bedroom on hearing a slight moaning noise coming from within. Concerned that perhaps Aunt Beatrice was feeling poorly like herself, Nellie quickly knocked on the door, but without waiting for an answer pushed the door open. Inside the room, her eyes already adjusted to the darkness, she could see not one shape in the bed, but two.

"What's the matter Clara-Jane, why are you not in bed?"
Nellie instantly recognised the voice of her Aunt Tilly and wondered why she was not in her own bed. Hastily Aunt Tilly sat up, her bare breasts displayed against the backdrop of moonlight creeping through the window. Quickly she covered herself with the bed sheet, hoping that she had rectified the situation before Nellie had noticed, but it was too late, Nellie had indeed noticed. Aunt Beatrice didn't move, but stayed well under the bedcovers.

"I don't feel well" whimpered Nellie. "My stomach hurts."
Usually if Nellie suggested that anything was amiss, more often or not both of her Aunts would immediately be at her side and fussing over her. On this occasion, this was not the case.

"Go back to your room Clara-Jane and we will be with you shortly. Just give us a minute" Aunt Beatrice ordered.
Nellie returned to her room and within several minutes was joined by her two Aunts, now dressed in their night attire.

Three days later and with no forewarning, nobody was more surprised than Nellie to find herself and her belongings, this time in a suitcase, being once again bundled into the back of the little black car. Nellie was a sharp-minded girl and noticed that she was the only one with a suitcase.

"Where are you taking me?" she worriedly enquired. "Where are we going?"

"We're taking you back to your Aunt and Uncle, Clara-Jane."
There was no further explanation. She had never learnt why she had been taken away in the first place and now she didn't know why she was being taken back.

Chapter 6

When Nellie returned to live in Penbryn Farm, she felt like a stranger. Three years was a long time to be away, life had moved on and during her absence things and people had changed. Nellie was now eleven and like her everybody else had grown up just that little bit more. Owen at seventeen was nearly a man, he was now quite tall and the hard, manual work on the farm had filled him out, giving him broad shoulders and muscles. Myvanwy was fifteen and out of all of Nellie's brothers and sisters had changed the least. She too had filled out and now had the body of a young woman, but was still the daydreamer that she had always been. Idris was fourteen and if Nellie hadn't known better, would have thought that he was Owen, they looked so alike. Joyce only fourteen months Nellie's senior, looked if at all possible even prettier than Nellie remembered. Life on the farm certainly seemed to agree with her. Cynthia, her Aunt and Uncle's daughter apart from looking chubbier, looked near enough exactly the same as she had before and was still consistently doted on by her mother.

The pretty dresses that Aunt Beatrice and Aunt Tilly had bought for Nellie were not really suitable for clambering up and down the mountain and sloshing around in the farmyard mud, so it wasn't long before they were so badly ripped and torn, that once again she was back in hand me down clothes. To be honest, it was something that Nellie was quite glad about, as she didn't like the teasing she had received from the other children at school. It wasn't only her clothes that were the point of ridicule, but also the way she spoke, so whether on purpose or not, within no time at all Nellie's Welsh accent had reappeared.

One morning Nellie was sat out on the back step shelling peas for her Aunt, when she noticed a familiar figure pushing open the five bar gate to the farmyard. Out of all the times, she had looked out of her bedroom window at 'Aberaeron', this time she knew that she wasn't mistaken. She jumped up so quickly, that she kicked over the colander of freshly podded peas and they scattered all over the step, some rolling off into the mud below. Nellie realised what she had done and knew that her Aunt would tell her off if she saw, but nothing deterred her.

"Rose, Rose" she excitedly shouted, reminiscent of the loud yell that had been the reason for her name in the first place.

Nellie covered the farmyard as quickly as she could and near enough sprung into her sister's arms, hugging her so tightly, that in the end Rose had to prise her away so that she could look at her face.

"Nellie, I can't believe it's you. Why you've changed so much. Not a day's gone by without me thinking of you. You know that don't you?" she appealingly looked into her sister's eyes.

"Yes, I know" responded Nellie with a lump in her throat, which for a few moments prevented her from saying anything else.

Looking down, Nellie could see a little boy of about five years old, looking up at her. There was no mistaking who his father was, with his dark curly hair and green eyes; he was the spitting image of Alfie. Her eyes were drawn to the pushchair that Rose was pushing and the two little girls inside, both around the same age with the same curly hair, but this time with Rose's dark eyes.

"Are these your babies?" asked Nellie.

"Yes they are" answered Rose proudly. "Aren't they beautiful? This little chap is Donald and he's nearly four and these are the twins Vera and Elsie and they are two and" smiled Rose as she patted her slightly swollen stomach, "there will soon be another one." Rose looked at her children and said "This is your Aunty Nellie. You've heard me talking about her haven't you?"

Donald with a sudden attack of shyness hid his head in his mother's skirt, unlike the twins who gave Nellie wonderful toothy grins.

As they approached the farmhouse, Nellie could see that Myvanwy had picked up the scattered peas and was just shelling the last few.

"Thought I'd best finish these off for you, before Aunt Grace saw them all over the place, otherwise you'd have been for it."

The hour and a half that Rose spent at the farm went by so quickly, but not before Nellie had been updated with news of her two elder brothers Arthur and Gareth. Arthur was still working in The Prince of Wales public house; he still had trouble with his breathing from time to time, but overall was coping very well. Gareth too was now married to Jane, a cousin of his friend Mel's and they also had a little girl of six months old, who was called Iris.

Nellie was sad when the time came for Rose and her little family to start their long walk home. However she was cheered by the fact that Uncle Henry had suggested that providing Rose and Alfie were in agreement, now that the children were older and if they were good, that sometimes he would let them walk over by themselves to see Rose. Nellie decided there and then that she was going to be very good, so that soon she would be able to visit Rose and play with her nephew and little nieces.

"Can you reach that plate down for me off of the top shelf Nellie?" requested Aunt Grace. "You may as well make those gangly legs of yours useful for something."
It was true, Nellie's growth had certainly sprouted over the last few years and she was at least a head's measure over Joyce, her next sister in line. At times she was becoming quite self-conscious over her height and her lean, skinny body did not help matters.

"When you've finished taken the eggs around Ferndale this morning Nellie, I want you to call in Mrs. Gregory's shop and buy a slab of rich, fruit cake for me. Mrs. Armitage is coming this afternoon and I should like to offer her a nice slice of cake to go with her cup of tea."

Nellie made her way down the mountain very carefully, desperately trying not to trip over as her basket was full with freshly laid eggs. Idris and Myvanwy had started off some fifteen minutes before Nellie and she could now see them nearing the bottom; Idris with a sack of potatoes and Myvanwy with a sack of cabbages. Nellie was grateful to be carrying the eggs, as although they were more breakable, at least they were not so heavy. As Nellie got to the top of Church Road, she waved at Mrs. Druary who was mopping down her front step. She had walked so cautiously all the way down from the farm and then just as she approached her regular customer, she tripped on the uneven pavement. Poor Nellie managed to save herself, but her basket of eggs took a severe jolt, resulting in two on the top smashing. Mrs Druary was a kindly lady and now that all her children had fled the nest, had a little bit more money than in days gone past. She guessed that Nellie would be in for a telling off if her Uncle knew that she had broken some of the eggs.

"Tell you what young Nellie. I'll give you the money for my usual half dozen, but only give me four and the two broken ones can be our little secret."

"Oh! Thank you Mrs. Druary, but are you sure?"

"Yes, yes I'm sure. Just make sure you look where you are going next time."

Her basket empty, Nellie made her way home and just as she started her climb back up the mountain, she remembered that she had to call into the shop to buy the cake for Aunt Grace. She retraced her footsteps and entered the shop, patiently waiting at the counter while Mrs. Gregory served Mrs. Evans the local gossip, who willingly notified the shopkeeper of the entire goings on for the week, without hardly taken a breath.

Eventually it was Nellie's turn to be served and all of a sudden her mind went blank. She knew that it was a slab of cake that she had come in for, but couldn't for the life of her remember the name of it.
"Yes" said Mrs. Gregory "what would you like?"
"My Aunt wants a slab of cake" Nellie nervously said. "It's the plain one, but the plain one with currants in."
Mrs. Gregory laughed out loud. "Well my child, I've never heard it called that before. I think you mean a slab of my rich, fruit cake."
Nellie felt herself colouring up, but was relieved when Mrs. Gregory brought the cake to the counter to wrap up and she recognised it as being the right one.

It hadn't taken Nellie long to settle back into life at Penbryn Farm, within a few weeks it was almost as if she had never been away. Nothing was ever mentioned again about Aunt Beatrice or Aunt Tilly and she sensed that it was best not to ask. As time moved on, Clara-Jane and her life at 'Aberaeron' all appeared to be a distant memory. Owen had never really recovered from losing his brother Edwin in the mining disaster; they had been more than brothers, they had been best friends. He was now twenty years old and when his elder brothers had been that age, they had loved nothing more than meeting up with their friends for a pint or going to the occasional dances to ogle the girls. That lifestyle was not for Owen; he was a loner. By this time Cynthia had married Jack Mason, quite a few years her senior and who already had a son by a previous marriage. Her mother and father had been totally against their getting married, but one night they eloped and the deed was done. Apparently Aunt Grace had sat in the chair by the fire, crying for days afterwards. Myvanwy and Idris had also left home, so now there was only Owen, Joyce and Nellie remaining at the farm. Myvanwy had gone into service at a large house over the valley and Idris had joined the army and was on his way to serve his country abroad in India.

As Nellie threw the last of the boiled, potato peelings out for the chickens, she glanced over towards the track and saw Owen bringing in the cows for milking. She was very fond of her brother, as he was of her. Leaving the bucket inside the barn, she quickly ran to meet him. Owen and Nellie understood each other, they were both a little on the quiet side and neither was embarrassed by silence. A few years ago there had been a very bad storm, which brought down the elm tree just on the edge of the small copse a few hundred yards behind the barn and often the two of them would sit there together, sometimes talking, sometimes both in deep thought.

"What you been up to today then Nellie? Did Mr. Bruce give you the cane?"

"No not me, but David Rees got it. Mr. Bruce turned around from the blackboard and caught him poking his tongue out at him. Fifteen of the best he got"

"Cor! I bet that stung a bit. Brings back memories, I can tell you."

"Did you get the cane then Owen?" asked Nellie "I never knew that."

"Yes I did on more than one occasion, but I didn't dare mention it when I got home, otherwise I would have copped for it again from Dad." Nellie watched and waited, while Owen milked the three cows, gently squeezing his thumb and finger together until the final drops emerged. He lifted the bucket and poured some of the milk into the tall white enamel jug that leant against the post.

"Here you are Nellie, can you take this into Aunt Grace? No doubt she will be waiting for it to make tea for everyone. And try not to spill any" he shouted after his sister, knowing how awkward she could be at times.

Aunt Grace looking out the kitchen window could see Uncle Henry running across the yard. "Goodness me" she muttered. "What on earth is he in such a hurry about?" Uncle Henry barged through the door waving a letter in his hand.

"We've got a letter. I think it's from Idris."

They were all anxious to have news of Idris. It had been over three months since they had last heard from him and at that time his training was complete he had been given his posting to the North West Frontier. Looking around, Uncle noticed that Owen was missing.

"Best get Owen, I'm sure he'll want to hear this."

Uncle gave a loud shout from the door, but Owen was obviously too far away to hear him.

"I think he's cleaning out the cow shed. Go and get him young Nellie! I'll open this when we 're all here."

All eyes were on Uncle Henry as he tore open the top of the envelope and took out the small piece of paper inside.

"Yes it is from Idris."

"Well go on" said Aunt Grace impatiently. "What does it say?"

Squinting his eyes, as nowadays his eyesight wasn't as good as it used to be, Uncle Henry read out the letter.

Dear Uncle Henry, Aunt Grace, Cynthia and my brothers and sisters,
I miss you all.

I have now arrived at my camp, although my sergeant says I am not allowed to tell you where I am or what I am doing. I didn't enjoy the long sea voyage and I was sick nearly every day.

This place is so different to Wales. You would not believe how hot and sticky it is here. I've seen funny trees with long, thin trunks and a funny bark. They don't have branches, just a big fan of leaves on the top. I think they are called Palm Trees.

I do miss you all very much and I don't know when I'll be coming home. I have made some new friends, so don't worry about me.

All the best

Idris xxx

P.S. I will write again as soon as I can.

Uncle Henry could still well remember the traumas of the First World War.

"I know they say it's a brave thing to do" Uncle Henry sighed, "but I do wish he hadn't joined the army. There's always trouble somewhere in the world."

"Shall I take the letter over to show Rose?" Nellie eagerly suggested, hoping for another chance to see her nephews and nieces.
The baby that Rose had been expecting three years ago, was now a beautiful, little boy called John. He was a happy child with such a cheeky smile that he could not fail to win a place in everyone's heart.
"Not today, love" replied her Uncle, "Maybe tomorrow, there's work to be done here today. I've got a lot of wood to chop up for the winter and you can help me stack it up in the barn."

Joyce had now left school and through a friend of her Aunt Grace's had managed to get herself a job as a chamber maid in the The Grand, the one and only hotel in Ferndale. Her shift started at eight o'clock in the morning, so Joyce usually left the farm around quarter past seven, so that she had plenty of time to walk down the mountain and put herself tidy before her due time to start work. This particular morning Joyce had company on her walk to work, as Nellie not wanting to miss a minute was up with the larks raring to get to Rose's house. As she climbed over the five bar gate, she heard her Aunt calling her and waving something in her hand.
"Nellie Edwards, you'd forget your head if it wasn't screwed on. Isn't this the reason that you're going?"
In her haste, Nellie had forgotten to pick up the letter from Idris.

The day had simply flown by for Nellie and probably also for her sister Rose and the children. Rose had made a lovely beef stew for their dinner, which Nellie had enjoyed immensely. The meat had been so tender; no doubt a perk of being the butcher's wife. Rose as expected, was a wonderful wife and mother to her children. Her young years looking after her brothers and sisters had held her in good stead. When it was time for Nellie to leave, she presented her with a bag of her home-made welsh cakes; a well known favourite of her younger sister.

As Nellie reached the brow of the road, in the distances she could see Owen sat on the fallen down tree trunk near the copse. Instead of going straight home, she made the detour to spend some time with her brother. Owen was so knowledgeable on country life and Nellie was amazed by how much he knew. He could tell a type of tree, by just examining the bark. Nellie could recognise them by their leaves, but their bark was a different matter. Often when they sat together on the trunk, he would point out to her different birds of prey hovering in the air; kestrels and sometimes kites, which according to Owen were quite rare.

It was obvious that Owen had not noticed Nellie approaching, he was sat on the end of the tree trunk apparently deep in thought with his hands resting on his lap.

"Phew! It's too hot for walking today", stated Nellie as she plonked herself down on the other end of the tree to her brother. The weather was indeed unusually warm for late September.

"Yes, we're having an Indian Summer "replied her brother.

"What does that mean?" questioned Nellie, forever seeking out information. "Is this like the weather that Idris is having in India; he mentioned in his letter that it was very hot and sticky?"

"To be honest, I don't know. Maybe you're right; perhaps that's where the saying comes from."

Nellie was chuffed with herself to think that she had possibly come up with an answer that her brother hadn't known. She always considered her brother to be so wisely and took it as quite a compliment if he ever gave her any praise..

In Nellie's eyes, Owen was the most handsome of all her brothers and if truth be known better looking than anybody else that she knew. He had wavy red hair, not carrot coloured like Bertie Bradshaw's in Nellie's class, but an enviable shade of copper. This halo of richness encompassed his face, highlighting his striking eyes and perfect nose, not dissimilar to a frame surrounding a beautiful painting. His eyes were blue and sparkly similar to Joyce's, only larger and more expressive. Owens' eyes were the window to his inner world and Nellie could read instantly, just by looking into his eyes, the type of mood he was in, or even sometimes what he was thinking. There had always been a special closeness between them.

Once again Owen appeared to be away in another place, his hands still resting on his lap. Remembering that she was holding the bag of welsh cakes that Rose had given to her, she asked him if he would like one.

"No thanks" mumbled Owen, trance like, in another world far away from the spot where they sat overlooking the road that wound its way passed the farmhouse and further on towards the small church of St. Mary's and the valley beyond.

Rose was quite glad that he had refused actually, as on the way home she had already eaten three and guessed that Aunt Grace would notice something amiss if anymore went missing.

Patting the tree trunk beside him, he motioned to Nellie.

"Come and sit by yer" he suggested. "Move up a bit."

Obediently, Nellie moved nearer to her brother and he took hold of her hand. Where his hands had been, she noticed a slight bulge in his trousers, but didn't wish to stare too long, as she knew that this was his private area. Owen sensing Nellie's embarrassment guided her hand towards his crotch and placed it down on the fabric of his trousers. She could feel the firmness underneath and instantly tried to withdraw her hand, but Owen increased the pressure of his hand on hers, keeping it there. She felt uncomfortable knowing that this was forbidden territory, but at the same time did not want to upset Owen. Nellie was aware of a pulsating throb beneath her fingers and within an instance she could feel warm flesh, as her brother's penis pushed itself through his open fly. Nellie could not help but look. She knew that this was wrong or maybe it wasn't, as Owen wouldn't do anything to hurt her, but at the same time she had never seen a man's private parts before and was intrigued.

"Don't be scared, Nellie. It's alright" her brother soothed.

Nellie wasn't so sure "I think I'd best be off. Aunt Grace may have seen me walking up the road and she'll be wondering where I've got to." She withdrew her hand and stood up.

"I can trust you can't I Nellie? You won't tell anyone will you? This is our little secret."

Nellie didn't know what to think, but nodded her head in agreement; anxious to get away from the brother she loved and trusted.

The incident between Nellie and Owen repeated itself on several more occasions, although not going any further than the first time. As Owen had suggested it became their little secret. However sometimes Nellie thought that Uncle Henry had an incline into what was going on and this worried her. She didn't want to hurt Owen's feelings, but she didn't want to upset Uncle either.

On leaving school Nellie joined her sister Joyce working in The Grand in Ferndale. They only worked together for a few months, as Joyce always a favourite with the clientele, was thrilled when one of the guests offered her a better position in his hotel in London. Nellie didn't enjoy working in The Grand so much once her sister had left and missed the little jokes they played on each other and their banter in general. If anything she was a little jealous when Joyce sent letters home, describing the wonderful life she was having in London. To lonely Nellie, everything seemed so exciting; the fashions, the cars; a million miles away from the dreary life in Ferndale, where the only person with anything interesting to say, if you were that way inclined, was Mrs. Evans the local gossip.

Over the last year, business at The Grand had been on a slow decline and eventually the management had no other option than to close down the establishment. Nellie was quite fortunate as she had been given a week's pay with her notice, but she was doubtful if she would be lucky enough to get another job.

'Oh well' thought Nellie 'I suppose it's back to mucking out the chickens and cows for me', which is exactly what did happen. So you can imagine Nellie's excitement when she received a letter from Joyce, saying that a friend of her boss was willing to offer Nellie a job as chamber maid in her guest house in London.

Chapter 7
The Cotswolds – 2006

The day room at Fir Trees Residential Home suddenly came to life as lunch was announced ready in the dining room. Chairs started shuffling, books, newspapers and knitting fell onto the floor as the elderly residents awoke from their naps. The carers certainly had their hands full, because as soon as the announcement was made, nearly all of the residents who were sat in the Day Room, decided that it was time to pay a visit to the toilet, a task that some of them needed assistance with.

Hearing the commotion, Nellie stirred from her sleep and started to panic.
"Where am I? What's happening?"
"It's alright Mum. You'd just dozed off for a few minutes."
"Did I?" replied Nellie surprised that she had fallen off to sleep. "That's funny; I thought I was back living in Wales. I must have been dreaming."
"Well before you nodded off Mum, you were telling me about your life as a little girl. You said that you had a secret that you wanted to tell me."
"Yes I did, didn't I?" Aware of all the commotion around her Nellie asked "What's happening? Where are all these people going?"
"It's lunch time Mum. They're going through into the dining room."
"I don't want anything to eat, I feel so full."
"Well maybe you should try just a little bit Mum. You haven't been eating very much lately have you? Let me move out of the way and this lady can take you through into the dining room."
"Hello Nellie" the young carer greeted Alison's mother. "You come with me. It's lasagne and chips today, one of your favourites Nellie."
Nellie and her wheelchair were manoeuvred around and headway was made towards the door.
"Don't leave me Alison, don't leave me. I don't want to be in this place by myself." fretted Nellie.
"It's alright Nellie, your daughter can come as well." the carer calmly informed her.
"Yes, I'm right behind you" assured Alison as they made their way through the narrow passageway to the dining room.

Once in the dining room, Nellie was seated at a small table on the left hand side, just inside the door.

"This isn't my usual place" complained Nellie. "I usually sit up there" she said pointing to a raised area at the far end of the room, reached by three steps leading up to it.

"Well I expect that they've put you here, because they know that I'm with you today and it will give us some privacy to chat amongst ourselves." suggested Alison, knowing full well that the real reason for the segregation was because Nellie was becoming disruptive and disturbing to the residents that she usually sat with for her meals.

"I want to sit with Nancy, I always sit with Nancy" Nellie's complaining continued.

"It's difficult at the moment Mum with you being in the wheelchair to get you up the steps. I expect when you are back using your legs again that they will let you sit with Nancy. Why don't you try your lasagne? It's very nice."

Nellie looked at the plate of food in front of her and eventually picked up her fork. She took one mouthful and then just moved the food around on her plate. Finally, determined that Alison was going to try and get her mother to eat something, she took the fork out of Nellie's hand, put some mince on the end of it and spoon fed it into her mother's mouth. Using this method, she did manage to get a few more mouthfuls swallowed. Feeding her mother like this, took Alison back to her own childhood when she too had not wanted to eat her dinner. A much younger version of the Nellie now sat by the side of her, had used the same technique to feed her. Nellie though, had made the whole process much more exciting by pretending that the spoon full of food had been a train and that Alison's mouth had been the big, dark tunnel that it was about to pass through.

Lunch over, Nellie and Alison returned to the Day Room, where the other guests were settling down to watch the film matinee of Ronald Colman and Greer Garson in 'Random Harvest'. Alison noticed her mother shudder.

"Are you feeling cold Mum?"

"Yes, I think I am a bit."

Alison told her mother that she would fetch her cardigan from her room, glad of the excuse for a quick break so that she could ring her partner Graham at home.

"Hello Graham, it's me."

"Hi, I'm glad you called. I was wondering how things were going. How's your Mum?"

"Not too good really, she doesn't look well. I don't know it's strange, she keeps telling me that she has a secret to tell me."

"Maybe's she's rambling on a bit love; it could be the tablets that she's taking."

"I don't know, I think there's more to it than that."

"Do you want me to come over?" enquired Graham.

"No, it's alright."

"I'm glad you said that" replied Graham. "I'm up to my ears at the moment. I left tidying the garage, as I thought it wasn't fair for you to come home after your day and cook dinner, so I'm making us one of my speciality Shepherd's Pies."

"Lovely, answered Alison.

She didn't have the nerve to dishearten him by saying that she had just had lunch with her mother at Fir Trees.

"Anyway I'd better go. I only popped out to get a cardigan for Mum, she'll be wondering where I've got to. I should be home by about five or five-thirty all being well. I'll give you a ring if I'm going to be any later."

Entering the Day Room Alison smiled to herself, as the chins of at least three quarters of the residents watching the film had now dropped down onto their chests and a few gentle snores could be heard coming from some. Her own mother was now back in a quandary, fretting and worrying, not knowing where she was.

"It's alright Mum, I'm back now. I only went to fetch you a cardigan. Here let me put this around your shoulders."

"Oh yes, I remember now. You're my daughter aren't you? Have I had lunch?"

"Yes we've had lunch" answered Alison "although you didn't eat very much Mum."

"No, no, I'm not hungry. I don't want anything to eat."

"The sun's trying to come out. Shall we go out into the garden and see how warm it is?"

"Yes alright then" Nellie replied. "I don't want to be cold though."

Alison picked up the blanket off of the back of the chair next to Nellie and placed it over her mothers legs, carefully tucking it in around the sides, so as not to get it caught in the wheels of the chair. Releasing the brake, she then pushed her mother out of the day room, leaving the remaining residents to their sweet dreams while the television blared out at a highly audible pitch.

Outside the sun was indeed trying to shine and during the short bursts when it broke through the scattered cloud, it felt quite warm. Alison pushed her mother around the perimeter of the residential home, admiring the hanging baskets and tubs full of flowers as they went. Parking the wheel chair in a sunny spot, Alison told her mother that she would fetch them a chilled glass of water from the dispenser in the hall, as she knew how important it was for her mother to take fluids to prevent dehydration. When Alison returned with two beakers of water, she could see her mother attentively looking across the parkland area amongst the dominating and very old oak and elm trees.

"Look, look!" instructed Nellie pointing in the direction that she had been gazing. "Can you see them?"

Alison followed her mother's pointing finger. "What are you looking at Mum?" she enquired, as Alison was certain her vision was better than her mother's and she couldn't see anything at all out of the ordinary.

"The little children. Look, over there; there's two boys and a little girl. Aren't they lovely and they are wearing such pretty clothes?"

As hard as she looked Alison could not see anything.

"I do hope they're not on their own. Where's their Mummy and Daddy? Oh, I expect that's them sat under the tree watching them."

Again Alison strained her eyes to look, but stare as she might there was nothing to see. Remembering stories that she had heard, about people near to their time of death recognising departed loved ones coming to collect them, she asked her mother if she knew who they were.

"No, I don't know them. I expect they are visiting somebody here." A smile came across Nellie's mouth and she laughed. "Can you see the little dog with them? Isn't he funny? He's going around and round chasing his tail."

"Yes I can see him" Alison acknowledged wondering if she was saying the right thing by agreeing with her mother. She decided that her decision had been correct; her mother was confused enough as it was and if seeing these make believe characters comforted her in any small way, then she could see no harm in that. However, she did quickly glance over her shoulders to make sure nobody was listening to their conversation, as she didn't want her own sanity to be doubted.

Over the course of the next hour or so, more imaginary figures were spotted ranging from rabbits and their young, to chickens and geese. All of a sudden Nellie stiffened in her chair as in her mind she could see a man walking towards her. She described him to Alison as a tramp like figure with a long scraggy beard.

"Don't let him near me" she wailed, "he frightens me."

Alison comforted Nellie as best she could. Fortunately the situation was reverted, by the sound of chinking cups, as afternoon tea was wheeled out to them on a trolley. Sipping her hot cup of tea, thankfully all nasty thoughts of the tramp were dismissed from Nellie's mind.

"What day is it?" Nellie asked again her usual question.

"It's Sunday, Mum" replied Alison. "No it's not, it's Monday. Dearie me, I'm getting as bad as you Mum."

Several times recently Alison had noticed that her memory wasn't as good as it had been and was concerned that maybe this was the first signs of dementia for herself. 'Is it hereditary?' she pondered. 'No I'm sure that I'm fine. It's just poor old Mum asks me the same questions over and over again that in the end I get confused. It's only natural' she convincingly told herself.

Nellie looked down at the large faced watch on her wrist with squinted eyes. Her eyesight was failing, due to a combination of cataracts and a degenerative disorder.

"Do you know it's twenty past three already."

Alison was amazed how quickly her mother's mental condition could change. One minute she did not know where she was, or what was what and now all of a sudden her sense of time was as good as anybody else's.

"Time's getting on and I realise that you will have to go home soon. Your husband will be wondering where you are. Does he know that you are with me?"

"Yes, he does. He was going to come over with me to see you today, but he was busy clearing out the garage."

"I'm sure he's got lots to do. I expect I shall see him soon. Anyway Alison, we seem to have gone away from the subject, but it is important that I tell you my secret."

Once again, Nellie seemed to be in full control of her senses. "Whatever does she want to tell me" thought Alison. "It's obviously something that is bothering her and she doesn't seem to be rambling like Graham suggested."

"Now, where had I got to?"

"You'd just been offered a job in a hotel in London Mum."

"Yes, that's right, in London."

Chapter 8
London – 1938

Nellie walked along the inside corridor of the train and slid open an empty carriage door. This was the first time that she had travelled on a train and she eyed up the two bench seats accommodating the length of the carriage. After some contemplation, she decided on the seat by the window, facing the direction in which the train would be travelling. She had heard that it was better to sit facing forwards rather than backwards to avoid the feeling of travel sickness.

She noticed the string luggage rack above her and attempted to lift her suitcase up into it. It was the same suitcase that Aunt Beatrice and Aunt Tilly had given her all those years before. As a little girl it had appeared to Nellie to be quite a large case and she could remember having difficulty carrying it, especially when it had been full. Now, proportions had changed and in hindsight, it did not seem very big at all. It was still quite heavy though and Nellie struggled to lift it above her head. At that moment she heard the carriage door sliding open and a tall, dark, smartly dressed gentleman with a moustache tossed his newspaper down onto the opposite bench and rushed to her aid.

Nellie had been very fortunate, as Mrs. O'Donavan her new employer had sent her money both for her train fare to London and for a taxi from Paddington station to the guest house in Euston. She was very grateful for this, as it had meant that she had been able to hang on to the week's pay that she had received on leaving The Grand, which meant Nellie had a tidy little nest egg for emergencies and rainy days. As it was a Sunday, Mr. Jones had also been very considerate and had allowed her brother-in-law Alfie to borrow his butcher's van to drive Nellie to the mainline station. Little John, had accompanied his father and the three of them had sat together on the front seat for the journey. Nellie was very impressed with the ease that Alfie handled the van, moving his feet from one pedal to the other and changing gears by altering the position of the stick that protruded out from the side of the steering wheel. Nellie felt that her life was taking on a new beginning and she wondered whether she herself would ever be able to drive a motor vehicle.

At eight years old, John was a typical boy and had a great enthusiasm for trains and was very excited about the prospect of standing on the platform and seeing a steam engine close up.

"Which way will it come from Dad?", "When will it be here?" he constantly asked.

Eventually he shouted in delight as he saw the big monster emerging from around the bend with clouds of black smoke puffing from its funnel. Sadly, as is often the case with small children, the end result was not as it should be. The shrillness of the whistle as it chugged nearer and the tremendous hissing sound of the steam expelling as it approached the platform edge, was just a little bit too frightening for John and he started to cry.

Nellie was having a day of mixed emotions. She was sad at leaving the family and the familiar surroundings, but at the same time, although very anxious and not knowing what to expect, was looking forward to the chance of starting what she hoped would be a new and brighter life. She sat back in her seat and decided that she was going to make the most of the long journey ahead of her. In her nineteen years, Nellie had never been outside of Wales and she was astounded at how different the passing countryside looked, as the train steamed on towards London. Gone were the mountains and rows of terraced houses and in their place rolling green fields, cows and sheep. The sky itself, now away from the depth of the valleys and the shadow of the mountains appeared brighter and today was glorious with strong sunshine.

'Maybe this is a good omen' thought Nellie to herself 'Maybe the sun will shine a little bit on me and my new life.'

The sound of the train's whistle could be heard and the man opposite jumped up to close the small sliding compartment at the top of the window.

"Best close this" he said to Nellie. In answer to Nellie's questioning look, he went on to explain "The whistle warns us when we are approaching a tunnel and if it's open the soot will come inside."

Nellie looked up and smiled. "Just as well you're here, I wouldn't have thought of that."

Nellie passed through places she had never heard of Bristol, Cheltenham Spa and Swindon, all of which seemed a million miles away from

Ferndale. Looking out of the window as the train sped through Reading, on her right hand side she saw a large factory with the name of Huntley & Palmers proudly displayed on the brickwork of the building. Nellie recognised this name instantly and knew that they manufactured biscuits, as she had often seen packets of them for sale in Mrs. Gregory's shop. Nellie was starting to get a bit stiff and fidgety from sitting on the train for so long. She was looking forward to reaching London, so that she could get up and move around. Her legs felt like they could do with a bit of a stretch. The closer she got to her destination, the more nervous and anxious she became thinking that she might not be able to find a taxi and get herself safely to her new address, The Shamrock Guest House in Euston.

The green countryside faded away and was replaced by buildings of an industrial nature and standing amongst these were tall, three-storey houses built of a reddish, brown stone. They were different to the familiar, terraced houses that Nellie had left behind, but similar by the fact that they too wore a grimy coating; a build up of dust from the factories and soot from the nearby trains that regularly trundled passed. Washing could be seen hanging from lines in the small backyards, not clean and fresh looking, in most cases a dowdy grey. Nellie was surprised. She knew the story of Dick Whittington's visit to London and the streets that were paved with gold and likewise had assumed that London was a city of hope and good fortune, but considering the view out of the train window she wondered if this was going to be the case.

Eventually in a cloud of steam, the train came to a standstill and Nellie stood up and hauled her suitcase from the rack. Convincing herself that she hadn't left anything behind, she opened the sliding door of the carriage compartment and made her way to the exit. Stepping down form the train, she looked around and was amazed at how big the station was.

'So this is Paddington?' she muttered to herself.
It was a far cry from her local station, with its one small platform and Mr. Armitage the station master, who ruled the running of the establishment with great precision and order. He was a well-known character of the community and knew almost everybody who stepped on and off his trains. Nellie's eyes moved upwards to take in the impressive, glass, arch-shaped roof that she could remember Owen telling her had been designed by the famous engineer Isambard Kingdom Brunel.

Like a sheep she followed the crowd emerging from the train. Everybody appeared to be in such a rush and on more than one occasion Nellie was jostled either from behind or in front. Never before had she heard so many different accents in one place, with not one familiar Welsh lilt catching her ear. She couldn't help noticing the smart clothes worn by the people around her and even though she was wearing her Sunday best, felt quite dowdy in comparison. Nellie with relief noticed a Taxi sign to the right in front of her and made her way towards it. Seeing the queue, she joined it and waited her turn.

"Where to Miss?" asked the taxi driver, in what Nellie assumed was a cockney accent.

She handed him the card with the address of the guest house in Euston.

"Right you are. We'll have you there in no time."

The taxi turned left as they came out of the station and joined the flow of traffic. Sitting in the back Nellie observed with interest the local landmarks, noticing that they had driven down Chapel Street and were now on the Marylebone Road. A short distance further on and the taxi pulled alongside the pavement and came to a halt.

"Here we are then Miss. This is where we say our goodbyes."

Nellie peered out of the window and could see a white house with black window frames. Its once white walls now had a grey hue about them and the black paintwork was chipped in places; all in all the entire house had seen better days. There were three steps leading up to the front door, with the words Shamrock Guest House etched on the fan light window above it. To the right-hand side, a green neon sign flashed 'vacancies' in the window. Nellie noticed more steps leading to a basement and nestled in the top of the roof two dormer windows. She paid the taxi driver and putting on a braver face than she felt inside, climbed the steps to the front door and rang the bell.

The door opened revealing a slight lady with pale skin and curly, shoulder-length black hair, pulled back either side and held in place by two tortoise shell combs. Her lips were painted red and her eyebrows plucked away to a bare minimum and replaced with thin, pencilled brown lines.

"Sure to goodness, you must be Nellie. I wasn't expecting you just yet." Glancing at her watch, she added "Is that the time already? Holy Mother of Jesus."

There had been no introduction, but Nellie rightly assumed that this must be Mrs. O'Donavan.

"Where's my manners? Come on in child, come on. Put your case down there. I dare say you could do with a cuppa after your long journey. Come through into the kitchen, I was just about to put the kettle on."
Indeed Nellie's mouth did feel quite parched, so obediently she followed her new employer down the passage and through the door at the far end. Immediately a smell of fresh baking wafted its way to Nellie's nostrils, which made her realise just how hungry she was. Several hours had passed since Nellie had eaten two slices of bread and jam at breakfast and now, encouraged by the aroma in the kitchen her stomach started to rumble. An array of pots, pans and crockery were piled up on the wooden shelves that lined the walls. A big cauldron bubbled away on the Aga and on the wooden table that dominated the centre of the kitchen, Nellie spied a tray of scones and a jam and cream sponge cake to die for.

A movement at the window caught Nellie's eyes and on turning her head, she saw a large black and white cat, which had jumped up onto the window sill. Realising that he was being given attention, he started to miaow and paw the window.

"That damn cat" complained Mrs. O'Donovan, "he always comes home for his dinner when I'm in the middle of something."
She opened the back door and in sauntered Charlie as he was called.

"It's my own fault" continued Mrs. O'Donovan "I shouldn't feed him so well and then perhaps he would catch some mice like the other cats in the street."
She mashed up some previously cooked fish, put it on a small, blue plate and bent down to give it to the cat. Nellie looked on thinking that she wouldn't have minded a bit of that for herself.

"Now where was I?" asked Mrs. O'Donovan who was promptly reminded when the kettle started to sing.
A steaming hot cup of tea was placed in front of Nellie and she just couldn't refuse when Mrs. O'Donovan offered her a slice of the sponge cake. While they drank tea, Nellie's new employer explained her duties to her. There was another girl who worked in the guest house and Mrs. O'Donovan suggested that tomorrow being her first day, for Nellie to shadow her and learn the ropes. Mrs O' Donovan collected their cups and placed them in the sink. Just as they were about to climb the stairs, the

front door opened and a man walked in. Nellie didn't know much about fashion, but she had heard the word 'dandy' before and staring at this apparition, thought that this might just be the right word to describe the man in front of her. His dark hair had a high shine to it and was combed back from his forehead and not dissimilar to Mrs. O' Donovan's eyebrows, had a thin line of hair above his lip. He was wearing a three-piece, brown pin-striped suit and in his hand he carried a trilby hat.

"Nellie this is my husband Mr. O'Donovan."

"Pleased to meet you sir" said Nellie offering her hand.

"The pleasure's all mine to be sure and please, it's Jimmy, none of that Mr. nonsense."

Nellie felt uncomfortable at the way her new employer leered at her and a shudder went up and down her spine. It was rare for Nellie to take an instant dislike to someone, but in Jimmy's case she did; there was something about him that she found distasteful.

At the very top of the house were the two dormer rooms that Nellie had seen from the outside and Mrs. O'Donovan opened the door of the one that was to be her bedroom.

"Lil, the other girl who works here has that room" Mrs. O'Donovan advised pointing to the next door, "but it's her afternoon off, so she's not in at the moment. I'm sure you'll get on just fine though, she's a pleasant enough girl."

Nellie stepped into her bedroom and looked around. It wasn't very big, but Nellie thought that she could be quite happy there. The window was small and high up, but the ruched lace curtain, allowed the light to penetrate through. A kitchen chair doubled up as a bedside table beside a single bed covered with a colourful, patchwork, crocheted blanket. There was a tall boy chest and a wardrobe, more than enough storage for Nellie's few outfits. On the wall hung by a chain was a mirror that immediately caught her eye. It showed a picture of a young lady in a bustled dress walking through a country garden full of lupins, foxgloves and roses. It reminded Nellie so much of the nursery rhyme 'Mary, Mary quite contrary how does your garden grow?' which she could fondly remember Rose singing to her when she was small.

"Well, I'll leave you to unpack as I'm sure you have a lot to do. Dinner will be at half-past six in the kitchen if you'd care to join us. I'm cooking a nice piece of roast beef today."

Nellie thanked Mrs. O'Donovan and assured her that she would like to have dinner with them. She then settled down to her unpacking, placing familiar items around to make the little room feel more like home. Pulling back the lace curtain from the window and standing on tip toe, she could just make out the roofs and chimneys of the houses around about. She wondered if there was a telephone box nearby, as she had promised to ring Joyce as soon as she got a chance, to tell her that she had arrived. Looking at the clock on the chair by her bed, she saw that it was already six o'clock and decided it was probably best if she rang her sister another time, as she didn't want to go out and get herself lost and then be late for dinner, especially not on her first day. Besides, glancing at her reflection in the mirror on the wall, her hair looked quite windswept and she could do with a quick wash to freshen herself up after her journey.

The next morning Nellie was awake long before she needed to be. The general hustle and bustle of the city streets wakening below her dormer window, edged on by her growing anticipation of her day ahead, soon put a stop to any chance of continued sleep. The previous day Mrs O'Donovan had issued Nellie with two uniforms; a burgundy dress edged with pink piping to be worn for chambermaid duties and a black dress with a white pinafore for when she was called upon to wait on customers in the dining room. Both were neatly pressed and hanging up on her wardrobe door.

As Nellie was making her bed she heard a light tap on her door. Opening it, she was met by a young girl with blonde, wavy hair and red lipstick like Mrs. O'Donovan's. A quick glance at her and Nellie surmised that she must be around the same age as herself or maybe a year or two older.
  "Hello, are you ready? We've got a busy day ahead of us. It's always the same Saturdays. Typical, Saturday is a good night down at The Odeon and by the time I finish here my poor old feet don't feel much like dancing. Won't put me off tonight though, I've got a new fella waiting for me. Real nice he is. By the way sorry, I'm Lil and Mrs. O'Donovan told me that you're Nellie. Is that right?"
Nellie nodded her head in agreement, immediately feeling slightly self-conscious in comparison to her new colleague. From the onset, Nellie could tell that Lil was certainly not one to be slow in coming forward and with her shapely figure and attractive looks Nellie felt even more like a

wilting wallflower. Nellie had hoped that moving away from Wales to start a new life, she would be able to shake off this feeling of inadequacy that always seemed to bear down upon her, but if today was anything to go by, she wasn't starting off very well.

'I bet she's got loads of friends' thought Nellie enviously, wishfully thinking that she could become one of them.

Nellie soon got into the routine of life at the Shamrock Guest House and really took a liking to Mrs O'Donovan. She acted more like a big sister towards her than an employer, always offering advice and keeping a watchful eye over her. Mrs O'Donovan was aware more than most just how easy it could be for innocents like Nellie to slip into the pitfalls of city life and with Nellie being such a good worker she certainly did not want to lose her.

As it turned out Joyce, Nellie's sister did not work too far away and lived on the direct route of the fifty-seven bus, which Nellie could catch at the top of the road. Unfortunately for Nellie, life in London was still not making out to be as exciting as she had hoped. It didn't seem to be very often that Joyce's time off coincided with hers and to be honest, by now Joyce had made new friends of her own, whose company if truth be known, she preferred to Nellie's.

The friendship with Lil too had never matured to anything further than work and even that at times did not seem to be working out too well. Nellie always thought if a job's worth doing its worth doing well and never was a speck of dust missed in the rooms that she cleaned. Furniture was pulled away from the walls, skirting boards dusted down and the windows cleaned on a regular basis. Lil on the other hand was never quite so industrious with a duster and did just the bare minimum of changing the bed sheets, clearing out any rubbish, a quick wipe around and a shake of Vim in the bathroom. Although Nellie never made comment on Lil's sloppy efforts, it still niggled, as at the end of the day it meant more work for her when it was her turn to clean the rooms that Lil had haphazardly given the once over to.

Glancing outside as Nellie cleared away some plates from the dining room; she could see the rain trickling like a rivulet down the window panes.

'Typical' she thought, especially as it was her afternoon off.
The streets of London always seemed gloomy to Nellie, the tall opposing buildings blocked out the sunlight even on a good day, so on a day like today, everything looked even more grey than usual.

Dining room duties were not a favourite of Nellie's. She wasn't over keen having to wait upon the guest house clientele and preferred to keep more in the background. Nellie always felt awkward placing the plates on the tables in front of the diners, as more often or not she managed to dip her thumb in the gravy as she set them down.

An appetising smell of apple pie wafted out from the kitchen. Mrs O'Donovan prided herself on her home-made cooking and as Nellie well knew her apple pies were definitely something special. A large saucepan of thick, yellow custard sat cooling on the kitchen table in readiness to pour over the freshly cooked pie. Nellie was alone in the kitchen and the temptation to just dip her finger into the custard for a quick taste was overwhelming. Thinking better of it, she returned to the dining room to collect some more plates. The next time though, the smell of the apple pie and the steaming custard was all too much for Nellie and with her inner self telling her that nobody would know, she picked up the spoon lying idly in the custard and licked it clean, carefully wiping her mouth with her hand afterwards, to dismiss any evidence of her crime. When Nellie returned with the second load of plates, Mrs O'Donovan was bending down in front of the Aga removing the apple pie.
"Have you been at this custard?" she enquired after Nellie.
"No Mrs O'Donovan" replied Nellie trying desperately not to look sheepish.
As Nellie retreated back to the dining room, she could hear Mrs O'Donovan muttering "strange" under her breath. It was years later that it dawned on Nellie that her employer must have guessed that she was the culprit; as if the custard had not been disturbed, a skin would have formed on it. In later life, Nellie could still feel her cheeks flushing whenever she thought about it.

Pulling her headscarf over her head and buttoning her coat, Nellie set off down the street in the direction of The Regal, the local cinema. This week they were showing 'Dark Victory' starring Bette Davis and George Brent. A passing car drove through a puddle and splashed her all up her legs, which not only annoyed her, but made her feel even more cold and wet. She tried to rub her nylon stockings clean, but the water being grimy left an obvious mark. Nellie was a little apprehensive about going to the cinema on her own, but what choice did she have. She had been a couple of times with her sister and loved getting lost in the romance and sophistication of the big screen, so different to her own life. A couple of hours spent at the cinema would fuel her imagination for several days ahead. Yes it would have been nice to have gone with a gang of girls or even just one friend, but if Nellie waited for an invite she knew it could be a long wait, so on her Jack Jones it was.

Entering the cinema and noticing the lack of a queue, Nellie guessed that she had probably missed the start of the film, but it didn't matter as the films were continuous so she would be able to catch up on the beginning the next time around. Very often, she would idle her time by sitting through the film twice anyway, especially on days like today when it was too wet to walk in the park and not wanting to spend her afternoon off in her room at the Guest House.

The gleam of light shining through the cinema door as Nellie opened it, made the usherette immediately aware that a late comer had arrived and came up the steps with her torch to meet Nellie. Unaccustomed to the darkness inside, but with the aid of the usherette's torch, a seat at the far end of the stalls was pointed out to her. Aware of her above average height and not wishing to disturb the other cinema goers' view, Nellie hunched her head and shoulders down in an attempt to make herself smaller and headed towards the appointed seat. Considering her duty done, the usherette turned and retraced her steps up the stairs, leaving Nellie without a beam of light to see where she was heading. Bang! With a loud thump Nellie's forehead made contact with the far wall. Embarrassed she quickly sat down, aware of some sniggering around her.

Nellie was a great fan of Bette Davies and was soon absorbed into the film, a moving story about a high living socialite Judith Treherne, whose eyesight was failing and who had been diagnosed with a brain tumour. As the story unfolded she fell in love with her surgeon Dr. Frederick Steale, but tragedy struck again when she was told that she only had a year left to live. By the end although feeling slightly foolish, as by this time a man had taken up the seat next to her, Nellie felt quite emotional and relentlessly snivelled into her handkerchief. Just at the point of the heroine being diagnosed with the brain tumour during the second showing of the film, Nellie felt something brushing against her leg. She realised that it was the man next to her, but innocently thought that he probably was just fidgeting or maybe had an itch that couldn't be ignored. The second time it happened Nellie was not so lenient with her assumptions, especially when she could actually see his hand resting on her knee. Nellie jumped to her feet with a hard jolt, making the seat she had been sat on flip back vertically with a loud thud, as it made its connection with the back rest. Being at the end of the row, she had to clamber over the offending gentleman as she made her exit.

The weather outside was slightly better now, at least the rain had stopped, but Nellie had to watch her step to avoid the puddles and splashing cars. Looking over her shoulder, she could not see him, but she was sure that the man had followed her out of the cinema. Nellie's anxiety rose and she quickened her step almost to a running pace, still looking over her shoulder at regular intervals. When Nellie realised that no suitor had caught up with her, eventually she calmed down, only to realise that in her haste she had just run, not paying attention to which direction and now found herself totally lost.

Some days the guest house seemed busier than others, but there was always a steady traffic of customers through its doors.

"Room two needs cleaning Nellie" instructed Mr. O'Donovan on finding Nellie cleaning out one of the rooms in the basement.

"No, it's fine. I did it this morning"

"We've had guests since then Nellie and it needs doing again I can assure you. As quick as you can now please."

It was beyond Nellie's understanding why people would pay good money for a room when they didn't even stay the night. The sordid reasoning for this would become clear to Nellie as the years passed by and her innocence departed, as too the purpose of the little rubbery things that she sometimes found floating in the chamber pots underneath the beds.

Nellie was a bit peeved that it was always her and not Lil who was asked to clean extra rooms. Mr. O'Donavan certainly seemed to take a preference to Lil over her, which thankful for small mercies she was glad about. He really made her squirm, even now as she climbed up the steps from the basement, she could feel his eyes burning on her legs, probably hoping for a quick glimpse of her knickers. As the weeks slipped by, Nellie became quite disgruntled with the unfair distribution on the workload between herself and Lil and everything came to a crunch when Mrs. O'Donovan took herself off to Ireland for a little break.

Lately Lil had taken to wearing extra makeup to work and even the odd splash of perfume, which this week in Mrs. O'Donovan's absence smelt stronger than ever. For some time now Nellie had had her suspicions that something was going on between her colleague and her employer, as more than once she had caught them giving each other the occasional glance, or whispering to each other when she had come across them on the landing. It was no wonder that Lil got through her jobs quickly, as not only did she not make a very good job of them, but Mr O'Donovan very often it seemed helped her.

Nellie was very fond of Mrs O. Donovan, who had always shown her kindness and had treated her fairly. One afternoon as Nellie was taking some bed linen out from the cupboard at the far end of the landing, unbeknown to Lil and Mr. O'Donovan, she spied them leaving one of the bedrooms. This in itself aroused suspicion in Nellie's mind, but this thought was increased one hundred per cent when she saw Mr O'Donovan lower his head to give Lil a quick peck on the lips, followed by a gently tap on her bottom, as she flirtatiously moved away. Before Lil had reached the top stair in her descent back down to continue with what she should have already been doing in the dining room, Nellie was upon the two of them. Her face was flushed red, not so much from embarrassment of the fact that she had been spying on them, but from anger at their indiscretion and the effect it would have on Mrs. O'Donovan, should she ever find out what the pair of them had been up to.

"You Mr. O'Donovan" she hissed "should be ashamed of yourself acting like this."

Nellie had never taken to calling him by his first name Jimmy, as he had suggested she should on her first day. Her anger far from subsiding and without a thought that she might lose her job for speaking her mind she continued.

"Lil's only a slip of a girl. You're old enough to be her father and on top of that you're a married man in case you've forgotten. What do you think Mrs. O'Donavan would make of all these shenanigans?"

"Now don't be silly Nellie, you're mistaken. It's not what you think."

"I don't think so Mr. O'Donovan; it's you that's mistaken. Why I only have to take one look at Lil's blushing face to know I'm right. She wouldn't be looking like that if she had nothing to hide now would she?" and with that Nellie dropped the bed linen that she was holding and stormed off to her bedroom.

In the calmness of her room Nellie's anger got the better of her and she burst into tears. She did think that maybe it would be best to just ignore the incident that she had witnessed, but how could she carry on working with Lil and Mr O'Donovan knowing full well that they were cheating on Mrs. Donovan. Considering further the dilemma that faced her, Nellie thought that maybe it would be kinder if Mrs O'Donovan never found out about the affair. Nellie was convinced though, even if she didn't say anything, somebody else would and her employer understandably would be extremely upset.

Nellie was jolted from her thoughts by a sudden knock on the door. Opening it she was confronted by Mr. O'Donavan himself.

"Listen Nellie, we need to talk"

"I don't think so. I've already come to my decision. As from today, I shall be leaving. I think that's the best decision for all of us, so please could you either sort out my wages now, or have them posted on to me. I shall give you the address where I shall be."

"Nellie, please don't do that. Mrs O'Donavan would think it odd if you just up and left and I know that she would be upset to think that you had gone without her being here to say goodbye to you."

"Mr. O'Donovan" said Nellie sternly. "I'm doing you a favour here. If I wait until your wife comes back, I shall have to say something to her about your conduct, so this way I am leaving it up to your conscience and hope that you come to your senses and do the right thing. Not that I expect you to. I don't think you realise just how fortunate you are to have such a loyal wife as Mrs. O'Donovan."

Nellie felt she had said quite enough and started to close the door on

Mr. O' Donavan, but not without telling him that she needed half an hour to pack her things and then she would meet him in the hallway, either to collect her wages or to give him the forwarding address to send them to.

Chapter 9
South Wales 1939

It was with some apprehension that Nellie clambered down off of the train, hauling her suitcase behind her. Quitting her job so suddenly and with nowhere else to go, Nellie was hoping that her Aunt and Uncle would take her in for a little while. She was not sure how much of a welcome she would get, especially as she had not warned them of her arrival. No doubt Uncle Henry would be cross that she had given up her job without another one to go to. She still hadn't touched her nest egg, the week's wages from when she had left The Grand Hotel prior to going to London, so hopefully if she offered to pay for her keep that would go some way to paving her way back into his favour.

Nellie looked around at the familiar countryside. The blackened terraced houses, the craggy mountains sparsely scattered with grazing sheep and the distinct smell of coal dust immediately made her feel like she had come home. Nothing has changed Nellie thought, but she realised that something had changed. When she had left here fifteen months previous, she knew that never in a million years would she have had the nerve to challenge Mr. O'Donovan the way that she had. Something had definitely changed and that something was Nellie. She had left the valleys as a child and had come back transformed into a young woman.

Nellie approached the five bar gate at the entrance to her Uncle's farm and well before she was within reach of its latch, the geese had started their welcoming or warning chant, however their mood took them. Nellie hoped for the former as she pushed open the gate. Hearing all the commotion, Uncle Henry peered out of the barn where he had been milking the cows. Screening his eyes from the low lying sun as it set over the distant mountain, he started to wave as he recognised the familiar figure.

"What's brought you here Nellie? Is everything alright? We weren't expecting you?"

'So many questions' thought Nellie, but felt more secure as she sank into her Uncle's embrace. It had been in the back of her mind that he might turn her away, but feeling the strength of his ardent welcome, she did not think this would be likely. The farmhouse door opened and Aunt Grace appeared looking in Nellie's mind slightly disgruntled.

"Good Grief! Look what the cats dragged home. I hope you're not bringing any trouble to our doorstep young lady."

"Grace, leave the girl alone. She looks dead beat and well in need of a cup of tea after her journey I dare say."

Aunt Grace poured the tea out from the big, brown tea-pot that permanently stood warming on the range. As they sipped their tea, Nellie related the goings on at the guest house and her reason for walking out. She had been right in her assumption that Uncle was not best pleased.

"Nellie, I can imagine it was a difficult situation, but you had a good job there girl. You should at least have stayed until you had found something else. You're old enough now to stand on your own two feet. You can't expect to keep running back to us every time something doesn't agree with you."

Having said his piece, it was agreed that Nellie could stay, for the time being at least.

Nellie was surprised to hear that Owen had moved away to England, much to Uncle's distain.

"Somewhere up north, that's where he's gone. Thought he could get more money up there. Bit of a cheek I think it is after all we've done for him. Who was it who gave you all a roof over your heads when you needed one? Me and your Aunt that's who and now that my joints won't let me do so much as I used to, he's upped sticks and left."

Nellie sympathised with her Uncle's ill feeling for her brother, but secretly felt quite relieved that he had left the farm. She had reservations about meeting up with him again, especially remembering the things he had made her do on the fallen down tree stump behind the farm; their little secret. In fact, just thinking about it she could feel the heat radiating up her neck and into her cheeks and felt sure that her Uncle and Aunt would notice her change of colour. Nellie had a better understanding of life nowadays and realised that it was not right for a brother and sister to have behaved the way that she and Own had done. She felt embarrassed and guilty for herself and anger towards the brother that she had doted upon and trusted.

Waking up one morning a week or so after her return to Wales, as Nellie lay in bed relishing the last final moment, before getting up to milk the cows, London seemed another life away. It was like a different world, comparing the two was impossible, as there were no similarities whatsoever. In London, she woke up to the cacophony of market traders setting up their stalls, milk bottles hastily being dumped on doorsteps, traffic and shouting. Here it was completely different, so quiet. Living on top of the mountain any noise from the streets in the valley below, was well silenced before it reached her bedroom window. In fact Nellie thought if it wasn't for the animated gaggling of the geese advising all and sundry that it was time for breakfast and the gentle mooing of the cows making it known that it was their milking hour, she could quite possibly have slept through until lunchtime. A luxury she knew was out of the question, especially as Uncle expected her to help out on the farm as long as she was living with him.

Nellie felt quite at ease living back at Penbryn Farm and particularly enjoyed being able to see her elder sister Rose. The pair of them had so much to catch up on; Rose and Alfie's children, their own brothers and sisters, as well as the local gossip of the last fifteen months. Many a cup of tea and Rose's delicious welsh cakes had been drunk and munched on since Nellie's homecoming. Nellie knew though that her time at Penbryn Farm was limited and really having had a taste for a different type of life than that which the valleys could offer, was pleased when the news came that she had been accepted as an auxiliary nurse at Headlands Rest Home in Swansea and was to start the following Monday.

Arriving the following week at the entrance to Headlands, a convalescent home for working men and their dependants, Nellie felt a lot surer of herself than when she had pulled up in the taxi outside the Shamrock Guest House in Euston. In those days, she had felt quite insecure and lonely, not helped either by the vastness and unfamiliarity of a city the size of London. Swansea seemed altogether more inviting, whether it was because of the stunning views of the bay and the Gower Peninsula that she could see from the high advantage point of Headlands Rest Home, or just the pure fact that she was in Wales, Nellie couldn't decide.

Headlands Rest Home itself was an imposing Victorian building made up of granite stone inset with dark wooden beams. The central part of the building rose up into two pinnacles with windows on three levels. Flagging on either side, were two buildings of two storeys, which Nellie assumed might be the hospital wards.

Immediately on entering the front door, Nellie got a whiff of very strong disinfectant and partly because of its age, the building acknowledged a sad, worn appearance. She guessed it was hygienically maintained to a very high standard, as would surely be expected of a place where poorly people were sent to recuperate. Her thoughts were confirmed when a lady in a navy uniform and starched white matron's hat came rushing towards her, briefly stopping to wipe her finger along the dado rail in the hallway.

"Can't be too careful in a hospital, everything must be so clean. Can't be having specs of dust like this around" she said holding up her blackened finger for Nellie to see.

"I'm guessing that you must be Nellie Edwards and a dust around here will be your first job. You will find all the cleaning materials in that cupboard under the stairs, but first I will show you to your room, so that you can get rid of that suitcase you're carrying."

Nellie enjoyed her life at Headlands. On accepting the post, she wasn't too sure exactly what to expect of a convalescent home. She imagined it to be much like a hospital with a lot of sick people to care for and was not too sure how she would be able to cope with it all. Her mind had been jolted back to the occasion when Owen had badly gashed his leg with a scythe, while cutting back the long grass in the top field. Aunt Grace without hesitation had the situation under control, bathing the wound clean and wrapping it tightly with make do bandages from one of Uncle's old shirts that she had just put to one side with the intention of cutting up into dusters. Nellie, for the other part had been totally useless and had been no help whatsoever. Scared by the commotion and the sight of blood, she had kept well out of the way hiding behind the barn door. Even when she heard Aunt Grace calling her to help, she pretended that she was out of earshot and didn't come forward. Later on when she eventually emerged from the barn, she had felt sick by the sight of the dark, red, blood droplets that etched a zig-zag trail across the farmyard. Nellie always carried this notion in her head, not sure where it had come from, or indeed whether it was true, but somewhere in her mind she had been told that if you saw blood, you must hold your collar until you either saw a four-legged animal or an ambulance, otherwise a similar grisly episode would happen to her. Fortunately for Nellie living on a farm, it wasn't long before she set eyes on the required four-legged animal, but still she wished for the heavens to open soon with a good downpour of rain to wash away the drops of blood that remained.

As it turned out Nellie coped very well with her duties at Headlands Rest Home. Unlike her first thoughts, although the patients had at one time been very sick, most now were well on the mend and enjoyed a bit of light heartedness around the wards. Matron too, although very strict with cleanliness and rules of how the wards were to be run, was not altogether against a bit of fun and banter from time to time.

Nellie particularly took a liking to Lillian, who worked alongside her. Whatever the task; changing beds, cleaning lavatories, everything was fun if Lillian was around; even the most onerous duties were always made light of. Everybody liked Lillian; being quick witted she always managed to say the right thing, but also had the ability to be comforting and reassuring whenever the need arose. The patients, especially the men, thought she was an absolute angel. In fact if she had been nursing them at the peak of their illnesses, when their temperatures had been running high, a lot of them may well have thought that they had died and gone to heaven.

Nellie had always been very conscious of her short, straight hair and had been forever envious of those lucky girls who had been adorned with curls, none more so than Lillian. Lillian had been graced with the most beautiful head of shiny black ringlets which fell down her back in rivulets like a Grecian goddess. Of course it was only on days off that Lillian could let her hair roam free, as work days it was tightly secured under her uniform hat. Everything about Lillian was adorable; if her hair alone was not enough; she had also been blessed with the clearest, china white skin and eyes of sapphire blue, encased by long, dark lashes. Nellie had come across girls before, who she had thought were pretty, but normally what they gained in looks they lost in personality. Lillian though was the exception, in Nellie's eyes and Nellie was not alone in her thinking, Lillian seemed to have it all.

One Tuesday morning, as Nellie and Lillian emerged from mopping down the men's toilet block, they saw a group of four auxiliaries standing together in the corridor whispering. Not wanting to miss out Lillian approached them to see what all the fuss was about. Nellie herself wouldn't have had the nerve, for they may have been talking about her. Confident as Lillian was, this thought would never have occurred to her.

"Nell, come here" instructed Lillian. "Jean's just been telling us that Alice Greeves has got nits. What do you think of that?"
Before Nellie had time to open her mouth in any sort of opinion, Matron was at the door shouting for the six girls to go down to the washroom.

"Now! Don't dawdle. This is a state of emergency" yelled Matron at their retreating backs.

In the washrooms, they were made to sit on a wooden chair behind a screen, while a nurse went through their hair with a special comb to drag out any unwanted louse eggs from their heads. Everyone afterwards regardless whether or not any nits were found, were made to wash their hair in paraffin as a precaution. For once in her life Nellie was quite glad that her hair was short and straight as her hair was clean of any parasites, although she still had to endure the paraffin rinse. Poor Lillian was not so fortunate; nits were present on the comb when the nurse dragged it through her hair. She was devastated when her lovely, long ringlets were cut off to ear level; washing her hair in paraffin was nothing compared to that.

Lillian was so upset and Nellie guessed that it was partly because she had a soft spot for George one of the patients recovering from Tuberculosis. It was obvious to Nellie that Lillian's affection was reciprocated, as she could tell by the way George's eyes always lit up when Lillian was present and followed her around the ward.

"Come on now Lillian, it's not so bad. At least your hair will grow back and you'll soon have your lovely ringlets back. Look at me, I'm always going to look like this; my straight hair is never going to change."

"I look so awful Nellie" sniffed Lillian from a red nose and red rimmed eyes to match.

"Of course you don't. I think your hair suits you like that and you've still got your beautiful blue eyes and if it's George that you're worried about, there's certainly no need to worry there. Anyone can see how madly he is in love with you and short or long hair isn't going to make one iota of difference there.

"Do you think so Nell? Do you really think so?" asked Lillian, her usual little smile coming back to her lips.

Lillian wasn't the only girl, who was embarrassed by the smell of paraffin still obvious on their hair. It wasn't only Lillian who had eyes for one of the male patients and even the not so successful ones like

Nellie who hadn't yet earned the yearnings of an admirer, still lived in hope. To counteract the smell on themselves, one of the girls came up with the idea of washing all the corridors down with paraffin, which they did.

Everything was soon to change and change it did on Sunday September third, not just for the staff at Headlands Rest Home, but for a much larger circle entirely. It was quarter past eleven in the morning. Nellie was just coming to the end of her tea break, having enjoyed listening to the other girls' tales of their antics from the night before. All of a sudden the music on the radio went dead and for a few seconds there was silence. Like most people in Britain, Nellie was aware that these were ominous times and the news two days earlier that the German battleship 'Schleswig-Holstein' had opened fire on the Polish garrison of the Westerplatte Fort in Danzig, had only accentuated the fact that war could be imminent. The radio station restored, everybody's worst nightmare was confirmed when Prime Minister Neville Chamberlain informed his countrymen that Britain and Germany were indeed at war. Nellie's concerns were not for herself at this time, but for her brother Idris who was still abroad with the army and for her sister Joyce who was still living in London, as without a doubt London being the capital of England would surely be a prime target for the Germans' bombs.

During the First World War Headlands Rest Home had been acquired by the St. John's Ambulance Association as an Auxiliary War Hospital and during this time two thousand, five hundred casualties from British, Australian, New Zealand and Canadian forces had been treated there. Similarly once again at the end of 1939 Headlands was requisitioned by the Military Authorities and once more Nellie found herself looking for a new job.

Following her departure from Headlands Nellie moved to Cardiff where she found work in a hostel catering for the Land Army Girls. Although the work had been hard in the rest home, it had also been fun most days and she missed the girls, especially Lillian. The women she worked with at the Hostel were all a lot older than her and married with children, so again Nellie felt that she lacked a common interest with them and once again found herself out on a limb. The Land Army Girls seemed a lively bunch and were around her age, but even with them she felt like an outsider, different. They were all friends; going off in groups together in the morning and coming back again in the evenings. As soon as they entered the hostel the surroundings changed from one of mediocre tedium to laughter, teasing and recklessness.

Nellie's routine at the hostel was similar to the one she had filled at The Shamrock Guest House, cleaning rooms, changing bed linen and serving meals. Meals were self service, so Nellie had to make sure early in the morning that everything was laid out for the girls to help themselves and packed lunches ready for them to take with them out to the fields. In the evenings, a hot meal was prepared and served to the land girls on their return. It was canteen style so Nellie did not have to wait on the tables, but she still managed to sometimes dip her thumb in the gravy as she handed over the plates. Thankfully the girls were too taken up with chatting and laughter to notice.

As time went by a few of the girls noticed Nellie and to be truthful felt a little sorry for her, she appeared so shy and awkward and obviously lonely. One evening after the evening meal, Margaret a lively lass from Liverpool and one of the main stays of the bunch approached Nellie.

"Nearly finished?"

"Yes, Just got to take these last dishes through and that's me done for the day."

"Good. Well why don't you come and join us for a natter. The girls are a friendly lot really. They won't bite your head off honest."

Nellie was very glad of Margaret's invitation and over the next few weeks it became a regular habit for Nellie to join them at the end of her shift. Just being in their company had made such a difference to her dull and dreary life. She had even had a puff once or twice on Margaret's cigarette, but wasn't quite sure if she liked it or not. All the same, she had decided that on payday she would buy a packet of ten so that she could really be one of the girls.

"Budge up there Jane, make a bit of room for Nellie. She looks shattered after looking after us lot" instructed Margaret. "Come and join us Nellie, we're just about to have a sing song" and with that the girls burst into their signature Land Army Song:

Back to the land, we must all lend a hand.

To the farms and the fields we must go.
There's a job to be done,
Though we can't fire a gun
We can still do our bit with a hoe ...
Back to the land, with it's clay and it's sand,
It's granite and gravel and grit,
You grow barley and wheat
And potatoes to eat
To make sure that the nation keep fit ...
We will tell you once more
You can help the war
If you come with us back to the land.

Huddled around the fire on that chilly night Nellie and the Land Army Girls had so much fun. The hilarity that evening was non-stop, so much so that Nellie's poor sides ached. Jane and Ann were relating a tale that had happened to Alice earlier in the day on the farm where the three of them had been working. They were both laughing so much that it was difficult to get the gist of the story. As soon as one would start to recount the story, the other would burst into laughter, which in turn made everyone listening fall apart. It was difficult to know which was the funnier, the tale of Alice who had apparently fallen face down in the pig muck after being butted in her rear end by a goat, or Jane and Ann's hilarious attempt at story telling.
"Gosh! You all seem to have so much fun. It's a bit different to what goes on here when you lot are not around" said Nellie.
"Well!" said Margaret taking control as usual, "Why don't you join the Land Army? It's got to be better than working here and you've probably got more experience of farming than any of us had put together when we started."

That conversation planted the seed in Nellie's mind and that was how she found herself turning up for her next job several weeks later in the uniform of the Land Army.

Chapter 10
The Land Army

Looking out of the window of the bus Nellie could see that they were approaching a village, which she assumed having seen a signpost a little way back, must be Trelawr, her destination. The conductor, knowing Nellie had requested to be told when they reached Trelawr, put up his hand to attract her attention and shouted.
"Here's your stop Miss."
The conductor kindly hauled Nellie's case down from the rack. She thanked him, as she descended down the bus steps and gave him a wave as the bus pulled away and set off on its onward journey.

Nellie looked around and surveyed the place that was to be her home for the unforeseeable future; not quite her home, as her directions informed her that the Dykewell Farm was a good two mile walk from the village. Trelawr appeared to be quite small with just the one road running through and a few houses scattered around. There was a church with a Norman tower on the opposite side of the road and a Public House called The Crown just in front of her. She couldn't see a shop, but hoped that there would be one somewhere close. Everywhere was very quiet, not a soul to be seen. Nellie involuntarily shuddered as she walked along the street, feeling very much 'the stranger in town' and wondered if although she could not see anyone, if anyone was indeed watching her from behind the small windows of the nearby cottages.

It was the beginning of May and really the weather should have been warming up a bit, but there was a certain dampness in the air that made Nellie feel quite chilly, so she set her case down and buttoned up her coat. It was only a thin mackintosh, part of her standard issue Land Army Uniform. In addition to the mackintosh, Nellie had been issued with two green jerseys, two pairs of corduroy breeches, two overall coats, two pairs of dungarees, six pairs of stockings, three shirts, two towels, one pair of ankle boots and one pair of brown leather brogue shoes, a pair of gumboots, a brown felt slouch hat with an enamelled metal cap badge and a Women's Land Army armlet, which was to be worn on the left arm. Nellie was already dressed in her uniform, but the rest of it plus some of her other clothes were packed tightly into her suitcase, so it was no wonder that it was heavy and made her arms ache.

Nearing the edge of the village, Nellie came to a single lane track on the left hand side of the road and looking again at her directions she guessed that this must be the track leading up to Dykewell Farm. Sitting on the corner between the track and the road was a young lad of about twelve years old. His hands were black with grease as he struggled to put his bicycle chain back on.

"Excuse me" enquired Nellie, anxious to gain his attention. "Is this the right way to Dykewell Farm?" Looking again at her notes "Mr. Bradwell's farm" she added.

"Yes that's right Miss. It's that white building you can see over there." Nellie stretched her neck and following the winding of the track along and up the hill she could see a whitewash building that had to be the farm she was looking for. Her heart sank, as not only did the house look isolated, but also it was a good trek from the village. Nellie had been hoping when she joined the Land Army that she would have been able to stay in a hostel like the one that she had been working in. She had so enjoyed the lively company of the girls and so much wanted to be one of them and part of that kind of life. However, looking ahead at Dykewell Farm, it didn't see that there was going to be any such fun at the farm or indeed at the nearby village. Her Land Army representative, Mrs. Ryan had already told her that she was the only Land Army volunteer staying at the farm, so although she had tried to change matters and make her life jollier, it looked almost certain that Nellie's lonely existence was set to continue.

The air temperature did not do anything to make it feel like a spring day, but the trees along the track were full of new buds, catkins and pussy willow. Seeing the trees made Nellie think of her brother Owen. She remembered his great knowledge of the countryside; how he could tell the type of tree just by studying its bark. She hadn't heard from him at all since his move to the north of England; maybe like her he too had had some pangs of guilt over what had passed between them. Nellie felt now that she could forgive him and would like to see him again. He was after all her brother and she possibly more than most knew what it was like to feel lonely. She didn't wish for Owen to feel the emptiness that she sometimes felt and at the end of the day, everyone wanted to feel loved and maybe that was all that Owen had wanted, but because of his shyness thought he had found it, but in the wrong person.

Turning around the next corner Nellie stepped up from the track to make way for a tractor heading her way. As it came alongside her she could see that the driver was about thirty five, had a ruddy complexion and a big smile.

"Hello! Judging from your uniform I would guess that you must be Nellie our new Land Army girl. Sorry I'm late. I had planned to meet you off the bus, but one of our cows went into labour. I'll just go down to the next gate and turn this thing around and then I'll be back to give you a lift."

The tractor engine revved up again as he pulled away.

"Oh! By the way" he said turning back over his shoulder "in case you hadn't realised I'm Jack Bradwell."

On his return Mr. Bradwell jumped down from the tractor, took Nellie's case from her and swung it up on to the front of the tractor.

"There's not much room in the front I'm afraid; you'll have to stand on the back, but it'll be a lot quicker than walking."

Standing next to Mr. Bradwell, Nellie whiffed the familiar odour akin to farmers; it brought back pleasant memories of her Uncle Henry. To a lot of people this mixture of manure, animals and sweat might appear offensive, but to her she found the smell quite comforting and distinctly masculine.

"Have you had any experience of farming, or are you one of those town girls that doesn't know the difference between the front and the back end of a cow?"

"I know a bit. I used to live with my Uncle on his farm, so I know how to milk a cow if that's what you mean" Nellie cockily replied.

"That'll come in handy then. We've got cows, pigs and chickens at Dykewell and we also grow a few crops, mainly potatoes though."

The tractor bumped its way into the farmyard. The door of the farmhouse opened and a lady appeared waving.

"That's my wife Betty" informed Mr. Bradwell. "Oh! And that little nipper" he said pointing towards a small boy of around four or five, who was eagerly trying to push past his mother in the doorway "is our son Richard. I'm hoping one day he might take over this place, but think I've still got a fair few years before that day arrives. Mind you, might not be the type of life that he'll be wanting once he's grown up."

Nellie followed Mrs. Bradwell into the kitchen looking forward to the cup of tea that she had been offered.

"Do you take sugar? Is one enough, we're all trying to cut down with the rationing?"

"No! None for me thank you"

"Did you have far to come?" asked Mrs. Bradwell with an intention of keeping the conversation going.

"Only from Cardiff. I had been working at a Hostel for the Land Army Girls, that's how I first got interested in joining up. They always seemed to have such good fun together."

"Might not be quite so lively here I'm afraid" Mrs. Bradwell advised. "Not too much going on in these parts. Occasionally there is a bit of a social at The Crown, but that's about it. Of course the black outs don't help matters. We tend to make our own entertainment, but usually by the time Jack's finished on the farm, he's usually too tired to want to do much. In fairness I'm not far different myself. Still it will be nice for me to have some female company around."

Nellie was a bit disappointed to say the least that it didn't look very much like she was going to have the fun that she had desperately hoped this change of employment would bring her. On a brighter note she had instantly taken a liking to Jack and Betty, as she had been told to call them and thought that maybe it wasn't going to be all bad after all.

Nellie's daily routine usually started at five in the morning. She would bring the cows in for milking, which was alright if they were in the lower fields, but if they were in the top field it was quite a business to group them together and bring them back down the track to the milking parlour. After milking, all the equipment and buckets had to be cleaned and the stools and floor scrubbed down. That finished with, she would then move on to the chicken house where she would mix up the feed for the chickens and collect the eggs. All this had to be done before breakfast. Sometimes Jack would do the early morning milking, which meant that Nellie would take the horse and cart down the village to deliver the milk while he was having breakfast. This was Nellie's most favourite chore and she would have liked to have done it more often than she was asked to, but I suppose Jack thought that there was no reason having a dog and barking yourself, so normally the early wake-up call was down to Nellie.

"Will you play with me Nellie?" Richard asked. "Mummy's cooking and she says she hasn't got time."

"Come on then, five minutes. You get your bat and we'll have a game of cricket. I know that's your favourite game."

A big smile appeared across the little boy's face, his previous bored look making a quick disappearance, as he ran towards the shed to get his bat.

"Thanks Nellie, you're so good with him. I know how much he keeps pestering until he gets his own way" laughed Betty. "Couldn't do me a favour in a minute could you? Take Jack's sandwiches up to the top field. I told him that I would take them to him, but I've just put some scones in the oven and I don't want them to burn."

"Course I will. Shall I take Richard with me as well?"

"That's a good idea. If you could wear him out a bit, chances are I might get him to bed a bit earlier tonight."

Walking back to the farm, Richard was getting a little tired. In order to take his mind off of his aching legs and to make him walk the full distance, Nellie made up a game of 'Spot the Rabbit' for he was too heavy for her to carry.

"There's one" shouted Richard excitedly "and another" he exclaimed even more excited than the first time, pointing straight in front of them where the track curved around to the left. Rounding the bend Nellie could see a figure walking towards them, which looked like Mickey Dunn. As the distance between them became less, she realised that it was him and put up her hand to wave. Nellie liked Mickey. She didn't know him that well, but had seen him a couple of times in the pub and he had always said hello to her.

"Out for a walk are you? Nice day for it."

"No, not really. We've just been up to the top field to take Richard's Dad his sandwiches haven't we?" Nellie replied looking down at Richard for confirmation.

"Now we're going back for a game of cricket" Richard shouted out.

Nellie laughed. "His Mum thought that this walk would tire him out, but doesn't sound like there's much chance of that does it? It will be lunchtime when we get back and then some of us have to work young man and not play cricket? Actually, it's not too bad today" she said speaking to Mickey. "Once I've done the afternoon milking I've got some time off."

"Would you like to come down The Crown tonight? I shall be there playing darts and I could do with a partner."

"Yes! Thank you" said Nellie. "I'm not sure if I'll be any good though."

"That doesn't matter; shall I meet you there about half past seven? I'd walk up to meet you, but I've got a job on and I don't think I'll be back much before then."

Bending down to Richard's level Mickey said to the small boy "So you like cricket then do you?"

"Yes I do. I had a new bat for my birthday."

"Well maybe one of these days Nellie will bring you down to watch me play cricket on the village green when we have a match and maybe when you're a bit taller you could join the team."

"Will you Nellie, will you?" Richard pleaded "Please".

"Oh! I don't know. We shall have to see. It's up to your Mum and Dad really. I'll see you later then Mickey at half past seven when you finish work."

Nellie didn't know exactly what Mickey did for a living. She had noticed that his hands looked quite rough, but was sure he would have mentioned if he had been farming like her. Most young men were away fighting for their country and she wondered why Mickey was not doing the same.

That afternoon biding her time doing the milking, Nellie wondered if maybe she could consider that she had been asked out on a date. Telling herself not to be so silly, she shifted her stool and lined herself up with the next cow's teats, but even so couldn't stop contemplating over what she might wear.

"Have a nice time then love" said Betty as Nellie buttoned up her coat in readiness to set off down the track. "You look really nice. Hope he's worth it?" she added.

Nellie could feel herself flushing.

"Oh! Don't be silly. It's only a game of darts you know."

Walking down the track Nellie's stomach felt full of butterflies and she could do with spending a penny again. She always felt like that when she was nervous. Looking at her watch it was quarter past seven. She didn't want to be late, but didn't want to be early either and certainly not the first person in the pub. Calculating the distant she had remaining to walk, she roughly calculated that all being well she would be just about right.

In the distant skies Nellie could hear the drone of a plane. She listened more closely and realised by its sound that it was a German plane, which was getting frightfully close to her. To avoid being gunned down she had no other option than to throw herself in the ditch. Nellie lay in the ditch completely still, not daring to breath let alone move. She could tell that the plane was flying directly over her head, then it appeared to move away and by the sound of it, circled the village a couple of times. Eventually, she breathed a sigh of relief as it flew away into the distance. After a few more minutes, Nellie considered that as the plane had not returned, maybe it was now safe to creep out from her hiding place and continue on to the pub. She shook herself down and pulled off some bracken that had stuck to her coat and hair and walked briskly on towards the village to more safe surroundings.

At the best of times, Nellie didn't like going into strange places on her own and generally felt unnerved. Tonight was no different, in fact if anything she was even more nervous, as by now she had convinced herself that maybe she was going on a date with Mickey. Nellie entered the door and as always in a small village, everyone turned around to see who had just walked in.

"What's happened to you?" asked Mickey pulling some straw out of her hair and drying to rub some mud off of her face.
A few of the regulars now had a smirk on their faces and poor Nellie realised that it was at her expense.
"It was that plane" she said. "The German plane. Didn't you hear it? It circled around a couple of times. I had to hide in the ditch so that they wouldn't see me" she explained.
By this time the landlady, a friendly blond woman in her fifties, who was always heavily made up came out of the back room and declared "Goodness me! What on earth's happened to you?"
Mickey stood in and generously explained what had happened.
"Oh! You poor dear" sympathised the landlady. "Come with me into the back room and let me clean you up."

The landlady fussed around Nellie, brushing her down and removing odd bits of straw from her hair. She fetched a damp flannel from the bathroom at the back and rubbed gently on Nellie's face to remove the smudges of dirt. Looking down at her legs, Nellie was upset to see that her one and only pair of nylon stockings, were literally ruined with holes and ladders running right down to her ankles.

"I don't think nail polish will be able to save those luvvie" advised the land lady. "Tell you what, take them off I've got an idea."
Nellie obligingly removed her torn stockings, while the landlady rummaged around in a small bag next to her mirror on the small occasional table.

"Here it is" she said "This will do the job. My sister told me about this trick; all the girls do it when they can't get their hands on a pair of stockings. Now keep still I've got to get this straight."
Nellie stood as still as she could and raised her skirt as the land lady knelt down and drew a line up the centre of her leg with her brown eyebrow pencil. Looking at the land lady's handiwork, Nellie was very pleased with the result.

"That's great. Thank you so much. You can't really tell the difference can you? I don't know if I shall be able to manage to draw them on myself though?"

"Oh! I'm sure you will luvvie. As they say "Where there's a will there's a way" and all that. It just needs a bit of practice."

Nellie made her way back through to the bar to join Mickey and thanks to the landlady once again felt presentable. She even managed to make a joke at her own expense saying that she must have straw for brains, judging by how much had fallen out of her hair.
Mickey laughed as did some of the regulars and he said "Well you look a picture again now."

"Yes" agreed another man sat at the bar "Don't let those Jerry's get to you."

"Too true" said another "Shoot them out of the skies, that's what I say. Shoot them down before they do harm to our courageous boys fighting for their Queen and country."

"Here, Here!" several men agreed.
Mickey appeared slightly subdued, but Nellie thought no more of it when he took her arm and suggested that they took their drinks over to a small table by the window.

Little Richard had never forgotten the suggestion of the man that he had seen on the track, that Nellie should take him to one of the cricket matches on the village green and had pestered her ever since. Nellie having finished the afternoon milking session, now had the remainder of the day to please herself. It was a beautiful summer's day and she wasn't in the mood for reading. She knew by rights that she ought to sit down and write some long overdue letters to the family, but although she loved to receive letters, she wasn't the best at replying. Nellie guessed being a Sunday there would more than likely be a match being played on the village green. Thinking that Betty might be more than glad for her to take Richard off of her hands for several hours, she walked towards the farmhouse in search of her.

"You truly are a saint Nellie, do you know that? Jack will be taking the horse and cart down to the village to pick up some supplies shortly, he could give you a lift. I'll go and give Richard a shout. You'll have made his day I know that."

When Nellie and Richard reached the green, the match was in full swing. Cricket wasn't a game that Nellie understood, but she liked the idea of village life and the community gathering together. Looking at the scoreboard, she thought that Trelawr was probably in the lead, but with no understanding of the scoring and for that matter even the game, she wasn't too sure.

After all Richard's pestering to come and watch the cricket match, the actual spectating of the game did not impress him too much and he soon became fidgety. Obviously watching the game was not half as much fun as playing it, especially when you had sole possession of the bat, as was often the case with Richard. Fortunately for Nellie, a young mother close by to her, with far more paternal experience than she, had the sensible idea of bringing her little boy's cricket bat and ball with them. Richard soon found a way to make his introduction and within seconds both boys happily immersed themselves in their own game of cricket, which was to them a lot much more pleasurable. Nellie gave a sigh of relief having avoided a close call of an afternoon of her employer's son's whinging.

The Umpire blew his whistle and half-time was declared. The men all made their way across the pitch towards the refreshment table. Realising that Nellie too had developed quite a thirst, she called across to Richard to say that they would go and get themselves a glass of lemonade. Trestle tables had been laid up with a few sandwiches and scones. Before the war, the selection would have been more varied and abundant, but rationing had put a stop to all of that.

"Hello lad! I see you've managed to get Nellie to bring you to the match then?"

Nellie glanced over her shoulder to see who was talking to Richard and her eyes found Mickey.

"Hello Mickey. Yes, to be honest though I think he prefers to play cricket rather than sit and watch."

"Is that right? I'll have to see what I can do. We're always looking for new players, especially with the war taking our best men away. May have to grow a few inches though little fella. Here let me pay for those" said Mickey and handed over some coins to the lady serving refreshments.

Over the last few months, Nellie had grown quite fond of Mickey and they often used to meet up at The Crown, either to play darts or just sit together and chat. Mickey always made some excuse and never actually came up as far as the farm to meet her, but would always be waiting for her in the gateway half way down the track. Making their way home after the cricket match, all Richard could talk about was cricket and he could not wait to grow a few more inches so that he could join Trelawr's cricket team.

"Well you'd better make sure that you eat all your vegetables if you want to grow taller" Nellie advised, knowing that the little lad was not too keen on his greens.

Reaching Dykewell Farm Richard put a spurt on and ran towards the house, not being able to contain his excitement anymore.

"Dad, Dad" Nellie could hear him shouting as she walked through the door herself.

"Mickey says I can join the cricket team. He says I need to grow a bit more though, so I am going to eat all my vegetables" turning to his Mum as he mentioned the word vegetables.

"Who's this Mickey? Jack enquired. "Not Mickey Dunn is it?" he said questioning Nellie.

With the mention of Mickey's name Betty moved towards the sink and busied herself washing cups, that to Nellie appeared to have already been washed.

"Yes" answered Nellie "That's right. He's a friend of mine."

"Friend of yours is he? Well! He certainly wouldn't be a friend of mine. I'm sure you could find someone better than him to hang around with girl."

His piece said, Jack turned and stormed out of the kitchen. Betty wiped her hands on her apron and motioned to Richard that it was time for his bath. Nellie could sense some sort of friction, but could not understand the reason. She thought it probably best to make herself scarce, so went up to her room.

Nellie continued to see Mickey, but she never mentioned to him the scene in the kitchen and Jack's reaction. It did seem to her that something was not quite right between Jack and Mickey, as he was never keen to come up to the farm to meet her, or walk her all the way home; their meeting place was always the gateway halfway down the track. Nellie had now learnt though that Mickey worked in forestry, which accounted for the hardness of his hands that she had noticed earlier.

One evening Nellie and Mickey were walking back up the track to Dykewell farm hand in hand. Nellie felt gloriously happy; she and Mickey had spent the afternoon sat on the riverbank, just the two of them. There had been a lot of kissing and Mickey she knew would have liked to have taken their relationship a step further, but she wasn't quite ready for that. For Nellie, everything was just fine, in fact much more than fine; she knew that she was falling in love with Mickey and for the first time she thought that he might even be a little bit in love with her.

Mickey stopped walking and took her again in his arms. Enjoying the tenderness of each other's lips, they had been oblivious to the sound of Jack's horse and cart until it was almost upon them. Nellie put her hand up to wave as she guessed that Jack would realise that she was on her way back to the farm and stop to give her a lift. Jack did not stop, if anything the horse speeded up as he passed them with Jack not even acknowledging her wave.

"What's up with him?" Nellie asked

"Don't bother about it, I'm not" said Mickey flirtatiously grabbing her again for another kiss.

Nellie eventually arrived back at the farm happier than she had ever felt. She felt grown up; she could sense her womanly attraction and most importantly she felt loved. In Nellie's eyes Mickey was a handsome man and she was very proud to think that she was 'his girl.' Her euphoria was very quickly brought to a halt.

"You're seeing him, aren't you? Friends you told me and I thought that was bad enough. Well I tell you girl it's got to stop."

Jack had taken Nellie by a surprise and for a split second the cat had got her tongue.

"Is that why you didn't stop to give me a lift, 'cos I was with him? What's wrong with him Jack? Why are you so against him?"

"What's wrong with him? How long have you got to listen? You've got to put a stop to it, do you hear?"

"I don't think it's any of your business. Mickey makes me very happy and it's up to me who I choose to go out with not you."

"Is that what you think? Well I'll tell you this for nothing. If I see you with that 'conch' again or even as much as hear that you are still seeing him, I won't have you working on my farm, do you hear?"

Nellie hadn't quite finished and would have liked to have given Jack a piece of her mind, but before she had the chance he had stormed out of the room slamming the door behind him. Determined she would have the last word, as nobody was going to tell her who she could or not go out with, the next day she made an appointment to see Mrs. Ryan the Land Army representative and asked for a transfer.

A week after her disagreement with Jack or more correctly Jack's disagreement with her, Nellie was packed up and once again on a bus heading this time to a farm in Pontypridd. Nellie's vision of living in a hostel and having lots of fun with other land army girls was still not going to happen, as once again, she would be living with her employers. Her new employer Mr. Jefferies was apparently a sick man and needed help, as he was no longer able to run the farm by himself.

Travelling on the bus Nellie thought over her time spent at Dykewell Farm. In spite of everything, although it hadn't matched up to what she had been hoping, she had been happy there. Betty had been so easy to get on with and Nellie right from the first day had never felt a stranger in her company. She had always too found no fault with Jack until recent times. Nellie felt guilty that she had left without saying good-bye to little

Richard, but at the time he had been away staying with his grandmother. The person she knew she would miss the most would be of course Mickey. She hoped that they would stay in touch and write to each other, but realistically considering the distance between them, although not vast, with the war and rationing it would not be easy.

Much to Nellie's disappointment she never heard from Mickey again. She had sent several letters to him but a reply had never come back. In fact her last letter had been returned to sender as 'not known at this address.' She often thought about him and indeed the situation at Dykewell Farm that had been responsible for her rapid departure. She remembered Jack calling Mickey a 'conch' and wondered if in fact he was a conscientious objector. His forestry work would back that up, as that was one of the types of work conscientious objectors were made to do if they refused to join the forces. Nellie also thought back to the strained atmosphere in The Crown that night, the night that she had hidden in the ditch to avoid being seen by the German plane. Something else niggled on Nellie's mind. Maybe it was possible that Mickey had refrained from fighting in the war; an action that was indeed frowned upon by most and considered to be a cowardly action, but she didn't think that that this was the only reason for Jack's total dislike of him.

Her mind regressed back to that time in the kitchen when Richard had come home so excited about the possibility of playing in the village cricket team. It came back to Nellie how Betty had turned away and aimlessly started washing the dishes at the mention of Mickey's name. In retrospect she had seemed embarrassed to look Jack in the eye. Thinking back, although she hadn't picked up on it before, Betty had always come across as a little edgy whenever Nellie had been going out to meet her friends at The Crown. She had never actually named who she was going to meet, but no doubt Betty had assumed correctly that it was Mickey.

Nellie's thoughts digressed to Mickey. Her heart would still miss a beat when she allowed herself to think of him. Nellie's fingers touched her hair and she remembered how Mickey's hair had curled around his ears. It suddenly dawned on her that little Richard's hair had fallen the same way.
'That's it' she thought to herself. 'No it can't be?' she questioned.

The more she thought about it, the more convinced she became. Their hair was the same, even their eyes now she came to think about it. They both had a tendency to scratch their head when they were uncertain of something and their mutual love of cricket was yet another factor. Of course she would never know the full truth behind Jack's reasons for hating Mickey so much. Maybe he was a 'conch', but Nellie was beginning to think that maybe there was more to it than met the eye. 'Could Mickey be the father of little Richard and not Jack?'

Nellie found the work on Mr. Jefferies farm a lot harder than she had been used to with Jack at Dykewell. Mr Jefferies was in his early sixties, but due to his poor health was not able to do very much around the farm. His wife too suffered badly with arthritis and her hands were badly malformed due to the painful disease. It was more than she could bear, to cope with the household chores let alone help out on the farm. Mr Jefferies only kept one cow, which was sufficient to supply milk for the farm, so Nellie no longer had a herd of cows to milk twice a day, which was a blessing. She did however have six pigs to feed and muck out. Cleaning out the sty was not a pleasant task and certainly not one of Nellie's favourites, but like everything else it had to be done so she got on with it.

One day the sty seemed messier than ever and the smell so bad she could even taste it in her mouth. The more she pitched in her fork to clear the muck and straw, the bigger the pile became. It was a hot afternoon and the sweat was accumulating on her forehead, her shirt felt clammy to her back and there was dampness under her arms. Nellie's shoulders and arms ached, but she knew it would be some while before she could have a soak in a hot tub, as she still had the cow to milk and the chickens to feed. A sound of ringing alerted her and brought her to her senses. Tiredly Nellie stretched out her arm to turn off the alarm clock, realising that her day of hard toil had all been a dream and her real day's work had not yet begun; that pigsty still needed mucking out.

Usually when she had a day off, to get away from the farm, Nellie would walk the four miles or so across the mountain to the nearest town. She enjoyed walking, it gave her time to dwell over things that had happened, put the world straight and more often or not, time to daydream. In her pretend life, she always had an entourage of friends, wore the latest fashion in clothes and was forever going to dances. At these dances she had a never ending string of admirers waiting to dance with her.

One afternoon, Nellie was disturbed from her daydreaming by the sound of voices shouting to her. Looking up she noticed a group of men of around about her age, sat on a bench smoking. They called to her and Nellie obligingly went across to them. On first impression the men appeared to be a friendly bunch and when one of them stood up and offered her his seat, Nellie gladly took it. Nellie wasn't one to always find it easy to talk to strangers, but she was soon put at ease by their banter and felt more than comfortable to spend a bit of time with them. They asked her name, where she'd been, where she was going to? All questions Nellie was happy to answer, glad of having the company and feeling that at long last maybe she was making some friends. Nellie guessed that the men had been drinking by the alcoholic fumes she could smell on their breath. This just made them funnier in Nellie's view and their hilarity soon rubbed off on her, encouraging her too to say things that in turn made them laugh. A good hour Nellie must have spent sitting with her new friends on the bench and she felt invigorated by their companionship. Still all good things must come to an end and looking at her watch she decided it was time to take her leave, as she still had a good two mile walk in front of her before she reached the farm.

As Nellie walked away, she felt a hard force on her back which pushed her to the ground. Before she had time to get her breath or realise what had happened, one of the men was on top of her. He roughly turned her over and she could feel his wet, slobbery lips on hers. Nellie immediate reaction was to push him off, but he had her arms pinned to the ground and her strength was no match for his. The others did not come to her rescue, but she could hear them laughing and jeering this monster on. Nellie was petrified and at the same time cross with herself that she had gone to talk with them at all. She hadn't intended to give them the wrong impression, but obviously she had. She could now feel the pressure of the man's body becoming lighter as one of the other men pulled him off.
 "Thank God" she thought to herself.
Nellie was mistaken, her nightmare continued as the second man pushed himself onto her, placing his hand over her mouth to prevent her from screaming. She could feel his course hand fondling her breast through her thin blouse and could feel his leg writhing up her skirt. Nellie knew she

had to do something, she could not allow this to go on, but what? Her strength was no match and if she somehow escaped this man, there were still the others standing around. It was a risk, but the only thing she could think of was to feign faintness. One or two of the onlookers noticed how limp Nellie's body had become and became frightened. Nellie didn't know if they thought she had just fainted, or whether they thought it was something more sinister, but thankfully they pulled the man off of her and she could hear them all running away, leaving her alone to pick up the pieces.

It was sometime before Nellie felt that it was safe enough to move. Understandably the tears started to flow and her body trembled with relief knowing that her nightmare was at last over. She was cross with herself for being so stupid. Why had she stopped to talk to them in the first place, especially in such an isolated area? Feeling inside as dishevelled as she looked on the outside, Nellie continued on her walk back to the farm. She could hear a car approaching and was petrified when it started to slow down, thinking that it might be her attackers returning to look for her. Never had Nellie been so pleased to see Mr. Jefferies as that day when he opened the door of his van and told her to jump in. If Mr. Jefferies noticed the state she was in, he never commented on it. Likewise she also never mentioned the incident to anyone. Firstly, as she was too embarrassed to repeat it and secondly she was frightened that people would think badly of her.

Nellie could never settle after her near rape encounter. No longer did she feel safe making the four mile walk to the town on her days off, for fear of a similar episode occurring. She threw herself into her work in an attempt to alleviate the boredom and loneliness that she so often suffered. Eventually she felt that she could not put up with this isolated existence any longer and much as she didn't want to let Mr. Jefferies and his wife down, Nellie gave him notice of her intentions to leave.

Chapter 11

Sadly Uncle Henry and Aunt Grace had both since died, so this time Nellie could not return to Penbryn Farm as she had done in the past. Nellie had made arrangements with Cynthia, her Uncle and Aunt's daughter, that she could for the time being have lodgings with her and her husband Jack in Maesteg.

Times had been hard for Cynthia. Soon after eloping with Jack, she had found herself pregnant and was over the moon when she gave birth to a little boy, who they named Trevor. Trevor was a happy baby, no trouble at all. Cynthia absolutely doted on her offspring and considered every minute she spent with him a gift from God. Ten months after Trevor's birth, Cynthia was struck down with grief when she had found his little body lying limp and lifeless in his cot. As like her mother Grace, history repeated itself and Cynthia too was not able to conceive anymore children. Jack's son from a previous relationship, now a teenager, would sometimes visit, but he was quite off-hand and rude to Cynthia and certainly no substitute for Trevor

Although it had always been assumed that Cynthia being the only daughter of Henry and Grace would automatically inherit the farm, when Henry eventually died, having outlived Grace by three years, it was discovered that he had never actually owned the farm, it had by all accounts been rented. A small amount of savings did come Cynthia's way but Jack, who was never able to hold down a job for long, soon managed to drink and gamble it away.

Cynthia did what she could to make ends meet. She cleaned houses and took in laundry, but often Jack would help himself to money he found in her purse and flitter it away on beer and bets, leaving her short. Lately, she had started to hide a little away each week in an old tea caddy for emergencies, if not every day didn't seem an emergency for Cynthia trying so hard to put food on the table. Only yesterday when she had gone to take a little out to pay the never, never man, had she found the caddy empty. Having Nellie to stay with them and bringing some extra money into the household, would be for Cynthia like manna from heaven.

Nellie walked up the street towards Cynthia's house, glancing at each house number looking out for number ninety-two. The street was like so many others in the mining communities of Wales, home to a long row of identical terrace houses on each side of the road. A feeling of déjà vu hit Nellie, it was as if time stood still and she was once again in Baker Street, the street where she had been born, where her mother had died and where afterwards her elder sister Rose had gallantly taken on the task of caring for them all.

Half way up the street, Nellie passed a huge crater, the devastation caused by a stray German bomb. It had completely destroyed one house and half of another; just a pile of rubble was left from what had once been a safe haven for the families that had lived inside. Nellie shuddered to realise how close to danger Cynthia had been and wished that this war would soon be over.

She thought of her brother Idris and her brother Gareth who too was now fighting for his King and country. Her thoughts also went out to Joyce, who was still living in London, which Nellie knew was being blasted with more than its fair share of bombings. Nellie had pleaded with her sister to leave the city and move back to Wales, but Joyce had now married and with her husband away in North Africa, she was determined to stay and look after her invalided mother-in-law.

The door of number ninety-two was well swept and clean. It was obvious too that the windows had recently undergone a polish. Nellie tapped on the door and it was quickly opened by Cynthia, who had been looking out for her. Nellie had not seen Cynthia for a number of years, although they had corresponded with each other from time to time. She was quite taken back, by the thin almost gaunt women who faced her. Cynthia's hair had always had such a shine to it, but nowadays it had lost its lustre and looked quite dull and lifeless. Nellie could remember the pampering that Aunt Grace had bestowed on her only daughter and the time that had been spent putting rags into Cynthia's hair to make it pretty with curls. Cynthia's hair now hung straight around her face and her whole appearance gave the impression that she had no self-worth at all.

Nellie followed Cynthia through the front door. Without being shown she knew exactly the layout of the small house, as with all the terraced houses being alike on the outside so were they the same on the inside.

"It really is good to see you Nellie. It will be so nice to have another female to have a natter with. I don't see that much of Jack truth be known. He spends more time in the pub than at home here with me."

"It will be nice for me as well Cynthia. You wouldn't believe how lonely it got on the farm at times. I think even the pigs got fed up of listening to me. They were all I had to talk to a lot of the time."

After a cup of tea and a plate of welsh cakes specially made for the occasion, Cynthia took Nellie up the stairs to the room at the back of the house which was to be hers. She unpacked her case and hung her clothes in the wardrobe at the side of the single bed. A bowl and pitcher of water was on the small chest in her room, so Nellie thought she might as well take advantage of it and freshen herself up a bit. She had been up early that morning and hadn't really slept that well the night before either, so between lack of sleep and maybe dust from her journey, her eyes felt quite dry and were beginning to sting a little. She thought splashing some cool water on them might help. Nellie had just finished washing and was rubbing in some Pond's cold cream onto her face when she heard the front door slam.

"Cynthia! Is my tea ready?"

Nellie guessed that this must be Jack home and thought by his tone that he sounded a bit gruff. This was followed by a mumble of lower voices, with the level of Jack's raising as the conversation continued. Nellie sensed that all was not well. She had never liked Jack and had heard say that he treated his wife badly; it seemed that the rumours could very well be substantiated. Not being the type to sit in her room until the fracas was over, Nellie decided to descend the stairs and intervene.

Cynthia's eyes glanced towards the doorway as Nellie approached and embarrassed that her guest must obviously had overheard the argument; put her head down in shame. Following his wife's gaze Jack turned around and saw Nellie looking at him.

"Hello Nellie, you've arrived then?" and with that he grabbed his jacket off of the back of the kitchen chair, leaving his untouched dinner on the plate. "I'll be back later" he shouted from a distance half way up the hallway.

"What was all that about?" enquired Nellie. "I heard the shouting."

"Oh! He was complaining about his dinner. Thought it wasn't good enough for the 'man of the house."

Nellie viewed the plate on the table, which consisted of several rashers of bacon, two eggs and some fried potatoes with two slices of bread and margarine on the side. Cynthia lifted the plate from the table and set it down on the draining board in the back scullery. Returning she nodded to Nellie to follow her through into the middle room where she wearily sat down on the rocking chair by the hearth and sighed.

"I just don't know what else I can do", poor Cynthia exasperatedly explained. "I've given him my egg from the rations as well as his own, plus he's had more than his fair share of the bacon and still he's not happy. I think he thinks I'm a bloody magician. He hardly gives me any money you know, keeps most of it back for his drinking and gambling. That's where he's gone now, down the pub. You mark my words."

Cynthia went on to say about the missing money from the tea caddy and Nellie recognised that all was certainly not well. Nellie remembered just how much Cynthia as a young girl had idolised Jack and felt sorry for her that it had all come to this.

"Well now I'm here I can help a bit. I start my new job at the munitions factory on Monday and I'm sure some weeks I'll be able to give you a bit extra. Look we can't let that bacon go to waste, what do you say to me making us both a nice bacon sandwich with it?"

Nellie thought working at the Royal Ordnance Factory in Bridgend was great and enjoyed every minute she spent there. She never appeared aware of the danger of working in a munitions factory, or if she did she never showed it. The munitions factories were a constant nightly target for the raids by the German bombers and when the sirens blew warning of an imminent attack, Nellie and the younger workers would run to the shelters laughing and singing, glad of the break from their repetitive work and a chance to have a good natter and a hot drink. The older women more aware of the danger would get cross with them, but being carefree they never took too much notice.

The factory more commonly known as 'The Admiralty' employed forty thousand people many of which were women, making it the largest employer of factory workers at the time in the whole of the United Kingdom. The factory stretched over three massive sites and also housed a huge underground munitions storage base, which was an overspill of the Royal Arsenal in Woolwich. The Bridgend factory was a filling factory and components from ordnance establishments across the length and breadth of the country were brought into Bridgend for the final assembly. The principal customer of 'The Admiralty' was the Navy who secured nearly half of the factory's production of munitions for light guns, smoke, signals and heavy shells. The Army received amongst other things medium rounds, demolition charges, smoke, mortar rounds, rocket components and grenades, with the Royal Air Force taking bombs and detonators.

It was a crisp morning as Nellie stood waiting for the bus to take her to work. Bridgend was a little way from Maesteg, but the factory provided a special bus to bring in its workers from the surrounding area. Nellie shuddered and her teeth chattered with the cold; she wrapped her coat closer hoping to keep the cold at bay. Her feet felt like blocks of ice and she stamped alternate feet in an effort to get her blood circulating again. 'These five in the morning starts are a killer' she thought and was relieved to see her bus make an appearance around the corner at the top of the road by the cinema.

Climbing onto the bus, Nellie could see her friend Elsie waving and gesticulating that there was an empty place next to her. Elsie had been given the role of showing Nellie the ropes when she had first started at the factory and ever since they had become firm friends. Elsie was a good one to know if you ever need to participate in any gossip, as nothing got past her ears. Nellie often used to wonder where she got it all from, as they worked side by side in the factory, more often or not for ten hours at a time and she never seemed to pick up on any interesting snippets.

There's a dance on Friday night in the skittle alley at the back of The Nag's Head in William Street. You'll never guess who's going to be singing there?"
Nellie shook her head when no names came to mind.
"Only Johnnie Bevan" exclaimed Elsie excitedly.

Johnnie worked as one of the supervisors at the factory. He was a few years older than the two friends and very good-looking according to their young eyes. Both of them believed that he was the best thing to have happened since sliced bread. Whenever he peered over Nellie's shoulder to inspect her work, she got herself into quite a tizzy and her stomach felt as if a hundred butterflies were flying around inside of it. Elsie was never quite so lost for words as Nellie and usually managed to come out with something ad lib, that would bring a smile to Johnnie's lips and make his deep brown eyes shine even more brightly.

"Apparently" Elsie continued "he's got his own band together."
"You're kidding me. Not really?" Nellie questioned in amazement.
"Yes, he's got together with Bill Jenkins, you know the tall, lanky chap in packing, Ray Stubbs from maintenance and somebody else; I'm not sure who."
"Are you going to go?"
"You bet I am. Wild horses wouldn't drag me away. You're coming as well aren't you, you've got to?"
"Sounds good to me. Is Johnnie the lead singer?"
"Yeah! Jill Braddock's heard him and says he sounds just like Bing Crosby. She says he's really, really good. Just think those dishy looks and he can sing as well. What more could a girl ask for?"

Nellie was really looking forward to the dance on Friday and both she and Elsie were counting the hours left to work until they could go home and put their glad rags on in readiness for the big event.

Having sorted through her meagre wardrobe, Nellie disappointedly came down the stairs and found Cynthia in the back kitchen peeling potatoes for dinner.
"Well I haven't got a clue what I am going to wear" she despondently mentioned to Cynthia. "I'm working days too this week, so even if I could afford to use up some coupons I couldn't get to the shops."
Putting the small peeling knife down on the cupboard, Cynthia wiped her wet hands on her apron.
"What you fretting about now girl, I'm sure we can sort something out. Come on show me what you've got and let's see what we can do."

Cynthia thumbed her way through the rail of clothes in Nellie's wardrobe stopping at a navy blue pencil skirt with a small kick pleat at the back.
"What about this?" she asked, pulling it out for Nellie to see. "This always looks real smart on you. Being tall and slim, it's just the right style for you."

"Well I could wear that I suppose" replied Nellie uncertainly, "but what could I wear with it? I used to wear it with my black and white polka dot blouse, but that's seen better days; it's quite threadbare."
Cynthia thought for a moment and then her face lit up with inspiration.
"Hang on a second I may just be able to help there."
She turned on her heel and strode through into her bedroom. Nellie followed suit and wondered what on earth Cynthia was doing looking through her pile of clothes and bedding that had been put to one side for mending.
"Here it is" Cynthia triumphantly remarked. "I thought it was here. What do you think of this then?"
Nellie didn't quite know what to think and thought Cynthia had taken leave of her senses.
"But it's a pillow case Cynthia, a pillow case."
"Ah! Might look like a pillow case now, but it won't by the time I've finished with it."
Nellie's face lit up. She remembered how good Cynthia had always been with a needle and she had every confidence that from nothing, Cynthia would magic something up for her.

End of shift on Friday was eventually signalled by the sound of the factory claxon and everybody on the day shift was happy to down tools and hand over to the arriving night shift. The bus trip back to Maesteg seemed to take for ever and Nellie only half listening to Elsie's non-stop chatter, couldn't stop wondering what Cynthia had made for her out of the old pillow case.
'I hope it's alright; what if it doesn't fit?' she inwardly asked herself. Mentally she worked her way through her wardrobe and drawers, wondering what she could wear, should things not turn out successfully. Of course Nellie need not have concerned herself. Returning back to the little terraced house, Cynthia proudly presented her with a lovely white blouse, freshly ironed. It had a V-neck collar and short sleeves, both of which were edged in lace.
Nellie looked at it admiringly
"Oh! Cynthia, thank you, thank you. You are so clever, do you know that? Nobody would ever know that this morning this was an old pillow case, you're a real marvel. Gosh! It looks brand new."

There had been no need for Nellie to show her thanks so enthusiastically, as Cynthia was able to read the delight in her cousin's face and that was more than enough for her.

Nellie felt good about herself as she made her way to meet Elsie at The Nag's Head. Elsie lived with her parents a couple of streets the other side of the public house, so they had agreed that they would wait for each other just inside the skittle alley, as it was a bit too cold to be hanging around outside. The blouse that Cynthia had made for Nellie looked a treat with her navy skirt and her best navy shoes, the ones with a small heel that gave a nice shape to her legs. Nellie didn't like to wear shoes with heels more than two inches, as she was conscious of her height and didn't want to tower over any prospective suitors. Not having any nylons to wear, she remembered the trick that the landlady in The Crown at Trelawr had taught her; the one of drawing a line up the back of her leg with an eyebrow pencil to create an impression of a seam. Before now she had rubbed gravy browning into her legs as well to make them looked tanned, but it hadn't been too successful and neither was Cynthia very happy when it had rubbed off on her white sheets.

Over recent years Cynthia had let her own appearance slip, but she knew just how much Nellie was looking forward to this evening and offered to set her hair in rollers. Cynthia had a real knack with hair, maybe all the hours of sitting around while Aunt Grace had tied her hair in rags all those years ago, had rubbed off a little on her. Nellie couldn't believe the finished effect when she looked in the mirror. Cynthia bless her, had managed to recreate the look of Veronica Lake the film star. Nellie's straight, lank hair at least for the moment was in the distant past, and the image reflecting back at her showed an attractive young woman, with a side parting and soft waves cascading down each side of her face. Nellie was pleased that she had stopped off in the chemist and bought the Vitapointe leave in conditioner that one of the girls at the factory had told her about. It really had made a difference and her normal drab hair now positively gleamed.

Opening the door to the skittle alley, Nellie's eyes took a while to adjust to the light. Elsie though was already inside and quickly noticed her and tugged on her sleeve.

"There's quite a few here. Let's move nearer to the bar and get a drink. It's a bit of a squash though."

The two girls shouldered their way through the crowd, stepping around couples and friends grouped together. Elsie heard her name being called and following the sound of the voice, saw Brian Towers at the bar with a couple of his mates.

"Come over here" he invited them. "There's a space here if we shove up" he said nudging his friends along the bar a few steps. Would you two ladies like a drink?"

"Thanks Brian. A small shandy please" answered Elsie flirtatiously, managing to look at Brian, while the same time extending her smile to his mates.

"Yes, a shandy would be very nice" agreed Nellie.

The atmosphere was very lively. Nellie found it hard to hear what was being said, as her ears were caught up in the hum of everybody else's chatter. The band hadn't yet started and everybody eagerly awaited their performance, none more so than Nellie and Elsie and daresay quite a number of the other girls filling the skittle alley that evening. A record player balanced precariously on a small table at the far end of the room. Some couples were already up dancing, being mindful not to step too close to the player, as the vibration of their movements were likely to make the needle jump.

The air was full of smoke and having in recent months taken up the habit, the smell made Nellie quite fanciful for a cigarette. She opened her bag and took out a full packet of ten Kensitas. Offering them around, it was only Elsie who took one, as the men in the group who smoked, preferred their own non-tipped variety.

"Look there's an empty table over there by the stage, shall we grab it? Johnnie and the boys should be coming on any minute."
The men preferred for the time being to stay propping up the bar, but Elsie and Nellie picked up their drinks and made their way over. No sooner had they sat themselves down on the hard wooden chairs when everyone started to clap and whistle and the band jumped up onto the stage.

"Cor! Doesn't he look different? I think he looks even more handsome if that's possible" said Elsie, her wide eyes glued to the Adonis image in front of her.

Nellie looked at her friend and laughed. Elsie was never one to keep quiet about her emotions and always said what she thought, without a care for who might be listening. Nellie on the other hand was the complete opposite and apart from the odd bit of banter with Elsie, in general kept her feelings to herself.

The band struck a few chords and very quickly the small dance area was awash with gyrating bodies. Persona exuded itself from Elsie and within no time she had had several offers to dance, unlike Nellie. Nellie didn't mind; in fact she was quite glad to sit out the dances. Dancing wasn't really her cup of tea; it made her feel awkward and ungainly and she was quite sure that she had been born with two left feet. She watched the couples sway in time to the music and really although she pretended otherwise to herself, deep down wished that she had more confidence and co-ordination and could do likewise.

Nellie was rescued from her thoughts by the sound of Elsie dropping herself down heavily onto the neighbouring chair.

"Phew! Need a rest after that. Sid's a great dancer; he really knows how to swing a girl around. I've got stitch in my side after that."

Elsie did not need long to get her breath back and for her stitch to subside.

"Oh! Look. Jill Braddock's over there."

Nellie craned her neck, but couldn't make out their colleague from the factory over the sea of bodies.

"By the bar. There see her now she's waving at us. I'll just pop over and say hello. Might as well get a drink while I'm there" she said glancing at her empty glass. "Do you want one?"

"No, I'm fine thanks. I haven't finished this one yet."

Johnnie and his band had now switched from the up beat songs and had now moved onto singing slow ballads. Elsie had still not returned to the table and Nellie scanned over the crowd to see if she could find her. Jill was chatting with some other girls that Nellie recognised from the factory, but Elsie wasn't one of them. Her eyes moved around and then she spotted Elsie back at the bar with Brian and his friends. She seemed to be getting on very well, with one of them in particular; a stocky fair-haired chap, the one that had seemed to have a lot to say for himself earlier she recalled. They seemed to be getting on very well, certainly laughing a lot and Nellie could see that he had his arm draped across her friend's shoulder. Recognising Elsie's flirty behaviour, she guessed that he was probably the real reason for her having left Nellie on her own and not to see Jill Braddock at all.

Sitting on her own, especially near to the stage, where everyone's eyes were directed, she felt a little bit obvious and hoped Elsie would soon come back. She wouldn't have felt so bad if the band had been playing faster songs, but now that they were playing slow ones, with couples closely dancing around her, she felt a bit like a wilting wallflower. The current song came to an end. Some of the couples who had either had enough of dancing, or were in search of a new partner moved off the dance floor. Others eager not to give up on their chosen partner, hung around on the dance floor for the next number to be introduced. The mood slowed right down and Johnnie introduced the next song.

"We're moving on now to a popular number which is in the charts at the moment by Vaughn Monroe. It's a favourite of mine and I hope it is for you as well. Ladies and Gentlemen, 'The Very Thought Of You.'

Nellie could have sworn that Johnnie had looked straight at her when he introduced the song; in fact he still appeared to be looking at her now.
'Don't be silly', she told herself 'he's probably looking at someone behind you.'
Nellie peered over her shoulder, but couldn't see another girl close by, but guessed that there must be one there. She let her mind wander and for a few seconds, she was that girl at the end of Johnnie's gaze, the one that held the key to his heart. She soon regained her senses and told herself off for being so daft.

Johnnie moved slowly and confidently across the stage in Nellie's direction.
'Gosh! He is good' she thought to herself. 'He really could go a long way if he had the right opportunity.'
Nellie felt quite unnerved, as he did seem to be looking at her as he sang.
'Don't be stupid girl; it's all in your imagination.'

Johnnie stepped down off of the stage and everybody's eyes were on him. Nellie sensed him moving her way and felt the same old butterflies start fluttering in her stomach. He stood briefly at the vacant chair beside her and then lowered himself onto it. Gently taking Nellie's hand he pulled her to her feet and motioned for her to sit on his knee. Dreamlike, Nellie did as she was told, totally caught up in the moment. Listening to him singing she forgot about the crowd looking on, for her it was just the two of them alone in the world. She could not believe what was happening, but managed to convince herself that for his part it was just his act and that hers was the face he recognised in the crowd. Nobody was more surprised than Nellie when Johnnie planted a kiss on her cheek at the end of the song before returning to the stage.

Before she had had time to recover, Elsie was back.

"Whatever was all that about?"

"Don't be silly, it was nothing. It's only because he recognised me from the factory."

"Wish I'd stayed put now and hadn't gone over there; he might have chosen me then."

Nellie could tell that Elsie thought that she was a far more likely proposition for Johnnie's advances than her and Nellie agreed that she was probably right.

The interval came and Nellie found herself once again abandoned as Elsie had gone off in search of richer pickings, namely men. Picking up her handbag, she thought she would go to the lady's room to spend a penny and maybe put on some fresh lipstick. When she returned to her table Johnnie was standing there.

"There you are. I thought for one minute you'd had enough of my awful singing and gone home."

"No not at all. I thought you were very good. I never realised you could sing."

"Well nice of you to say so. Can I get you a drink; I notice your glass is empty?"

Nellie thanked him and he went in search of a refill for the two of them. Nellie was grateful for small mercies that at least she had just checked herself in the mirror and refreshed her lipstick. Unusual for her, she started to feel quite good about herself and even if Johnnie was only being kind to her, at least she would have a bit of company for a while and not be on her own.

Johnnie returned with the drinks and sat down next to her. Nellie had been concerned that she would dry up and have nothing useful to say; she needn't have worried on that particular score, as there were no pregnant pauses and the conversation between the two of them flowed. Soon Johnnie's short break was over and he was being called back to the stage for the second half of his performance.

The end of the evening came all too soon in Nellie's opinion. Johnnie and the band took their final bow and left the stage, as exhausted dancers wound their way back to their tables. Elsie had not made another appearance, but Nellie had noticed her from time to time dancing with a variety of different partners. It emerged that Brian's friend, the fair-haired one that she had been laughing with earlier, was her final choice of the evening and Nellie could see them in a tight clinch in one of the less well-lit corners of the skittle alley.

Nellie stood up and took her coat off the back of her chair. She put in her left arm and was pulling the garment around trying to find the other armhole, when she felt somebody helping her into it.
"Thank you" she said turning to face her aid.
"If you can hang on a few minutes, while we pack the gear away, I'll walk you home if you like?"
Nellie was flabbergasted. 'If I would like?' thought Nellie. 'If I would like? Of course I would like.'
Somehow Nellie managed to answer in a composed fashion and sat back down while she waited for Johnnie to finish.
The skittle alley was almost empty, apart from a couple of hangers on at the bar making their last mouthful of beer last, in the hope that the landlord might bend the rules and let them have another pint.
"I'll see you Monday then Nellie" Elsie instructed. "Brian's walking down your way, if you want to walk back with him."
"No I'm alright. I'm waiting for Johnnie. He said that he would walk me home."
"Johnnie? Johnnie Bevan?"
"Yes" said Nellie with a warm glow on her face. "I can't quite believe it myself."
Nobody else would have noticed, but knowing Elsie the way she did, immediately Nellie could see her expression turned sour.

"Oh!" she said disdainfully. "Well Reg is waiting for me. So best be off. See you."

There was the beginning of a sharp frost on the ground as Nellie and Johnnie left The Nag's Head. The ground beneath them sparkled like diamonds, symbolic Nellie mused to the fairy tale she found herself in. Nellie shuddered with the cold and her teeth started to chatter slightly.

"Are you cold?" Johnnie caringly questioned.

"Just a bit" she answered. "It's my circulation; it's never been that good."

"Come here" he said taking the opportunity to put his arm around Nellie. "Maybe I can warm you up a bit."

The easy conversation that they had experienced during the interval continued and both of them seemed to be enjoying the other's company.

"So where did you live before you came to Maesteg Nellie?"

Nellie explained to him a little of her life, not in any great detail, just some of the basics. She told him that her mother had died at her birth and of her father's death in the mining accident a few years later.

"So who looked after you then?" Johnnie enquired.

"My elder sister Rose did for a while, but when we were evicted from the house my Uncle Henry and Aunt Grace took the youngest amongst us in. It's actually Cynthia their daughter who I am lodging with now."

Johnnie reciprocated with information about himself. He had always lived in Maesteg and had desperately wished to join the forces, as much to see some of the world as to fight for his country. Due to health reasons his application had been refused, which is how he came to be working in the munitions factory. His father and apparently his grandfather before him owned a butcher's shop. Nellie jumped on this point in common and with a degree of pride told him that her sister Rose and her husband Alfie, since Mr. Jones' death, also owned a butcher's shop.

Nellie was a little disheartened to find that even though they had been walking slowly, they had now turned into the street where she lived. She would have liked the walk home to have lasted longer; even the icy night temperature was not able to deter her happiness. The nearer they got to number ninety-two, she was saddened to think that soon Johnnie would be taking his arm from her shoulder and no doubt that would be the end of it. How on earth would she face him at the factory the next time their paths crossed?

Nellie's worries were uncalled for. On reaching her doorway, Johnnie turned her around to face him.

"Nellie" he softly said to her. "I've really enjoyed talking to you tonight, but playing with the band didn't really give us a lot of time together, did it?"

She couldn't believe that she had heard him right and felt that her face must have given away what she thought. Before she could answer she felt the desire to swallow hard.

"Yes, it's been really nice and thank you so much for walking me home."

Nellie had hardly got the words out of her mouth when Johnnie gripped her firmly and pulled her towards him. In an instant his lips were upon hers. So taken aback was she that she thought her legs were going to buckle underneath her. The butterflies in her stomach went into a state of overdrive, enough to make her feel quite queasy with pleasure.

Their embrace finally came to an end and still holding her Johnnie asked if she would like to go to the pictures with him on Tuesday.

"That's a date then" he advised, gave Nellie another quick peck on the cheek and sauntered off up the road.

The next morning Nellie lay in her bed going over the happenings of the previous night and still couldn't quite believe the events that had occurred. In reality she should have still been tired, as it wasn't until about four in the morning that she had managed to stop her mind racing and sleep had finally come to her. She knew that Cynthia was quite behind with the ironing that she took in and Nellie had every intention that morning to help her out with it, but for now all she wanted to do was lie in her bed and cosily reminisce and enjoy her new found status.

'Johnnie Bevan's girlfriend' she proudly thought to herself. 'What will everyone say at the factory when word gets out?'

Suddenly a dark thought came to her, her insecurity striking again.

'What if I've got it all wrong? Maybe it was just a dare to see if I would let him kiss me.'

She could feel her heart start to hammer and upset moving up through her chest, forming a lump in her throat.

'No, don't be silly' she chastised herself 'Johnnie wouldn't do that; he isn't that sort of person and anyway if that was the case he wouldn't be taking me to the pictures on Tuesday'

Nellie looked at her alarm clock and thought that she really must get up. She raised her head off the pillow and rolled over onto her elbow to ease herself out of bed. Downstairs she could once again hear Jack's raised voice, no doubt having another go at poor Cynthia over some demeanour in his view. Hearing the commotion below, she thought it best to stay where she was for a while longer, until the arguing subsided. Quarter of an hour or so later, all seemed quiet so Nellie got herself washed and dressed and went down the stairs. Jack was sat on the rocking chair, his body leaning forward hunched over the fire.

"Hope you've got some warm clothes on girl" he snapped, rubbing his hands together over the barely visible flames. "There's no coal in the house, she's spent all the money" he snarled pointing at the kitchen door, where poor Cynthia was washing up the dishes. "Don't know what on earth she spends it on" he continued "it's not as if she even puts a good meal on the table for me. That's my boots I'm having to burn on there, an old pair they may be, but I shouldn't have to burn them for a bit of warmth now should I? Well as soon as that hand comes around to eleven" he said looking at the clock "I'm off down the pub; it'll be a lot warmer down there I'm sure."

Nellie didn't answer him. She didn't think he was worth spending her breath on. Instead she walked out to the kitchen and gave Cynthia, her cousin an understanding hug.

"Show me what needs ironing Cynthia and I'll do it for you."

"There's no need for you to do that Nellie, especially on your day off."

"I don't mind at all" she replied and when her eyes settled on a bundle of clothes dumped on a nearby chair she walked towards them and picked them up. "Is this them?"

Cynthia and Nellie continued their chores in silence, conscious of Jack sat in the preceding room. As the clock struck eleven o'clock, without a heed of a goodbye to either one of them they heard the front door slam.

"Thank God for that" said Cynthia and let out a loud sigh of relief.

"I don't know how you put up with him, I really don't" sympathised Nellie. "He's just so rude to you. You'd be better off without him."

"Don't think I haven't thought of that" admitted Cynthia, "but I've no money and where would I go? To be honest though I don't think I could ever leave him; there's a part of me in here" she said touching her heart "that still loves him."

"You're a saint Cynthia, do you know that? Either that or a fool."

"Anyway let's forget about him, I want to hear all about last night. Did you have a nice time? You looked a real picture when you left here. Let's put the kettle on and have a cuppa and you can tell me all about it."

They sat at the kitchen table together and Nellie related the whole tale; how good a singer Johnnie was, how he had made her sit on his knee and how he had walked her home.

"And will you be seeing this Johnnie again?"

"Yes" Nellie grinned not being able to contain her excitement. "He's asked me to go to the pictures with him on Tuesday."

"I just knew it" said Cynthia, "I just knew it. Even having to put up with Jack and his grumpy mood, your face was still glowing this morning. I just knew something good had happened."

A couple of weeks had past since the dance at The Nag's Head and Nellie and Johnnie were still seeing each other. Now that she was recognised as Johnnie's girl, Nellie felt like a different person. For the first time in her life she felt special, she felt accepted and most of all she felt loved. She was so content with her life and just hoped that this bubble that encapsulated her would never burst.

Nellie and Elsie still worked side by side on the conveyor belt at the factory, but for some reason that Nellie could not quite put her finger on; their friendship of late did not seem so easygoing. Nellie had first noticed a strain in their relationship on the Monday following the dance when Johnnie had walked her home. She felt somewhat elated going into work that morning, as both she and Elsie, so she thought, would have so much to talk about; for her Johnnie and for Elsie, Reg. Unusually for Elsie, who normally could not wait to relate any goings on in her life, more often or not in more detail than Nellie wished to know, that particular morning Nellie had to prise the details from her friend and she had hardly mentioned her and Johnnie. Nellie had felt quite disillusioned, as she considered Elsie to be her best friend and had thought that she would have shown more interest.

Nellie spied Johnnie in his role of supervisor, walking up the factory line on his afternoon inspection round. In the beginning when they had first started dating, when he arrived at Nellie's station, he would stop and rest his hands on her shoulder as he checked her work. Lately though he had stopped showing this level of familiarity towards her, at least while at work. Nellie suspected it was because he was acting in a professional manner, which secretly she couldn't help admire and made her even more proud to be known as his girlfriend. As he neared Nellie, he gave a cursory glance over her shoulder and just added "Fine" as he stepped across to Elsie.

"Not sure if I'm doing this right Johnnie? What do you think?" Elsie asked smiling coyly up at him.

"Can't be good at everything I suppose" Johnnie responded with an emphasis on the word everything, which incidentally did not go unnoticed by Nellie. Johnnie then bent down and whispered something into Elsie's ear and a private joke was shared between the two of them.

Nellie could not concentrate on her work, which without her realising had come to a halt, causing a small pile of components to build up in front of her. She glared at Johnnie and Elsie trying hard to listen to their muted conversation and asked herself if she was just being over reactive, or whether she had good reason to be. Johnnie stood upright and patted Elsie's shoulder before taking his leave to continue on his inspection further up the line.

"What was all that about?"

"What was what about?" retorted Elsie.

"You know exactly what I mean. Looking at Johnnie as if butter wouldn't melt in your mouth. What would Reg say if he could see you flirting like that and more to the point you know that Johnnie's going out with me?"

"All's fair in love and war. Haven't you heard that expression?"

With that Elsie turned up her chin and faced the other direction. Both of the girls finished their shift in silence and Nellie for one was glad when the claxon sounded to announce the end of the day.

Normally Nellie and Elsie would pack up their things, collect their coats and walk off together to catch the bus back home. Today though, no sooner had they stopped work was Elsie on her feet and gone. 'She can please herself' Nellie thought, but inside felt quite hurt by her friend's earlier behaviour and the fact that they she had chosen to ignore her.

Nellie trailing behind the other workers slowly made her way to the cloakroom. She took her new grey coat off of the peg. It was very stylish and had cost Nellie quite a few coupons, but she had been struck by the nipped in waist and thought it worth the extravagance. She knew by rights that it was far too good for work and really she ought to keep it for best, but since going out with Johnnie she had been very watchful over her appearance and wanted to look her best at all times. Doing up the buttons of her coat, she noticed that Elsie's jacket was still on the peg next to hers. Having left so quickly, Nellie had assumed that Elsie would be at the front of the bus queue by now. She raised her hand to the coat to take it down from the peg and then thought better of it. 'No why should I bother?' she decided withdrawing her hand from her friend's coat. 'If she doesn't want to talk to me, she can come back and get it herself.'

Reaching the bus queue, Nellie looked for Elsie still wondering if she shouldn't remind her that she had forgotten her coat, but couldn't see her anywhere. Usually the factory bus was waiting for them as they came out, but for some reason today it hadn't yet arrived. As it turned out, this was a good thing as suddenly Nellie realised that she had left her sandwich tin at her work station and rushed back inside to retrieve it.

Walking back through the factory she noticed Johnnie's office door was ajar and thought she would just pop her head around it and say Cheerio. Nellie couldn't hear any voices so guessed he was in there alone. She pushed the door open and stepped through and immediately saw Johnnie standing by the metal filing cabinet, his back facing her. However, he was definitely not alone, but in a tight and apparently passionate embrace with somebody. From the angle where she stood, Nellie could not recognise the person and for a second or two even questioned if it was Johnnie. Although she didn't want to believe what her eyes were telling her, reason told her that the strong, wide shoulders and the recognisable way the dark hair curled around the ears, that it was her Johnnie. At first Nellie was speechless but then in a small voice she managed to question in a whisper.
   "Johnnie?"
The man in front of her shot around and her worst fears were confirmed. It was indeed Johnnie and now she had a good view also of the woman her boyfriend had been kissing.

"Johnnie!" she screamed, "How could you? And as for you Elsie, well you're nothing more than a trollop. Do you hear me? A good for nothing trollop?"

Nellie could feel the tears welling up inside of her and her mouth start to tremble. There was no way her pride would allow these two to see her cry and so before she had said everything she would have liked to have said to the two traitors she made her escape.

'They're just not worth it' she thought to herself. 'They're welcome to each other,' but if she was honest with herself, she would have known that was not how she truly felt.

By the time Nellie reached Cynthia and Jack's house, whether through anger or upset over the deceit of her boyfriend and best friend, she wasn't sure which, she just wanted to throw herself down on her bed and have a good cry. Opening the front door of number ninety-two, she could tell immediately that she was walking into yet another argument between Jack and his wife. As she turned from the hall into the middle room, she could see Jack shaking Cynthia roughly and Cynthia trying her utmost to push him away, but her strength was no match for his. Nellie for the time being forgot her own upset, although probably it was her growing anger that made her take her next action. She strode across to where Jack was so cruelly bullying Cynthia and with unprecedented strength heaved the bulk of Jack's body away from the weeping Cynthia. Jack swirled himself around.

"And you can leave well alone Nellie. This is none of your business."

Nellie was consumed with anger and hatred towards this man. She was thankful that he had given her lodgings, but as she rightly guessed, it was not done out of charity on his behalf, more likely because he would have a bit more money to spend on his gambling and drinking habits. Unable to stop herself, Nellie lashed out some home truths of her own to Jack, concerning his lazy ways and his abusive treatment towards his wife. Jack's temper neither had diminished and as he heaved himself away from Nellie's grasp, he lifted his arm and landed a punch on the left side of Nellie's face. The force from the punch was so fierce that Nellie stumbled backwards, knocking over a wooden chair as she fell to the ground. Jack never wasted any time to see if she was hurt, just did as he always did, grabbed his jacket and went off in search of a pint.

The next morning as she woke, Nellie put her hand to her face where Jack had landed his punch. It felt so sore and she could feel that it was swollen. Her eye too she knew had taken some of the impact and she could tell that it was partly closed. She eased herself out of bed and picked up the small hand mirror by the wash stand. Viewing her reflection, indeed she looked a sight. Her one saving grace was that today being Saturday she wasn't due to work at the factory. She would have hated for Johnnie to see her looking like this and then she remembered the other awful part of the day before.

Thankfully she found Cynthia alone in the kitchen; Jack had already left the house. Cynthia on hearing her enter looked up from her ironing.
"Oh! Look at you, you poor thing. Does it hurt?"
"I must admit I have had better days" answered Nellie feeling the teapot to see if it was still warm.
"You should have left him Nellie, not interfered. You know what he's like, especially after a few drinks."
"That's no excuse Cynthia and well you know it. He can't go on treating you like he does and he's certainly not going to start on me."
"He doesn't mean to do it"
"Make excuses for him if you like, but I'm not going to. Look at my face. As soon as I've finished this cup of tea, I'm off to the police station to report him for assault."

Later that day a policeman arrived to question Jack. Cynthia sat quietly at the table, frightened as to what would happen to Jack if he was prosecuted and frightened as to what he might do to her if he wasn't. The policeman could tell that Nellie was telling the truth and it was quite obvious from her injuries that she had been the target of someone's anger. Many a time in his line of business had he been in contact with men who thought nothing of venting their anger and strength on women and children and in his mind Jack didn't seem the slightest bit different to any of them.

Turning to Nellie the policeman asked, "Well it's up to you Miss, do you want to press charges? I think there's a strong case against Mr. Mason here, but unless you want to proceed my hands are tied."
Nellie's face was still very sore and the bruising had since come out on her eye making it quite black. She definitely wanted to see Jack charged;

someone had to stand up to the bully and it wasn't likely to be Cynthia, so she thought it was her place to do it. She glanced at Cynthia, who by now was softly weeping and wiping away the tears with what had once been a white handkerchief, but now had tendencies of grey. In Nellie's mind Cynthia would be far better off without Jack Mason, but in reality was that really her choice to make. Her mind went back to a previous conversation that she had had with her cousin, to a time when Cynthia had told her that even with everything considered, a small part of her heart still loved Jack. Nellie questioned herself 'Was she really able to take that away and more so did she really have the right?'

"No officer, I'm sorry to have wasted your time. I've changed my mind. I won't be pressing charges"

The policeman left. The atmosphere was so heavy it could be cut with a knife. Not a word was uttered by Jack, Cynthia or Nellie. Eventually Jack looked at Nellie and the silence was broken.

"I think it'll be best for all of us if you pack your bags and leave."

Nellie looked across to Cynthia, who raised herself out of the chair and walked across the room to stand alongside her husband.

"Yes I think its best Nellie."

Nellie found herself a room with a family a couple of streets over. Her relationship with Elsie never recovered, made worse by the fact that Elsie dumped Johnnie after only going out with him a few times; certainly not more than three. When Nellie found this out she was livid. It was not only because she felt deceived by the pair of them but in addition, she felt that Elsie had taken Johnnie away from her, not because she had liked him, but more to make a point that she could have any man she wanted.

Life at the factory was just not the same without Elsie's friendship. Nowadays it was all work and no play. Neither did Nellie enjoy living in rooms, much as her room was clean and the family she lived with pleasant, it was not half the same as living with family and she missed Cynthia's company. Nellie was far from happy and she felt yet again it was time to move on.

Chapter 12
The Cotswolds – 2006

Nellie shuddered. The last of the afternoon sun had gone behind a cloud and with the slight breeze that was building up, the temperature had suddenly dropped. One of Nellie's used and screwed up tissues escaped from the side of the seat of her wheelchair, where she had irresponsibly stuffed it out of sight earlier. Landing on the ground the breeze caught it and with a combination of bouncing and floating it finally came to rest against the leg of a nearby bench. Alison not one to be able to stand litter or graffiti for that matter marring the countryside, quickly walked over to the offending article and placed it in the litter bin.

"There you are" admonished Jane the carer. "So you've been sat out here enjoying the sunshine have you? I've been looking everywhere for you Nellie."

"Yes I have" said Nellie. "It's gone a bit chilly now though. This is my daughter Alison. Have you met her?"

Jane knowingly smiled at Alison.

"Course I have Nellie, Alison's always here visiting you. You're very lucky you know to have such a good daughter. Come on; let's lift your feet up here onto the supports. That's right; don't want you banging your knees on the doors as I wheel you through do we?"

Jane wheeled Nellie through the main doors of the residential home.

"Now Nellie, let's just go to the toilet and check your catheter bag, before I take you through to join the others in the dining room."

Alison stayed behind in the reception area, while Jane took care of her mother's needs. Alison knew that she had made the right choice in sending her mother to Fir Trees Residential Home. Reading the notice board, she was amazed at just how many activities were arranged for the residents; bingo, keep fit, singsongs, quizzes and from time to time excursions to the local theatre or places of interest. At Christmas time, the local church choir always came in to give a carol concert and other entertainers were also very generous with their time and would sometimes put on a small show.

Alison glanced at her watch and was surprised to see that it was already half-past five, so engrossed had she been in her mother's story that she had not kept track of the time. Taking advantage of Nellie being in Jane's care for a few moments, she took the opportunity to ring Graham.

"Hello. It's me."

"I was just thinking of you. Are you on your way home?"

"'No sorry I'm not, that's why I'm ringing. I think I might be quite a while yet. Mum's just about to have her tea, but I can't leave her just yet she's insistent on telling me this secret. It's really strange you know, at times her memory seems quite vivid and I don't want to leave her half way through, as come tomorrow more than likely she will have forgotten again whatever it was that she was trying to tell me."

"I wonder what it can be. Strange she's never mentioned it before."

"Yes that's what I was thinking. Some things she has told me are quite fascinating; I just hope I can remember it all when I get home so that I can tell you. I shouldn't be too much longer, but you go ahead and have your dinner, don't wait for me."

"No I'll hang on Alison, it's not a problem, but what about you? You must be starving?"

"Actually to be honest, I had some lunch here, so I'm fine, but you have yours."

"No it wouldn't be the same eating on my own. I'd rather wait for you and besides I've drawn a heart and written "I love you" in the mash potato and if I take a helping out you won't be able to see it."

"Oh! Graham. You're such a softie, I do love you."

Alison looked up and could see Jane manoeuvring her mother's wheelchair out from the toilets.

"Best go, Mum's just coming back. I'll try not to be too late. Love you."

"Love you too" said Graham.

On seeing her mother exit the toilets, it dawned on Alison that she too could do with using the facilities.

"I'll just spend a penny myself Mum and I'll be with you" Alison whispered in her mother's ear.

"I'll wheel Nellie back into the day room to wait for you then Alison and then you can go through to the dining room together."

Opening the door to the toilet, Alison was faced with a raised up toilet seat, with support railings and other paraphernalia around, no doubt all very necessary for getting the elderly residents on and off the toilet. Alison checked the second cubicle hoping that she would find a normal toilet inside, but she found there also the same bespoke contraption as had been in the first one. If Nellie had an en-suite in her room, she could have used that, but unfortunately at the time she had booked Nellie in to Fir Trees, no such rooms had been available, at least not on the ground floor. There had been a vacant en-suite room on the first floor, but with Nellie's fear of lifts and not being able to contemplate the stairs, it wasn't really an option. If it wasn't for the fact that Fir Trees had come with such high recommendation, Alison might have looked elsewhere to place her Mother, but considering that toilet facilities were just outside Nellie's room she had settled for FirTrees.

Returning to the day room, Alison found Nellie once again getting herself in a state.

"Oh! There you are" said Nellie with a sigh of relief. "I thought you'd gone home without saying goodbye and I haven't told you everything yet have I? I've still got my secret to tell you. I have to tell you Alison, it's important that you hear what I have to say. It will explain a lot of things to you and I'm hoping that when you hear it, you will understand a little of why I've behaved the way I have and somehow find it in your heart to forgive me."

Nellie started to sob again and fumbled around in the seat of her wheelchair looking once more for the tissue that had earlier worked itself free and blown away.

"Here you are Mum, have mine" Alison said handing over a clean tissue that she had found in her pocket. "Come on there's no need for tears, wipe them away and blow your nose."

At that moment Jane reappeared to escort Nellie through to join the other residents in the dining room waiting for their tea to be served.

"Let's be having you then Nellie, time for tea."

"I don't want any" sniffed Nellie, "I want to stay with my daughter"

"Alison can come with you love, I'm sure she could do with a cup of tea."

"No, No" replied Nellie agitatedly. "I want to talk to my daughter in private. It's important. I want to go to my room. Please take me to my room Alison."

Alison looked at Jane.

"Is that alright if I take Mum to her room?"

"Yes of course it is. I'll tell you what I'll do. I'll bring a plate of sandwiches up to you Nellie and some tea. What about you Alison, would you like a sandwich as well?"

"Not for me thanks" Alison answered remembering that Graham had a shepherd's pie waiting for her at home, "but I wouldn't say no to a cup of tea."

"Has she gone?" whispered Nellie referring to Jane once she was back in her room. "I don't want any prying ears listening."

"No there's nobody here, just you and me."

"Good. Now where was I again? Oh! I do wish my memory was better, I keep forgetting things."

"Well you've being doing very well up until now telling your story Mum" encouraged Alison. "You'd got to the bit where you'd just discovered Johnnie with Elsie at the munitions factory."

"Yes that was awful. I was upset. You can't trust men you know. There only after one thing and if you don't give it to them, they're soon off looking elsewhere for it. As for her, I don't know why I was friends with her in the first place; man mad she was."

"I must admit it couldn't have been very nice for you to find them together like that and you were obviously very fond of Johnnie" agreed Alison.

"Well that's all history now as they say. Did I tell you about Cynthia's husband giving me a black eye?"

"Yes that's as far as you got. The police came and in the end because of Cynthia you decided not to press charges. After that Cynthia and Jack told you to leave and you found lodgings a couple of streets away."

Nellie sat motionless with her hand on her chin, as she tried to recollect the events of her life well over fifty years before.

"Mmm! It was such a shame really. For a short while life seemed to be really good. Well probably not good in a lot of people's eyes, but it was good for me. I had a boyfriend, a good friend in Elsie or so I thought and a job I enjoyed, but that's life I suppose all good things come to an end."

"So what happened after that?"

"Well! Let's see. What happened after that? Yes I remember, it was 1946."

Chapter 13
Tripoli – 1946

Nellie arched her shoulders back and tilted her head upwards to take in the warm rays of the sun on her face, as she perched herself on a wooden crate and waited. Her uniform was a bit on the thick side for the current climate and she felt that she could well do with taking her jacket off, but knowing that very soon; along with the other members of her group she would be called to board the plane, thought best to keep it on. Nellie also assumed, more than likely correctly that she might be reprimanded if she wasn't in full uniform at the time of boarding.

Gazing across the runway Nellie became mesmerised by the row of palm trees near the boundary fence of the aerodrome. She watched their lush, green fronds gently swaying, slightly distorting her view of the crystal, blue sea behind. Her thoughts took her back to Penbryn Farm where she had lived as a child with her Uncle Henry and Aunt Grace. She remembered the letter that they had all been so excited to receive form Idris her brother, who had been serving at the time in India. She recalled his description of some funny trees with large fans, so unlike anything that he had ever before seen in Wales. Nellie realised now as she sat waiting to board the plane that would take her from Cairo to Tripoli that these trees were the same as her brother had written about all those years before.

Nellie thought back to her days in the munitions factory in Bridgend, had it really been only just three months ago, such a short period of time considering. She couldn't believe how much her life had changed and for the better at that. It wasn't only her life that had changed for the better; with the ending of World War 11 the previous September most peoples' lives had taken a turn for the better.

After the Johnnie and Elsie incident, Nellie had made up her mind that she was going to move on and look for other employment. One Saturday afternoon in October, as was her normal routine to escape the solitude provided by the four walls of the room where she boarded, Nellie was traipsing around the shops in Maesteg, mostly window shopping. She passed by the Forces Recruitment Office and her eyes caught a large poster on a white, yellow and blue background in the window. Nellie stopped and looked closer and saw a girl in a smart uniform with a peaked cap shaking hands with a smiling soldier. The poster was an advertisement for the ATS/EFI (Auxiliary Territorial Service – Expeditionary Forces Institute) and it was asking for N.A.A.F.I. (Navy Army Air Force Institute) girls to work abroad. Immediately Nellie's interest arose and she thought that this could be just what she was looking for, so read on. The age requirement was between twenty and forty-three, so at twenty-six she was within the limit. The vacancies were for canteen staff, drivers, shorthand typists, clerks and ledger clerks. Nellie didn't have any skills to talk about in clerical work and neither could she drive, although no doubt training would be offered. There was no reason though why she couldn't work in a canteen, as she could pour a cup of tea as good as the next person and surely her past experience in the hotels would be to her advantage. A red band at the bottom ran across the width of the poster saying 'Ask at the Counter for N.A.A.F.I. Overseas Pamphlet'. Without further hesitation Nellie opened the door and walked through, a decision that was to change her life.

Nellie was over the moon when she received notification that she had passed her medical and had been accepted to join the ATS/EFI. Kitted out in her uniform Nellie felt special and very proud to be referred to as Private Edwards. She completed her training course in Shropshire and then travelled by train to Liverpool where she met up with the ship that was to take her to Cairo, her very first posting.

Nellie had loved the voyage by sea and unlike her brother Idris' accounts of a similar journey, was not in the least bit sea-sick, although some unfortunate fellow travellers were not so lucky. She had been amazed to see the dolphins playing around the bows of the ship and the flying fish leaping out of the water, a sight she would never forget.

On the passage over the ship sailed past the rock of Gibraltar on its way through the Mediterranean Sea towards Malta, where it briefly docked giving Nellie the chance to get a brief glimpse of the city. She thought the Grand Harbour in Valetta was the most impressive sight that she had ever seen and the pretty, little white houses that dotted the coastline a far cry from the dismal, dust covered terraced houses that she had left behind in Wales.

"Private Edwards stand in line."

Suddenly brought to her senses by the sergeant standing at the top of the by now already formed queue of girls waiting to board the plane, Nellie immediately leapt to her feet, grabbed her army issue holdall and made her way over to join them.

Time had gone very quickly since her arrival in Cairo just a few weeks earlier. Her time there had been brief. A short posting of six weeks working in the canteen of a transit camp and getting used to a life abroad. It was really a bit of an induction course after her initial training, but now this morning she was about to leave to take up her permanent position at The Marina Barracks in Tripoli.

Nellie had never flown before and it was with some degree of trepidation that she followed the line of girls into the hold of the Lancaster Bomber, where during wartime the bombs had been housed. There were a few benches placed inside that had already been taken up by the first section of girls to enter the plane, Nellie had no alternative, but to make herself as comfortable as possible on the cold floor of the plane. The huge door at the rear was finally closed and the engines were switched on. The great plane, to begin with slowly started to roll along the runway gradually getting faster. As its speed increased a loud rumbling distinguished any chance of talking amongst the girls and everything around started to shake. Sitting on the floor Nellie could feel the vibration transcend through her body; her mouth felt dry with anxiety and she swallowed hard as the huge bird lifted its front wheel off of the tarmac and made its journey upwards into the blue sky. Nellie felt that if there had been a window that she could have peered out of, giving her some idea of height and distance, she would have felt slightly better, but as that was not an option, she just sat quietly thinking to herself that she would be glad when the flight was over. As the bomber reached a higher altitude the air thinned and the temperature in the hold became quite chilly. Unlike earlier when Nellie had felt quite warm sat in the sun, she was now quite relieved to feel the cosiness of her uniform around her. The Lancaster bomber started to descend and Nellie could sense the need for her ears to pop. She tried rubbing each ear in turn with her finger to relieve the pressure, but with no result. The plane finely hit the ground with quite a jolt causing Nellie to tip over onto her side. She was more than a trifle relieved when the motion of the plane slowed down and it eventually came to a standstill on the runway at Castel Benito Aerodrome in Tripoli. The huge rear doors were once again opened and Nellie being last on was first off; watching her step she walked down the ramp. She was glad to feel the sunshine again on her chilled skin and took a deep breath. The warm air that she inhaled through her nostrils was dry and made her feel quite stuffy.

Disembarking from the plane, the new arrivals congregated together awaiting further instruction. Nobody was more surprised than Nellie when a regimental band started to play. As they neared the main buildings, the girls were greeted by several dignitaries representing the forces stationed in Tripoli. The girls looked at each other in surprise and several of them started to giggle as the whole affair tickled their fancies, especially when cameras were pointed in their direction. They were asked to group together for a photograph and as per usual being one of the tallest, Nellie was asked to stand at the far end at the back, with another girl of similar stature at the opposite end.
'We must look like two book-ends' Nellie thought to herself.
When the band had struck their final chord, a tall man with a handlebar moustache and in full military regalia stepped away from the adjoining welcoming committee and introduced himself as Major Gilbert Walshawe. In his speech he announced the reason for all the excitement. Apparently the girls as they discovered, were the first British women to arrive in Tripoli and not only did their arrival make the local papers, but the papers back home as well.

An army lorry from the nearby Marina Barracks was waiting adjacent to the main buildings to transport them back to their base for the foreseeable future. Nellie threw her holdall up onto the lorry first and then hitching up her skirt clambered up into the back. Some of the other girls had been more sensible and had travelled in trousers.

The Marina Barracks were approximately a mile and a half away from the town and Nellie thought herself very lucky to be sharing a billet with Ethel from Derbyshire and Clarissa from Surrey. All three girls came from completely different backgrounds. Ethel was the daughter of a builder and spoke with a strong Derbyshire accent, while Clarissa's father was a doctor in Surrey and she spoke in Nellie's terms 'quite posh'. Despite any differences in their upbringings they all got on famously right from the word go.

Ethel, having previous knowledge of typing was allocated to the offices, Clarissa prior to joining up had worked on the buses as a driver, so she was given the role of chauffeuring the officers, while Nellie was set to work as a N.A.A.F.I. Counter Assistant.

The N.A.A..F.I. canteen where Nellie worked was at The Castle Club aptly named because it was based within the boundary walls of Tripoli's Red Castle (Assai-al Hamra). Nellie really enjoyed her work, in fact she thought it the best job she had ever had. It was a lively place to work with the soldiers popping in during breaks as well as off duty, for some char and a wad, slang for tea and a sandwich normally made up of fish or meat paste. As well as serving beverages and snacks, with pie, beans and chips being amongst the favourites, the canteen also supplied sundries that the servicemen needed, which were not supplied by the service such as razor blades, matches and cigarettes.

Life in the canteen offered so much hilarity and banter between the staff and the customers, a far cry from the lonely hours Nellie had spent by herself in the Land Army. The soldiers used to frequent the canteen, as much for a game of cards or darts as refreshments and Nellie soon earned herself a reputation of being quite a hot darts player, thanks to Mickey Dunn's tuition years before at The Crown in Trelawr. She wondered if the canteen had been so much fun during the war when imminent danger had been all around, but she gathered from soldiers that had been stationed there at the time, that in general unless their units had suffered a loss; it usually had been quite similar.

Another frequent visitor who came to the canteen on a daily basis was a medium size, beige mongrel dog with the most appealing chocolate brown eyes. Nobody knew who he belonged to, if indeed anyone. The staff of course could not resist his doleful looks and Whippy as this dog became known was well fed on scraps saved from the leftovers on plates. He had got his name partly because of his likeness to a Whippet and partly because of his long, thin tail, which when he became excited would lash out quite a whipping to the legs of whoever he was greeting at the time.

The summer months, particularly July and August could be quite stifling. Sleep was hard to come by with night temperatures hardly dropping below seventy-seven degrees Fahrenheit. The little breeze gained from opening a window had to be carefully balanced against the influx of preying mosquitoes. The canteen was no different and Nellie could feel her cleavage feeling quite moist with perspiration. The ceiling fan rotated around, but only for a second or two as the blades passed directly over her head did Nellie feel any benefit. She opened another window, knowing undoubtedly that it was an invitation for a further invasion of flies. The temptation of the cakes and sticky buns, although partly covered by a glass canopy under the counter were far too easy a target for them and Nellie constantly had to swot them with a rolled up newspaper. Usually on days like this, especially when on the day shift, as soon as work was over Nellie would go down to The Lido Beach and relax on the golden sands or paddle in the sea. Nellie had never learnt to swim, so going in up to her knees was her limit. Even if she went down to the Lido on her own, she knew that once there she would find friends who she could sit with. There was a large group of them, male and female alike, who all used to hang around together. Nellie nowadays wasn't the odd one out; she was one of the crowd and was extremely happy to be included.

Nellie moved from behind the counter to collect two empty cups and saucers from the table outside. Walking back through the canteen she noticed Whippy patiently waiting at the back door. When he saw her, he started to bark and wag his tail, so as there weren't any customers waiting, Nellie took the scraps that she had been saving outside for him. As usual Whippy was overjoyed to see her and quickly wolfed down the offerings he had been given.

"You could do with a drink of water, couldn't you my boy. Wait here and I'll fetch you some."

Nellie kept a couple of old tin bowls under the sink especially for the purpose of feeding and watering Whippy and she bent down and took one out. She filled it with water and just as she turned to take it back outside, she noticed a customer just coming through the door.

"Won't be a moment" she said with a nod, sure that the man wouldn't mind waiting.

"Right" she said on her return "What can I get you?"

"Two cornets please, vanilla."

Nellie took the man's money and rang up the amount in the till and returned with his change. She then took two cones from the tower on the counter and proceeded to the ice-cream dispenser and filled the two cones with creamy, whipped ice-cream.

"You've not given me enough" exclaimed the man looking at the loose change in his hand.

"No" replied Nellie "that's exactly right for the note you gave me."

"I know damn well it wasn't. You've short changed me."

"Look" said Nellie quite put out that he should doubt her, as she was always very careful when giving change "Whenever I'm given a note I always leave it on the till shelf until I've taken out the change, so as not to make that mistake."

The argument went on for several more minutes, the boiling temperatures not helping in any way to quell their rising tempers. Eventually an agreement was struck and Nellie handed over the two ice-cream cones. Imagine the man's surprise when he looked down to see two half eaten cones; Nellie absent-mindedly had been licking them as she argued.

Later on back at the billet, Nellie in fits of laughter related the story of the licked ice-creams to Ethel and Clarissa as they put their make up on in readiness to go out for the evening.

"Oh! My God" laughed Clarissa "what on earth did he say?"

"Well he couldn't say much could he? I'd eaten them. I did give him another two though free of charge."

"Nellie you are such a scream" said Ethel with tears rolling down her face. "You do make me laugh."

To Nellie this was one of the best compliments her friend Ethel could have paid her. She knew no malice was meant and didn't mind her friends laughing at her expense. She felt accepted.

The three friends with their glad rags on set off in the direction of the mess. Once a month, sometimes more, a dance was held, which was always considered a good do and one that Nellie, Ethel and Clarissa didn't like to miss. Usually the male species outnumbered the female specie by three to one, so they were never short of partners to dance with.

"Is there a band playing tonight" asked Clarissa "or is it just records?"

"I think there's a band tonight" answered Ethel. Somebody mentioned to me this morning that in September a big show is being put on and rumour has it that Bob Hope and Gracie Fields will be performing."

"Really, I hope I'm not on duty that night" said Clarissa and Nellie at the same time and all three girls laughed.

"Great minds think alike" said Ethel.

The mess was already in full swing by the time the three friends arrived. They saw the crowd that they usually met up with leaning against the bar, so made their way over to them, Clarissa and Ethel wiggling their hips in time to the music as they walked.

"Name your poison" shouted Archie a sandy haired soldier from Yorkshire.

"Is it your round then Archie? Mine's a martini please" said Clarissa.

"Small sherry for me please."

"What about you Taffy?"

Taffy had become Nellie's nick-name with a few of the soldiers, obviously arising from her welsh accent.

"A shandy for me thanks Archie."

The group stood around chatting, catching up on camp gossip and in general having a fun time. Nellie really enjoyed her life nowadays; to her it was what she had always dreamed for and relished every minute. She hadn't believed her luck on receiving her posting to find that it was to be abroad, to a place with lots of sun, sea and sand. Sometimes the heat could be a little hard to cope with, but Nellie would never have chosen to swop it for the rain and drizzle of Wales.

"Come On, let's dance" suggested Clarissa. "They're playing 'The Candy Man' my favourite."

"We'll come with you ladies" answered Fred and Charlie.

Ethel in agreement put her glass down on the bar.

"Are you coming Nellie?"

"You go on" said Nellie. "I'd rather stay here, you know I've got two left feet."

Nellie had never learnt to dance, not being able to master the co-ordination. She wasn't over concerned though with Clarissa and Ethel taking to the dance floor, as if truth be known she was happier staying at the bar with the men. It wasn't that she was a flirt; at least she didn't think she was, although other people might have considered her behaviour differently. Much as Nellie thought Clarissa and Ethel were great, in general she did prefer men's company to women's. Women always chattered on about fashion, boyfriends, latest songs, who was dating who, subjects she never really had any great interest in. Men on the other hand talked about more serious matters and Nellie would enjoy standing her corner in a good debate and equally insisted on buying her round of drinks. Being normally the only girl amongst them, she would regularly be the target for a bit of leg pulling, which she happily took in her stride. The present company of men were considered Nellie's friends and frequently she would meet up with them at the Lido beach. Nellie never felt the odd one out in their company. as they thought of her as one of them. She knew she had been accepted when no apologies were made for telling the odd risqué joke in front of her and not one of them was surprised when in return Nellie could relate an equally risqué one back, although often mixing up the punch line or forgetting it altogether.

"Well that's me finished for the day" said Jean, a pretty blonde girl from Lancashire, who worked with Nellie at the N.A.A.F.I. canteen. "Can't say I shall be sorry to get out of this uniform. Doesn't do much for a girl's esteem does it?"

"No you could be right there" agreed Nellie eyeing her colleague up and down.

It was true; the N.A.A.F.I. uniform was indeed not too flattering. The straight, royal blue cotton dress was quite shapeless and the belt at the back didn't help matters. The only significant effort to break up the plainness was the white piping that edged the short sleeves and the N.A.A.F.I. crest with the words 'Servientur Servietium' on the lapel.

Jean emerged from the toilet transformed in a pretty, pink floral dress.

"That's better, I feel a bit more human now. Didn't want to be seen walking through the town in that awful dress" she said referring to her uniform. "A girl just never knows who she may bump into."
Nellie admiringly looked at Jean's pretty dress and wondered where she had got it from. Nellie herself could do with a few new clothes, but western clothes were not to be found easily in Tripoli. Sometimes on her way back to her billet, she would wander through the Medina, the old

walled city, occasionally stopping to view the stalls in the bustling market place, but never had she spotted anything in the clothes line that she would wish to buy.

"Did you bring that dress with you Jean? Surely you didn't buy it here?"

"Well yes and no really. I bought the material in the market and there's an Italian lady I know who's very good with a needle. I drew a picture of what I wanted and she made it up for me."

"I would have never guessed it was home-made, said Nellie examining the garment more closely. She's made a really good job of it. Does she take in sewing for other people; do you think she would mind making something for me?"

"I'm sure she wouldn't mind. Signora Fabrini's always glad of a bit of extra money, being a widow with three small children to bring up. Here pass me that pen and paper and I'll draw you a map of where she lives. It's not far from here, just a bit further up than the fortress."

A couple of days later, Nellie was wasting a bit of time walking through the market and on one of the stalls she came across some white, cotton tea towels with a red check running through them.

"How much for three of these?", Nellie asked the vendor. "No, no too much"' she replied to his inflated price, but after a bit of bartering agreed to buy them for a lower price.

Recently at the Lido beach, Nellie had seen girls sporting shorts with matching bra tops rather than the normal swimsuit style. Nellie had liked this idea, as not only did they look smart and showed off the figure, but also the exposed midriff would be a lot cooler in the blazing temperatures. The tea towels in the cool, cotton material would be perfect she thought for Signora Fabrini to run a similar outfit up for her.

Later that evening with the package of material under one arm and Jean's rough map in the other, Nellie set off in search of the dressmaker's house. There was still quite a lot of heat in the sun, although it was not half as fierce as it had been earlier in the day. She'd saved a bit of time walking from her barracks to the town, as Archie had been passing in a jeep and had stopped to give her a lift. Making her way through the dry and dusty streets of the Medina, she gave a wide berth to a snake charmer playing an Arabian melody on his flute. As she came alongside the terracotta pot, temporary home of the large, reptile being, it rose up above the rim and turned its flat head from side to side. The snake's black beady eyes seemed to entrap Nellie in its stare and she shuddered and quickened her step.

Nellie had known her way to the fortress, but now that she was amidst its maze of courtyards and buildings, she stopped to look at Jean's map. Finding herself on the other side of the fortress, all she could see ahead of her was a barren track up through wasteland. Nellie studied the map again, not sure if she was on the right course.
'This must be right' she thought 'there's nothing else around.'
Her eyes followed the track and about quarter of a mile in the distance she could see a few odd buildings dotted around. Thinking that Signora Fabrini must live in one of them she set off in their direction. As Nellie neared the buildings she saw that there were three houses close together and two more further on. Looking again at her map for confirmation, she decided that the house she was looking for must be amongst the first three. Two of the houses were single storey, white washed buildings and the third, property was two storey and sand coloured. It was quite large in comparison to the other two, with arched windows top and bottom and a balcony running along the whole of the top. Similarly there was a veranda running across the full length of the ground floor. It appeared to Nellie that this was the place she was looking for.

As Nellie drew nearer, she could see quite a lot of activity going on at the house. A number of girls maybe eight or ten, all scantily dressed littered the balcony and veranda. Some of them had on bikinis decorated with hanging beads, others a little more covered, although only slightly with fine, gossamer over shirts. The sun, a large orange ball, was now setting over the horizon and the temperature had noticeably dropped, but with it still being a very warm evening, Nellie did not pay too much significance to their choice of attire. She could feel the girls' eyes watching her every move and she began to feel quite uncomfortable. One of the girls, thin with long, dark shiny hair held to the side with the red flower of a bougainvillea, straddled the white balustrade in front of the house. Sensing Nellie's footsteps behind her, she turned and without a smile, glared at the stranger in the camp.

Nervously Nellie asked "I'm looking for Signora Fabrini, she does dressmaking."

Without uttering a word, the girl inhaled on her cigarette and blew the smoke in Nellie's direction. With the cigarette still in her hand she pointed to a door at the far end of the building. With the same attitude, Nellie didn't speak either and just followed the direction of the girl's pointed finger.

Knocking on the door, Nellie was greeted by a small boy of about seven dressed in a white vest, which going by the stains on it looked like he had eaten spaghetti bolognese for his dinner, shorts and no shoes. Before she had time to ask if this was the right address for Signora Fabrini, a beckoning voice came from behind the young boy, telling her she supposed to enter.

Being Italian, Signora Fabrini did not speak any English, but having already thought that this might possibly be the case; Nellie had had the foresight to make a rough drawing of the shorts and bra outfit that she wanted and showed this to the dressmaker. Lack of a common language made conversation a little stinted between the two women, but with a display of hands they managed to get by.
"Signora Fabrini" the dressmaker said, tapping her index finger lightly on her chest. She then pointed the same finger at Nellie and putting two and two together Nellie guessed that she wanted to know her name.
"Nellie, my name is Nellie."
"Nilli" repeated Signora Fabrini in a heavy Italian accent. "Parla inglese?"
"Si' agreed Nellie, thinking it would be too much like hard work to try and explain that she actually came from Wales. Truth be known though, Nellie's welsh was very limited and English had always been her first language, so it was not necessary to confuse the issue.
Within no time at all, Signora Fabrini had measured Nellie up and noted down the measurements. She then held up three fingers to Nellie and Nellie got her drift that the garment would be ready in three days time. Moving towards the door Nellie practiced the few Italian words that she could remember.
"Grazie. Arrivederci."
"Arrivederci Miss. Nilli"

Outside again Nellie could once more feel the eyes of the girls lounging on the balcony and veranda burning into her. She found their hostility unnerving, but then thought that it must be her imagination, as after all why would they not like her, they didn't even know her? However the catcalls sounding in her wake did leave her in a state of growing apprehension.

Checking the time on her watch as she made her way back down the track, she noticed that it was ten minutes to nine. If she got a spurt on she might just meet up with Archie again on his way back through and be able to scrounge a lift back to camp. Rounding the corner by the church, Nellie was right and Archie bless him had parked up his jeep and was waiting for her.

"Thanks Archie, you're a real friend" Nellie told him as she clambered up into the jeep.

"I wasn't sure if I'd missed you or not, but I thought I would give it just a few minutes more and just as well I did. Did you find the place alright?"

Nellie told him that she had and also explained to him about the scantily dressed girls on the veranda.

"I thought it was a bit odd really for there to be just young girls hanging around. Usually you find people of all different ages living together or next door, children, parents, and grandparents even. I would have expected to have seen some old men sat out together having a smoke and a chat, but nothing just these young girls. They didn't seem too pleasant either and when I left they were jeering and whistling at me."

Nellie looked over to Archie who was laughing loudly.

"'Oh! Nellie you are so naive. I always say that you make me laugh" he said holding his side with one hand and using the other to steer.

"What's so funny?" asked Nellie innocently.

"Signora Fabrini must be Madam Louisa's widowed sister-in-law. I heard that she had taken her in when her husband was killed. Nellie where you've been for your dressmaking is the local brothel"

Nellie looked at Archie with such a shocked expression that he laughed even harder. Nellie though had moved on and wondered how on earth she would be able to face picking up her new swimwear in three days time and why on earth hadn't Jean warned her.

"Ready for the off then Nellie? Let's get this show on the road" said Billy.

Nellie had felt quite pleased with herself when a month earlier she had been put in charge of the mobile canteen visiting all the surrounding camps. Not being able to drive, Billy an elderly colleague in his late fifties accompanied Nellie on the rounds and drove the N.A.A.F.I. wagon. Despite their difference in ages Nellie and Billy enjoyed each others company and worked together well as a team.

It was not possible to offer such a great selection of snacks and accessories on the mobile canteen as in the canteen at the Castle Club. A major disappointment to the servicemen was that unlike the main canteen, beer was not sold. However, this didn't deter the volume of customers that always rushed up to the mobile canteen as soon as it parked up on the camp. At busy times like these Nellie was always grateful of Billy's assistance to help work through the waiting crowd quicker.

One morning at one of their regular camps, Nellie and Billy were just getting to a quieter period having worked their way through what had been a very long queue. Nellie had her back to the counter holding a cup under the spout of the large, tea urn when she heard a voice with a familiar welsh lilt cry out.
"Nellie Edwards. I just don't believe it. Is it really you?"
On hearing her name Nellie quickly turned around a little too fast, spilling some of the hot tea onto her hand.
"'Ouch!" she gasped, drawing her hand to her mouth and licking it. Looking in the direction of the voice, with likewise amazement she recognised her old friend from the munitions factory in Bridgend.
"Jill Braddock. What on earth are you doing here?"
"I could ask you the same question?"
"Well as you can see I'm in the N.A.A.F.I.. Billy here" she said pointing at her driver in an attempt of an introduction "and I drive this mobile canteen around the camps. I've been out here now let's see it must be a little over a year now. I joined up straight after leaving the factory actually. What about you?"
"Similar really. I stayed on at the factory a bit longer until it closed down and then I joined the WAAF. To begin with I was stationed at Fairford in Gloucestershire, but about six months ago I was posted out here. Not for much longer though. I'm going back to England next week. Got a posting to RAF Innsworth, which isn't far from where I used to be

in Fairford. Better make the most of this lovely sunshine for what little time I have left."

Nellie was trying to talk to her old friend and serve the customers at the same time, with neither getting her full concentration.

"Why don't you get yourself a cup of tea Nellie and grab that bench over there. You obviously haven't seen your friend for sometime and I'm sure you've got lots to catch up on. I'll be fine here, the queue's died down now and if I get busy I'll just give you a shout."

"Are you sure Billy?" asked Nellie.

"Of course I'm sure, now take this" he instructed handing Nellie a cup of tea and get yourself over there before I change my mind."

"Thanks" said Jill smiling up at Billy, who acknowledged her with a wink.

The two girls chatted non-stop for the next fifteen minutes and could very well have continued for the rest of the day had they not been approached by an airman from the United States Air Force.

"So this is where you're hanging out is it Jill?" the airman enquired in a mesmerising drawl.

"Hi Chad. Gosh is that the time" panicked Jill looking at her watch. "Sorry Nellie, but I really have to get back otherwise the sergeant will have my guts for garters. It's been great seeing you though; maybe we'll catch up again before I go back."

A clearing of a throat interrupted Jill's flow of talk.

"Aren't you gonna introduce me to this lovely lady before you dash off?"

"Sorry Chad. This is Nellie, Nellie Edwards an old friend of mine from Wales. Nellie, Chad Munroe the biggest flirt on the camp" teased Jill looking at Nellie.

"Pleased to meet you" nodded Nellie.

"Oh! Believe me the pleasure is all mine."

"Well now that you've met my friend Nellie Chad, I expect you to look out for her when I'm gone."

"At your service Ma'am" Chad replied with a mock salute to Nellie. "Your wish is my command. Can I start off as I mean to go on and buy you another cup of what is it you English drink? Tea?"

"Welsh" Jill and Nellie corrected him simultaneously.

"Welsh? Oh yeah! Wales. I remember that tiny country on the bottom, left hand side of England."

"Thanks for the offer, but I really must get back to work myself as well" answered Nellie gently pointing to the canteen wagon. "It's time we moved on to our next camp, but maybe I'll catch up with you again sometime."

"I sure hope so Ma'am, I sure hope so."

Visiting the camp the following week, Nellie looked out for Jill in the hope that they would have another chance to grab a cup of tea and a natter, but she never saw her so assumed that she had been posted back to England. She never met up with Chad again either. Whenever she heard an American voice she would search out the face in case it was him, but it never was. Nellie wondered if he was still around or whether he had also been posted somewhere else, but not knowing him that well did not like to ask.

.

"Anything you can do, I can do better lala lah lala lah lala la la. Weren't those singers good last night? Do you know if I'd been blindfolded I would have thought that I was listening to the Andrews Sisters?" said Dorothy as she washed up crockery in the canteen.

"Yes I thought they were excellent" agreed Nellie. "I thought the comedian was good too. Often they tell the same old jokes, but he had me in stitches. Does you good to have a laugh now and again doesn't it?"

The canteen staff were in high spirits that morning, having enjoyed such a splendid time at the camp concert the previous night. Dorothy started again to sing the wartime hit, while Nellie with her colleagues Ada and Diana acted as backing singers behind her, shaking their tea towels in unison. Finishing their rendition of the popular wartime song, they turned and got on with the work that they were supposed to be doing. Billy not wanting to miss his moment of fun, grabbed the broom from the wall by the back door and pretending it was the love of his life, serenaded it with Bing Crosby's hit 'Moonlight Becomes You.' He held the broom stick lovingly and caressed it from top to bottom, even planting a passionate kiss on its course bristles. The girls couldn't stand up; they were doubled over laughing at Billy's antics. The door of the canteen opened and in walked Archie.

"What are you lot up to?" he asked with a big grin across his face. "I could hear all the commotion outside. Talk about coming here for a bit of peace and quiet on your break."

"'Sorry Archie' ' apologised Dorothy. "My fault really. We got a bit carried away after the show last night. Fancied ourselves on the stage and the like."

"Why don't you do it then? To be honest, I didn't think you were half bad. I've certainly seen a lot worse."

"Thanks" said Ada. "Was that meant to be a compliment?"

Walking to the counter for a refill Archie replied "No honestly, think about it. They're always on the look out for concert parties to go around the camps. I'm sure if you asked around there would be a few other budding starlets on camp who would jump at the idea as well."

The four girls and Billy looked at each other, mulling over the idea that they themselves would never have thought of.

"Why not" said Billy. "What we got to lose and it could be a bit of fun?"

"We'd be doing our bit for the troops really wouldn't we?" agreed Diana. "After all we've still got to keep everyone's spirits up. Even though the war's over, everyone's still far away from home."

"Oh! I don't know if I could get up on a stage and sing in front of an audience. It's one thing doing it here with no one watching, but that would be a completely different story."

"You'd be fine Nellie. I say we give it a go" said Dorothy enthusiastically.

"Me too" said Ada. I'll ask around to see if I can drum up a few more to join us.

"I'm still not sure. We'll have to practise somewhere" Nellie reluctantly agreed.

"There's room out the back in the store room, I'm sure we could use that" suggested Billy.

"We'll have to think of a name for ourselves" Dorothy excitedly proposed.

Archie dragged his refilled cup of tea standing on the counter towards him. Feeling peckish, he eyed the selection of cakes underneath and made his decision.

"Give me one of those as well please Nellie."

"One of these?" questioned Nellie with cake slice poised in front of a large, cream slice.

"No" answered Archie. "Looks a bit too fattening for me, a macaroon please."

"That's it. That's what we'll call ourselves" decided Ada The Macaroons.

The Mad Macaroons would be more fitting for us daft lot I should think" laughed Billy loudly.

"That's it then" confirmed Archie holding himself first upright and then following on with a stupendous bow he announced in a loud voice, "Ladies and Gentleman, may I present to you The Mad Macaroons.

Chapter 14

At every available opportunity The Mad Macaroons practised in the store room behind the N.A.A.F.I. canteen. Nellie, Dorothy, Ada, Diana and Billy had now been joined by a further five equally enthusiastic, amateur performers, so now The Mad Macaroons concert party had grown in size to become a troop of ten. A lot of hard work and serious preparation had been put into planning their performance, as more than anything they wanted to put on a decent show. The routine consisted of a variety of acts from vocals to comedy, juggling and several comedy sketches. The girls had laughed so much at Billy's act with the broom that it became a definite choice to be kept in. To much disagreement at first by Nellie, the rest of the troop had voted for her to be the lead vocalist singing a few solo songs. Nellie's confidence had not been boosted at all, when in practice whilst attempting to hit the high notes Whippy could be heard howling profusely outside the store room door.

Just five weeks after their decision to form The Mad Macaroons, a date had been set for their first concert. It was to be held on Saturday evening in the mess at Marina Barracks. All too soon the evening was upon the excited, yet at the same time very nervous group of amateur performers. A makeshift stage had been erected at the far end of the mess and on the right a small area had been cordoned off with red curtains, to give the entertainers a designated space for putting on their makeup and storing their props. For modesty's sake all costume changes had to be done in the general toilets, so everyone hoped that there wasn't a mad rush by the audience to use them during the scene changes.

Nerves were paramount as the troop changed into their outfits for the opening scene, the atmosphere heavy with tension. Chairs could be heard scraping the floor as the audience arrived and settled down in anticipation of the evening ahead. Nellie noted the time five minutes to eight, just five more minutes before the start. Her hands felt quite clammy and she wiped them on the side of her dress. Her heart was racing and she was convinced that she would faint and collapse in a heap as soon as she walked out onto the stage. The bar manager interrupted Nellie's thoughts when he parted the red curtains and popped his head through.

"It's eight o'clock ladies and gentleman, are we ready to get this show on the road?"

Nellie looked at Ada, who likewise glanced at Dorothy, all of whom pulled a face and wished the floor would open up and swallow them, saving them from making fools of themselves.

"Yes, come on" encouraged Diana "we can't put all our hard work to waste now can we?"

Acting as compere for the evening the bar manager jumped up onto the stage and signalled for hush.

"Ladies and gentlemen please can I have your attention" he called across the audience and little by little the drone of the surrounding chatter ceased. "We are very lucky to have with us tonight" the compere continued "our very own concert party. All the artists you are about to see are stationed here on Marina Barracks. They are a newly formed group who in their spare time will be going out to perform for service people like ourselves in the neighbouring camps."

"Hope they're better than ENSA" (Entertainments National Service Association) heckled someone from the audience "You know what that stands for Every Night Something Awful."

"Tonight is their first, ever show, so give them a chance folks" insisted the compere. "Please put your hands together and give a warm welcome to The Mad Macaroons."

Nellie and the rest of the concert party emerged from the curtain and stepped up on to the stage amidst raucous applause.

"Actually I don't think that went too bad" admitted Billy as The Mad Macaroons with their debut performance over, gathered again behind the red curtain. The applause continued, interspersed with shrill whistles.

"Did it show when I forgot the words in 'White Cliffs of Dover?'" questioned Nellie. "I had to hum along until I got to a bit I remembered."

"I never noticed a thing" said Ada. "You were brilliant Nellie. What do you thing gang, our very own Vera Lynn?"

The others agreed making Nellie feel a lot better and they all hugged each other, happy with the knowledge that if the ongoing applause was anything to go by, their first show it seemed had been a great success.

"I could do with a drink after all of that, I'm quite parched" stated Billy. "Who says we don't make our way to the bar and toast our new found fame?"

"That sounds a good idea" said Dorothy. "Not too sure about the fame bit just yet though?"

Reaching the bar The Mad Macaroons were not able to buy themselves a drink, because everybody wanted to express their thanks and buy a drink for them. First night nerves well forgotten, Nellie and the other members of the concert party thoroughly enjoyed the recognition of their newly found success.

The Mad Macaroons soon became quite well known around the military camps in the vicinity and were thrilled to be invited to entertain at the United States Air Force base some ten miles away. It was general knowledge that the American base was far larger than any English base in the area and its facilities so say much grander.

The concert party keen not to allow their performances to become staid and repetitive, were forever learning new songs and acts to entertain their audiences. Nellie and the girls of the troop were practicing a new sketch about char ladies and were planning to act it out for the first time at the American base. The door of the store room opened and hidden by an enormous bundle of clothes, Diana bustled her way through.

"I've got the overalls. I reckon we'll have a good laugh when we try these on for size."

"You're just in time Diana, we were just about to start rehearsal for that sketch, so now we can make it a dress rehearsal" added Dorothy who had appointed herself head director of the char ladies' sketch.

Each girl was given a nylon overall that on most of them came down nearly as far as their ankles, but on Nellie a few inches shorter due to her height. The girls laughed at each other when they saw how funny they all looked.

"And don't think that's the end of it," said Diana "you've have to wear these as well" she added handed each girl an elasticised white mop cap.

The sketch was very amusing and the girls had a job to act it without creasing up with laughter themselves. Nellie being the lankiest amongst them was nominated to play the part of Agnes, the stooge who walked around in a daze, cigarette constantly hanging out of her mouth and who came out with the daftest comments at the most inopportune moments.

"Girls that is just so funny" chuckled Archie, who had sneaked in through the door and taken up role of spectator from the one and only chair in the corner of the store room. "That really is going to go down a bundle with the G.I.'s."

The concert party had been given permission to use one of the army vehicles to transport themselves and their props around the various camps where they were booked to perform. As the van approached the main gates of the American base, the sentry guard stepped outside his box, raised a white gloved hand and bid them to stop.

"Evening mate" said their driver. "I've got The Mad Macaroons here, they're entertaining you lot tonight."

The guard peered through the driver's, open door and touched the peak of his cap in salute to the passengers inside.

"Howdy, everyone's really looking forward to seeing the show tonight. Your reputation precedes you." Looking at the driver he added "Take the first on the right and then second on the left. Hanger number two is the one you want and you'll see it straight in front of you." Turning back again at the performers he said "Might just catch a bit of the show myself later, if I can get off duty in time."

The van pulled away from the main gates and the sentry stood back and saluted.

"Blimey, quite makes you feel like royalty doesn't it?" said Ada.

"And our reputation precedes us" mocked Billy in an American drawl. "What about that then?"

The concert party were met at the hanger and led through into the inside. The interior of the hanger was immense and half of it had been partitioned off and it was in the top half that Nellie and her friends were going to stage their act.

"Gosh!" exclaimed Dorothy. "Have you ever seen anything like this?" she announced looking around at the full size stage and all the professional lighting gear. "Are you sure this isn't the London Palladium?"

Their host showed them into another room to the side of the stage where there was plenty of space for them to get changed and ready for the show.

"I'll organise some tea to be sent through for you. I understand you English like your tea."

"That would be lovely" said Diana thanking their host. "I certainly wouldn't say no to a nice, hot brew."

Listening backstage the concert party could tell by the level of chatter and noise emerging from the theatre area behind them, that tonight a larger than normal audience was gathering.

"Right let's go" said Billy "it's time to show them what we can do."

Every member of the concert party was involved in the opening song of the show. One by one they followed each other out of the changing room and up onto the stage. The noise from the audience, a mixture of clapping, stamping, whistling and shouting was deafening. The girls walking up the steps to the stage just looked at each other and smiled, knowing that any words that they spoke would just be drowned out by the rumpus below.

The opening song had been followed by a stand-up comedian and Nellie was the next in line to sing a solo. The Mad Macaroons were having a fantastic reception from their American audience, better than they had ever expected. Relief was paramount amongst the artists, enough in fact for nerves to subside so that even they could begin to enjoy themselves a little.

The show was going so well that Nellie mounted the stage with more confidence than she could ever remember experiencing. She had brushed her hair to the side into a Veronica Lake style, similar to the way her cousin Cynthia had done it, the evening she had gone with her friend Elsie to see Johnnie Bevan sing in The Nag's Head in Maesteg. Who would have thought that a few years later, Nellie Edwards would actually be on the stage herself singing a solo.

The song Nellie had chosen to sing was 'We'll Gather Lilac', so to help set the scene she wore a lilac dress and a comb with a lilac flower attached in her hair. Nellie walked across the stage, again to great applause and took up centre stage position in front of the microphone. The lights dimmed and gradually the applause died down and all was quiet except for a few wolf whistles. The main spotlight came on and focused directly onto Nellie. She hadn't noticed when she had been on the stage before, but now as she stood alone on the vast stage, everything appeared quite daunting. Nellie knew that in front of her and soon to be listening to her singing all by herself, were around five hundred people, but with the lights extinguished, the only knowledge she had of their presence, were red cigarette ends glowing here and there. The music began and Nellie counted the beat for her cue. Initially for the first few notes her voice wavered, but soon she was away with the song and her uncertainty a thing of the past.

The last act of the first half was the comedy sketch of the char ladies, with Nellie playing the stooge Agnes. As Archie had rightly predicted it went down a bundle with the American audience. Nellie was quite a hit with the G.I.'s and she felt sure that sometimes they must have missed her punch line, as they were already laughing before the words left her mouth.

Back in the changing rooms during the interval, the concert party quickly discussed their routines for the following half. A knock on the door interrupted them. The door opened and the man who had originally shown them around the hanger appeared.

"Is one of you called Nellie?" he asked "Only I have been asked to give her this." he added holding out in front of him a piece of white card and a flower, obviously taken from one of the small vases on the tables outside in the hanger.

Nellie stepped forward and took the white card and flower from him. Looking down she read "Hi Nellie, remember me Chad. I'm waiting outside the door if you have a second."

"Oh! It's from Chad" she said to the questioning onlookers. "How long have we got until the second half? Have I got time to just pop out and see him?"

"We're back on in five minutes" informed Dorothy, but looking down at her list added, "You're Okay. You're not needed until the eighth act."

Nellie opened the door and immediately saw Chad standing a little way in front of her with a big smile on his face.

"How you doing little lady? Long time no see."

"I'm fine thanks Chad. How are you? I did look out for you when I visited the camp where I saw you with Jill.'"

"No sorry I couldn't tell you as I didn't know myself, but I got sent to another camp about fifty miles west, left the same week as Jill."

"So you're back here now?"

"For the moment, but next week I'm on the move again."

"Oh!" said Nellie disappointedly. Having just met Chad again, she was reluctant to let him go before she had a chance to get to know him a bit better.

"Not far though this time. In fact I shall be just down the road from you at Marina Barracks. I trust you're still there?"

"Yes" answered Nellie with relief. "I sure am" she said trying to mimic his American accent not too successfully with her strong welsh one.

"The show's just great" congratulated Chad "The guys are loving it."

Shock appeared on Nellie's face, as all of a sudden she remembered in her haste to come out and meet Chad; she was still dressed in the awful drab overall and elasticised mop cap from the char ladies sketch. It wasn't fetching on the stage, let alone down here.

Chad immediately sensed her embarrassment. "Don't worry; you look real cute to me."

Nellie could feel her face start to flush and without warning the auditorium felt uncomfortably hot. She gave her excuses saying that she really must get back to the others, but not before she had agreed to catch up with Chad again after the final curtain went down.

The show was coming to a close and Nellie was back on stage to sing the final song 'Every Time We Say Goodbye'. Strangely she felt more apprehensive singing a solo this time than she had done previously. Her stomach churned and the butterflies were back and she couldn't make out whether it was nervousness from being on the stage in front of such a large audience or excitement from meeting up with Chad again. The remaining nine members of the Mad Macaroons walked up the steps of the stage to join Nellie in singing the last few lines in a grand finale. The applause was again deafening as the concert party took their farewell bow. The compere retuned to the stage to thank them for giving such a wonderful performance, but it was quite a few minutes before he could make himself heard above the appreciative crowd.

Back in their dressing room the concert party kissed and hugged each other, pleased that it had all gone so well. The compere put his head around the door and told them that he hoped that they didn't have to rush off, as there were free drinks waiting at the bar for them.

"Blimey, makes you feel like a real star doesn't it" said Ada.

"Yeah" agreed Dorothy and with a twinkle in her eye added "C'mon let's get a move on, can't waste time with all those lovely yanks out there waiting for our company."

Nellie spotted Chad as soon as she left the dressing room standing just a couple of paces away.

"Over here Nellie" he shouted waving his hand to indicate his whereabouts. "Thought I'd best stand close to the door. I didn't want you getting picked up by any of these red blooded males before I could reach you myself."
Nellie just smiled at him, not knowing quite what to say.
"You girls were real swell, you especially Nellie. The guys were good as well, but not half as pretty."
"Thanks" said Nellie. "It was quite nerve-racking to begin with, we've never sung anywhere as big as this before."
"Well you'd better get used to it 'cos gee I can see Hollywood looming for you my girl."
"Oh! Don't be silly" laughed Nellie nudging his arm. "Can we get a drink my throat's a bit dry."

Nellie awoke early the next morning. Even though it had been a late night, she had found sleep difficult to come by. Her head was full to the brim with happenings of the night before; how well the show had gone and more excitedly she remembered the time she had spent with Chad afterwards. When she had first been introduced to Chad by her friend Jill whilst on the rounds with her N.A.A.F.I. mobile canteen, much as he had seemed very pleasant, she hadn't really thought anymore about him. Her thoughts now however were changing and she found it hard to put him out of her mind. She tried to fathom out exactly what it was that she liked about him. He had a friendly face, but you could hardly call him good looking and height wise he was probably no taller than she was herself. She felt comfortable with him though; he put her at ease and maybe that went a lot further than superficial looks.

The relationship between Nellie and Chad quickly developed from being friends to spending every available moment together. Occasionally if they both had time off in the afternoon they would go downtown to the cinema where the troops could see films for free. The cinema though was often crowded and would get very warm inside. More often or not they preferred to go to the early evening showing, either at the Field Bakery Unit, the American Hospital or the aerodrome where mobile cinemas showed movies outside. The selection of films on offer was far better and showed all the new releases. The night before Nellie and Chad had watched the film 'Mrs. Miniver' in the open air at the American Hospital. Greer Garson had played the part of Mrs Miniver, the middle-class wife of Clem Miniver an architect, played by Walter Pidgeon. The story was about a British family's struggle to survive in World War II. At times the plot was very sad, causing Nellie to sniffle into her handkerchief much to Chad's amusement.

Nellie had found that practicing and attending shows with the Mad Macaroons was taken up far too much of her valuable free time. Much as in the days prior to Chad, she had not minded and enjoyed every minute, nowadays she felt differently and wanted to spend as much time as possible with him. It was a great disappointment to the rest of the concert party when she informed them that she wanted to leave. They tried every way possible to convince her to change her mind, but Nellie understood where her priorities lay and that was with Chad. Much as her decision to leave was a big blow to the concert party, a new lady called Pamela soon took her place as the lead vocalist and The Mad Macaroons went on from strength to strength.

Nellie had also been transferred back to work in the N.A.A.F.I. canteen at the Castle Club, which she was more than pleased about, as again it gave her more opportunity to see Chad. One morning as she was outside wiping the tables down with a wet cloth, she was grabbed around the waist from behind and a kiss was planted on her left cheek. She knew instantly that it was Chad and her heart quickened its pace.

"What are you doing here Sergeant Munroe? I thought you were meant to be on duty."

"I am so I can't stop" replied Chad.

"I really enjoyed the film last night. Greer Garson is such a good actress isn't she?"

"So did I, but I preferred what we did afterwards to watching the film."

"Ssh!" scorned Nellie people will hear you."

Nellie was concerned that people would hear and get the wrong idea. They had never gone further than a kiss and a cuddle, but she knew that Chad would like to take their relationship to the next step, but she herself wasn't quite sure if she was ready. She felt confident that Chad accepted her decision and was willing to wait for the time being. She remembered her friend Jill saying that Chad was the biggest flirt on the camp, but she didn't have any worries on that score, as not once had he given her cause to doubt him. Obviously on Jill's part it had just been a friendly taunt.

"I just popped in to see if you fancy meeting me at the ice-cream parlour this afternoon when you finish?"

"Yes alright, on one condition though."

"And what might that be?"

"That I can have a chocolate and vanilla with extra nuts on top."

"That's a date then Ma'am. What time do you finish?"

"Half past two today, so I'll meet you there about three."

Chad gave Nellie a quick peck on the other cheek and walked away, only to glance back over his shoulder a few steps further away to proudly take a last glimpse of his girl.

At three o'clock on the dot Nellie arrived at the ice-cream parlour to find Chad already there waiting for her.

"Is it still a chocolate and vanilla ice-cream with extra nuts, or has the lady changed her mine?"

"No I haven't changed my mind that's exactly right."

Finishing their cones Chad suggested that they take a walk along the path that ran alongside the beach. The slight breeze coming off the sea and the shade from the palm trees lining the path made it a cool and pleasant place to walk and several other couples, old and young alike had the same idea as them. Whether it was the warm air, the sparkling blue sea or even the simple ambience of Tripoli Nellie wasn't sure, but everything felt so romantic, so right. As they walked along hand in hand, Nellie took a sideways look at Chad's profile. She asked herself what it was about him that she found so very attractive. He wasn't tall, not what you would call good-looking even, but saying that there was a certain something about his face that appealed to her. Chad turned and smiled at her, at the same time squeezing her hand, letting her know that he was happy to be spending his time with her. Nellie understood at that moment that it was the little things about him that she loved. The way one of his eyes scrunched up slightly more than the other when he laughed, his cheeky face that no doubt as a child had been full of mischief, but now as a man was etched with fun, his tentative ways towards her and most of all the knowledge that he cared for her and that here was someone at last that she could trust forever.

Chad seemed deep in thought as they walked along the path.

"Penny for your thoughts."

'Sorry what's that?" asked Chad coming out of his reverie.

"I said penny for your thoughts" replied Nellie "you are obviously deep in thought over something."

"No nothing really. I was just thinking about your name. It's a strange name Nellie; I've never heard anyone being called it before."

"Not as strange as Chad" she responded disconcertedly. "Is that your proper name or is it short for something?"

"My real name is Chadwick, Chadwick Munroe, but everyone calls me Chad."

"Same with me" replied Nellie. "My real name is Ellen."

"Gee! That's a real pretty name, so why are you called Nellie?"
Apparently my sister Joyce, who's eighteen months older than me, could never say Ellen, somehow it always came out as Nellen and I guess along the way it changed somehow to Nellie and that's what I have always been called."

"Is it just you and Joyce or do you have any other brothers and sisters?"
Nellie felt at ease talking to Chad and he was a keen listener. Without realising she had soon told him quite a bit about her brothers and sisters and their sad upbringing.

"You poor thing" he said stopping suddenly and embracing her "It must be real tough growing up without a Ma and Pa."

"I suppose like they say what you've never had you don't miss" Nellie answered flippantly, but then added "Actually that's not true, no not true at all. There's been many a time I wished things could have been different. Anyway enough about me, what about you?"

"I've just got a brother, Denver. Actually I should say had a brother. He was killed in Pearl Harbour I still can't get used to it."

"I'm sorry; it must be hard for you."

"Sure is, for Ma and Pa too, but mostly for his wife Delores and his young son Frankie. Poor boy never ever knew his father; he was born six months after he was killed."

"That's really tragic. I'm so glad the war's over, it brought heartache to so many people that didn't deserve it; ruined so many lives."

"You're right there. I try and do whatever I can to help Delores and Frankie out, but nothing can make up for their loss."

Nellie felt like her life was taking on a new beginning. She looked at everything in a different light, everything was fun, never had she been so happy, so contented. Never before had she been in love. She realised now the feelings that she had experienced for Mickey Dunn and Johnnie Bevan were nothing in comparison to the way she felt about Chad. There was no doubt about it, Nellie was in love and the world was a wonderful place to be. She felt like she had climbed the highest mountain and everything she surveyed was her oyster. Nothing and she meant nothing was ever going to spoil this wonderful euphoria. She understood that this feeling was not one sided either and that Chad felt exactly the same way as she did. She led back on her pillow and let her thoughts wander uncontrollably into the life that the two of them would one day share together. She pictured two small children, a boy with light brown hair like his father's and a little girl with darker hair just like her own. The happy family walked with hands joined together along the riverbank. Mum and Dad on the outside, obviously so proud of their off springs, while the children skipped along contentedly between them.

Nellie could afford a little time to daydream, as today she was on late shift and didn't need to be at work until half past two. Leaning over to check the time on her clock, she thought to herself that she really ought to be getting up, as she wanted to go to the market before work and also had made arrangements to meet Chad for a quick coffee afterwards.
 "Just another ten minutes and then I'll get up" she told herself and rolled over, once again to indulge her senses and let her imagination take over.

Chad and Nellie sat at a table on the outside of the other strategically placed tables at the café where they had arranged to meet. There was no conversation between them, relaxed enough now with each others company, no longer was it necessary for them to talk at every given moment. Their eyes gazed on three small, local children all bare footed who were playing just in front of them, two boys and a girl. The two, slightly elder boys kicked a ball between themselves and the little girl soon started to cry, as selfishly like older siblings can sometimes be, they refused to let her join in their game. A woman presumable their mother, hearing the commotion poked her head through a nearby, open doorway and witnessing events shouted out at the children. Nellie and Chad could not understand her native tongue, but guessed that the boys were getting a stripping down for preventing their sister from playing with them. The boys ignored their mother's suggestion and continued kicking the ball between them. The little girl, knowing that her mother's eyes were watching and knowing that she had her approval raced towards the ball in an effort to join in. The taller of the two boys beat her to it and kicked it out of her reach. Witnessing this, the mother stormed out of the doorway and before any of the children could catch up with the rolling ball, was upon it and picking it up. All three of the children, stopped in their tracks wondering what was going to happen next. Their mother turned around, her finger wagging vigorously in their direction, shouted some expletive and with the ball under her arm strode back to the house. The children looked on with dismay; all three started to cry and then ran after her in her wake.

"Time I was off" said Nellie picking up her handbag. "I'll get these."
"No you won't, my treat."
Nellie knew better than to argue, so said no more when Chad stood up and fished out his wallet from his back pocket. As he turned and walked away in the direction of the counter, Nellie saw something flutter down from his pocket and land on the chair he had just vacated. Leaning over she picked up the small piece of paper and turned it over. It was a photograph of a small boy of about four or five. Nellie instantly recognised similarities between the small boy and Chad; same colour hair, same cheeky face. 'This must be his nephew Frankie' Nellie thought. 'Chad's obviously very fond of him. How sweet to carry his photo in his wallet.'
Nellie studied the boy's photo in more detail and felt a warmth inside of her. Nellie's ease for daydreaming surfaced once again and Nellie wondered if when she and Chad had their little boy if he would look anything like this one.
Chad returned to the table.

"This must have fallen out of your wallet" she said handing the photo of the small boy up to him.
"Oh! Thanks" he said turning it over and examining the picture. "He's a cute little guy isn't he?"
"He's lovely" agreed Nellie 'and you too' she thought to herself, once again thanking her lucky stars that she had found such a wonderful, caring man.

It had been an exceptionally busy Friday night in the N.A.A.F.I. canteen and Nellie was relieved when the last customer left and she was able to lock the door behind him and pull down the shutters. She had been so looking forward to the week-end and thought it was never going to arrive, so in one way it had been good that she had been so busy, as the time had flown by quicker. It was a rare occurrence for both she and Chad to manage to get the same days off and this weekend they could look forward to two blissful days together. Neither of them had to be back on duty until Monday morning and Chad had promised her that he would make it a very special week-end.

Chad had told Nellie that he would meet her at her billet at eleven o'clock. He wasn't giving many clues away, but did tell her to wear some sensible shoes as there might be a bit of walking and to pack her swimsuit and a towel. Nellie wasn't the slightest bit concerned about where they would be going or what they would be doing; just spending time together was precious enough for her.

It was half past ten, another half an hour to go before the hands on her watch reached the appointed time. Nellie was already ready and just given her hair a final brush when she heard a continuous car horn sounding outside. Chad wouldn't be hear for another thirty minutes, so looking out of the window she was quite surprised to see Chad waving at her from the driver's seat of an American Jeep. Nellie waved back, grabbed the bag that she had packed with a few things that she thought she might need for the day and rushed outside.
    "Your carriage awaits you Ma'am."
    "Where did you get this from? I was expecting you on foot."
    "Well you should know by now that a man of my calibre is well able to participate in a bit of negotiation and have a few surprises up his sleeve. Jump in; this little beauty is ours for the day."

Clarissa by this time had been woken up from her lie in by the disturbance outside. Realising that the noise was down to Nellie and Chad setting off on their day out she came to the door and shouted.
    "Have a nice day you two. Don't do anything I wouldn't do."
    "Don't think you'll be up to much today Clarissa, not unless you take those curlers out" teased Chad laughing loudly.
Clarissa put her hand to her head and in shock realised that she did indeed still have her curlers in. A troop of soldiers were marching past and she fled inside before any of them got close enough to recognise her.

Driving around with the N.A.A.F.I. mobile canteen, Nellie had seen quite a lot of the surrounding countryside. Much of it seemed very similar, sand, desert, sea and yet more sand. Chad was a confident driver and Nellie felt quite at ease with him. They turned right off of the coast road and climbed higher and higher up towards the looming mountain range. The higher they drove the better the view and rounding a bend, Chad pulled the Jeep off the road and came to a stop on a gravelled area. They got out, stretched their legs and took in the view. The mountain side was quite barren consisting of mainly scrubland interspersed with pine trees. Even though the layout of the land had a certain wilderness quality to it, still it managed to capture its own form of beauty. Beyond lay small nestling villages, communities of whitewashed houses dotted here and there. The sea, a serene shade of sapphire blue streaked with turquoise stretched out in front of them, merging gently with the sky on the horizon, making the melodramatic change in nature hardly noticeable. To the left stretching further than the eye could see, the desert covered the ground like a golden carpet, dramatically broken up by sculptured mounds of sand dunes. Nellie felt as if she was on the outside of nature looking in. Being so high up on the mountain ledge, birds flew past at the same level and she could hear their wings gently flapping as they glided past and skilfully kept themselves airborne.

"This is absolutely amazing Chad. I have never seen anything so beautiful. Thank you for bringing me here" she said and gave him a quick kiss on the lips.

"Is that all I'm getting?" he jokingly enquired. "At the very least I would have expected a kiss like this" and placed his lips gently against Nellie's for a kiss of a much stronger nature. Loosening his grip, he added "I thought we'd take a walk from here, better get started otherwise many more of these passionate interludes and I won't have any energy left."

They continued their walk for half an hour or so, not meeting one single soul. Everything was just so peaceful and it felt like the world belonged to them and them alone. Through a gap in the trees, a small lagoon about a hundred and fifty yards below caught their eye.

"I'd like to go down there. Do you think there's a path down to it? Maybe we could have a swim in that lagoon if it looks safe."

Chad looked around and noticed a small single vehicle track leading down on the far side of the lagoon.

"Let's go back and get the Jeep, as it looks the perfect spot for us to have the picnic lunch, which I've organised for us."
Nellie squeezed his arm.
"You've packed lunch for us as well. Chad you're such an old romantic and I love you very much."
She had surprised herself just how easy the words had come out, but she didn't care; she did love him and the words needed to be said.
The bank of the lagoon was the most perfect location. Sitting there having lunch with Chad made Nellie feel like a star in a Hollywood film and she cherished every moment, not wanting it to come to an end.. The sun played tricks on their eyes as it dappled through the leaves of the over hanging trees that provided Nellie and Chad with some welcome shade and privacy.
"Have another sandwich" suggested Chad as he picked up a plate and offered it to Nellie.
"I don't think I could eat another thing, I feel fit to burst as it is."
"Drop more wine?"
"Mmm! I dare say I could force a little more down" answered Nellie holding her glass up for a refill, "but just a drop."

Nellie had been more than a little surprised when Chad had carried out a wicker hamper from the back of the Jeep. He had thought of just about everything. Laying a tartan blanket on the ground he had motioned for Nellie to sit on it, while he unpacked the hamper which consisted of sandwiches, breaded chicken legs, crisps, cakes, two bottles of wine and some beer. He had even thought to pack proper plates and glasses. It was such a perfect day, Nellie couldn't have wished for anything more. After lunch they just lazed together on the blanket, so relaxed that they both fell off to sleep for nearly an hour.
"Isn't this swell?" said Chad as he woke up and stretched his arms. "Don't have to rush off anywhere, nobody to tell us what to do, just you and me and all of this" he announced circling his arms to encompass their beautiful surroundings. "That water sure looks inviting, fancy a swim?"
"You go in first and see how deep it is. You know I can't swim, but I don't mind having a paddle if it's shallow."

Drying themselves off with their towels and with no hurry to be anywhere else, they sat back down on the blanket and opened another bottle of wine.

"This is the life isn't it?" said Nellie. "Do you know if we did this everyday for the next fifty years, I still don't think I would be tired of it?"

"Oh! I forget something" said Chad hunting in the bottom of the wicker hamper.

"Here you are I bought these for you. I hope they haven't melted" and handed over a bag of confectionery to Nellie.

"What are they?" she asked.

"Hershey's Kisses."

Nellie opened the bag with her teeth and took out a bite-size piece of chocolate wrapped in a lightweight, aluminium foil with a narrow strand of paper protruding from the top. Pulling the strand of paper, the sweet unwrapped and she popped it into her mouth.

"Mmm! These are lovely. Are they American I've never seen them before."

"Yeah! They haven't been around for a while though. They were originally made in" taking the bag from Nellie he read, "1907, but during the war the aluminium that they used to make the wrappers was scarce, so they've only recently stated making them again."

"Take one for yourself" instructed Nellie and Chad dutifully unwrapped one and likewise popped it into his mouth.

"I wonder why they call them kisses" pondered Nellie.

"I don't know the answer to that Ma'am, but I know the type of kisses I prefer", Chad added leaning across to Nellie and gently pressed her down on the blanket.

Nellie could feel her body becoming aroused and did not want their kisses and caresses to stop. The couple were well camouflaged and shaded by the trees, so it was highly unlikely that their rising passion could be seen by any passers by. Nellie's whole body yearned for Chad to explore her more and the stronger his kisses became, the more Nellie knew that this time she didn't want him to stop.

She had a sudden flashback to the abuse she had received from her brother Owen and to the time when she had nearly been raped on the road back to Mr. Jefferies farm in Pontypridd. Nellie had moved on enough to realise that she couldn't dwell on happenings from her past, especially those that could spoil her future. Those incidents held bad memories for her. It still upset her to think of these wrongs that had been carried out; purely for the gratification of others, without a consideration to how she might be affected. She was cross with herself for even thinking again about those awful incidents, as they couldn't in any way at all, compare to the love and it was love, real love that she felt for Chad and he felt for her.

Murmuring softly as her desire magnified to a level of unprecedented intensity, Nellie knew this time that she had reached the point of no return and huskily she spoke the words that Chad had been hoping to hear.
"Don't stop Chad, please don't stop."

Chapter 15

It would have been more than easy for Nellie to have turned over and gone back to sleep that morning when her alarm had gone off. Lately she had been feeling so tired, but had put it down to all the time she had been spending with Chad, burning the candle at both ends. She was on early shift, so reluctantly she had forced herself to get out of bed, as it was her turn to open up the canteen. At least tonight, knowing that Chad was on duty, she could come home, have a bath, wash her hair and even possibly an early night might be in store.

"You couldn't do a full English could you Nellie?" asked Jean. "I just want to finish mopping this floor down."

"Yes of course I can." replied Nellie. "How do you like your eggs?" she asked turning towards the customer.

Nellie went to the refrigerator and took out some bacon and sausages. Undoing the packaging of white paper, she snipped a sausage from one of the links and peeled off two rashers of bacon and popped them into the waiting frying pan. Normally when the bacon started to sizzle, the smell of it would make Nellie feel quite peckish, as usually in the morning she had little more for breakfast than a cup of tea. She rolled the sausage in the pan to brown its sides evenly and flipped over the bacon. Suddenly Nellie could feel herself coming over quite queasy and the smell of the bacon cooking was not helping at all.

"Sorry Jean" she shouted to her colleague, "You're going to have to finish this for me" and made a dash to the toilet.

"Are you alright?" asked Jean quite concerned when Nellie eventually emerged from the toilet.

"Yes, I'm sure I'll be fine now. Must have caught a bug or something."

"Well sit yourself down there for a minute; I'll make you a nice cup of coffee."

Jean brought the cup of coffee over to Nellie and placed it in front of her.

"There you are that should make you feel better."

Nellie picked up the spoon from the saucer and stirred the contents in the cup. The steam and strong aroma of the coffee swirled its way up towards Nellie's nostrils, hesitating slightly she picked up the cup and took a small sip. She could feel the warm coffee coursing its way down her throat, through her chest until eventually it hit her stomach. There it felt as if it turned a somersault and Nellie could now feel it regurgitating and tracing its way back up through her body. Nellie's hands felt all clammy, her head felt oddly cold. She could hear Jean shouting something to her, but everything seemed as if at a distance. Suddenly Jean was beside her.

"God what's the matter with you my girl, you're not well at all are you?"
Seeing the colour drain from Nellie's face she instructed her to put her head down between her knees.

"Now stay like that for a while, you'll feel better in a moment."
Sitting quietly for a few minutes, eventually the feeling of faintness wore off, but Nellie felt sick again and had to make another dash to the toilet. By the time she came out, Jean had already bundled Nellie's things together and they were waiting for her on the side counter.

"How are you feeling now?"

"A little better thanks."

"Well I think you should go along right now and see the camp doctor. I can manage here just fine, so you go and see the quack and after that get yourself off home."
Normally Nellie would have argued and dismissed the idea, but she knew herself that she did not feel right, so this time she did take notice.

Nellie sat in the doctor's waiting room waiting her turn. Luckily there was only one other patient in front of her and she didn't have to wait too long.

"Good morning Private Edwards. Please, take a seat" said the doctor indicating the chair in front of the desk he himself sat behind. "Now what can I do for you?"
Nellie described to the doctor how she had been feeling that morning.

"I see" he thoughtfully replied. "Best I examine you I think. Pop behind that curtain and strip down to your underwear please."
Dutifully Nellie did as she was bid and waited for the doctor to finish off writing his notes.

"Jump up on the bed please and lie down. That's right."
The doctor felt around her stomach pressing here and there.

"Mmm!" he said not giving anything away. "Tell me, when did you last have a period?"

"About eight or nine weeks ago," answered Nellie thinking back "but I'm never very regular. I've gone that long before without anything."

The doctor asked Nellie to remove her bra and felt around her breasts.

"Does that hurt?"

"Just a little tender. I noticed it a little while ago; I think I may have strained some muscles."

"Mmm!" added the doctor for a second time. "Okay well pop your clothes on and come and see me back at the desk."

Nellie sat down in front of the doctor. By this time she was feeling a lot better, whatever it had been that was making her feel so strange had thankfully now passed over. The doctor head down, busily finished writing up his notes. Nellie thought this quite rude of him, as he knew that she was sat there patiently waiting.

"Nothing serious I hope?" she asked interrupting his flow of writing.

Looking up the doctor put down his pen and leant back in his chair.

"No nothing serious, all quite normal really."

Nellie felt a surge of relief falling over her, obviously as she had expected it was just a minor upset.

"If you give this piece of paper to the nurse on your way out," the doctor continued "she will organise a few more tests to make sure, but I think I know what your problem is Private Edwards. I think you are more than likely pregnant."

Nellie's hand went to her mouth in shock.

"Pregnant? Are you sure?"

"Well like I said, get the nurse to sort these tests on your way out and come back, let's see it's Tuesday today, come back on Friday morning and I should have your results by then."

In a complete daze Nellie stood up and walked out of the doctor's surgery and if it hadn't been for the nurse calling her, would have forgotten all about the tests.

Although in one sense of the word Nellie was feeling a lot better, with the recent news weighing heavy on her shoulders, she returned to her billet and led down on her bed.

'I can't be pregnant' she tried to convince herself. 'I just can't be', but realistically she knew that it could be a possibility. She had always left Chad to take care of such matters, but thinking back, so fierce had been their ardour at times, she now wondered if he actually had. 'This should be one of the happiest moments of my life' she told herself, as she could feel her tears welling up. 'What on earth am I going to do?'

Nellie lay on her bed for some time and her emotions went full circle several times over, tying to resolve and make sense of what challenges lay ahead of her. She thought back to her sister Rose and her children who themselves were now teenagers and older.
'Look at Rose, she had four children and she probably wasn't any older than me at the time' Nellie told herself, trying desperately to convince herself that if she was pregnant, it wasn't the end of the world and that she would cope. 'I suppose it was a bit different though for Rose, she was married to Alfie, but then I've got Chad.' Her thoughts reverted back to Chad. 'I won't tell him until I've been back to the doctors and am absolutely sure. I won't tell anybody for the time being. Chad will be over the moon I know he will be. I am silly; I don't know why I'm even worrying. Chances are the doctor's got it all wrong and if he hasn't well I've still got Chad.'

Nellie returned to work the next day and understandably Jean was full of questions regarding her health.
　"I'm fine now thanks Jean. Like I said it must have been one of those twenty-four hour bugs."
　"Well I hope so, but you still look a bit peaky to me. You just let me know if you feel the slightest bit funny again. I don't want you passing out in someone's egg and chips."
　"I suppose you could say if that happened I really would have egg on my face wouldn't I?" joked Nellie.
Jean laughed with her, but still gave her friend a serious caution to take things easy.

Nellie didn't want to take things easy; she wanted to bury herself as much as possible in her work. Anything to keep her from thinking about what the doctor had told her and her looming return appointment on Friday. In order to prevent Jean from asking any more questions when she told her that she would need time off to see the doctor on Friday, she booked the day off, making an excuse that she was meeting up with some friends. After three nights of fairly, sleepless nights, Friday arrived. Nellie had been awake since the early hours, contemplating the news she would receive from the doctor. Deep down, she hoped that his original diagnosis was incorrect, as she felt embarrassed that everyone would know that she was pregnant and not married. Nellie had moved on a lot during her time in the N.A.A.F.I., no longer was she the timid and self-conscious girl she had once been, but mulling over the crisis she could very well be facing, part of that sad, little girl form the welsh valleys returned to haunt her.

"Come in Private Edwards", instructed the doctor, "please take a seat."
Nellie nervously sat down, her hands folded together on her lap, secretly praying that the news the doctor was about to impart was what she wanted to hear.

"I've read through your results Private Edwards and it is as I thought. It seems congratulations are the order of the day; you are indeed pregnant. Seven weeks gone I should say."

In a trance Nellie walked back to her billet. Entering the door, she was greeted by Ethel, one of the girls that she shared her billet with.
"Hi! Nellie."
Like Nellie, Ethel too was dating an American airman and had unconsciously picked up some of his Americanisms.
"Message from Chad. He said for you to meet him at The Lido Bar at six and if you fancied it maybe the two of you could take in a film."
"Thanks" said Nellie. "I'll see how I feel later. I'm just going to have a lie down."
"Still not feeling well" asked Ethel. "I thought you'd got over that bug you had earlier in the week."
"It's nothing much. I just got a headache, need a bit of peace and quiet."
"Okay." said Ethel quietly "I'll try not to make too much noise."

'Nothing much,' thought Nellie, 'nothing much. Who am I trying to kid?' Reality of her situation had struck home; Nellie was at her wit's end.
'What a mess' she told herself. 'I thought everything was too good to be true. I should have known better, good things just don't happen to me. God, what a mess?'
Nellie's poor tormented mind analysed every minute detail of her agonising predicament. The questions kept mounting up. How was she going to break the news to Chad? How would he take it? What would happen with her job once news got out that she was pregnant? She'd be sent back to the England that was for sure. Where would she go? She couldn't possibly expect Rose to help; Rose who had given up so much for Nellie and her siblings all those years before. She had a bit of money

saved, but how long would it last her, especially with a baby to look after? Ethel interrupted her thoughts.

"It's five o'clock Nellie. How's your head now? Time to get ready if you're planning on meeting Chad in an hour."

"Are you going down The Lido Ethel?"

"Yes I am. Just waiting for my nail polish to dry and then I'll be off."

"You couldn't give Chad a message for me, could you?"

"Course I can."

"Tell him I'll catch up with him tomorrow. Explain that I've got a bit of a headache."

Much as Nellie knew that she was going to have to face Chad at some stage, tonight just wasn't the right time. She had to get her own head in order first and the way she felt at the moment, she wasn't at all sure just how long that was going to take. Nellie's mind continued to torture her, but eventually everything just appeared so obvious and fell into place.
'Why on earth am I being so silly? I don't know why I have been getting myself into such a state. It's not as if Chad and I have had a one night stand, we've been together for nine months now and I know that he loves me as much as I love him. I'll tell him tomorrow. He is just going to be so thrilled, I just know he is. He idolises Frankie his late brother's little boy. Not many Uncles would carry around a picture of their nephew in their wallets. I could see that little boy looking so much like him, but just imagine when this little one is born, I'm sure he or she will be the spitting image of its father and I know how proud that will make him. Yes, tomorrow I shall tell Chad that he is going to be a Daddy.'
With an easy mind, Nellie nestled down amongst the sheets on her bed and sleep soon came to her. She dozed off dreaming of her certain life with Chas and their newborn child. I expect we'll live in America she mused and closing her eyes Nellie had pleasant dreams of a white, clapboard house with a small rear garden littered with toys.

Nellie awoke the next morning in a far more positive frame of mind, in fact she felt on top of the world. She couldn't understand why she had felt so anxious the day before and put it down to the change in her hormones. Yes it wasn't exactly the way she had planned for things to happen, but what did it matter. She and Chad were so right for each other and well now that she was expecting their child, it would just hurry things along a little. Nellie was convinced that it would have only been a matter of time anyway until Chad had popped the question, so what difference did it make if it happened sooner rather than later. Jumping out of bed she put the kettle on to make a cup of tea.

"How are you this morning? Feeling better?" asked Ethel.
"Yes much thanks. Did you see Chad last night? What did he say?"
"He was really sorry to hear that you weren't feeling too good. In fact he never stayed long; he'd disappeared by about seven."
"He didn't say anything else?"
"Yes he did actually" smiled Ethel knowing that Nellie was anxious to hear what his plans were for the day. "He told me to tell you that if you were feeling better to, meet him at the coffee shop in the Medina at half past twelve."
Nellie felt her stomach take a flutter. Considering her new condition, she thought surely it was too early for the baby to be kicking and realised as always, it was just the excitement of seeing Chad, even more so today with such exciting news to tell him.

Chad was on his feet to welcome Nellie as soon as he caught sight of her. Giving her a kiss on the cheek he asked if she was feeling better, to which she confirmed that she was.
"Can I get you a beer; I've just ordered one for myself?"
"I think I would prefer an orange juice if that's alright."
"'Lunch? Have you eaten?"
Thinking about it Nellie realised that she was feeling a little peckish and considering after all that she was now eating for two, informed Chad that she wouldn't mind a sandwich. Finishing his light meal, Chad replaced his fork on the plate and pushed it away from him. Fumbling in his breast pocket he pulled out his cigarettes and offered one to Nellie.
"No thanks, not for me."
'Good God girl! What's the matter with you? No drinking, no smoking, you'll be telling me next that you've joined the Franciscan Nuns. If I didn't know better I'd be thinking that you were pregnant" he laughed.
Hearing this, at first Nellie thought maybe this was an ideal time to tell him that she was, but decided against it with so many people seated close by and within earshot. She wanted the moment to be special and decided to wait for a more opportune time.

"Fancy a walk?" Nellie suggested hoping that when they were alone the right moment would present itself.

"Okay. Where would you like to go?"

"I thought along the beach and around to that quiet cove where the fishermen sometimes come in would be nice."

Hand in hand the two of them walked along the far end of the beach, leaving behind those who preferred to sunbathe, play ball games and meet up with friends for a laugh and a joke at The Lido Bar on the front. Nellie felt so happy, contented maybe was a better choice of word. As long as she had Chad and his love, their baby and the wonderful future she knew lay ahead for the three of them, she couldn't ask for more. Everything was just perfect. Nellie actually was not even the slightest bit worried about telling Chad that she was pregnant, her tummy felt a bit jittery, but she knew that it was nothing more than excitement, as Chad would be as happy as her.

The sun was not quite as fierce as it sometimes could be, its rays gently warming their skin rather than burning. Waves gently rolled in from the sea, appearing little more than a ripple by the time they cascaded over Chad and Nellie's bare feet as they walked along the soft sand. It felt like the two of them were totally alone in the world; the peace of their surroundings only broken by the sound of the gulls calling to each other in their search for food and the calming rush of the sea.

As they approached the rocks, Nellie knew that the time had come to tell Chad about the baby, their baby. Once they rounded the rocks and entered the cove beyond, it was likely that there would be people milling around watching the fishermen unload their daily catch.

"Chad, I heard some good news this week. I wasn't sure to start with, but yes it is good news, very good news."

"What on earth are you babbling on about Nellie?"

"I'm pregnant Chad. We're pregnant. Isn't it exciting?"

Chad stopped in his tracks, grabbed Nellie by both arms and swung her around.

"You can't be?"

"I am Chad, the doctor's confirmed it. Isn't it wonderful? I know it's taken us a bit by surprise, but we're right for each other, I know we are. Everything will work out just fine."

"No Nellie it won't, not by a long shot" screamed Chad.

Nellie was completely taken aback by Chad's reaction. It wasn't at all what she had been expecting, but still she continued.

"What do you mean Chad? It's just come as a bit of a shock that's all. There's no reason why we can't get married. We certainly won't be the first couple to have a baby on the way before the wedding, or the last."

"I can't marry you Nellie."

Nellie was now in a state of shock herself. Her beautiful world was collapsing around her, one huge, crumbling block after the other. Chad roughly let her go and walked over to the rocks and sat down on a large boulder, head in his hands.

"Chad" Nellie desperately called after him. "We need to talk. Why can't you marry me?"

"Because Nellie, because I'm already married. I thought you knew."

"Married?"' she questioned. Nellie was totally speechless, her mouth hung open.

"I thought you knew" repeated Chad. "That little boy in the photograph that you picked up in the café, he's my son Joe and I have a daughter as well called Lois."

Nellie could not take in what she was hearing and collapsed in a bundle on the sand.

"Your son? But I thought he was your nephew Frankie, you never told me he was your son."

Nellie was a time bomb of emotions, all clambering to explode at the same time. She was angry because Chad had lied to her, or at the very least hidden the truth. She was cross with herself for having been taken in so easily and most of all she felt let down, badly let down and on top of all of that she was still pregnant and from how it looked, listening to Chad, very much on her own.

Nellie looked down on Chad, unable to hide her disappointment and the tears that streamed down her face.

"I thought you loved me Chad, why have you lied to me?"

"'I haven't lied to you. I honestly thought you knew I was married. I thought like me you just wanted a bit of fun. I have a lovely wife and two kids back home, me and you were never going anywhere Nellie, it was never gonna happen. You must have realised that?"

"No Chad, no I didn't."

Nellie turned away from Chad and made her way back up the beach, this time all alone. She could find no words to say to Chad. Utterly distressed her brain was not able to function in any format that would express the full depth of her disappointment. In her mind it all seemed like a bad dream and she was sure that at any minute she would hear Chad calling her name and running after her, telling her that he loved her, that he had only been joking and of course he wasn't married. She could hear his voice telling her that she was the only girl for him, but of course in the sad reality of things she heard no such thing.

Nellie was in a daze, she couldn't remember walking back to her billet at all. Her whole body was numb and her mind just seemed to shut down with all the chaos and torment going on inside it. She slumped down onto her bed, too traumatised even to cry. Chad for nearly a year had been her life, he had meant the world to her and now she had nothing. Nobody to love, nobody to share things with, nobody to confide in and she also had the added complication, as at that moment that is how it felt, of a baby growing inside of her. Clarissa and Ethel she knew were good friends and no doubt would help her in any way they could, but realistically what could they do apart from listen to her and sympathise? It wasn't sympathy she wanted, it was Chad and anyway she didn't want anyone to know what had happened between them. How could she tell them that she was pregnant by a married man, who wanted nothing more to do with her? She knew only too well how gossip tore around the camp like wild fire and Nellie didn't want to be the subject of the same ridicule that she knew other, poor unfortunate souls before her had been.

Two weeks had gone by since Nellie had broken the news about the baby to Chad and not one word had she heard from him. Often in the past while working at the canteen, she would see Chad passing on his way somewhere or other and if he didn't have time to call in for a coffee, he would always pop his head in the door or tap on the window and wave, but for the last couple of weeks she had neither caught sight nor sound of him. Nellie had been unable to hide her emotions from her two friends Clarissa and Ethel who shared her billet and inevitably they asked her what was the matter. Eventually she confided and told them about her break up with Chad, even the fact that he was married, but Nellie could not bring herself to tell them that she was pregnant. For a time she put herself into denial and pushed the truth of the matter to the back of her mind, hoping that somehow, maybe by magic the problem would go away. Clarissa and Ethel tried as best they could to cheer Nellie up and were forever asking her to go out with them down to the beach or for a drink in the evenings, but Nellie refused, making excuses that she wanted to wash her hair, finish her book or have an early night.

Another week had elapsed and still nothing had been heard from Chad. Being thin anyway, Nellie soon noticed her body shape starting to change. Her stomach was no longer flat and her before, non-existent breasts were starting to fill out and become quite rounded. She smiled and her attention once again reverted back to Chad and the tender moments they had shared. At first, Nellie had been a little embarrassed by the fact that she had little bust to speak of, but Chad had boosted her morale by saying that good things came in small packages and that anyway more than a handful was a waste. Understanding that it was not possible to keep her pregnancy secret for much longer, she had decided to tell Clarissa and Ethel that evening. She had also made an appointment to see her commanding officer the following Monday morning. The doctor may have already informed him of her condition she wasn't sure, but she knew that she had to face the fact that being pregnant she wouldn't be able to stay in the N.A.A.F.I.

Poor Nellie could not think more than one day at a time. She didn't have a clue what she was going to do, or how her future lay. There was one thing on her mind though, one thing that she knew she had to do before she told anyone else. She had to see Chad again. The more she thought about it, the more she believed that Chad had behaved the way he had, because the news had been so unexpected for him. After all having a baby was no small task and quite a responsibility in itself. In fairness Nellie thought she herself had had a few days to think about the news and time to digest it, whereas for poor Chad it must have been quite a bombshell. Being Saturday lunchtime, Nellie guessed that more than likely if Chad wasn't working, he would be at the bar near the army hospital playing pool, so she decided that she would walk down there and speak to him, give him one last chance. Nellie hadn't forgotten that Chad had told her that he was married with two children, but inwardly she had managed to convince herself that his marriage couldn't be that strong,, as if it had have been, he wouldn't have taken up with her in the first place.

No Nellie, believed that there was still a chance that things would work out between them.

Nellie opened the door and walked through into the bar, all eyes were upon her. Walking into a bar by herself wasn't something that Nellie usually did and she felt uncomfortable, especially when she didn't recognise anyone. Making her way through the tables and chairs, she moved towards the back room where she knew the pool table was. With relief she saw a couple of Chad's friends leaning over the table.

"Howdy Nellie, how you doing?" shouted Floyd, one of the airmen who Chad often hung around with.

"I'm fine" lied Nellie. "I was looking for Chad, have you seen him?"

Floyd set his cue down on the table. Walking over to Nellie, he gently took her by the arm and guided her over to a solitary table.

"Nellie darling" he softly spoke to her. Chad's not here."

"Oh! Is he working? Never mind I'll catch him some other time" and she rose to go.

Once again Floyd grabbed her arm and made her sit back down.

"No Nellie, he's not working. Didn't he tell you? He went back to the States about ten days ago. He put in for a voluntary posting."

Chapter 16
Berkshire, England 1949

Hearing the news that Chad had gone back to America completely shattered Nellie. Learning that he had actually asked to be posted was evidence enough, even for her, that he was running away from the situation that they both found themselves in.

Nellie had been at her wits end, not knowing which way to turn. Clarissa and Ethel had tried their best to comfort her and say the right things, but at the end of the day it was up to Nellie and her alone it seemed now that Chad had chosen to desert her, who had to make the final decision; a decision that try as she might, she didn't know the answer to. Her head loaded with so many questions and what ifs, felt like sponge; she couldn't think straight at all. She had heard of a lady in one of the back streets in the Medina, who for a price would carry out an abortion. It wasn't that Nellie was necessarily against abortion, but she couldn't bring herself to take such action, through fear as much as anything else. Her other option of going ahead with the birth, neither filled her with confidence. She remembered only too vividly the stories that Rose her elder sister had related to her, of their own mother's tragic death through complications at Nellie's own birth, and the thought of history repeating itself scared her silly.

Nellie stepped off the train at Reading Station. In the end time had run out and it had become too late for an abortion and as Nellie suspected, considering her circumstances, the N.A.A.F.I. dismissed her. Clarissa proved to be a real friend in Nellie's time of need and learning that Nellie had nowhere to go once she arrived back in England, gave her the telephone number and address of her Aunt who ran a Bed and Breakfast in Reading.

"Give her a ring as soon as you get back to England" Clarissa had told her. "I'll send her a letter off today to explain, but knowing the post, you might arrive before it. She'll let you stay there for a while Nellie, I know she will and look here's my father's number, being a doctor he might be able to help in some way."

As soon as the boat bringing Nellie back from Cairo docked, she found a telephone box and called Clarissa's Aunt. She only had to mention her name and no further explanation was necessary as Clarissa's letter had already arrived. Nellie was so thankful for both Clarissa's and her Aunt's kindness. She would of course pay her way. She wasn't a charity case, but if it hadn't been for them she just couldn't think where she would have ended up. As she'd previously considered, she couldn't possible rely on Rose's kindness again and well she'd burnt her bridges with her cousin Cynthia and her husband Jack, when she'd called the police over Jack's assault on her. To be honest, Nellie didn't want the family to know that she was pregnant; although she expected that they wouldn't turn her away, she just couldn't bear to pass her shame on to them.

Breakfast was the only meal served at the Bed and Breakfast, so Nellie usually ate a sandwich or a small snack of beans or cheese on toast at a nearby café to keep herself going throughout the day. She knew with a baby on the way that she should be eating more nutritiously, but trying to make her savings last, it was the best she could do. She always made sure that she bought some fruit at the market and would eat at least one piece a day.

Nellie diligently tried to find work, but her shape now made it obvious that she was pregnant and employers just didn't want to know. Returning one afternoon following another unsuccessful trek around the local shops and cafes looking for employment, Nellie bumped into her landlady, Clarissa's Aunt, in the hallway. Mrs Harvey was more than just a little concerned about her niece's friend. In her opinion she looked a little on the peaky side and she guessed that Nellie was probably not looking after herself well enough

'The poor girl. She seems such a lovely lass as well, not the sort that deserves everything she's been lumbered with' she thought to herself.

"No luck today, love?" Mrs. Harvey enquired in a concerned voice.

"'No nothing again. I just don't know what else I can do. Trouble is it's not likely to get any better once I have this one." Nellie replied patting her swollen tummy.

"Come on through to the kitchen" said Mrs. Harvey. "I've just made a pot of tea, would you like one?"

"Yes please" answered Nellie, glad of the company as much as the cup of tea on offer.

"I've been having a think" said Mrs. Harvey, "I can't afford to pay very much, but how about you helping me here in the Bed and Breakfast. Just a few light duties, don't want you overdoing things in your

condition, but maybe you could help with some of the washing and ironing and the odd bit of dusting. In return, you can have your room here for free and you can join Mr. Harvey and me for your evening meal. At least that way I'll know that you're getting some proper food inside of you. I'll give you a bit of pocket money as well; it won't be much mind you, but at least you'll have a little something of your own to spend."
Nellie's eyes lit up at her landlady's suggestion.

"Of course you realise Nellie don't you, that you'll have to find somewhere else before the baby's born, as it wouldn't be fair on our other guests to have a newborn keeping them awake at all hours."

"Yes, I haven't forgotten you telling me that Mrs. Harvey. Will it be alright to stay here until four weeks before I'm due?"

"Yes love, of course it will. I only wish things were different, but I have to think of the business."

"I quite understand, please don't worry. You've been more than helpful and thank you so much for your offer of work. When would you like me to start? I do have to go to the doctors in the morning for a check up though."

"That's fine. Come and find me when you get back. Have you thought anymore of what you're going to do once the baby's born?"

Nellie's eyes started to fill up. She knew that she was going to have to make a decision at some time on not only her future, but also that of her unborn child. The thought of it was always constantly in her mind. She tried not to think about it, because it was a decision she just could not come to terms with. How could she give up her child, her own flesh and blood, Chad's flesh and blood as well, the only man she had ever loved? Realistically Nellie understood that time was running out and if she couldn't get a job now, it certainly wouldn't be any easier when she had a baby to look after.

"There, there" said Mrs. Harvey handing her a clean handkerchief from her fresh pile of ironing stacked on the kitchen table. "Don't go upsetting yourself pet, it's not good for the baby or you for that matter."
Mention of the baby made Nellie feel worse and she started to sob.

"I just don't know what I am going to do. I'd like to keep the baby, of course I would, but I can't see that it's going to happen. I thought I would ask the doctor tomorrow if he knows of somewhere where I could go at least for the birth. I can't really think any further than that at the moment. I suppose if I'm honest, I don't want to. It's just all too painful."

"Would you like me to have a word with my brother, the doctor? He might be able to help on that score." Mrs. Harvey cautiously asked while she topped up Nellie's cup with some more tea.

"If you wouldn't mind, thank you. I don't really know Reading, so I'm not sure what to do or where to go."

'It's no trouble honestly. You go to the doctor's tomorrow and get yourself checked. I'm wondering if you're not nearer to your time than you think; judging by the size of your tummy you look quite far gone to me. Why don't you have a lay down after your tea; you look quite whacked to me. Mr. Harvey and I will be having dinner at six, so get yourself down here for then and join us. Hope you like liver and bacon?"

The next day Nellie nervously lay on the bed in the doctor's surgery awaiting his examination. She hadn't seen a doctor since leaving Tripoli, so hoped everything was alright. It was times like this that Nellie really missed a mother's love and attention, even to have had a sister or good friend to lend her support would have been something, but Nellie had nobody.

The doctor felt all around Nellie's stomach, which even she had noticed was getting larger by the day.

"I'm just going to measure you" the doctor told Nellie. "That will give us a more accurate date of how many weeks pregnant you are. Mmm! When did you say your baby was due? Was it the last week in September?"

"Yes that's what the doctor in Tripoli told me."
The doctor pulled his stethoscope from inside his white coat and placed the ends in his ear.

"Just going to check the baby's heartbeat now. Nothing to worry about Miss. Edwards. Just try and relax."

"Mmm!" said the doctor and placed his stethoscope on another area of Nellie's stomach "Mmm!"

'Why do doctors only ever say Mmm?' thought Nellie with memories of the doctor in Tripoli doing exactly the same.

Once again the examination complete, the doctor left Nellie to get dressed and moved back towards his desk.

"Right Miss. Edwards. I agree with your date of the last week in September. At first I thought it might have been earlier considering your size, but I can actually tell you that I have just heard two heartbeats, you're expecting twins. I would imagine, as there's two of them in there pushing for space, they could very well arrive a little early."

Understandably Nellie left the surgery in a state of shock and didn't think for one moment to ask the doctor about suitable maternity homes. Returning back to the Bed and Breakfast she broke the news to the waiting Mrs. Harvey.

"Surely you must have some family you can contact; a girl needs her Mum at a time like this."

"I haven't got a Mum" sniffled Nellie, the thought of which made her feel even more desolate. "She died at my birth." Nellie's worst fears came gushing out. "Mrs. Harvey, what if the same happens to me? What if I die? It's got to be more dangerous having twins hasn't it?"

"Now, now don't you go upsetting yourself. Medicine is moving on all the time, you'll be fine, just fine. What about one of your sisters, couldn't you write to one of them?"

"No" Nellie vehemently replied. "I don't want anyone to know. At least not until I have decided what to do about the babies. If I have to give them up, I couldn't face everybody knowing. It would break my heart."

This latest remark set Nellie off on a new flood of tears.

"What on earth am I going to do Mrs. Harvey? I thought that maybe there was a chance I would be able to manage with one baby, but now that there's going to be two, what on earth can I do?"

"Now, now love. Just get yourself through today for the time being. You've been handed quite a bit to think about. I'm sure things will seem a lot clearer tomorrow when you've had a good night's sleep. I'll ring my brother tonight and have a word with him. At least if we can find somewhere for you to have the babies, that would be one less thing for you to worry about now wouldn't it? Let's just take one step at a time shall we?"

Clarissa's father did suggest two numbers of possible maternity homes that Nellie could try in Surrey, but when she telephoned to make enquiries, both of them were full. Nellie was finding her pregnancy quite hard going and although Mrs. Harvey had been more than helpful towards her, Nellie could sense that with her time coming closer, she was becoming anxious for her to find alternative accommodation. Talking one day to the lady on the fruit stall in the market, Nellie learnt of an establishment called Shipways House on the outskirts of Reading that took in unmarried mothers. Apparently the market trader's niece had found herself in a similar position the previous year and that is where she had gone for the birth of her child.

"I wouldn't say it's the best of places my girl, but at least you'll have a roof over your head."
Nellie thanked her and added that she would certainly give it a try. Options were running out for Nellie, so she hoped and prayed that Shipways House would take her in.

Shipways House reminded Nellie of the fever hospital she had spent time in as a child. All the expectant mothers shared one large ward, beds either side of a long room. They didn't engage in too much conversation; their spirits had been broken and troubled times lay ahead. Some of the women Nellie knew were pregnant as a result of rape; others like her had been badly let down by men that they had thought loved them. Whatever their circumstances, the staff working at Shipways, looked down their noses at them and in some cases considered them to be little more than prostitutes.

Nellie's time was now very close and the closer it came the more fearful she was not only of the birth and what that entailed, but also of the decision that she knew she had to make. The Matron of the hospital as well as the workers, relentlessly pressurised Nellie and the other unmarried mothers, that the best thing was for them to give up their babies. It was common knowledge that some maternity hospitals handed over babies given up by their mothers to wealthy couples, in exchange for a handsome donation. Nellie guessed that if this hospital acted in the same way, no wonder with her having twins they were keen for her to give them up, as that likely would mean double the donation.

In 1948 the government had granted unmarried mothers the same benefits as married mothers, albeit a very meagre allowance. Most unmarried mothers, not helped by the stigma their status carried, were too frightened to go it alone, especially without the support of a family, as the allowance was not enough to realistically keep a growing child.

The day before, a lady half-way up the ward had given birth to a little girl and as Nellie made her way to the bathroom, she couldn't resist looking at the little bundle, sleeping soundly, comforted by her recent feed. Nellie was fascinated by her feet and hands that constantly scrunched up with contentment; her fingernails so miniscule, yet so perfect. Nellie felt a warm glow inside of her and couldn't believe that she too would soon be giving birth to not one but two of these little beings. She wondered if she would have a beautiful little girl like this one, would she have two girls, two boys or even one of each? What did it matter as long as they were healthy?

"I've called her Elizabeth" said the proud Mum.

"Elizabeth" repeated Nellie "that's a lovely name. Are you keeping her?"

"Yes I'm keeping her. My Mum and Dad said they would help. They weren't too pleased when they first found out that I was pregnant, but they soon came around and now that they've seen her, well there's no way any of us could give her up. Have you decided what you're going to do? Don't let these dragons here" she said referring to the Matron and her staff "persuade you into doing something you will regret."

"I don't know. I really don't know what to do. There's nothing I would love more than to keep them, but I'm having twins and I just don't know how I would manage on my own with two. Sometimes I think I am being selfish wanting to keep them. What could I offer them? Maybe it would be better if I did give them up to a nice couple who could give them so much more."

Nellie found it difficult to say more on the subject as she could feel a lump forming in her throat.

"Is there nobody that could help you?"

Before Nellie could answer, the lady in the next bed started wailing profusely. Both women looked on with heart felt sympathy, as they knew that three days earlier the poor women had given her child away and still couldn't come to terms with her loss. Nellie would have liked to console the women, but just didn't know the right words to say, especially with the situation being so close to her own heart. She had heard that some mothers who gave up their babies cried for weeks on end.

The duty nurse strode over to the distressed women.

"Now come on Laura. Stop all this nonsense at once. You're upsetting all the other women. It's no good crying over spilt milk. What's done's done. It was your choice, now pull yourself together."

"God, they're such hard cows" commented the new mother. "They can't be human; they've no feelings whatsoever."

Hearing the women crying had upset Nellie as she knew that possibly she would have the same grief herself to endure. Returning from the bathroom, Nellie led on her bed and tried once again to make up her mind as to the best decision for her two unborn children.

'Why has it got to be like this?' she tormented herself. 'If only Chad hadn't been married or even if he had just told me he was married I would never have got myself into this situation in the first place.'

Nellie could not prevent the river of tears that streamed down her face. She tried with difficulty to turn her swollen body over and bury her head in the pillow, so that onlookers wouldn't notice her grief.

'If it had been one baby, I could have probably managed, but two I just don't think I can. I can't keep one of them without the other, how could a mother make such a choice?'

So many unanswered questions went through Nellie's head. She found a little comfort thinking that maybe if she did give up her twins that they would be adopted as a pair and at least have the comfort of each other, but common sense told her that this was unlikely. Eventually after much soul searching Nellie came to her decision, a decision that she was going to have to live with for the rest of her life. The next time the Matron asked her if she had come to a decision, Nellie reluctantly agreed that she would give her babies up when they were born.

Nellie had been feeling uncomfortable all day; her tummy and back were aching constantly. One minute she would be sat down, the next walking around the ward to try and ease the discomfort. At half-past four, just as tea was being brought around the ward, Nellie's contractions had become so severe that she knew without doubt that her babies were definitely about to make their entrance into the world. Nellie felt frightened. The pain was intense and she just wanted it all to be over. Not having had a child before she wondered if this level of pain was normal, or was she experiencing the same problems that her own mother had suffered and consequently died from. Although beforehand Nellie had told the nursing staff of her mother's history and her concerns for her own children's birth, nobody now seemed in the least bit bothered with attempting to put Nellie's mind at ease and tell her the words that she so wanted to hear, that everything would be alright. Nellie not only feared for her own life, but also for the lives of her two unborn babies. Already they felt so much a part of her and the protection she wanted to give them was overwhelming.

With a final push, the first baby appeared.
"First one's a boy" said the midwife in an uninterested manner.
Nellie desperately tried to get a glimpse of him before he was rushed away, but saw nothing except a little bit of dark hair. Within ten minutes Nellie gave birth to her second child, another boy. Similarly to the first, he too was whisked away before Nellie had chance to see him.
"Let me see my babies" Nellie yelled in an anguished tone.
"Later" snapped the midwife. "Get some rest."
"Please, let me see them. Are they alright?"
Nobody answered Nellie and once cleaned up she was left alone. Nellie was exhausted, but even so she found sleep impossible with not being allowed to see her two sons, let alone know if they were alright. One of the young nurses, who thankfully had more feelings than the majority of them at Shipways, returned a little later to check on Nellie. Seeing her anguished state, the nurse slipped out and checked on the two baby boys, returning with the news that they were both fine and healthy. Satisfied with the knowledge Nellie finally slept.

Nellie looked down at her first born snuggled against her breast, his tiny rosebud lips suckling for all his worth. As soon as she had set eyes on her two sons all her previous fears of not being able to look after them vanished. Everything just came so naturally to her and both of them gave her contentment beyond whch, she could never before have contemplated enjoying. She never minded being woken up in the middle of the night if one or sometimes both of them cried, as she loved them so much. Sometimes she would lie awake in her bed willing them to stir, so that she would have an excuse to pick them up, give them a cuddle and show them a mother's love. Nellie knew in those moments that she could never give up her boys, although she had signed the adoption papers they would just have to be changed. She remembered her own childhood of being passed from pillar to post and didn't want the same happening to them. As a child Nellie just got on with life and took whatever was handed out to her, but as an adult looking back, she could see that her dysfunctional childhood had not gone without leaving its scar.

Nellie studied her son Richard's face as he continued to feed. She couldn't see anything of herself in his looks, but without a doubt he had her sister Rose's long eyelashes and dark eyes. His brother James, already full from his feed was fast asleep in the cot to the side of Nellie's bed. On first sight of James, Nellie could instantly recognise his father Chad in his face. There could be no mistake as to his parentage; the resemblence even in one so young was striking. In the beginning Nellie had been quite tearful to think that Chad would never see his two sons and that the twins would never know their father. It didn't take long for her perception to alter and to remember her anger at Chad's abandonment of her, when she had most needed him. In some way Nellie's revenge was satisfied, by the fact that he would never get the chance to see his sons.

At the sound of heavy footsteps marching down the wooden floorboards of the ward, Nellie's eyes averted from her son feeding to see Matron flagged by two nurses coming towards her. Matron stood at the foot of her bed while one nurse leant over the cot to the side of Nellie and lifted out the sleeping James. Before Nellie had time to ask what she was doing, the other nurse was tugging at Richard, trying to release him from Nellie's cradling arms. Noticing Nellie resistance, Matron moved forward, grabbed Nellie from behind and held her down while the nurse prised Richard away from Nellie as he fed on her breast.
"What are you doing?" screamed Nellie. "Where are you taking my babies?" she shouted after the nurses who were striding back down the ward, one carrying Richard the other James, both of who were crying for their mother.
"You signed the papers Miss. Edwards" Matron sharply advised. "It's time for them to be taking away now. Arrangements have been made for their adoptions."
"No, No" wailed Nellie. "I've changed my mind. I want to keep them. Bring them back. Please bring my babies back. You can't take them away from me. They need me and I love them. I love them so much. Please bring them back, I want to keep them."

"Too late for that. As I said arrangements have been made and we have your signature on the papers to say that you agreed, so that's the end of it."

Nellie threw herself out of bed to chase after her babies. Nobody was going to take them away from her. Having witnessed similar incidents before, the Matron quickly grasped the situation and before Nellie had a chance to reach the end of her bed, she had grabbed her firmly and was shouting for assistance. Two burly nurses ran forward and helped Matron to restrain her.

Understandably Nellie was inconsolable, never had she been so grief stricken. It was as if her heart had literally been ripped out and she could feel an excruciating pain from the gaping hole left behind. In that instance, as Nellie sobbed until her last ounce of strength spilled from her body, a part of her, if not two parts, one for each son died within her. Nellie would never again be a whole person, her grief and guilt would continue to plague her for her remaining days.

Chapter 17
The Cotswolds – 2006

Alison reached out to hold her mother's hand in a fruitless endeavour to console her.

"How could I let them take my babies away? They were so tiny and so beautiful Alison. I failed them at the time they needed me so much. How could I have done that? How could I?"

"Oh Mum! Come on try not to upset yourself so much. Things were different in those days. You had been badly let down, you were all alone. What else could you have done?"

Much as Alison tried to comfort Nellie, at the same time she was shocked by the events that had been related to her. She had never suspected that her mother's secret, the secret that she so desperately wanted to tell her, would have been anything as revealing as this. She had so many questions to ask. Did her father know about the boys? Had Nellie ever tried to find them? In the past, Alison had often considered some of her mother's revelations to have been made up or exaggerated, but she could tell by her mother's obvious upset, that was not the case this particular time.

"I should have kept them. I wanted to keep them, but they wouldn't let me. They just took them away and I never saw them again. I've got nothing to remind me of them, not even a lock of their hair."
Nellie fumbled around in the sleeve of her cardigan for another tissue to replace the current one that was now very sodden and crumbling into holes. Not finding one, her frail, speckled hand moved down to check the side of her wheelchair, in case one had carelessly lodged itself between her body and the arm rest of her chair. Seeing her frustration, Alison pulled out an unopened packet of tissues from her own pocket.

"Here Mum, have these" Alison said as she tore along the blue dotted perforation and pulled a tissue half way out from the packet.

"Thank you" Nellie sniffed. "You must think I'm so awful Alison."

"No I don't Mum. Of course I don't."
Alison grasped her mother's small hand inside her two hands and gave it a gentle squeeze.

"You did what you thought was best. At the time I'm sure you believed that somebody else could give them a better life, could provide more for them. It was a very unselfish decision that you made for them

Mum and I can see just how much suffering and grief, making that choice must have caused you."

"But Alison, you don't understand you've never had children. My boys would never have known their mother's love, nobody else no matter how much money they had, would ever be able to give them that."

Before Alison had time to answer, the tears again started to flow in torrents down Nellie's cheeks.

"I think of them so often, not a day goes past without me wondering where they are, what they look like now, even if they are still alive. I used to sit on the bench in the High Street and watch all the young men walking by; those of similar age to Richard and James, wondering if any of them were my sons. James as a baby looked so much like Chad that I felt sure I would recognise him at once, but I never saw anyone who even remotely resembled either of them."

"Richard and James?" questioned Alison. "Was that their names?"

"Yes" sniffed her mother, "but I don't know whether they kept those names, or if they were given new ones" and with that came another onslaught of fresh tears.

Not seeming to notice her mother's renewed anxiety, Alison continued.

"Is that why you always told me that I should have been born a boy and not a girl? Is that why you planned to call me Richard and didn't have any girls' names chosen?"

"Yes, I suppose it was. Alison, I am so sorry. I haven't treated you very well over the years."

"I must admit" agreed Alison "as a child knowing that you always wanted a son did make me feel a bit unwanted."

Nellie's emotions were running so high that she found it difficult to continue the conversation, but between sobs eventually with difficulty she managed to formulate the words.

"What can I say to make things up to you? I've been such an awful mother to you and at times so horrible. I shouldn't have behaved like that towards you; it wasn't your fault at all. Bless you; you've always been so kind and patient with me. Nobody could have had a better daughter than you Alison. I do love you, in my own way I always have. It's just that I didn't feel that I deserved you after abandoning my two boys. I was so ashamed of myself; anything could have happened to them. I had no idea who adopted them, whether they were able to stay together and be brought up as brothers or not. In my hopes they both went to good homes and were brought up with plenty of love and affection, but realistically I know that may not have been the case. Oh! Alison, you read such terrible stories in the newspapers, they could have been abused, anything could have happened to them."

"Did Dad know anything about this Mum? Did you ever tell him?"

"No I didn't. I know I should have done and often wanted to, but I felt so ashamed. Nobody knows anything of this, only you. I have never to this day stopped carrying the guilt around with me. It has weighed so heavy on my shoulders for sixty years. Your Dad was a kind man and needless to say, I know that if I had let him into my secret that he would have been alright about it and understood."

Nellie broke down again.

"Everything will be okay Mum. You've had an awful lot of pain to deal with and I'm sure you will feel a lot better now that it is out in the open."

"But it's too late really isn't it? I can't tell your Dad the truth now can I? He was such a good man, he deserved better than me."

"Of course he didn't Mum. You're being silly now; you know you are. Nobody adored you more than Dad, he idolised you?"

"Yes I know he did" agreed Nellie, but he was never my real true love you see. It was not fair of me to marry him. I should have let him find someone else, someone who could have loved him for all the right reasons, for the good, kind man that he was. See Alison, I have been selfish, very selfish and sadly at your Dad's expense. For all of Chad's faults and I know he abandoned me and the twins, but it was always him who held my heart, who I really loved. For me your Dad was second best, nothing more and because of that I didn't treat him as well as I should have done either."

"Well if it's any comfort, I am sure Dad thought that you were the right women for him."

Alison was trying her best to make things easier for her mother. She knew from her own experience how difficult and spiteful at times her mother could be. Graham didn't call her T.O.B., The Old Bat for nothing. Alison recalled having thought to herself after her father had passed away, just how demanding her mother was. She realised that this was likely nothing new and that her poor father more than likely had silently taken the brunt of Nellie's sharp tongue and high demands all through their married life.

Nellie and Alison's conversation was halted by a small tap on the door.

"Alright to come in" asked Jane carrying a tray with the promised two cups of tea and plate of sandwiches.

"Thank you Jane, that's so kind of you. Here put it down here" instructed Alison as she pulled a small footstool across the room.

"Everything alright?" Jane enquired noticing Nellie's distressed face.

"Yes, we're fine thanks" answered Alison "Just going back over old times, some happy memories and some not so."

"I'll leave you to it then. Ring the bell if you need anything."

Alison stirred her mother's cup of tea and handed it to her.

"Can you manage that, Mum? Try and keep it steady. How about a sandwich, would you like one of these?" suggested Alison desperately trying to encourage her mother to eat.

"No, nothing for me thanks. You have them."

"No I'd better not start picking, as Graham has cooked a shepherd's pie for dinner and I've already had lasagne as it is."

"Graham, I must see Graham. I know at times I have been so unpleasant to him. It was wrong of me. I've been so stupid, being horrible to the ones who love me most. Please tell him how very sorry I am. Do you think he would come and see me and then I could tell him myself? That's the least I could do isn't it?" Nellie said lifting her face up to look at Alison.

"I'll see if he will come tomorrow. He may be at work, I'm not sure, but if he is, we'll both come over at the week-end. Don't worry he's got a thick skin. I don't expect he's taken any of your comments to heart."

"Well he should have done. I've been such an interfering old fool. I realise that now. I should never have kept pestering you two to have children; it was none of my business."

"Well yes I agree with you on that one Mum, it wasn't."

"It was just I suppose having lost my two boys, I could never understand why you didn't want children of your own. It just didn't seem right to me when I had such a big, empty hole in my heart from all the pain and suffering of not having my twins close to me and there was you and Graham who could have a lovely family and didn't seem to want it. I realise now how selfish I was, thinking that grandchildren would in some small way replace the love that I had not been able to give to Richard and James."

"I can see what you are saying Mum, but we all have our own choices in life to make and what might be right for one person is not necessarily right for another. Graham and I are happy just being the two of us. Maybe if we had met when we were younger, things might have been different, who knows? At the end of the day though Mum, I love Graham and he loves me and that's what really matters."

"Yes, you're right dear. I can see that now. I'm so sorry."

"It's alright Mum, don't go upsetting yourself again. You know the saying "Love means never having to say you're sorry.""

"Yes and there's another one" sniffed Nellie, "The truth hurts."

A silent interlude hung over Alison and Nellie as they both mulled over their own individual thoughts.

"Did you ever try to find the twins Mum?"

"I did actually, not long after your father died. It was something that I had always wanted to do, but just didn't know how to go about it. Then one day I was reading the Sunday newspaper and this advert jumped out at me. It was for an agency specialising in connecting adopted children with their birth parents. I knew there and then that I just had to give them a ring. Whether or not I would have had the courage if your Dad had still been alive I don't know, but ring them I did. The agency were very helpful, the lady I spoke to sounded so kind. They sent back various forms for me to fill in, which I did with all the information I knew. The usual stuff you know like name, father's name if known, date of births etc. All those details were then filed on their records, so that if Richard or James ever contacted them trying to find me, our details would be matched together. I hoped with all my heart that one day I would get a phone call to say that they had been found, but realistically I knew that it was like looking for a needle in a haystack."

"Did you ever hear anything of Chad Mum, I don't suppose you did?"

"No, nothing at all. I had hoped in the early days that he might have considered writing to me; the NAFFI would have forwarded it on if he had, but no he never did. I suppose he just wanted to forget me and get on with his life in America with his wife and children. In a small way, I could accept that he didn't want anything more to do with me, but to this day I have never been able to understand how he could turn his back on Richard and James. That hurt so much. If he had only seen them with his own eyes, I am sure that he would have thought differently. They were just so small, so helpless and so loveable; little angels that's what they reminded me of."

"Did you put Chad's name on their birth certificates?"

"No that's another thing. He was definitely their father, there was no getting away from that, but because I was unable to contact him and get him to acknowledge the fact, on their birth certificates it had to be shown as father unknown."

Nellie started to cry again, the sad emotions of remembering the stark events appearing all too evident.

"Alison, that was the worst part for me not having their father's name on their certificates. That piece of paper was all Richard and James would have if they ever did try and find their parents. They knew nothing about me, what kind of a person I was, what my circumstances were. Alison for all they might think I could have been a prostitute."

"I'm sure Mum if they ever come looking for you, they will realise that life was different in those days. You went through some hard times and I am sure that they will understand."

"Maybe you are right. When I sent the forms back to the agency, I sent with them two letters, one for Richard and one for James. You would not believe how difficult it was for me to write those letters. I just didn't know where to start. My heart spilled out onto those few sheets of Basildon Bond paper I can tell you and I remember the ink being smudged in places where my tears had fallen. I tried to explain to them how much I had loved them and how I had wanted to keep them, but being alone I wasn't able to offer them the life and opportunities that they deserved. I told them about Chad, their father and how much I had loved him and that if I had known at the time he was married, I would never have gone out with him in the first place. It was so difficult putting into words all that I wanted to say, it brought everything back. I felt that I had to be truthful and say that Chad had abandoned me when I told him that I was pregnant, but at the same time I didn't want to make him sound bad. He is after all their father and I didn't wish to influence their opinions of him."

"I think that was a good idea Mum to write the letters and when you think about it Richard and James would be grown men by now. If they were born in 1949, let's see they would be", there was a slight pause while Alison made her calculations, "fifty-seven by now and certainly worldly enough I'm sure to make their own assumptions. You must try though Mum not to be too upset that you haven't heard anything from Richard and James. I know it's very hard, but as you said earlier, you don't know their circumstances either do you? They could have been adopted by the same family or by two different ones and you have to face facts that their adopted parents may never have told them that they were adopted. It does happen."

"Yes you're right of course Alison and to be honest it's helped telling you today, but I think at long last I've resigned myself to thinking that I am never going to see them again. Time's running out for me now, I'm an old lady. All I can wish for is that my two boys have had a good and happy life, even though sadly I was never a part of it."

Alison pushed up the sleeve of her jumper to check the time.

"Gosh! I didn't realise it was as late as that. Do you know it's five past seven already. I'd better give Graham a ring, he'll be wondering what on earth has happened to me."

"You get going now Alison. I'll be alright. To be honest, all this talking has made me feel quite tired. I think maybe I'll have an early night. Would you ask Jane on your way out to come and help me get ready for bed?"

"Are you sure Mum? I don't mind staying a bit longer, Graham won't mind as long as I give him a ring."

"Yes I'm sure. You get off home; I've taken up enough of your time already with my silly ways."

Alison stood up, bent over and gave her mother a tender kiss on the cheek.

"Now you try and get a good night's sleep Mum. It's been a big day for both of us and don't you forget I love you and I always have."

"And I love you too Alison and Alison thank you. Thank you so much for putting up all of these years with my stupid, selfish ways."

Alison answered with a smile and moved towards the door with a gentle glow in her heart. How strange after all of these years, that her mother had told her that she loved her and not just once either."

"Alison" whispered Nellie. "Don't forget to ask Graham if he would come and see me. I'll understand if he doesn't want to, but it would mean so much to me to be able to apologise to him and thank him for making my lovely daughter so happy."

"Yes I will Mum. See you tomorrow."

Alison left her mother's door ajar ready for Jane when she came to put Nellie to bed. She felt the beginnings of what might become a migraine, so was relieved to be back out in the fresh air again. Although the window in her mother's room had been open, it had still felt quite stuffy. Just as she walked across the car park, rummaging in her bag for the car keys, her mobile started to ring. Glancing down she saw instantly that it was Graham calling.

"Hello I was just about to call you. I'm on my way home, unlocking the car door as we speak."

"That's fine then. I was just beginning to start worrying. How did it go?"

"Not sure where to start really. Probably best if I tell you when I get home."

"A bit heavy was it?"

"Yes, that would about sum it all up quite well."

"Sounds like a drink is the order of the day then. What would you like, a white wine? I'll have a chilled glass waiting here for your arrival."

"Think I could do with something a bit stronger."

"That bad eh?"

"Mmm! You could say that; certainly a big surprise. I'll have a gin and tonic and Graham, make it a double. Actually thinking about it, maybe you ought to pour one for yourself as well."

It had been nearly half past two in the morning and quite a few gin and tonics later, by the time Alison and Graham had eventually climbed into bed. Alison turned over and snuggled into her pillow and somewhere in the distance of her dream she could hear a telephone ringing. The ringing continued and eventually woke her. She then realised that the ringing was in fact coming form the telephone in the hall. She sprang out of bed and looked at her watch which read five past eight. Her sudden jolt had woken Graham, who as usual being such a sound sleeper had not stirred until then.

"What's the matter, why are you getting up?" he sleepily asked, rubbing his eyes.

"The phone's ringing, can't you hear it?"

Alison quickly ran down the stairs with that sense of foreboding that always comes with a phone call at an unusual hour. Upstairs in the bedroom, Graham strained his ears, but could not really pick up the conversation to know who was calling. It didn't take him long to guess though, when he heard Alison just before she put the phone down, tell the caller that she would be straight over.

"Is it Nellie?"

"Yes" murmured Alison. "That was Carol the Matron at Fir Trees. She said that Mum's going down hill fast and that I really should get over there."

Graham sat up in bed. Although on the one hand they had always been expecting a phone call of this nature, now that it had actually happened it didn't fail to surprise them both.

"I didn't realise that she was that bad. I'll come with you. You have a shower first and I'll go downstairs and put the kettle on."

"It seems so hard to take in" said Alison as she walked into the kitchen after showering. She has been a bit strange the last few days, but last night when I left her, apart from feeling really tired, she didn't seem too bad. In fact I thought she had turned the corner and was slightly better."

"Here, you sip this" Graham said "and I'll just pop upstairs and get ready. There's a slice of toast in the toaster if you want it."

"No, I don't think I could eat anything at the moment, I'll just have this tea."

Fifty minutes later, Alison and Graham were in the corridor just outside Nellie's room, in conversation with the Matron.

"Alison dear, I know this is hard, but I think you should prepare yourself for the worst."

Tears welled up in Alison's eyes and she was glad of Graham's protective arm around her shoulders. Alison's hand moved upwards to cover her mouth in an attempt to conceal her anguish.

"I thought she seemed a bit brighter yesterday. I can't believe that she has gone downhill so fast."

"Her pulse is still strong, she's a tough old girl you're Mum, as I'm sure you know, but her breathing has become quite laboured."

"Can we see her please?" asked Alison.

"Yes of course you can, but as I said just prepare yourselves a little. She is now falling in and out of consciousness and at times is quite distressed. She keeps calling out the names Richard and James. Do they mean anything to you?"

"Yes, yes they do" replied Alison with a small smile on her lips, "It's a long story."

"Nellie dear, can you hear me?" Matron asked as she pushed open the door to Nellie's room. "Your daughter and son-in-law have come to see you."

Nellie's head moved to and fro aimlessly on the pillow. She looked so frail and deathly against the crispness of the white bed linen. Alison, even though Matron had tried to warn her, was still surprised by her mother's sharp decline. Nellie's face looked gaunt and skeletal. Her appearance was probably not helped by the fact that her teeth were in a glass on the side of the sink in the far corner of the room, rather than in her mouth. Alison had no intention of pressing the issue as she could see that her mother was past caring what she looked like. Normally she would have hated anybody to see her without them.

"Can you hear me?" Matron again prompted. "Your daughter Alison is here to see you."

"No, don't wake her. It's alright I'll just sit here with here until she wakes up."

"Okay. If you want anything just give me a shout."

"Thanks" said Graham.

Alison pulled over the straight backed chair to the side of her mother's bed and picked up her hand. It felt quite cold.

"Are you warm enough Mum? Would you like another blanket? Actually Graham we could close that window for starters, would you mind?"

Nellie became quite fidgety and rather than pull the bed clothes up around her, started throwing them off. Alison rubbed her mother's hands between her own to try and warm them up. This act of tenderness appeared to bring Nellie back to consciousness.

"Hello Mum, it's Alison and Graham's here with me. You asked to see him yesterday."

Witnessing her mother's struggle to raise herself up, Alison leant over and plumped up the pillows behind her and helped raise Nellie back onto them. By this time, Graham had settled himself down on the only other chair in the room, a green, wing-backed arm chair. Alison could see her mother having difficulty making out the shape of the person in the corner and without her glasses; she knew that her short sightedness would not allow her to recognise him.

"Come a bit closer Graham, Mum can't see you."

Graham stood up and moved over to Nellie's bed as per Alison's instructions.

"Hello Nellie, How are you feeling? You've been a bit poorly lately haven't you?"

Nellie nodded in agreement and undid her hands from Alison's grasp and offered them out to Graham, who took them in his own.

"Oh! You are a bit cold Nellie. We'll see if we can find you another blanket in a minute."

"Thank you for coming" whispered Nellie, her little face looking so pitiful, causing Alison to swallow hard herself in an attempt to prevent her own tears from coming.

Graham could see that Nellie was trying to talk but just didn't have enough strength.

"There's no need to say anything Nellie. Alison has told me everything and don't you worry, everything is fine and we love you very much. That's all you need to know. You try and rest now. We'll still be here when you wake up."

Alison looked over to Graham and a warm smile spread across her mouth. There was no need for any words to travel between them; Graham knew that her smile was saying thank you and he replied with a loving wink.

Alison and Graham spent a long day at Nellie's bedside. The staff at Fir Trees were very considerate and brought in cups of tea and at lunchtime a plate of sandwiches for them. Neither Alison nor Graham felt very much like eating and only picked at a couple of them. Nellie's room was eerily quiet, disturbed only by Nellie's at times heavy breathing, which as the day wore on was getting noticeably weaker. Outside was a completely different story. It was a beautiful summer's day and the birds' constant twittering was a welcome exchange to the stillness of approaching death.

Jane the carer entered the room and motioned for Alison and Graham to follow her outside.

"It's been a long day for you two hasn't it? Why don't you give yourselves a bit of a break? I'll stay here with your Mum; she won't be on her own. Nothing's going to happen in the next hour anyway, so why don't you too have a bit of fresh air. The Clinton Arms is open on the village green, go and get yourselves a beer."

Graham looked at Alison. "I think that would be a good idea Alison. As Jane says it's unlikely that there will be any sudden change and even if there was, Jane's got our mobile numbers and we could be back in two minutes."

"Yes alright. My head does feel a bit muggy; I could do with a breather. You will stay with her though won't you Jane? I would hate for anything to happen to her while she was on her own."

"Of course I will. Now off you go and have a little bit of time on your own."

Alison and Graham carried their drinks from the bar over to a small table in the corner by the window. Even though it was only late afternoon, because of the low, beamed ceilings and small windows, it was necessary for the wall lights to be on.

"We could have sat outside I suppose being such a nice day" suggested Graham.

"If you don't mind I prefer it in here. It's a lot quieter; no noisy kids running around."

"Yes there is that" agreed Graham.

"Do you know" started Alison "I find it all so sad. It was only yesterday when Mum and I had that heart to heart that I really for the first time felt close to her and now………."

Sensing that Alison found it difficult to continue, Graham placed his pint on the table and reached across for her hand.

"I know what you mean love, but just be glad that you had that conversation with her when you did. At least perhaps you understand more about your Mum now and why she thought it necessary to treat you, well us really, the way she did."

"Yes I suppose so, but it doesn't make it any easier really."

"No maybe not, but when you think about it, perhaps Richard and John"

"James" corrected Alison.

"Yes sorry James. Maybe for all we know, they did know that they were adopted and maybe they have been looking for their mother. It's too late for them to find Nellie now by the looks of things, but at least Alison you did have that chance."

"Yes you're right, of course you are. I'm just feeling a little sorry for myself. Having at last found my real mother so to speak, the one who loves me, I just don't want to lose her."

"I know you don't, but she is an old lady Alison. Eighty seven is a good age by anybody's standards and you wouldn't want to see her suffer would you?"

"No as usual you are right" answered Alison, so glad of his support.

Alison and Graham crept quietly back into Nellie's room.

"How is she" asked Alison.

Jane didn't say anything in front of Nellie, but slowly shook her head in a negative fashion and mouthed "Not long now."

Although the news was expected and really what they all knew to be imminent, Alison could not help but take an emotional gulp of air.

"Speak to her Alison; she will know you are here. She can still hear you."

Jane raised herself from the chair at the side of Nellie's bed and Alison sat down in her place. Once again she took her mother's hand, it felt very cold and her lips now had a twinge of blue about them.

"I'm back Mum. Graham and I just popped out for a breath of fresh air. We walked down to the little pub on the village green and had a beer. It's a lovely day outside, really sunny."

"Is it? Your Dad always liked a pint, do you remember?" Nellie reminisced for a brief moment coming out of her increasing sleep pattern.

"Yes I do and I can also remember that I liked to sip the froth off of the top of it when I was a little girl."

"Yes" Nellie sleepily remembered "You did."

The few words that Alison and Nellie imparted with each other seemed to drain Nellie greatly of her energy and once again, her eyes heavily closed, giving way once more to slumber.

Alison and Graham continued to watch over Nellie in silence, preferring for her to rest quietly. Some time later, Nellie's eyes once more struggled to open, but it was such an obvious effort for her, heavy as they were.

"Alison, are you still here?"

"Yes I'm here Mum."

"I'm so tired" Nellie wearily whispered, "so very tired. I think it's time for me now. I'm ready to go upstairs. Will you come with me?"

Alison glanced across to Graham and they both realised what Nellie was really trying to say. She had had enough of the fighting and was now ready to drift away peacefully.

"I'm sorry Mum, but I can't go with you. It's not the right time for me yet. There are still things I need to do."

"But I don't want to go by myself."

"You'll be fine Mum, just fine. Dad's waiting for you I know he is."

"Yes Gerald, he was my husband wasn't he."

"Yes your husband and my Dad."

"And you never know maybe Chad will be there to meet you as well."

No I don't think so" murmured Nellie, but I know your Dad will be. He always did love me."

And with that Nellie gave a deep sigh and expelled her last breath of air.

"Oh! God, Graham I think she's gone."

"Yes I know. Would you like me to go and get some help?"

"No, just let me have a minute or two to sit with her please."

Alison stayed holding her mother's limp hand, while so many thoughts and memories passed through her mind. It seemed so strange, although she was a grown women in her fifties, now that both her parents had passed away she felt all alone in the world. In a way she was now an orphan and for the first time shared a feeling of empathy with her half brothers Richard and James and not least Nellie herself.

Nellie's funeral took place the following Wednesday afternoon in the village church. The weather had taken a turn for the worse and grey, ominous clouds hung overhead. Not sure whether down to the inclement weather or the prospect of the service to come, but Alison shuddered as she followed Nellie's light oak coffin along the dark red, tiled aisle of the church. Alison had chosen white lilies to adorn the top of her mother's coffin. Lilies had not been her first choice; ideally she would have preferred daffodils reminiscent of Nellie's welsh background, but in June they were out of season. Ordering her mother's floral tribute had been the hardest part of the whole sad occasion for Alison. It somehow brought everything home, that this was the final thing that she could do for her mother, the last gift that she would ever give her.

Inside the church, the few mourners present occupied the first three rows of wooden pews. Glancing around, Alison counted approximately twenty-five in total, not a very good farewell in Alison's mind to celebrate nearly eighty-seven years of life. Realistically, it was hardly surprising that there were not more mourners as Nellie had already outlived her brothers and sisters and most of her friends and acquaintances. Alison was pleased to see that two of her cousins had made the journey from Wales, Gary who was her Aunty Joyce's eldest son, and Vera, one of Aunt Rose's daughters, who in herself must be now in her seventies. She also recognised Jane and several of the carers from Fir Trees in the congregation, as well as a couple of hers and Graham's friends, who she knew were there as much for support to them as they were to mourn Nellie.

By early evening the grey clouds had blown over and the sun was at last, for the final few hours of the day at least, poking its way through. It had been a long day for Alison and Graham, but now at last they were back home, just the two of them in Acorn Cottage. Neither of them felt much like eating, so Graham opened a bottle of wine and Alison laid out some olives, nuts and cubes of cheese on a small platter, which they took out to the patio table on the cobbled terrace.

"Mmm! That tastes good" said Alison as she sipped her glass of chilled wine. "I needed that."

"Yes it was a funny old day really wasn't it. Your Mum would have really enjoyed herself if she had been there. It was nice to see Vera and Gary; must be quite a few years since we last saw them?"

"Must have been at Uncle Idris' funeral I suspect and that must have been three years or more ago."

"Same old story isn't it? It's sad that families only seem to get together at funerals and the likes, as everyone has such a good time when they do actually meet up."

"I suppose we all lead such busy lives nowadays and as you get older you tend to drift apart."

"Yes and I suppose" added Graham "if you have kids they take up your time and then when grandchildren come along you're needed for babysitting duties."

"Just as well we didn't have any then, as Mum took up most of our time."

"Maybe she would have been different though if we had become parents, you don't know. She told you herself that grandchildren would have given her something to love, maybe life would have been different."

"Well, we'll never know now will we?"

Graham picked up the bottle of wine to replenish their glasses.

"It's empty already. I didn't realise that we had drunk that much. Anyway I for one thought that it had gone down rather well, shall I get another one from the fridge?"

"Yes why not; seems like a perfectly good idea to me."

Graham returned with the empty wine bottle to the kitchen and left Alison alone with her thoughts. Her eyes fell on the recently planted flower tubs, which she had busied herself planting up when her mother had first become ill. 'So much has happened so quickly' she thought to herself. Finishing the remaining drops of wine from her glass, she looked over her shoulder to see if Graham was on his way back with the other bottle. Thinking that he was taken rather a long time she jokingly shouted, "What's keeping you? A girl could die of thirst out here."
A moment later Graham re-appeared looking deep in thought.

"Bottle of wine" Alison prompted holding up her empty glass, noticing Graham emerging from the back door empty handed.

"Oh" Graham said patting his head in recognition of his forgetfulness.

On his return Alison asked him "Are you alright? You look deep in thought."

"Yes. Well I don't know really. It all seems a bit odd."

"What does?"

"Well when I went into the kitchen the phone started ringing."

"I thought you were a long time. Who was it?"

Graham sat down and refilled both of their glasses.

"It was a lady called Margaret Horcott."

"Horcott? Doesn't ring any bells with me?"

"No it wouldn't. It all seems a bit confusing; I can't really get my head around it. She's from an adoption agency in Windsor."

"What did she say?" enquired Alison.

"She sounded very nice, but was rather non-committal really. She asked if my name was Graham Richard Henderson and when I confirmed that it was, asked if my parents were June and Arthur Henderson of 6 Harbour View, Sidmouth in Devon, which as you know they were."

"Strange. What else did she say?"

"Not much more to be honest. She said that she had some rather delicate information to go over with me and that she felt it would be better to tell me face to face."

"How odd. God! I thought we'd had enough surprises with all Mum's revelations. I don't know if I can take any more."

"Yes quite. Anyway I've made an appointment to see her in her office next Tuesday at half past three. It all sounds quite intriguing, although for the life of me I can't fathom out how I'm involved with anything that she's got to tell me. I don't even know anyone who's been adopted."

"Would you like me to come with you?"

"No that's fine. I've got a meeting in London in the morning anyway, so it's quite handy I can call in there on my way back home."

"If you're sure. I could always drive up and meet you in Windsor."

"Gosh! You're making it sound like this woman's got some awful news to impart. I'll be fine honest, don't worry. She's probably found out that I'm the long lost relative and sole survivor of some multi-millionaire who's left me all of his money."

"Oh! I hadn't thought of that. That would be nice."

"Well whatever it is, we shall find out soon enough on Tuesday. Hey! Maybe my Mum like yours had a little dalliance before she married as well and I'm about to be told about a brother or sister I didn't know I had?"

"Well be warned as my poor old Mum said 'Truth Hurts.'

18 Chapter

The day after Nellie's funeral was a damp, greyish type of day, not exactly raining but drizzling. Graham was busy going through some customer files upstairs in the small bedroom that doubled up as his office whenever he was working from home. Alison felt that she ought to make good use of her time, but looking out of the kitchen window considered it not the best of days for gardening. She could see as she peered through the window, dried droplets of water that had obviously splashed up at some point from the sink directly underneath. Looking around she noticed smudged finger prints also marking the glass panes of the French doors leading out to the patio. Alison blamed Graham for that. She was forever telling him to shut the door using the handle, rather than pushing it shut. Again she thought that it wasn't the best day for cleaning windows either. Deep down Alison knew what would be the best thing for her to do; something that she hadn't been looking forward to doing, but something that couldn't be put off for any longer. She had to go back to Fir Trees Residential Home and sort out her mother's belongings. It was no point in keeping the room on any longer than necessary and besides, until it was cleared out she was still being charged for it.

Alison reversed 'Doris' her blue fiesta out of the drive and set off, probably for the very last time, in the direction of Cirencester and Fir Trees. She hated driving in this kind of weather, not enough rain to keep the windscreen wipers going and too much to warrant not using them. The continuous screeching of the blades against the window was a constant irritation to her. She switched on the radio in an attempt to drown out the drone of the wipers. All but one of the stations had bad interference and the only programme being clearly broadcast, was yet another debate on the rights and wrongs of the war in Iraq. Alison turned the radio off and risked being mesmerised by the continuous scratching of the windscreen wipers.

It felt strange and lonely entering her mother's room, knowing that she no longer occupied it and memories of her last visit came flooding back to her. A lump came to Alison's throat, but she took a deep breath in an attempt to compose herself and decided it was best to get on with the job in hand. First she took down the photographs hanging on the wall. Graham had suggested that they put them there, so that Nellie could see them better when she lay in bed. There was a lovely one of her parents, taken Alison remembered in the garden of a pub in Jersey that her Mum and Dad used to frequent when on holidays. There was another one of Alison taking at a friend's wedding a few years earlier. Alison hated the photograph and certainly wouldn't have given it wall space, but for some unknown reason it had been one of Nellie's favourites.

Alison moved across to Nellie's wardrobe and started to remove the clothes, some of which had never been worn and even still had the labels on. Alison put a couple of garments to one side, as rather than give them to a charity shop; she thought she could make use of them herself.

'After all as they say charity begins at home' she told herself.

Hearing the door rub against the carpet on opening, Alison turned to see Jane the carer in the doorway.

"Hello Alison, I thought I heard someone in here. How are you?"

"Not too bad thanks. I haven't been looking forward to emptying Mum's room, but it's got to be done hasn't it?"

"Yes it's not the easiest of tasks is it? What are you planning on doing with your Mum's clothes?"

"There's a few things I will probably keep, but the rest I thought I would give to a charity shop. Do you know if there is one close by; maybe I could drop them off on my way home?"

"Well if it's alright with you, I am sure some of the ladies here would be very grateful for them. Unlike your Mum, some of them don't have daughters or relatives to take them shopping and their clothes wear out and they don't have any to replace them."

"Yes of course. What would you like me to do, fold them up and leave them on the bed?"

"Just leave them hanging in the wardrobe and I'll collect them later. It will be one job less for you anyway. Would you like a cup of tea?"

"I'd love one thanks, if it's not too much trouble."

"Course it isn't."

A lot of Nellie's things Alison put straight into a black, bin bag. Her mother had always been a hoarder and all sorts were found in her drawers; sweets, nibbled bars of chocolate, pens, half used tissues, raffle tickets and bingo cards, to name a few. Alison pulled out two biscuit tins from the bottom of the wardrobe. The one she could remember from her childhood days. It was navy blue with white Grecian figures draped in

robes on the lid. Before even opening it Alison knew what it contained, old photographs from years before. She didn't feel that she wanted to look at them on her own, but thought maybe later when at home with Graham, that then maybe they would go through them. Opening the second tin, she discovered that too was full of photographs, although more recent ones. Feeling around, to make sure that nothing was still in the wardrobe, Alison's hand touched on something. She dragged it out and saw that it was a cardboard, concertina folder. Briefly glancing inside, she realised that it was Nellie's old household bills dating back prior to her move to Fir Trees. Alison couldn't recollect having brought the folder over from her mother's old home when she had initially moved her belongings to Fir Trees.
'Surely I would have thrown out any old bills out at the time, not kept them.'
She could only assume that for some reason Nellie had smuggled it over herself. Alison placed it in the box of items to take home, making a note to check through it, just in case there was anything of any significance in it.

Alison took one final glance around the room, she didn't think she had left anything behind, so she walked out of the door and pulled it to. For in instance she felt extremely lonely. It was as if she was closing the final chapter on her mother's life; the end of an era.   It was impossible for Alison to leave Fir Trees without one final visit to see Matron to thank her and the staff for all that they had done for Nellie. Alison well knew that her mother could be tiresome at times, but they had always showed her such care and attention that there had never been any call for complaint. Alison made a mental note to arrange for some flowers to be sent to them in the morning, as a token of gratitude from herself and Nellie.

Graham had not had a good morning. The meeting in London had certainly not been as plain sailing as he would have hoped and on top of that it had run over time. Thankfully Margaret Horcott's instructions had been spot on and he easily found the address that she had given to him. He slowly drove past the three-story, grey building with its three, exact rows of windows equally interspaced between the floors.
'Definitely a relic of the sixties' he thought.

One of Graham's reasons for not wanting to be late for his meeting with Margaret Horcott was parking. He had thought that it might well be a problem, so was greatly relieved to see a blue parking sign indicating a public car park in the next street down. Graham looked at the clock on the dashboard. He needn't have worried after all; it was still only ten minutes to three, forty minutes before the allotted time of the meeting.

Looking across the street, he noticed a small café and thought that he may as well use the time having a coffee and a cigarette. He could do with unwinding a bit and getting his thoughts together, especially as he had no inclination whatsoever of what this meeting was all about.

Graham chose a table at the far end of the café, which was partially concealed by a large, rubber plant that had definitely seen better days. He bent down and felt the compost in the pot and realised his initial assumption had been correct, it definitely was in desperate need of water. 'Alison would have a fit' he thought to himself, knowing his partner's love of plants.

Thoughts turning to Alison; he took out his phone from his inside pocket, scrolled down to their home number and pressed the call button.
"Hello love. Thought I would give you a quick ring. I found the place, no problem. I'm just having a quick coffee before I go in. What are you up to?"
"Nothing much really. I've just made a cup of tea as well. I thought I might have a look through that tin of old photographs I brought back from Mum's room."
"Well don't you go upsetting yourself. I know what you're like."
"No I won't. If I remember rightly, most of the photographs date back to before I was born. There's probably a few of me as a little girl. If there's any funny ones, I'll keep them out to show you when you get home."
"I hope this meeting doesn't take too long. I suppose I'd better get going" said Graham looking at the clock on the wall behind the counter.
"Good Luck and I'm sure it's nothing to worry about."
"No, I'm not worried, not worried at all. I am intrigued though. Still all will be revealed very soon."

"Will you give me a ring when you come out? I'm dying to know what it's all about and also then I'll know what time to expect you home. I'll have the gin ready in case you need it" joked Alison.

Walking through the main doors, Graham immediately noticed an array of brass plaques to the side of the lift, indicating the companies who operated from within the building. Working from left to right, his eyes soon focused on Connection Intermediary Services the company which Margaret Horcott worked for. Their offices were on the third floor, so Graham opted to take the lift.

Graham introduced himself to the receptionist and was invited to take a seat on the soft, brown leather sofa. The receptionist spoke quietly into her telephone and Graham assumed that she was announcing his arrival to Margaret Horcott. He hardly had time to make himself comfortable, before a lady appeared through the office door to the side of him. She turned towards him and held out her hand.

"Mr. Henderson?"

"Yes" replied Graham standing up to shake hands.

"I'm Margaret Horcott, we spoke on the telephone. Thank you for sparing me your time. Please, come into my office."

Graham followed the lady through. He thought her to be very smart and was immediately taken by her professional attitude. In his line of business, he often saw business manners falling somewhat to the wayside, something that irritated Graham immensely being one of the old school. Margaret Horcott was above average height and quite slim; an attractive lady, smartly dressed. Graham guessed that she must be in her early sixties and thought that she had preserved herself extremely well.

"Please sit down Mr. Henderson" she instructed, pointing at two leather sofas the same as the one in the reception area. They were placed corner to corner in a right angle with a stylish chrome and glass coffee table in front.

"Thank you Miss. Or sorry is it Mrs. Horcott?"

"Please call me Margaret. Is it alright if I call you Graham? I find these meetings go a lot better if we can stand aside from the formalities."

"Yes of course, please do."

"Well I am sure you must be wondering why I have asked you here today, so let's get on shall we? As you may or may not know Connection Intermediary Services and companies like ours work very closely with the Adoption Agencies and Adoption Support Services. It is the role of Intermediary Services such as Connection, to carry out research and bring together adopted adults and birth relatives, who wish to be reunited."

"No, I didn't know" said Graham. "In fact to be honest I don't know much at all about the legalities of adoption. It's not something that I have had any dealings with."

Margaret Horcott looked straight into his eyes and continued.

"Well, the laws regarding adoption have changed over recent years. Of course adoption legislation has been around in the U.K. since 1926, but it was only in 1975 that adopted adults were given the right to find out about their birth relatives. This did not work the other way around though, so birth relatives were still not able to trace adoptees. That all changed however in 1991 with the introduction of the Adoption Contact Register. This enabled adopted adults and adult birth relatives to register their wish for contact with each other. Over the past few months" continued Margaret "both myself and my colleagues have been trying to find information on the birth relatives of a gentleman called Neil Cartwright who registered on the Adoption Contact Register. Our research told us that he was born at a maternity hospital near Reading in September1949 to a single lady, father unknown. The hospital is no longer standing, but it mainly took in unmarried mothers and was run in close conjunction with Bradstoke Orphanage in Theale. Putting two and two together, it does not take a lot of imagination to work out where a lot of the babies ended up and Neil was no exception to this rule."

Graham looked puzzled.

"It's all very interesting, but what has all of this got to do with me? Presumably it does, otherwise you would not have asked me here."

"Please bear with me Graham, these matters are very sensitive and should not be rushed."

"Of course" said Graham "sorry."

He hastily looked at his watch. He had hoped to miss the rush hour as the A34 was notorious at that time of day.

"You mentioned earlier Graham that you had never had any exposure to adoption, so it was not something that your parents Mr. and Mrs. Henderson ever discussed with you?"

"No, why should they?" asked Graham.

Suddenly his puzzled expression lifted and recognition seemed to set in.

"Hey, surely you're not trying to tell me that I was adopted are you?"

Noticing the seriousness on Margaret's face he added "My God! You are, aren't you?"

Margaret stared back at him with her most comforting expression.

"There's no easy way to say this Graham at the best of times, but even more so when it comes out of the blue like this, but yes I'm afraid to say you were. I'm sorry. Your parents who brought you up were not your birth parents. You were adopted as a six week old baby in nineteen forty-nine."

"But this is preposterous. How come they never said anything to me?"

"I know it must be very difficult for you to understand, but some parents never do tell. More than likely it was because they loved you so very much that they were frightened that if they told you the truth, you would go in search of your birth parents and they might lose you. Try not to be too angry with them."

"No I'm not angry. It's just so much to take in. I have so many questions that I would like to ask them, but they're not here anymore. They both died a number of years ago, so looks like any explanation well and truly went to their graves with them."

"I'm sorry. Obviously then you can't ask them any questions, but I may be able to help you."

"What do you mean? Do you know who my parents were?"

"Not your parents Graham, but I should soon have some detailed information regarding your birth mother."

"Go on" instructed Graham leaning forward.

"As I was saying, we sought Neil's original birth certificate, not the short one he was given on his adoption, but the long version. This gave us his date of birth, place of birth and known details of his parents. In brackets at the bottom was the word "twin", so this told us that Neil had at least one sibling, either a boy or girl who was his twin."

"I think I know what you are going to say" said Graham with his eyes beginning to water, "This Neil, his birthday is September 15th isn't it, same as mine? This is unbelievable. You're going to tell me that he is my twin brother aren't you?"

"Yes. You both share the same Mother. You too were born at the same maternity hospital and then taken to Bradstoke Orphanage, from where your parents as you know them June and Arthur adopted you."

"I'm sorry" sniffed Graham, taking a big, white handkerchief from his pocket. "I just never expected anything like this when I came here today. I'm finding it hard to take it all in."

"Don't worry Graham" Margaret calmly said. "It's perfectly normal to have a reaction like yours. Would you like a coffee? No doubt you could do with something stronger, but I'm afraid tea, coffee or water is about all we can stretch to here."

"Coffee will be fine, thanks."

Margaret Horcott picked up the telephone on the desk and asked the receptionist to bring in a tray of coffee.

Back at Acorn Cottage, Alison mused herself going through Nellie's old photographs. She picked up a black and white one of herself taken when she had been about nine months.

'How on earth could Mum dress me in anything like that' she inwardly asked, looking at herself in the most awful three pointed, knitted hat imaginable. 'I look like a pixie. Must keep that one out to show Graham.' Alison's stomach gave a little flutter when she thought of Graham. She felt so anxious for him. This phone call from the Adoption Agency had been so out of the blue; neither of them for one moment could conceive what it was all about. Alison hated the idea of Graham finding out on his own. She just had an uneasy feeling about the situation and would with all honesty have preferred to be with him.

Sifting through the tin of photographs, one photograph slightly larger than the normal size caught Alison's attention. She looked at it and instantly recognised the lady shown in the head and shoulders portrait. It was the one and only photograph that Nellie had of her mother Jessie, the mother who had died given her life. Strong, kind eyes peered out at Alison and straight away she was aware of closeness between herself and the grandmother that she never knew. Jessie had been an attractive lady by all accounts and Alison could not help but agree. Relatives in the past had often said that they could see a resemblence between Alison and her grandmother, but at the time she had never been able to see it herself. She could now though, now that she was getting older. The photograph had probably been taken when Jessie had been ten years or so younger than Alison was at the present time. Life in the 1900's had been a lot harder for Jessie, harder than Alison thankfully would ever experience, so looking at the photograph Jessie and Alison could well be mistaken for being of the same age. For the first time Alison could see the resemblence between the two of them. The same thick, dark hair, similar eyes and when Alison pulled back her own hair to emulate her grandmother's bun, the hairline was exact.

Another photograph bought a smile to Alison's lips. It was one of her mother and five more ladies dressed in overalls and mop caps. Alison turned the photograph over and on the back in her mother's writing she read 'Tripoli 1948.'

'I know what this is' recalled Alison. This is Mum when she was in the concert party The Mad Macaroons. I remember her telling me about this; it was the Char Ladies' Sketch. Oh! Mum look at the state of you, you look so gormless. It's no wonder everyone laughed so much.'

To that day Alison could never understand how her mother, who had always claimed to be self conscious, could ever have got up on a stage and sung to a large audience. Alison knew that she herself would never be able to do such a thing.

There was just one last photograph lying face down in the tin. Alison struggled to pick it up, but eventually managed to curl the corner and lever it out. The lady in the shorts and bikini top was without doubt her mother, but she did not know the man whose arm was casually draped around Nellie's shoulder. The couple were stood on a beach, in front of a bar, called from the sign above the counter, The Lido Beach Bar. She turned the photograph over in the hope that once again Nellie had written some detail on the back and sure enough there it was, 'Tripoli 1948 – Myself and Chad'. Alison drew the photograph closer to her and again looked at the couple displayed.

'So you're the one who broke my mother's heart.'

Alison wanted to despise this man who looked out at her from years ago, but seeing how happy her mother and he looked, she thought that maybe their relationship had not been totally bad. He wasn't good looking by any stretch of the imagination, but he did have a cheeky, endearing face and Alison could see the reason for her mother's attraction.

Alison piled all the photographs back into the tin, keeping out the one of herself in the funny hat and the one of Chad and her mother. She replaced the lid and stored the tin in the cupboard underneath the stairs. Walking back through the lounge on her way to the kitchen, Alison stood the two photographs that she wanted to show Graham on the mantelpiece. Glancing at the timer on the video she read twenty-five past four and thought that Graham's meeting should surely soon be coming to a close.

"Thanks, that was a lovely cup of coffee" commented Graham placing the cup and saucer back on the tray. "So this Neil, does he know about me?"

"He is aware that we have been searching for his twin sibling and he does know that contact is being made. Further than that, no he does not have any information at all about you. Neil has expressed an interest in meeting you, but that and any information passed back to him is purely your decision. Without your consent our hands are tied. It's entirely up to you whether you would like further contact with your twin and how much information is divulged to him. What are your feelings regarding contact Graham? Neil is happy for me to give you his telephone number should you wish to call him; I also have an email address for him. Sometimes people find it hard to make the first move, so if you do wish to meet him and prefer, I would be more than happy to set a meeting up for you."

Graham leant back on the sofa and ran his hands through his hair.

"I don't know Margaret, I just don't know. It's too soon. I can't get my head around everything."

"Of course, take your time. It's not necessary to decide at this moment. Go home and think about it. I am sure there's probably somebody who you might like to talk things over with first."

"Yes, sorry but I think I would. We've only recently lost my wife's, well my partner to be exact, Mother and her parting came with a few surprises of its own."

"I'm sorry. I can see that you're going through a tough period."

"Yes, it's not been easy."

"As I mentioned, I should soon have some information on your birth mother. Several years ago she registered on the Adoption Contact Register, so obviously she very much wants to find you and Neil."

"Really?"

"Yes, really. For mothers, especially unmarried ones, giving up their child is often the hardest choice they will ever have to make, but saying that, they also consider it at the time to be the right one. It is something they often regret for a lifetime, believe me I know from stories that I have been told. Never a day goes by that those mothers don't think of their lost children and their images are forever etched on their hearts."

"Do you know why she gave us up? Was it because she wasn't married? Did she say who our father was and what happened to him?

All of a sudden, a bombardment of questions came into Graham's head, spilling out of his mouth in a torrent.

"Graham, I don't know, but I have learnt that when your Mother sent her application form to the Adoption Contact Register, she also sent with it two letters, one each for both of her sons. I haven't actually received these letters yet, they are coming from another office, but as soon as they arrive I will forward them on to you and Neil. I would assume that those letters may well hold the answers to some of your questions. At least you will know her side of the story."

"Yes, I suppose I will."

Graham stood up.

"It's been quite a day hasn't it?"

"Yes it has" agreed Margaret "And I hope you find some comfort in your mother's letter when you read it."

"Thank you Margaret. I'll give you a ring in a day or two and let you know my feelings regarding meeting Neil. Is that alright?"

"That's fine. A few more days is not going to make any difference and don't forget the choice is yours."

Graham walked towards the door of Margaret's office, opened it and turned around to face Margaret.

"Margaret, will you be speaking to Neil abut our meeting today?"

"Yes I will, but as I said until you give your consent, no information will be passed on."

"Well tell him could you that I think I'm warming to the idea of having a brother?"

"Yes, I will Graham. I most certainly will" smiled Margaret, secretly pleased with herself that another reunion was looking likely to becoming a success.

Alison had anxiously been waiting for Graham's return. He had phoned her before setting off from the car park, but had only briefly related details of his meeting with Margaret Horcott. She didn't press for him to tell her more, as she could denote from his tone of voice that he was understandably a bit shocked and she was more concerned that he concentrated on his driving and got home in one piece. Hearing the sound of Graham's car reversing onto the drive, she ran out to meet him.

"Hello darling. Not quite the long, lost rich Uncle you expected then?" she teased noting back to Graham's flippant remark when Margaret Horcott had first rang.

"No, certainly wasn't. Who'd have thought it? I couldn't believe that it was all happening again, so soon after the shock with your Mum. Is life ever going to be normal again for us?"

"Come on" said Alison "let me take that" putting her hand out to offload Graham of his brief case. "I've got chilled beer in the fridge, or do you want something else?"

"A beer would be great. I'll just pop upstairs though and have a quick shower and get changed. It might just get rid of some of these aches and pains" he said as he flexed his shoulders.

"That'll be stress" remarked Alison.

A quarter of an hour later Graham reappeared freshly showered and dressed in his favourite torn and paint stained shorts, which given half a chance Alison would have loved to throw in the bin. He walked across the garden and joined Alison, who was sat in the area by the willow tree, which they called their secret garden. The privet hedge had been cut and rounded into a semi-circular shape, dividing this small part of the garden from the rest. The secret garden edged onto the small brook and the combination of the sound of trickling water and the softness of the cushioned, wicker arm chairs made it a peaceful and comfortable place to relax.

Graham took a sip from his glass of beer.

"Mmm! That tastes good. You're having a beer as well are you? That's not like you. You normally have wine or a gin and tonic."

"Yes I know, but I was feeling a bit dry. I'm quite enjoying it actually. So what else did this Margaret Horcott say? Did she say what this brother of yours is like?" enquired Alison. "Have you got his phone number?"

"Can we talk about it tomorrow? I think I've had enough for one day."

"Yes sorry, if that's what you want. You know I said that I was going through Mum's old photos this afternoon; well I came across these two. Who do you think this is?" Alison asked handing over the photo of herself as a baby in the three cornered hat.

"It's never you is it? I just must keep this" teased Graham holding it up high out of Alison's reach.

"I came across this one as well" she said as she handed over the second photograph that she had not put back in the tin with the others.

"That's never Nellie?"

"It is."

Gosh! She was quite a looker wasn't she in her day? Who's the guy with her?"

"Look on the back" suggested Alison.

"Chad?" said Graham thinking. "Oh! Chad. Chad who left your Mum and scuttled back to America to be with his wife and kids?"

"The very same."

"He looks a bit of a con merchant if you ask me."

Alison took the photograph back and studied it again.

"Do you think so? He had a nice smile; I can see what Mum saw in him."

"Ah! Never judge a man by his smile."

Alison laughed. "No, it's you never judge a book by its cover."

Graham eased further back into his chair and stretched his legs out. He picked up his beer from the table and took another gulp.

"This is lovely" he pondered. "I can't think of anything I would rather do right now than sit here with my lovely wife, enjoy this lovely summer's evening and have a few drinks."

"Well there's just one problem there Mr. Henderson, I'm not your wife."

"No, that's true, but you could be if you wanted to."

"Is that a marriage proposal then?" Alison joked laughing at Graham, who she knew had never been interested in getting married again.

"Yes, why not?" replied Graham.

Alison looked at her partner of sixteen years and couldn't quite believe her ears. Marriage had never been a subject that they discussed. It had never held that much significance to either of them, but in more recent years, Alison's ideas had been changing and not that she would ever have said anything to Graham, but secretly she thought a proposal of marriage was the greatest honour that one person could bestow onto another.

"I won't for one minute say that yours is the most romantic of proposals, but if that's the best you can do, all I can say is yes please."

Graham stood up, offering his hand to Alison to help her from her chair and they sealed the proposal with a kiss to the gentle burbling of the brook, the chiming of the church bells and the mating call of the neighbour's cat.

"I'm sorry, I haven't got a ring. The idea just came to me. Maybe I was prompted by today's events and what with Nellie dying as well, it just made me realise just how very special you are to me and how I never want to lose you. Does that make sense?"

"Perfect sense and you know how special you are to me as well don't you?"

"I do. Hey! There is a bottle of champagne in the fridge, lets pop the cork and celebrate. Just stay exactly where you are the future Mrs. Henderson, I'll go and get it."

Alison proudly not for the first time that day looked down at the beautiful ring on the third finger of her left hand. It was absolutely gorgeous, a double row of baguette diamonds on a yellow, gold band. Each time Alison went into the bathroom, she could not resist holding her ring up to the three spotlights on the bathroom vanity unit to see the dazzling shades of blues, pinks, and mauves that radiated from the perfect diamonds. Alison had always admired rings on other people that sparkled like this one, but never thought that she would be lucky enough to ever have one herself. More importantly she loved everything that the ring represented; Graham loved her and would always be at her side and she his.

'Its sad really' thought Alison 'that Mum's no longer here. I would have loved to tell her that Graham and I were getting married and shown her my ring.'

In reality Alison knew that her mother probably would not have shown a lot of interest. She never had done at anything that Alison had been remotely excited about. Alison and her Mother's relationship had come to a better understanding at the very end, but prior to that Nellie had never seemed capable of sharing any happy experiences that her daughter may have sampled. Alison could guess the tone of her mother's reaction, probably something along the lines of 'How silly getting engaged at your age and what a waste of money buying a ring.' Alison didn't care. She wasn't going to allow any memories of her mother's comments to ever come close to hurting her again. Alison could not be happier and nothing was going to change that.

Graham had taken the following day after he had popped the question off work, with the intention that they went to Cirencester to buy Alison her ring and make their engagement official. Exiting the Brewery car park, the first jeweller's shop they came to was one from a high street chain. Alison made a conscious effort to appear interested looking in the display window, but she knew that these were not the type of rings that she would like. Being of a strong mind she was determined that she wanted something nice; after all a bit of money should be coming their way shortly from her mother's will, so why not?

"The nicest jeweller's I think is Appleby's next to the church" suggested Alison as she looped her arm through Graham's and manoeuvred him in the said direction.

Appleby's held a prominent position in the market place and its three large bay windows and their glittering displays proved that it was a prestigious concern.
"I like that one, isn't it lovely" squealed Alison excitedly.
"Which one?"
"Second one in, third tray from the back."
"Yes, nice" replied Graham feeling slightly worried as all the prices were well concealed.
"Let's go in" said Alison and was already half way through the door.
Graham's concern that Appleby's was not the cheapest of shops was confirmed when the lady assistant on hearing that they were looking for an engagement room, took them through to a private back room and offered them seats on plush red velvet chairs. Alison described the ring that she wanted to try, but then decided that it would be better if she accompanied the assistant to the window, as there might be a few more that she would like bringing out. A selection of rings was tried and with Alison not being able to make up her mind, further trays were brought from the display window. Graham had reservedly turned over the price ticket of one of the rings and knew then that he was in for an expensive ride.

"This is the one I like the best. It's my size too. Must be an omen. What do you think Graham?"

"Yes it's very nice" he agreed, where in fact he was more interested on turning over the small white ticket attached to view the price.

"Oh! It is lovely isn't it? I want something nice" continued Alison as I only intend on getting engaged once."

"I should hope so too. I think I'm pretty safe" Graham said to the assistant "we've been together fifteen years."

"Sixteen" corrected Alison.

"That's lovely" the assistant awkwardly replied, not sure really what she was expected to comment.

Graham eventually found the courage to look at the price ticket. It was more than double the amount he had intended to pay, but he could see how much it meant to Alison.

"Go on then, if it's what you want" thinking to himself that it was a good job his bonus was coming through at the end of the month.

Alison shrugged her shoulders and grinned at Graham, acting more like a teenager than a mature woman.

"You're what I want."

"Does that mean I can save my money and not buy the ring then?" Straight away from Alison's expression he knew differently, "I'll take that as a no then."

Alison twiddled her fingers admiring the sparkle one more time. Her thoughts reverted back to Graham and she wondered how he was getting on. She was finding it hard to concentrate on housework, as on top of worrying about Graham, at two o'clock she herself had an appointment with Mr. Robson her mother's solicitor to go through Nellie's will. Alison thought Graham might have rung by now as he knew that she would soon have to leave to see Mr. Robson; maybe the signal wasn't very good where he was. She hoped his credit hadn't run out as she knew he wasn't the best at remembering to top it up.

The last few days had been a rollercoaster for Graham trying to come to grips with the reality that the two people who he had always regarded as his parents were not actually blood relatives to him at all. He could not take it in; up until now his life had always been so normal. It was June and Arthur who had showered him with love, who had bought him his first bicycle, helped him through school and later university. How come he had never suspected anything; he had no reason to he supposed. Graham thought to himself that if anyone had asked a week ago, what he would be doing today, he would never have dreamt that his answer would be driving to a pub in Surrey to meet up with the brother that he never knew until now existed.

Graham had no difficulty finding Chequers, his and Neil's appointed meeting place, as he had been there once before on a business lunch with a client. He pulled into the car park and easily found a slot. Graham was not sure if he felt nervous or a bit excited. In his line of business he was used to meeting and talking to new people, but somehow this felt completely different; he didn't feel prepared or in control at all.

'Damn' thought Graham 'perhaps I should have brought some photos with me; at least it would have given us a starting point for our conversation. Well too late now. We're bound to meet up again anyway; he'll have to meet Alison at some stage and I expect he will want me to meet his family as well.'

Graham walked through the front door. He and Neil had exchanged brief descriptions of each other, but Graham for one was not highly convinced that he would recognise his brother from it. Inside, what had once been a typical pub with beams and inglenook fireplaces was now more of a trendy wine bar come eatery establishment. Dark, oak beams and floor boards had been ripped out and replaced with more modern pine. Chrome and glass tables with lime green chairs replaced the more sedate oak furniture that had been present at Graham's last visit.

Graham conspicuously looked around and his gaze found another man eyeing him up in the same way. The man stood up and Graham made his way over to him.

"Neil?"

"Yes."

Meeting for both of them was difficult and brought with it emotional sentiments that neither of them had quite expected. Hearing about each other they had felt nothing more than strangers, but seeing each other in the flesh was a totally different ball game.

Alison sat waiting in the reception of Saville, Cook and Robson, her late mother's solicitors. Her mind was still more on what was happening with Graham than her own meeting with Mr. Robson. After all, her mother's will she was sure would all be straight forward. The telephone on the reception desk rang and a middle-aged lady with a rather large bosom answered it, trying to sound posh, but with a definite undertone of a Gloucestershire burr. Alison smiled to herself; she had lived too long around these parts not to notice.

"Miss. Collier." said the large, bosomed receptionist in an attempt to gain Alison's attention "Mr. Robson is ready for you now. Please go through" she instructed pointing to the middle of three doors.

Alison approached the door and knocked. She heard a voice from within beckoning her inside.

"Miss. Collier, thank you for taking the time to come and see me" Mr. Robson addressed her, while at the same time shaking her hand. "Please before we start on the matter in hand, may I say how very sorry I was to hear of your mother's passing."

Alison thanked him and sat down in the chair being offered and her mother's solicitor continued.

"Miss. Collier I don't know if you are aware of the contents of your late mother's Last Will and Testament, but for the most part, it is quite straight forward, although not completely. In total your mother's estate came to £219,452.86. There are a few costs to come out of that amount, which I have of course listed here for you to see. After those costs have been deducted the amount remaining comes to £213,126.21."

Alison nodded her head. It was more than she was expecting. She knew that Nellie's house had been sold a few years ago, but with the care home fees, she hadn't expected it to be so much. Alison kept a close eye on her mother's current account, but she also had a few other investments and high interests accounts dotted around and these obviously must have done reasonably well over the last few years.

"Now Miss. Collier, you are the main beneficiary of your mother's will. As I said the will is not completely straight forward and this next part is somewhat delicate. Your mother as it appears had two sons before she married your father and to both of these sons she has bequeathed the sum of £25,000 each. I hope this is not too upsetting for you Miss. Collier."

"It's alright Mr. Robson I do know, not about the money I admit, but about her sons, although it was only when my mother was dying that I found out."

"Yes often the case. I'm afraid skeletons have a habit of coming out of the closet at such times. People like to pass on with a clear conscience it seems."

"Yes quite" muttered Alison.

"As you are probably aware then Miss. Collier, your mother gave up her two sons for adoption in 1949. There is a clause in the will to this effect, that should any of the aforementioned sons not be found within five years of your mother's death, then their share of the inheritance falls back to you."

"I see. So will you be trying to contact my half brothers?"

"Yes as executors of your mother's will, we do have a responsibility to try and locate them."

"I'm sorry, but I cannot help you very much. As I said it was only recently that I found out about them. Mum did tell me that a few years ago she registered on the Adoption Contact Register, so I don't know if that will be of any use to you."

"Thank you for that piece of information. It may be that you come across more pieces of the jig-saw, so to speak, when you go through your mother's personal possessions. That being the case I would be grateful if you could inform us of any findings."

"Yes of course," said Alison and thank you."

Alison started up 'Dora', her little, blue fiesta and quickly did a calculation in her head. 'So two hundred and thirteen minus fifty is' and after the passing of a few moments she came up with the answer 'one hundred and sixty three thousand pounds. The extra fifty would have been better, that was a bit of a blow, but still that's still a tidy, little sum.' She pushed the gear stick into first and 'Dora' begrudgingly moved forward.
'Well Dora' Alison confided, 'you've been a good friend to me, but I think we may soon be parting company' as she imagined herself in a sporty, little red Peugeot 307 convertible. She'd always fancied one of those and thought that she might just treat herself now.

Graham was already at home when Alison returned from the solicitors' office.

"I'm out here" he shouted in answer to Alison's call.

"Bar opened early then?" she asked noticing that Graham already had a half full glass of beer in front of him."

"Yes why not. The weekend's here. Anyway have we got anything to celebrate? How much did 'T.O.B.' leave you?"

"Don't call her that Graham. That's not nice, especially as she is no longer with us."

"No I'm sorry I shouldn't have. It was in bad taste. So how much?"

"I'll tell you in a minute" replied Alison slightly crossly and thought that she would make him wait a bit longer. "I want to know how you got on first. What was Neil like? What did you think of him?"

"Mmm! Not sure really. That's what I was sat here thinking about. There was something that I couldn't quite take to, but I can't put my finger on exactly what it was."

"Well I don't think you should make a judgement after so short a time, it was your first meeting after all. It was a big step for both of you. He was probably uptight and nervous and didn't come across in the best way. I bet when you see him the next time you will feel completely different about him."

"Yes, no doubt you're right and in fairness I don't know how I came across to him either."

"So, did he look like you, are you identical?"

"Not the slightest. You wouldn't even think we were brothers let alone twins."

"Really."

"Yeah! He's quite a few inches shorter than me, about five nine I would say and his hair was brown, but a lot lighter than mine."

"Yours is very dark, almost black."
It was strange though, he reminded me of somebody I've met before, but I've been racking my brain and nobody comes to mind."

"Maybe it's a twin thing. You read about strong senses and similarities that twins have for each other."
Possibly, I don't think it was that though. He definitely reminded me of someone I'm sure."

"Is he married?"

"Yes, second time around. His wife's called Eloise I think he said and they've got one daughter and his wife's expecting again."

"She must be quite a lot younger than him then."

"He seems to have done alright for himself;" Graham continued "he turned up in one of those big BMW jeep things."

"Nice."

"I got the impression the money's on his wife's side though. It's her father who owns a packaging company and that's who he works for."

"Have you arranged to meet him again?"

"We thought we would wait until we'd received the letters from our birth mother. You know the ones that Margaret Horcott is forwarding on to us."

"I would have thought you would have had them by now. He hasn't received his either then?"

"No. If nothing comes tomorrow, perhaps I will give Margaret a ring on Monday. Anyway how did you get on? I'll get you a glass of wine and then you can tell me all about it."

Alison told Graham the amount she had inherited and like her, he was slightly disappointed that she didn't inherit the full lot, but even so the money they did have would make their lives a lot more comfortable.

"You might still get the rest of the money anyway. It was quite a while ago that Nellie started looking for them and nobody has come forward yet?"

"Yes, I can hear what you are saying, but in another way I would be quite happy for them to have the money, as then I would have two brothers, or at least half brothers wouldn't I."

"You're absolutely right love and it's wrong to complain, we've done very well out of it. Let's raise a toast to Nellie, your Mum. Do you realise we'll be going to Spain next week for our holidays. It seems ages since we were at our villa last, don't you think?"

"It certainly does" agreed Alison, "So much has happened I suppose. The revelations of Mum's adopted twins, then her dying and now all this about you and your twin brother.

"Yes, but that's the way things go I suppose."

"You're right though, it will be fabulous to get out to Spain and feel some real sunshine, not this sort in England that comes out one day and then wants a rest for three. Actually Graham, I've been thinking."

"Steady on there."

"Graham, how many have you had?" Alison sternly asked.

"Only this one and one before."

"As I was saying, I've been thinking that now we've got Mum's money, why don't you give up work, pack it all up?"

"Are you serious?"

"Yes. Life's too short. Just think we could then go to Spain for six weeks at a time or for however long we chose. I think we've reached the time in our lives when we should start dipping into our capital and spoiling ourselves a bit. After all we haven't got any children to leave it too." Alison stopped in mid flow, "unless there's something you're not telling me. I don't think I could cope with any more family surprises."

"No, hardly, I agree no more shocks. It's a nice idea, I must admit. Do you think we could really afford to?"

"Yes, I do. We could invest Mum's money. I know the rates aren't as good as they have been, but we would get some income from it and you know we don't spend so much when we are in Spain."

"We'll look at the figures" responded Graham with his sensible hat on. "I'm not sure. We would have two houses to run and that doesn't come cheap."

"Come on Graham, at the end of the day we're not getting any younger and do we really need two houses? Now that I haven't got Mum to worry about, we could always sell this place; I'm sure we would get a good price for it and just think, then we could move permanently to Spain and wake up to the sunshine every single morning. How does that grab you?"

"It grabs me very nicely thank you. I'm warming to the idea all of the time. Do you think our finances would stretch to a yacht?"

"A dinghy's about all you'll get and don't forget we've got a wedding to pay for."

Chapter 19

Alison peered out of the front window of the cottage, looking up and down the street to see if there was any sign of the postman.
'He's late today' she thought hearing the church clock strike eleven.
Graham was upstairs in his office making a few business calls. Hearing him come to the end of his telephone call, Alison shouted up the stairs to ask him if he wanted a coffee.
"No thanks, not at the moment. I'll get a few more calls done first."
Alison went through to the kitchen, filled up the kettle and put it on the Aga to make herself one; she would always be able to manage another when Graham was ready to drink his. While she was waiting for the kettle to boil, she busied herself putting the box of breakfast cereals back into the cupboard and generally tidying up the work tops. She noticed her mother's concertina file on the chair, the one she had found in the wardrobe at Fir Trees. Picking it up, she placed it on the table thinking that she really must go through it and may as well start as she drank her coffee.

Looking through the file, A –Z fashion, Alison found that it contained mostly old domestic bills that she took out and put to one side with a mind to shred later. At the very back behind the alphabet section were a few blank compartments. Out of one of these Alison pulled out a folded, beige sheet, which looked like an official document. Carefully unfolding it, she identified it as her Mother's birth certificate.
'I've never seen this before', she uttered talking out loud to herself.
'Gosh! How interesting.'
Alison read the relevant section giving the name and maiden name for Nellie's mother and was saddened seeing the word deceased in brackets underneath it. It made her think again, just how hard her mother's life must have been for her. She could remember Nellie saying many a time that she didn't know how to love, as she herself had never been loved and with her mother dying when Nellie was so very young, Alison could appreciate a little of her mother's words.
'I suppose looking back, in a way that was Mum's way of saying sorry and trying to tell me why she found it so hard to love me. She couldn't have had a normal upbringing being shoved from pillar to post like she was poor thing. I could never understand though how she could say that she had never been loved. Yes she lacked her mother's love, I can

understand that but Dad and I loved her. Probably what she missed was love as a child and that would have been an important time in her life. Really that would go some way to explaining the guilt she felt for letting Richard and James go I suppose. I can remember her saying that they would never know the meaning of a mother's love. I don't know if I did either for that matter.'

Alison carried on studying the certificate in front of her.
'Look at this, it says that Mum's father, he would have been my Grandfather, was a Master of Hauliers in a coalmine. I thought he was in charge of the pit ponies form what Mum told me. I wonder if that's the same or something different, I shall have to look it up. And that's the address where Mum was born 3 Baker Street, Llanfaer, I wonder if it's still standing. Perhaps one day Graham and I could go to Wales and try and find it?'
Alison was completely fascinated reading all the facts about her family.
'I never knew my grandmother's maiden name was James. I've always fancied having a go at tracing the family tree, but Mum never knew very much abut her parents with them dying when she was only young. I remember her mentioning an uncle on her father's side, because it was him who she went to live with on the farm. I'm not sure if there was another brother as well, but I don't know anything about Grandmother's side. I wonder if she had any brothers or sisters?'

Alison neatly folded up the certificate and placed it back in the folder. In the next compartment she found her Mother and Father's wedding certificate and again found the information it contained intriguing. The following compartments were empty and Alison was just about to pack the folder away, when she noticed a brown envelope in the very last one. Alison pulled it out; it was addressed to her mother. She was just about to take its contents out and read them when she heard the postman put some letters through the letter box. Knowing that Graham was anxiously awaiting the correspondence from Margaret Horcott, Alison walked through the hall towards the front door, to see if indeed it was amongst the mail that had arrived. She bent down and picked up the scattered envelopes that had fallen onto the mat. There was one envelope slightly larger than the rest and it was addressed to Graham.

She walked up the stairs and peered through Graham's door that was ajar.

"I think this might be your letter from Margaret Horcott."

Graham swivelled around on his chair and took the letter from Alison. Thinking that he might prefer to read its contents alone, Alison said "Right, well I'll leave you to it then. I'll go downstairs and put the kettle on and make us both a cup of coffee. You know where I am if you need me."

"Thanks" said Graham appreciative for the time on his own.

Graham opened the envelope and read the letter from Margaret Horcott. He then pulled out an accompanying small, powder blue envelope. He looked down at the neat, looped handwriting, for the first time seeing his own mother's handwriting. His hands started to tremble as he read to who the letter was addressed, 'To Richard, My First Born Son.'

Graham opened the envelope and took out three sheets of Basildon Bond writing paper and placed them on the desk in front of him. He noticed a document of sorts inside and took that out as well. Graham rested his elbow on the desk and placed his hand across his mouth, rubbing his nose, as he started to read the same neat, looped handwriting that had addressed the envelope.

'My Dear Richard,

I hope you don't mind me calling you Richard, I realise that you may of course now be known by a different name, but to me you will always be my Richard.

This is the hardest letter that I have ever had to write and the words are not coming easily. I am finding it nearly as hard as the day that you and your brother James were taken away from me, but nothing will ever match the sorrow and anguish that I felt on that most memorable of days.

If you are reading this, then you are by now aware that I had to give you and your brother up for adoption. I hope that you don't feel too badly of me, but of course you have every right to. I cannot deny that. Please believe me when I say, that not a day goes past, even today so many years later, when I don't think badly of myself. I have so many regrets, a life time full of them. Every single night, I say a prayer for you both. I pray that your lives have been happy and enriched with opportunities. I pray that you were adopted by kind and loving parents, who gave you limitless love and attention. I could not bear to think that anything bad had happened to you as a result of my giving you up. I wholly believed, although so very painful, that it was the best option to give you a better start in life.

I feel I owe it to you and your brother to tell you the truth. It must be difficult growing up without knowledge of who you really are. You must have so many questions that you want to ask me. I truly hope with all my heart that you will find forgiveness for me and one day find the will to contact with me. I am getting on in years now and nothing would please me more than to meet up with you and see for myself the fine man I'm sure you've become.'

Graham slowly read through the letter, with every word learning more about his real mother, how much she had loved his father and how painful her ultimate decision had been. By the time he reached the third page, his eyes were watering so much that his vision became blurred.

'There is something else that you need to know. Several years after you and your twin brother were born; I did meet and marry a man. He's dead now; he died a number of years ago. This man and I had a daughter, Alison; she would be your half sister. She has been a wonderful daughter to me, but sadly I have to admit that I have not been a good mother in return. The guilt I carried inside for letting you and James go weighed so heavy, I felt that I never deserved to be happy ever again. When this little girl came along, I knew that it was not right for me to love her; I was not worthy of her. Loving her would have been an injustice to my two sons and I could not let that happen.

Richard, I sincerely hope that this letter has explained to you some of the things that you needed to know. Please remember that I love you so very much and I will continue to do so until my dying day. I know I have no right, no right at all to ask your forgiveness; you owe me nothing, but if you ever feel the need to come looking for me, rest assured you would be welcomed with open arms. I would never turn my back on you again.

Forever in my thoughts,

Your loving Mother xx

P.S. I have enclosed a copy of my birth certificate. It's just that I have a fear that I may die before you get a chance to read this letter and maybe one day in the future you may need it to prove that you are my son.

P.P.S. I am sorry about the smudges on the ink. As I said the words in this letter did not come easy, but the tears did.'

Graham wiped a stray tear away from his own eye as he gathered together the envelope and its contents.

It was some time before Graham emerged downstairs. The kettle had already boiled and by now had lost its heat, so Alison replaced it on the Aga.

"Everything alright?"

"Yes, very sad though. How she must have suffered, poor woman. To be honest, I was quite upset reading it. It must be far worse for people who have been looking for their parents a long time and built up their own opinions of their mothers. At least I didn't have time to make any really."

"I don't know. I should imagine it's a pretty painful process for everybody involved."

The kettle started to sing. Alison picked it up and poured hot water into the two mugs on the draining board.

"Cream or milk, Graham?"

"Cream please."

Alison opened the fridge door.

"Do you know your Mum's name?"

"Ellen."

"That's the same as my Mum. She was Ellen as well."

"But I thought your Mum was called Nellie?" Graham questioned.

"Yes she was. That was the name everybody knew her by, but her real name was Ellen."

"Well I never knew that."

Alison gave both mugs a stir, picked them up and walked over to the table to join Graham.

"Is that the letter?"

"Yes."

"What else did she say?"

"Usual story I guess. Fell in love with a man, didn't know he was married and then he left her when he found out that she was pregnant and went back to his wife and kids."

"Seemed to have happened a lot in those days, didn't it. Same happened to my Mum if you remember."

"Apparently I've got a half sister somewhere as well. Several years after she gave us up, she married and had a daughter."

"Really? Do you think you might try and find her?"

"Maybe, haven't thought about it."

"What did you say the name of the maternity hospital was where you and your brother were born?"

"Umm! Can't quite remember" answered Graham. "Ship something. It was Reading way?"

"Was it Shipways?"

"Yes that's it. Why are you asking?"

"While you were upstairs I've been going through Mums folder and in it I found a copy of her application to the Adoption Contact Register. I can't believe this, but Mum had her twins at Shipways as well. I can remember thinking when Mum told me that they were born in nineteen forty-nine that they would now be the same age as you."

"What a coincidence. Just think your Mum and my Mum could have been in beds next to each other. It's quite nice to think that they might have helped each other out during their difficult times when they were both alone, without family."

"Can I read her letter, would you mind?"

"No of course not" said Graham pushing it across to her.

Alison looked at the neat, looped handwriting and hesitated.

"She called you Richard?"

"Yes. Funny that, because my middle name's Richard. Makes me wonder if Mum and Dad knew that she intended to call me that and kept the name. Quite a nice gesture if they did, don't you think?"

Alison didn't answer

"And she named your brother James?"

"Mmm."

A cold sensation crept all around Alison's neck and alarm bells started to ring in her head. As her eyes followed the pages through, she could see the smudged ink, which she knew had been caused from teardrops falling, even before she got to the apology at the end. She could remember her own Mother describing her pain, as she had written her letters to her sons; the ones that she had sent with the application for the Adoption Contact Register. Alison's worst nightmare was near enough confirmed when she saw that Graham's real mother's daughter was called Alison.

"Your half- sister's name is Alison?"

"Yes, it's amazing don't you think? So many coincidences."

Noticing Alison's sudden loss of colour, a light suddenly dawned on Graham. Pushing back his chair with a loud scraping on the tiles, he quickly rose from the table and strode into the lounge.

"Bloody Hell" Graham shouted as he returned to the kitchen, "I knew he reminded me of someone. In his hand was the photograph of Chad and Alison's mother. "It's him! It's bloody him, that's who Neil reminded me of."

Alison put her head in her hands.

"Now let's not jump to conclusions. Let's try and think rationally. Do you know your mother's surname?

"Edwards. I've got her birth certificate here. She included a copy of it with her letter. "

Alison's hand shook as she took the certificate from Graham. Everything was going horribly wrong; her world was crashing around her. She knew from the documents she had found in her Mother's folder that Nellie, as well as sending letters to her two sons, had also enclosed a copy of her birth certificate. The details on the certificate jumped off the paper, Baker Street, Master Haulier, Jessica Edwards, nee James. In her hand was the exact copy of the birth certificate she herself had just been reading; the one she had taken out of her mother's folder.

Alison slumped down on the table, her head resting on her arms and wailed.

"I just can't believe this is happening. Things like this don't happen."

"You think it's true then?" asked Graham quietly. We haven't made a mistake?"

"No" said Alison. "No mistake. God Mum, you were right about one thing, the truth certainly does hurt."

Alison and Graham sat at the kitchen table for a very long time. Lunchtime came and went with neither giving a thought to food and still they had not found a solution to the terrible crisis they faced.

"I still love you Alison, nothing's going to change that."

"But I'm your bloody sister Graham, that's a different type of love. You realise that I can't marry you, not now. God think if we've had children. At least that's one saving grace I suppose."

Alison's frustration was turning to anger. She was aware that it was no more Graham's fault than her own, but that didn't stop her snapping at him.

"I'm sorry" admitted Alison. It's just that only a few days ago, everything was so perfect. You were thinking of packing up work, so that we could spend more time together. I was looking so forward to our holiday at the villa and now everything is such a damn mess."

Alison's eyes were red and puffy. The kitchen roll on the table was fast diminishing as she kept tearing off sheets to soak up her tears and blow her running nose. Graham too had needed a few sheets, as the upset hadn't passed him by unscathed either.

"I can't wear this anymore" sobbed Alison as she removed her precious engagement ring from her finger. "Why is life so cruel? We don't deserve any of this, not one bit of it."

"Please don't take it off" pleaded Graham.

"I have to Graham. There's not going to be a wedding now is there?"

"No, I suppose not, but I still love you Alison. If nothing else wear it as a reminder of that."

"I can't Graham. Don't be so stupid. It's not right."

Alison took one last look at her ring, before she slipped it off her finger. Walking over to the dresser, she slid it inside one of the small drawers until the next time she went upstairs and could put it away in the safe, in its little blue, velvet box.

"This is going to be quite some gossip when it gets around the village."

"It needn't be" replied Graham. "Who's going to tell them? I'm not for one. Alison let's just think about this. We've been living together for sixteen years and very happily at that. Why does anyone need to know? Why can't we go on just the same?"

"But it wouldn't be right Graham. I would know that it wasn't right, surely you must realise that."

"If two people are as happy as us, there can't be too much bad in that surely?"

"This is so difficult" sniffed Alison. "Life will never be the same for us again, will it Graham? Sex for example. We can't sleep together now, knowing all this. It would be immoral, apart from anything else."

Alison shuddered when the reality of the matter hit home; for sixteen years she had been sleeping with her half brother. She felt confused, cheated and the word 'bizarre' was prominent in her mind.

"Alison, listen to me. We'll just take each day as it comes and go from there. It's not that we do it very often anyway, between our bad backs and cramp." Graham smiled as he spoke trying his utmost to lighten the conversation.

"More what's on the television with you" Alison jibed back.

"That's more like it. What we have is more than just sex Alison; we're friends, good friends. Never forget that."

Graham smiled and stretched out his hand to touch Alison's. Alison quickly recoiled her hand.

"Would you like another coffee?" she asked clearing away their mugs.

"Let's have that bottle of red that Lorraine and Derek brought around when they were over for supper the other week. I know it's a bit early, but I think it will do our shattered nerves a bit of good. It looks quite a good one from the label."

Alison took a sip of the ruby red wine in her glass.

"It's quite full-bodied, pretty potent I should think."

"Good that's what we need. It's so weird to think I've known Nellie for all of these years and she's my Mum. I don't think I will ever be able to think of her like that. Hey! I just had a thought. You know what this means don't you?"

"What?"

"I'm due £25,000 from Nellie's will."

Alison nearly choked on her wine.

"Oh! My God, Neil. He's my brother as well. I hadn't thought of that. So much for people not knowing. We'll have to tell him. Mum left him £25,000 as well."

"Let's not rush into anything; certainly not until we get used to the idea ourselves and to be honest maybe it's best if we keep all of this to ourselves, especially if we want to stay together, which I hope we do."

"I'm not sure about that yet Graham, don't rush me."

"Okay, but at least don't worry yourself about Neil for the time being. Let's get ourselves sorted first, alright?"

"He's bound to find out, even if we don't tell him."

"How do you know that?"

"Mr. Robson, Mum's solicitor will be trying to find him. He told me the other day that as executor of her will, it was his responsibility to contact all beneficiaries. He'll be looking for you as well."

"He may never find him and even if he did, Neil may not necessarily add up the pieces and realise that you are the same Alison as the one mentioned in the letter. Don't forget he hasn't heard two sides of the story like you have."

"True, but what if he decided to trace his family tree, a lot of people do you know? I don't think it would be too hard for him to find me, as records are available for everything nowadays."

"Just put Neil to one side for the moment Alison. It's more important that we think about ourselves and our future. I can't impress on you enough Alison that I don't want to lose you. You know how much I love you. We get on so well, we always have. We can't throw all that away. It's ridiculous really, just think about it. We could have carried on living our lives never knowing that we were related; same as we have done up until now. I'm sure that must actually happen to some people. What about all those children who came from donated sperm, who knows who their fathers are? It must happen all the time, or if it doesn't now, I'm sure it will in the future. Christ, we'll be a race of inter-breeding morons. Come on Alison, what do you say? It might not be the best idea to have the wedding and all the trimmings which I know you would have liked, but we can be just as happy as we always have been, even more. This needn't change anything Alison. We shouldn't let it."

"You make it all sound so simple, but it's not. It's all such a farce. We'd be a farce, don't you get that Graham? I don't think I'll ever be able to show my face in the village shop again if any of this ever gets out. You know what an old gossip Mrs Giles is and I'm sure someone would want to make a killing at our expense and sell our story to the tabloids. I just couldn't handle that Graham, I know I couldn't."

"We could move. Get right away from Bampton St Mary, start again where nobody knows us. Hell, you suggested yourself only the other day that we should move to Spain. Let's do it. The world's our oyster Alison, it doesn't have to be Spain, we could go anywhere in the world."

The cogwheels in Alison's mind were in overdrive, trying to work everything out, trying to reason if there was a plausible solution to this horrendous scenario that they were caught up in.

"This is all so hard Graham; I just don't know what to do or think for the best. I love you, every bit as much as you love me, but everything's so different now. We're not the same two people we were when we woke up this morning; everything's changed. I can't imagine a life without you, which makes not being with you so hard. I couldn't bear to see you with somebody else that would just break my heart. I'm never happier than when I'm with you, you know that. Before we met, my life was nothing really. I just filled my time with work, looking after Mum, not a lot of play, quite a miserable life in a way. But together, we've had dreams, we've had expectations, we've had fun, we've had a fabulous life and I don't want to have to give that up."

"So what are you saying Alison? Are you agreeing with me?"

"Graham, I'm sorry. I really do wish that I had the same confidence as you that we could stay together and everything would be okay, but I don't have that."

"But you can Alison, you can. I just know it's possible. You have to believe me."

"I wish I could Graham, I really do."

"Maybe you'd feel differently if we went away, away from everything and everyone familiar. We're meant to be going to Spain on Saturday anyway, let's bring it forward. We could get a flight tomorrow, even tonight, I'll check the internet."

"But what about your work, you can't just take time off."

"Sod work! I'll just tell them there's been an emergency and I need time off. They can either take it as holidays or dock my wages. Who cares? Let's do it Alison. We'd both be more relaxed in Spain; you know how much we enjoy it there. It would give us time to think, to get to grips with what's happening to us."

Alison sucked in her cheeks as she thought over Graham's proposal. It wouldn't be a bad idea for them to get away on their own. They did have a lot to talk over and she didn't want either of them to make any rash decisions that they would live to regret.

Before Alison had made up her mind, Graham continued.

"Think of it as a trial period if you like, to see how we get on, if we feel comfortable with each other. I won't push you Alison I promise. I'll give you all the space you need, really I will. If it's sharing the same bed you're worried about, I'll sleep in the guest room. What do you say? Shall I ring the office and tell them I won't be in?"

Alison carefully considered the options. The problem had to be faced whether they were in Bampton St Mary or Spain. What was she frightened of? Graham was still the same, kind and affectionate man he always had been, so no change there.

"Ring your office Graham, you're right."

Graham moved around the table and planted a big kiss on Alison's cheek.

"That's fantastic Alison, I knew you'd come around."

"We'll go to Spain Graham," Alison began, "but you must understand I can't make any promises. I really don't see how we can keep all this secret and even if we could, I'm still not confident that we could get back to how we were. Too much has happened Graham, you must see that surely? I'll be honest with you if any of this got out, I don't think I could live with the repercussions. I can just see the headlines now "Truth Hurts for Brother And Sister in Incestuous Relationship."

"Alison we owe it to ourselves to at least give it a try. Why worry about other people? Who's going to take any notice of us, they're all too busy covering up their own clandestine lives."

"But this is slightly different Graham. We're not talking trivia here are we?"

"No, but we haven't committed any crime the way I see it. We've got to give it our best shot Alison; we love each other too much not to. At least let's take our holiday and see where life leads us from there. The world's a big place you know.

THE END

From the author of 'Truth Hurts' comes 'The Circle'.

Meet the ladies of the spiritual group The Circle, all who have different reasons for attending the Tuesday afternoon meetings.

Olive – who is looking forward to being reunited with her long departed husband and daughter.

Diana - three times married, who hopes the spirits, may be able to throw some light on where she can find husband number four.

Rosemary – a quiet, lonely spinster, who is desperate to form new friendships.

Elsie – who feels she has a real calling for the spirit world.

Pam – happy go lucky and renown for her inappropriate comments.

Brenda – who certainly has ulterior motives for developing her psychic abilities.

Carol – who seeks forgiveness, as she feels sure her extramarital sexual antics were the cause of her husband's untimely death.

………………….. and then another member joins the group.

Printed in Great Britain
by Amazon.co.uk, Ltd.,
Marston Gate.